Acclaim for

"I combed through the pages with delight. This book is going to cause a real buzz."

—Debbie Macomber, #1 *New York Times* bestselling author, on *The Enlightenment of Bees*

"A delicious romance, breath-catching world travel, family entanglements, and food writing that will have you wanting to leap into its pages for a seat at the table—*The Enlightenment of Bees* has everything a girl wants in the perfect book club read."

—Kimberly Stuart, author of *Heart Land* and *Sugar: A Novel*

"Linden is a gifted author and international aid worker whose travels around the world provide detailed settings for the unique locations in her novels."

—*CBA Market* on *Becoming the Talbot Sisters*

"This is more than a fluff 'sister chick' story. There is a depth to the story as each sister faces fears and digs deep to uncover the courage needed to find their path in life. There are numerous heartwarming scenes which demonstrate the bravery and selflessness that Waverley and Charlie exhibit along the way. Unexpected twists and a surprising mystery angle add to the enjoyment."

—*RT Book Reviews*, 4 stars, on *Becoming the Talbot Sisters*

"Linden's debut novel is a bittersweet tale of enduring friendship, family ties, and the complexities of love that will engage readers of thoughtful women's fiction."

—*Library Journal*, STARRED review, Debut of the Month, on *Ascension of Larks*

"Rachel Linden's *Ascension of Larks* is a lyrical novel about love and loss. This beautifully told story takes readers on a meaningful journey, marked by an artistic sense of place, a fragile mystery, and an emerging grace. I couldn't put the book down! Bravo, Rachel!"

—Leslie Gould, #1 bestselling and Christy Award–winning author

"This is a heartfelt, tender story with a strong, intelligent, and independent heroine at its center."

—*RT Book Reviews*, 4 stars, on *Ascension of Larks*

"Winsome kids and family friends add depth and warmth to the well-developed cast of characters. Readers will eagerly await future offerings from this promising new author."

—*Publishers Weekly*, STARRED review, on *Ascension of Larks*

"There is a beautiful redemptive strand running through the story."

—*CBA Market* on *Ascension of Larks*

The Enlightenment of Bees

Other Books by Rachel Linden

Becoming the Talbot Sisters

Ascension of Larks

The Enlightenment of Bees

Rachel Linden

Thomas Nelson
Since 1798

The Enlightenment of Bees

Published in Nashville, Tennessee, by Thomas Nelson. Thomas Nelson is a registered trademark of HarperCollins Christian Publishing, Inc.

Thomas Nelson titles may be purchased in bulk for educational, business, fund-raising, or sales promotional use. For information, please email SpecialMarkets@ThomasNelson.com.

ISBN 978-0-7852-2141-8 (e-book)

Library of Congress Cataloging-in-Publication Data

Names: Linden, Rachel, author.
Title: The enlightenment of bees / Rachel Linden.
Description: Nashville, Tennessee : Thomas Nelson, [2019]
Identifiers: LCCN 2019002201 | ISBN 9780785221401 (paperback)
Classification: LCC PS3612.I5327426 E55 2019 | DDC 813/.6--dc23 LC record available at https://lccn.loc.gov/2019002201

Printed in the United States of America

HB 03.02.2023

For my dearest Grandma Sally who makes the world a brighter and more lovely place

Do small things with great love.

—A FAVORITE MOTTO OF MOTHER TERESA OF KOLKATA

Part I

Seattle

Chapter 1

Early April

The day my world crumbles I am dreaming about piecrust. Cubes of chilled butter, ice bobbing in a Pyrex measuring cup of water, a pastry cutter to slice the butter and flour and salt into baby-pea-sized gobbets. A light touch, light as a feather. And honeybees.

Their contented hum is a droning undercurrent to the *ting ting* of my pastry cutter against the chilled bowl straight from the refrigerator. The air is heavy with the scent of lavender, sharp and pungent from the fields of purple stretching beyond my family's farmhouse kitchen window. One by one bees buzz through the open window and land on the rim of the bowl. I shoo them away. They are fat and slow as they fly off, legs laden with orange saddlebags of pollen, buzzing across the fields and over the silver waters of Puget Sound. On the lip of the bowl where they rested, each leaves a dot of honey that trickles down the glass in a slow golden rivulet.

When my ringing cell phone wakes me, I burrow out from under my duvet with a muffled exclamation and a shiver, scrambling to silence the cheery tune. My room feels like an icebox. I'd accidentally fallen asleep reading with the window open, and the wet April air wafts under the curtain, sharp and salty from the sea.

"H'llo," I stage-whisper, not wanting to rouse my housemate, Rosie, who I'm guessing is still asleep across the hall after her late-night performance in a jazz club on Capitol Hill.

"Good morning, Mia. Kate here." The activities director at Sunny Days Retirement Community where my grandmother, Nana Alice, lives.

"Good morning, Kate." I try to match her chipper tone, covering my confusion and erasing the sleep from my voice. I open and close my eyes like an owl; the insides of my eyelids feel like sandpaper. Splayed on the floor near my feet is Mary Berry's *Baking Bible*, open to the alluring chapter on traybakes and flapjacks. I must have fallen asleep reading it after my shift.

"Just checking to see if you're bringing baked goods for the residents today as usual," Kate says in a perky voice.

"Oh sure." I glance at the clock and startle. Ten forty! I was up at 4 a.m. for my four-hour baking shift at the Butter Emporium, an artisan bakery and coffee shop in historic Ballard where I'm an apprentice baker. On Sundays I deliver our day-old baked goods to Sunny Days.

"Be there in a jiffy." I hang up, already throwing on a plaid flannel shirt over my fitted tee. I rub a smudge of flour off the elbow and twist my hair up into a messy bun. Olga, the Ukrainian woman who cuts my hair, bluntly describes it as "crazy vitch hair" with a disapproving shake of her own militantly subdued blonde bob. I think it's more accurate to label it unruly, a disheveled sort of curly, like I'm in a perpetually brisk breeze.

In college my English lit professor told me that my hair was the color of an Irish peat bog stream, which sounded a little insulting until I looked it up. He was right. A rich brown with glints of red and gold, the color leached from the peat bogs. It matches my eyes, hazel shot through with green. Ethan swears they're so wide and innocent that I look like a Japanese anime character or a dewy forest creature, like Bambi.

I snatch my phone on the way out the door and dictate a text.

Happy 6 years to us! How's the meeting going? Love you!

Ethan's been in meetings all weekend. The Internet start-up he founded with a couple of friends right out of college is potentially being bought by a tech company from San Jose, and the decision makers flew to Seattle on Friday to hammer out the details. And later today, when it's all over, we are celebrating our six-year dating anniversary. At the thought my heart skips a beat. I have a premonition, a shiver of delight down my spine, that today could be a very special day indeed. I am over the moon at the anticipation of it at last.

With the box of baked goods securely fastened to my white Cannondale, I pedal fast across the north slope of Queen Anne, the genteel Seattle neighborhood where I live. Even the chilly gray spring weather doesn't stop me from relishing the speed and the freedom and the feeling of flying, like the gulls that circle high over Puget Sound.

Near the Trader Joe's grocery store on Queen Anne Avenue, a familiar figure is standing on the corner, sporting an afro and a purple T-shirt with a peace sign and the slogan Kindness Is Karma.

"Angie!" I wave and she waves back. She's holding aloft copies of *Real Change*, the magazine pages fluttering in the breeze. Her German shepherd, Cargo, is lying on the pavement at her feet, his nose touching her shoes.

"How are sales this morning?" I ask, wheeling to a stop and opening my pastry box. I hand her a mascarpone and strawberry Danish, her favorite.

Angie shrugs. "Good enough. Me and Cargo can't complain."

I place a mini lemon bundt cake in front of Cargo, who wags his tail appreciatively.

Angie and I met a year ago when I started volunteering at Hope House, a women and children's shelter in downtown Seattle. Originally from Florida, she's been living in Seattle for five years, all of them on the street.

"Well, I've got to scoot. I'm late with my delivery today." I scratch Cargo behind the ears and turn to go. "See you around."

I mount my bike, then hesitate, wishing as always that I could give Angie more than a pastry every week. She's making good strides at Hope House, in her AA meetings, and with *Real Change*, but I wish I could wave a magic wand and untangle the complicated mess of her substance addiction, childhood abuse, family dysfunction, and mental illness.

"Bye, girl." Angie waves. "Thanks for stopping. See you next week."

Now even tardier, I pedal fast through picturesque neighborhoods of neatly kept historic Craftsman houses nestled up to million-dollar newly built townhomes, the product of the tech boom in Seattle and the seemingly insatiable demand for housing in the city. Zipping along the peaceful streets, I hum the Beatles' "Love Me Do" under my breath. One of Ethan's favorites. How many times has he sung it to me, strumming his guitar with that endearing smile, slow and sweet as maple syrup?

"Love, love me do," I belt out, flying down the hill toward Sunny Days. For a moment I let go of the handlebars and spread my arms wide, turning my smiling face to the sun as it just barely peeks through the gray clouds. I feel almost giddy with the promise of what I hope is to come, as though gravity itself is lightening, as though any moment I might take off into the air and soar. I have a fabulous feeling about today.

Chapter 2

Nana Alice?" After delivering the pastries to the kitchen, I rap lightly on my grandmother's studio apartment door. A moment later she opens it, wheeling into the doorway with her cherry-red walker, which she's dubbed *Greased Lightning.*

"Mia," she says, beaming with delight. "I just got back from my hike."

Nana Alice is my father's mother and one of my favorite people on earth. At eighty-two, she's spry and pert, more sugar than spice with her white hair a pouf of cotton candy on her head and her bright hazel eyes fixed on me. Today she is wearing a hot pink Patagonia fleece and yoga pants after her morning hike in Discovery Park with a vanload of residents.

"We saw a seal pup along the shore," she tells me. "They're so cute, look just like puppies, but they carry leprosy. The nature guide told us that. He had very muscular calves."

Nana Alice has lived at Sunny Days for almost four years, ever since my uncle Carl caught her perched on the roof of her house, cleaning her own gutters. At his insistence she relocated, settling somewhat unwillingly into this gracious and tasteful assisted-living residence for seniors. Nestled on the north slope of Queen Anne hill, it's just a mile from her former home, the cottage that Rosie and I currently rent from her for a mercifully discounted price.

"I was just about to make a cup of coffee." She pulls her walker aside and waves me in. "You want a cup before we watch our show? I think we're judging pastry week today, isn't that right?"

Nana Alice and I have a standing weekly date to watch reruns of *The Great British Bake Off* and act as amateur judges.

"Nana Alice, I can't stay today," I say apologetically. "Remember, Ethan and I are celebrating our anniversary?"

"Oh, that's right." Her eyes brighten with anticipation. "A big day ahead, we hope! Well then, you'd best get home and put on a nice dress." She casts a pointed look at what she refers to as my lumberjack attire. She is a liberated modern woman but was still raised in a time when ladies never went out without a pressed skirt and combed hair.

"Here, I brought you some treats." I offer her a small white Butter Emporium bag, and she peeks inside.

"Ooh, those buttermilk lemon bars are my favorite."

"I made that batch, so taste them and tell me what you think. I think I got the filling right. It's zesty, but the shortbread layer is a little tough."

As I was growing up, Nana Alice was the domestic paragon by which I measured all else. For years she owned a bakery on the top of Queen Anne hill. It was called Alice's Wonderland Bakery and featured a vaguely Carrollian theme with marzipan mushrooms and a stuffed white rabbit with red glass eyes—the rabbit was, in retrospect, rather unsettling. As a girl I loved to visit the bakery for a free butterscotch oatmeal cookie and a hug from Nana Alice, her apron always floury and stained with vanilla extract. Sometimes she would even let me operate the big stainless steel mixer.

"Tomorrow I've got medical tests all morning," Nana Alice says, folding over the top of the bag. "These will be a perfect treat while I wait."

"Tests for what? Is everything okay?"

She waves away my worry. "I'm sure it's nothing. Just a mammogram and an ultrasound. When you get old, going to the doctor is a full-time job." She sets the bag in the little basket on the front of *Greased Lightning*, then peers at me searchingly for a moment. "Are you ready if Ethan pops the question?"

I take a deep breath and nod. "Yes, I think so." How could I not be ready? Any qualms I've had about our differing visions of the future I've laid aside long ago. After six years we've learned how to compromise. We're good together. I love him. He loves me. It's that simple.

"Good." Nana Alice nods. She adores Ethan, who charmed her the first time they met by telling her she looks like Debbie Reynolds and bringing her dahlias he'd handpicked from a flower farm. Still, after six years, even she is chafing at the delay. "If we're not judging pastry, I think I'll head to the dining room for tea. There's a piano concert starting right now. The pianist isn't very good, but he tries, dear man." Nana Alice zips her fleece and maneuvers *Greased Lightning* into the hall. "I'll walk with you."

As we amble slowly down the hallway, she sighs. "You know, I envy you a little, Mia. All of your life still before you. You can do anything, go anywhere. That's a great gift. Time and youth and opportunity."

I wince. "Yeah, if I could just figure out what I want to do."

It's a sore subject for me. In the four years since college graduation, I've cycled through a variety of volunteer positions and a few short stints in different careers, but nothing has been the right fit. I finally started the apprenticeship at the bakery, but while I adore baking, it just doesn't feel big enough. I want to make a difference, change the world for the better. Making cookies doesn't seem quite grand enough.

"Your parents still hope you'll take over the farm one day," Nana Alice says.

"I just can't," I sigh, feeling the weight of their hopes and bridling just a bit under the gentle pressure.

My parents run an organic lavender farm on the Olympic Peninsula a few hours from Seattle. It provided the setting for an idyllic childhood, but is not where I want to settle down as an adult. I don't want to spend my days growing lavender and making honey. I envision a very different life, like my mother's younger sister, my aunt Frances.

Aunt Frannie has spent the last twenty-five years crisscrossing sub-Saharan Africa with a small team and a portable dental clinic in a Land Cruiser, reaching remote areas. Fiercely smart, witty, and independent, she is my hero, living a life so different from my parents' peaceful, ordered existence on the lavender farm.

I want to make the type of impact Aunt Frannie has made on people. I just have to figure out how exactly I can do that in a way that doesn't involve crowns and molars and novocaine.

"I'll figure it out someday, right?" I ask plaintively.

Nana Alice stops and takes my hand, her skin papery thin but her grip surprisingly strong. "My dear girl," she says, looking me in the eye, "don't be disheartened. You are a smart, gifted young lady with a tender heart. You were made to do good in this world. To love and be loved. Don't you forget it."

I glance away, blinking back the prickle of tears, and nod. She's been giving me this pep talk practically since I was in diapers. I believe her, I just wish I could see the end result of all her faith and expectation.

"I think your concert is starting." I gently place her hand back on *Greased Lightning.*

The opening strains of "I've Got You Under My Skin" drift across the lobby as we head toward the dining room. Outside the glass front doors rain drizzles steadily down. It's going to be a wet ride home. An older gentleman in a trench coat and a trilby is just coming in. He opens the door with a gust of cool air, fumbling to maneuver an open red tartan umbrella through the doorway in front of him. Nana Alice stops to let him cross our path, but he doesn't seem to see us. He gives the umbrella a thorough shake and then furls it smartly, spraying both of us with a shower of raindrops.

"Gracious, watch where you're going," Nana Alice protests.

"Why ladies, my apologies." He peers over the umbrella at us. Under the trilby his face is lined but good-humored, his pale blue eyes sharp. He looks about Nana Alice's age. His figure is lean and he walks nimbly but with a slight stoop. "I didn't see you there." He tips his hat to us. "Albert Prentice. I just moved into 4B."

Nana Alice gives him a startled look. "Albert Prentice?" she says. "I went to school with an Albert Prentice. Eleventh grade at Holy Cross. Sister Mary Teresa's English class. I was Alice Freeman then."

Albert takes a step back and removes his hat, holding it to his chest. "Alice Freeman," he says slowly, almost reverently. "Of course I remember you. We performed a scene from *Much Ado About Nothing*. You were radiant as Beatrice."

Nana Alice grips *Greased Lightning* and stands up a little straighter. "Well, your Benedick wasn't half bad either, if I recall correctly." She beams at Albert. "What a coincidence." She pauses. "Are you here alone?"

His eyes cloud. "My wife, Jeanne, died three months ago. Heart failure. And my kids think I can't manage on my own. Sixty years in our home in Laurelhurst, and now here I am." He shakes his head and puts his hat back on. "It's tough to start over at my age."

Nana Alice reaches forward and grips his hand, her gaze sympathetic. "Albert, you are among friends here. You come by my table for dinner tonight. I'll introduce you to everyone."

Albert looks pleased. "It would be my pleasure. Thank you, Alice. That's kind of you." He releases her hand, tips his hat to us, and heads toward the east wing, his stride jaunty.

When he's out of earshot, Nana Alice shakes her head in amazement. "Albert Prentice. Imagine that. And newly widowed, poor man."

"He's very handsome," I observe. "The ladies are going to swoon when they see him."

Nana nods. "Yes, and he still has his hair." She purses her lips. "He'll be the toast of the town around here."

"What about you," I tease gently. "He seemed awfully fond of your Beatrice."

"Pshaw," she says lightly. "That was ages ago. The girls all liked him, though, even then. They thought he looked like Paul Newman."

"He still does," I say, giving her a sideways glance.

Nana Alice tilts her head with an uncharacteristically coy smile. "I guess you're right," she says. "He does."

Chapter 3

"You look pretty." Ethan gives me a quick kiss as I slide into his vintage silver BMW idling against the curb.

"And you're very dapper." He's wearing his gray cashmere cardigan over a button-down shirt in sky blue that makes his eyes pop. Is this the outfit of a man about to propose? I can't decide, but he looks endearingly handsome in it.

"I thought we could go down to Pike Place," he says, darting a sideways glance at me.

"Sounds perfect." My heart is beating fast against my rib cage as we head toward downtown Seattle and the waterfront. Pike Place Market is one of Seattle's most iconic spots. After today it may be my favorite location in the world.

I clasp my hands between my knees and try to calm my nerves. I didn't take Nana Alice's admonition to put on a nice dress, but I'm glad I thought to put on waterproof mascara and my new spiffy red pair of TOMS canvas shoes.

"How'd the meetings go today?" I ask as we drive down Queen Anne hill.

"Great. They really like the concept and want to move forward on a contract." As he talks enthusiastically about the start-up, I try to focus on his explanation, but I can't stop thinking about what I hope is about to happen.

I fell for Ethan White the instant I saw him. It was the first week of my sophomore year as a sociology major at the University of Washington. Standing in the front of the line at Wow Bubble Tea in the University District, I was frantically rooting through my satchel in search of my wallet, which was nowhere to be found. Panicking, I was scrambling for loose change at the bottom of my bag when an arm reached around me and placed a five-dollar bill on the counter. I whirled around.

The owner of the arm was about my age, impeccably groomed and dressed like an investment banker on vacation. Khaki shorts and a Ralph Lauren polo shirt in a pale pink the exact shade of strawberry ice cream. He was adorable, with straight blond hair and broad shoulders, but it was his eyes that caught me; they were the color of the Caribbean, so clear and aqua blue I couldn't look away.

"I'm so sorry," I stammered, embarrassed by my cashless plight and a little tongue-tied by the star appeal of the man standing before me. "I think I left my wallet in my dorm. I'll pay you back."

He smiled, revealing a dimple in one cheek, and took a sip of his smoothie. "Don't worry about it," he said casually. "Happy to help a fellow Husky in distress." He motioned to an empty table in the corner. "Care to join me? I'm Ethan, by the way."

We talked for hours, sitting on the uncomfortably hard chairs until my bottom went numb. He was educated and cultured but not snobby, just sweet and earnest and funny, very funny. I couldn't remember the last time I'd laughed so hard. It was so easy between us, as easy as falling, as easy as breathing. We were friends for months first, but I sensed we both wanted more. I certainly did. The first time he kissed me, I saw sunspots.

I glance at Ethan in the driver's seat, his hair blowing in the wind, his eyes alight as he talks about the future of the start-up. My first love, this man I've given my heart and six years of my life to.

In an instant I glimpse the life ahead of us in a burst of images, the life we've sculpted from a hundred nights sitting on Ethan's plaid blanket side by side at Gas Works Park, dreaming of the future. The restored Craftsman cottage we'll buy in Green Lake. A French bulldog named Butterworth. Lazy Sunday mornings reading the *Seattle Times* over coffee and deliciously flaky morning buns from the Butter Emporium. Sampling craft beer and listening to Ethan's band perform in slightly grotty venues on Capitol Hill. And some years down the road, a little curly-haired girl and a blond boy with a dimple in his cheek. For a split second I picture my passport sitting in an unused suitcase under my bed, its pages still blank as a disappointed stare, but I push the thought away. This is the life I have chosen.

It may not fit my childhood fancies of exotic adventure and sacrifice, following in the footsteps of Aunt Frannie, but I adore Ethan. I don't want to live without him—the way he cups my face in his hands and looks at me like I'm the only thing in his world, the Beatles tunes he hums constantly under his breath, his practicality, ambition, and sensible can-do attitude. I want him so very much. I want *us* more than anything in the world.

I squeeze my eyes shut, envisioning Ethan down on one knee, holding a sparkling diamond solitaire. When he asks me, of course I will say yes.

"Oh Pike Place," I sigh happily, wandering hand in hand with Ethan through the long covered walkway lined with vendors' stalls. The market is usually jammed with tourists, but it's starting to close down for the day and is surprisingly empty this late in the afternoon.

"Scene of our first real date, remember?" Ethan says. "Clam chowder at the Athenian . . ."

"And coffee from the original Starbucks," I finish, squeezing his hand. He remembers. Coming here today can't be an accident.

Pike Place is a feast for the senses—the fresh briny smell of the seafood stalls with their glistening king salmon and octopus and prawns on beds of pebbled ice, a man in a straw fedora playing a Willy Nelson song on a banjo, fruit vendors handing out segments of tangerine, their produce piled like jewels behind them. We pass stalls with honey and beeswax skin care products, framed photographs of the Space Needle, orca whales made from recycled metal, handmade hippie jewelry.

Ethan seems distant and distracted. I try to lighten the mood, laughing and making witty observations, but I'm nervous. There's a fluttery sensation in the pit of my stomach, and my laughter sounds forced in my own ears.

He slows at one of the flower stalls run by diminutive Hmong ladies. Sitting behind a low wall of gorgeous seasonal flowers, they craft beautiful bouquets with quick, ever-moving hands. "Pick one," he urges, and I choose a gorgeous little bouquet of double daffodils and tulips, a riotous orb of sunny spring colors. Ethan reaches into his messenger bag for his wallet to pay for the flowers, but just then his phone rings.

He grabs the phone instead and glances at the number. "Oh, I have to take this. Here." He hands me the bag and ducks into a quiet corner of the hall. I fish around for his wallet and pay the woman. As I drop the wallet back into his bag, I spy something. A little ring box in unmistakable Tiffany blue. My heart does a grand jeté against my rib cage.

For an instant I panic. *Am I sure? Can I do this?* This is forever we are talking about. And then I brush aside those momentary nerves. Of course I'm sure. I close the bag.

Ethan rejoins me.

"Sorry about that. Just Vihaan checking in about some projected numbers from this morning," he says. He takes his bag and holds out his hand. I take it, and we continue through the market.

I eye him furtively as we walk. There's something in the set of his shoulders . . . He's seemed distant for weeks now, but when I've questioned him he's brushed it off as busyness, stress over the start-up, preoccupation with the possibility of investment from a major company in Silicon Valley. But now I understand. He's nervous about this monumental step we are finally about to take together.

As we near the end of the market hall, he turns to me. "Hey, can we ride the Ferris wheel?"

The Seattle Great Wheel was built just a few years ago down by Elliot Bay. At night it's lit up with different colors and always looks so jaunty and enticing, but we've never ridden it.

"Sure, sounds fun," I say, trying to sound light and nonchalant. This is where it will happen, then, dangling above Elliot Bay, all of the city spread out behind us. This is where our future will start.

Twenty minutes later our airy glass-and-steel gondola lifts us into the air above the Seattle waterfront. For a moment I forget everything else and lean forward eagerly, taking in the breathtaking panorama—the wide gray blue of Elliot Bay below us, flat and shiny as a new nickel, and beyond that the low green mound of Bainbridge Island. Farther west, beyond Bainbridge, the snow-capped Olympic Mountains rise jagged and majestic on the peninsula. And behind and below us lies Seattle, my beloved city. Our capsule pauses at the apex of the ride.

Ethan clears his throat. "Mia."

I snap to attention, sitting up straight and swallowing hard as Ethan reaches into his messenger bag and pulls out the Tiffany-blue box. It sits in his palm, a beautiful invitation, a promise.

Yes, I almost whisper before he asks the question. *I'll marry you.* The words sit on my tongue, lozenge shaped and weighty with commitment. I want them to be smooth when I utter them, round and smooth as pearls.

"Mia." His hands are trembling. Those beautiful hands that have interlaced with mine a thousand times, that can mix a perfect margarita, strum an Eric Clapton tune on the guitar. He meets my eyes, his the limpid blue of the Caribbean shallows. He opens the box, and I stifle a gasp. The round diamond solitaire sparkles in the sun, throwing rainbow glints of light across the white walls of our capsule.

Ethan opens his mouth, then glances down at the ring and pauses. His silence stretches long.

"Yes?" I prompt, but he doesn't say anything. "Ethan?" I stare at him in bewilderment.

He fiddles with the ring in the box, then looks up and meets my gaze with a pained expression. It's strange how many things begin and end without words. I learned once in a college communication class that only 35 percent of conversation is what you say. The rest is nonverbal. And so this is how I finally know. Not with a flood of words, not from a mouth twisted in grief, but with two eyes that slide from mine like oil on water.

Dread sinks like lead, cold and hard, in my stomach. *Oh no. Oh no. What is happening?*

"I can't," he says as our gondola starts the descent from the top with a jerk. "I'm sorry. I thought this was the right thing to do, but I can't . . . I can't seem to make myself propose." He looks so surprised. He fumbles with the box, snapping it closed. The click of that lid shatters all my hopes and expectations. "Mia, I need to take a break from us. I can't go forward with this right now."

After that I hear only the outline of his words. Going different directions. Been growing apart for a while now. Need time to figure things out. Will I give him space?

His words are rushed, a little pleading, as though he thinks he can rationalize me into agreement or at least understanding. But I can't make out the details over the ringing in my ears. This can't be happening.

I look down at the colorful buildings along the pier far below, the Seattle Aquarium, Miners Landing with its carousel and carnival music, Ye Olde Curiosity Shop where you can see a preserved walrus penis and purchase gaudy souvenirs from Seattle. I glance back at him, sure I've misunderstood, but he is waiting for an answer, looking at me pleadingly.

I know every bone and freckle of him, but I didn't see this coming. I didn't know this corner of his heart. I swallow and swallow again, unable to get my bearings. What can I possibly say? I feel dizzy, as though the gondola is listing to one side, leaning too far out over the water. I have the sensation for one brief second of falling. How long has he seen this coming? Did he really intend to propose and then at the last moment gain this flash of insight, this earth-shattering clarity?

"Please, Mia. I just need a little time to figure this out. I don't know what's wrong. I just need some space to get my head on straight." I can see the fear in his eyes, in the rapid throb of the pulse in his neck. He looks trapped by the circumstances, by his own words.

I dart a look around the gondola and then down again. Below us an Argosy dinner cruise ship is docked in the harbor and tiny people are gathering beside it. Beyond the pier lies the ferry terminal for the islands, and farther south the monolithic red container cranes of the port.

What about the ring in the little blue box? What about our future together? The Craftsman cottage and Butterworth and the flaky morning buns? I want to ask so many things, but in the end I just ask why.

"I don't know, Mia." He spreads his hands in a helpless gesture, those hands that have cupped my face so tenderly, brushed away tears with his knuckles when I cried. "I just don't know if this is right anymore. Please, give me time to figure it out." His tone is pleading for me to understand, but I don't, not at all. I cannot think of what to say to change his mind.

So as the Ferris wheel slowly completes its final rotation, I agree to give him space, three days to determine the course of our future. I agree because my heart is breaking. I can't seem to draw enough air into my lungs. I'm choking on the panic and grief welling up in my throat. The disappointment and fear taste bitter in my mouth, like the charred edges of burnt toast.

When our gondola finally bumps to a stop, I alight with as much courage and grace as I can muster. My eyes are like dikes for a sea of tears, my pride the little Dutch boy's finger trying to hold back the flood.

"Let me know," I tell Ethan finally, "when you figure it out."

He takes a step toward me, his expression pained, but I quickly step back, clutching my jacket. I glance at his messenger bag, picturing the little blue box sitting within like a broken promise.

"Mia, I'm sorry," he says.

I look away. If I see pity in his eyes, I know it will be the end of us. I will shatter. Instead, I gather the shreds of my dignity and the small but stubborn hope that he will realize his mistake and come back to me, and I walk away. I don't look back at the man I love and the ruined remains of what I thought would be the happiest day of my life.

Chapter 4

"How can this be happening?" I whisper to the empty living room. Three hours after the disastrous Ferris wheel ride, I am curled in the fetal position on the couch at the cottage, puffy and wrung out from incessant ugly crying. Cocooned in a fuzzy brown blanket my mother crocheted for me when I left home for college, I stare out the picture window at the cold drizzle. Floor lamps cast pools of light onto the Persian carpet and Bonnie Raitt warbles plaintively in the background. "I can't make you love me," she sings with such aching poignancy fresh tears well up in my eyes.

Six. Six years since Ethan first kissed me. Six years since this all began. So many anniversaries, so many opportunities, all ended in disappointment. There was always a reason—paying off school debt and getting on firm financial footing, the start-up that's taken all his time and energy for the past few years, his desire to be financially secure and able to provide a good life for us together. But the years ticked by with alarming rapidity and still no proposal, no start to our life together.

Were all the delays, all those years of waiting for the right time, actually because in his heart of hearts he didn't want to marry me?

The front door swings open with a sudden gust of cold air and Rosie rushes in carrying a bakery box from Trophy Cupcake.

"Sugar!" she exclaims dramatically in her big Texas twang. "I got your message. I came as soon as I could."

Clad in a canary-yellow wool coat that looks sensational with her burnished red hair, the exact color of a shiny copper penny, she kneels next to the couch and envelops me in a hug that smells of butter cream frosting and damp, salt-tinged wool. "Come into the kitchen and tell me everything. I've got cupcakes." She leans back and eyes my blanket-wrapped form lying prone on the couch. "You look like a pupa."

"This is my chrysalis," I mutter pitifully. "I'm waiting to be reborn."

"Come on then, my poor little caterpillar. Follow me." She sheds her coat on an armchair and breezes into the kitchen at the back of the house, waving the cupcake box enticingly. I shuffle obediently behind her, taking my blanket cocoon with me.

In the outdated but cozy kitchen, I slide onto the bench in the breakfast nook. Rosie places a single cupcake on a white plate in front of me. It is hummingbird flavor, my favorite, a combination of pineapple coconut cake with cream cheese frosting, but how can I eat when I'm suffocating in grief?

Carrying a French press of coffee to the table to steep, Rosie squeezes her tall, curvaceous frame onto the opposite bench. "Okay, sugar. Tell me all about it. What in the world happened?"

I tell her the whole messy, sordid tale, and when I'm done she reaches across the table and squeezes my hand.

"Mia," she says sympathetically, "I'm so sorry. If Ethan doesn't choose you, he is dumber than a box of rocks."

I smile wanly, appreciating the display of loyalty, then promptly burst into tears, sobbing uncontrollably over my cupcake so that salty drops dapple the frosted top. Rosie just sits with me and lets me cry. Finally, I take a napkin from the stack on the table and blow my nose, hiccupping softly. "I guess I just have to wait three days and see what he decides, right? I can't change anything now." I sniff. "Let's talk about something else. How was your day?"

"Well, I have some news," Rosie says carefully, pouring herself a now terribly overbrewed cup of coffee. "It's such bad timing to tell you now, I know, but I don't want to keep it from you either. I just heard back from the Humanitas Foundation." She looks up at me, and a surprised smile breaks over her face. "I got in. They said yes!"

"They said yes?" I repeat, staring at her, agape and aghast. Then I try to cover my reaction with a feeble "That's great!"

When Rosie first told me about her desire to apply for an around-the-world trip with a global humanitarian organization, I encouraged her to go for it. Up to this point, the extent of her philanthropy has been volunteering to be Seattle's tallest and sexiest elf and singing "Santa Baby" at charity galas around town at Christmas. Her international travel has included a week in St. Barts and five days at an all-inclusive resort in Jamaica, both gifts from her last boyfriend, an art dealer who turned out to be very married. I'm not one to talk, though. I've only ever been to Canada.

"It's just for nine weeks and then I'll be back," she reassures me. "I'll be gone from the end of April to July, so I need to find someone to sublet from me until I get back."

I nod numbly. My head is spinning with the speed of these changes. When Rosie first applied, I was a little envious that she might get to travel the world, but I also secretly believed I would be planning my wedding in her absence. The thought of Rosie leaving me in this time of uncertainty makes me feel panicky. I need my best friend by my side.

"I didn't think I'd actually get in." Rosie shakes her head, looking a little stunned too. "I'm a jazz singer, not an international aid expert or a pediatrician. I don't have hard skills like that."

"Maybe they wanted someone with softer skills." I nibble an edge of my cupcake. When your whole world crumbles, eat sugar.

That should be embroidered on a cushion somewhere. "Maybe they needed a jazz singer, cupcake froster, and plus-sized model all rolled into one. Maybe you fit the profile perfectly."

Rosie slants me an amused look. "Oh, I'm positive they were looking for just that combination. But this is my chance, Mia. I'm going to do good in the world—and maybe finally meet Mr. Right." She gives a wistful sigh. "Think about it, a select team of talented young professionals giving back to the world in exotic destinations. If that isn't a recipe for love, I don't know what is." She unwraps her Black Forest cupcake and frowns. "Maybe this time I'll get lucky and actually meet a good guy."

Rosie's love life has been a tumultuous series of mishaps and regrets. Her heart's desire is simple—to find a good, honest man, preferably one who's rich enough to own a yacht or a second home in Saint-Tropez, and to have a career as a jazz singer in New York City.

"What countries are you going to travel to?" I ask. It sounds so glamorous and important, jetting across the world to help people in need. While I very well may be sitting here single and alone in a blanket cocoon. I unwrap my cupcake and take a big bite.

Rosie swirls her finger around her cherry buttercream frosting and licks it off. "India, Thailand, and Mexico." She's practically fizzing with excitement.

"That sounds amazing," I say wistfully. For a second I am caught up in a whirl of exotic images—colorful saris, Buddhist temples, authentic tortillas, and ancient Aztec pyramids.

"Oh Mia, you could come too!" Rosie exclaims, sitting bolt upright. "I just remembered! Stella, the trip organizer, told us today that a girl from our team dropped out unexpectedly. They have an opening they're trying to fill last minute." She gazes at me expectantly.

I shake my head. "I can't just drop everything. I have my apprenticeship. And Ethan . . ." I stop, unsure how to finish that sentence.

Rosie nods and purses her lips, taking a sip of coffee. "I understand. Well, the opportunity is there if you change your mind. It would be so fun. Think about it. India, Thailand, and Mexico." Her tone is just slightly wheedling.

"I've always dreamed of going to India," I admit. "To follow in the footsteps of Mother Teresa. And I'd finally get to try real chai."

Rosie nods, popping the maraschino cherry from the top of her cupcake into her mouth with a flourish. "At least consider it," she says. "It could be the chance of a lifetime."

That night I dream again of bees. Swarms of them, golden and laden with pollen, swaying drunkenly through the brilliant blooming purple rows of lavender in the lazy summer sunshine. I'm standing in one of West Wind Farm's lavender fields. My arms are full of cut lavender, the sharp scent rising heavy and languid in the air. I dig my bare toes into the sun-warmed earth. Far off beyond the fields Puget Sound glistens gray, and beneath the overwhelming scent of lavender wafts the ever-present hint of a fresh salt breeze. I glance down and take a step back. I'm wearing a white satin wedding dress. A bee lands on the skirt of my dress, then another and another. I try to shake them off with one hand, the other clutching the bunches of lavender, but the bees cling to the rich fabric, climbing slowly and stubbornly up the dress. When I glance up, Ethan is standing at the end of my row, his back to me, staring out across the fields to the Sound, the breeze tousling his blond hair.

"Ethan, help me!" I call, struggling to shake off the honeybees.

He turns and looks at me, his eyes sad, then raises his hand in farewell and silently backs away.

Chapter 5

"Morning." I let myself in the back door of the Butter Emporium and greet Colleen and Hector, the two chief bakers. It's barely 5 a.m., but they've already been here for an hour or more, prepping for the day.

It's been three long days since the disastrous Ferris wheel ride. Three agonizing days of waiting, the minutes rolling by as slow and viscous as treacle. I have had no word from Ethan. I stow my fleece and satchel in the staff closet and join the others in the kitchen.

"Today you're going to do the pain au Nutella by yourself," Colleen announces, pausing for a moment from mixing up dough for Parmesan bacon scones.

I nod and go wash my hands, still feeling sleepy. Outside in the darkness a light drizzle is falling through the yellow glow of the streetlights. I've been training with Colleen and Hector for six months now. I've finished bread, scones, and cookies and have moved on to pastries, a tricky, temperamental class of baked goods.

"Hop to it, girl." Colleen jerks her head to a spot across from Hector at the huge stainless steel prep table. "Hector made you a chai latte."

I assume my place at my station and take a grateful sip. It's piping hot and perfect—earthy, creamy, and exotic tasting. For a moment I imagine myself in India with Rosie, sipping chai while watching the sun rise pink and orange over the Taj Mahal . . .

"Thanks, Hector."

He stands across the table from me, shaping boules of sourdough bread. He nods and gives me a wink, placing a boule into a lightly floured proofing basket to rise. "You're welcome, chica."

Making the pain au Nutella is a tedious, exacting process. First I cut six sticks of butter into half-inch pieces and beat them with a little flour in the big industrial mixer, making sure to keep it cool. Then I shape the butter into two even squares and set them to the side. I retrieve the croissant dough that has been waiting in the refrigerator since yesterday and roll out half the dough into a long rectangle, placing one butter square on the dough, then folding the dough over it. I press down the edges, sealing the butter inside, then carefully roll out the dough and butter combination into another long rectangle. With great concentration and precision, I fold the dough into thirds like a letter.

I cover it with plastic wrap and let it rest for twenty minutes while I repeat the process with the other half of the dough. Each batch of pain au Nutella requires at least three rounds of these precise steps, with twenty-minute rests in between. It is painstaking work, requiring a cool hand and a steady touch.

"Looking good," Colleen says, rolling out the scone dough as she keeps an eye on my process. "You've got the touch." She watches me work for a moment, her brow furrowed. I wonder if I'm doing something wrong, so I check my work thoroughly. Everything seems fine.

The slap of Hector turning the dough and the snick of Colleen making perfectly round scones with a metal biscuit cutter are the only sounds as I tidy my workstation and let my dough rest. It's still pitch dark outside, just beginning to lighten at the edges of the windows. It feels as though we are all alone in the quiet dark world, cozy in a warm pool of light, the air smelling of butter and parmesan from Colleen's scones.

I have loved baking for as long as I can remember. While some girls stayed up late reading Nancy Drew or Sweet Valley High under their covers, I was devouring *Baking Illustrated* and Rose Levy Beranbaum's iconic *The Cake Bible.*

Still, much as I love this apprenticeship, baking isn't momentous enough to be my life's work. It is making something to be consumed; it's about simple pleasures and momentary joys. But I find such contentment in the act of baking itself—the tactile reality of mixing the ingredients, the earthiness of kneading and shaping, getting my hands floury, making something delicious out of simple ingredients like flour, sugar, salt, and water. So until I figure out how I am supposed to really change the world, at least I can offer humanity perfectly chewy cookies and a nice flaky scone.

I hear a text message come through, and while my second batch of dough rests, I check my phone.

Hey, you free for a picnic tonight at Gas Works Park? I'll get sushi.

Ethan. I stare at the text under the bright kitchen lights, trying to discern its tone. I can't think straight. Gas Works Park is our favorite picnic spot, a quirky little snip of land on the north shore of Lake Union where the Seattle Gas Light Company gasification plant once stood. We have spent countless evenings there watching the sailboats and dreaming of the future. What does it mean that he's chosen this spot? Has he come to his senses and realized we are meant to be together, or is he breaking up with me for good, closing the loop in a familiar place? My heart is pounding with adrenaline.

And sushi? Ethan doesn't like sushi. He claims that any food that has to be strapped to rice with a seaweed seat belt is too adventurous for him. Is he trying to be nice, cater to my tastes as an apology . . . or as a consolation prize? I text what I hope sounds like a casual response.

Sure. What time?

A moment later my phone pings. 5 okay?

Great. I add a smiley face, then set the phone down and wrap my arms around my middle, around my apron, greasy with butter, trying to anchor myself, panicked by the blind hope swelling in my chest. I take one deep breath, then another. The air smells of crisping bacon. Delicious, but I can't focus.

I glance at Colleen and Hector rhythmically going about their work. Colleen looks up at me again with a troubled expression. She raises her eyebrows, and I shake my head. I don't want to talk about it, not until I know Ethan's decision. I fetch my chilled dough from the refrigerator. For better or worse, by tonight I'll have my answer. And until then, there are pastries to make.

A few hours later, my shift over, I'm tidying up my station when Colleen approaches me. "Mia, can I talk to you for a second?"

She glances beyond me across the table at Hector, and a look passes between them. A moment later he takes off his apron and announces he's taking a break, something I've never seen him do.

"Listen, Mia." Colleen scrubs her hands through her salt-and-pepper buzz cut and sighs. She looks tired. "There's no easy way to say this—we have to stop your apprenticeship."

"What? Why?" I stare at her in disbelief. "I thought it was going well. You said I have a natural touch." My mind races, trying to recall something I've done wrong. Were my buttermilk biscuits too dense last weekend? The walnut date bars too dry?

She holds up a hand. Her blunt nails are caked with dough. "It has nothing to do with you. You're one of the most promising young bakers I've ever seen. You have a natural feel for baking that can't be taught. And you're a hard worker, diligent and consistent. This decision comes straight from the new owners. They don't think we need another baker, and they don't want us spending time and resources to train you if we can't keep you on. They're cutting back hours, staff, everything, trying to make the bakery more profitable. I'm sorry." She presses her lips into a thin line and looks away.

The bakery was sold a few months ago to a couple from Southern California who'd previously run a chain of successful salad bars in LA. They promised no big changes, but apparently that doesn't include keeping my job. Fired. I've just been fired from baking. I am stunned, humiliated. "I don't know what to say," I stammer.

"I know, Mia. I'm sorry." Colleen clasps my shoulder and looks pained. "I'm supposed to tell you that you can go back to your counter job starting next week. But what I'm going to say instead, off the record, is that I think you should turn in your resignation and get out of here." She stares at me hard, as though trying to channel some inner fortitude into me in the face of this devastating news. "Find somewhere that will let you do what you love, because you're really good. Don't let this stop you, okay?" She gives my shoulder a firm squeeze.

I nod, heart pounding and tears blurring my vision. "Okay." I stumble to gather my things. I pass Hector lurking in the supply closet on my way out. He gives me a sympathetic nod, his eyes sad.

I take my satchel and fleece from the hook and let myself out into the watery sunlight, still reeling. How is it possible that in just a few short days my entire future could be crumbling away? By tonight there may be nothing left at all.

Chapter 6

"Hey, tiger." My older brother, Henry, answers the phone on the second ring. He's the first person I think to call when I leave work. I'm a mess, stunned by the loss of my apprenticeship and in knots over my impending picnic with Ethan. I need a cooler head to talk me down.

"I think I might be having the worst day of my life," I blurt out, bicycling at breakneck pace through historic Ballard.

"Really? What happened?" In the background I can hear one of the twins squawking. "Oliver, don't hit Auden with the rubber hammer," Henry admonishes. "No! Dude, what did I tell you? Gentle touches!"

Henry is a stay-at-home dad in one of the affluent suburbs of Chicago. His wife, Christine, has a high-powered job in marketing for Kraft Foods. Besides the twins, who are eighteen-month-old bundles of boundless energy, they have Madeleine, who is four, and a dwarf hamster named Rainbow Princess.

"For starters, I just got fired from the bakery." I quickly describe my morning, then detail Ethan's entire non-proposal, ending with, "So it's been three days. He just texted to ask me to meet. I'm absolutely petrified."

I turn onto the Ballard Bridge and wait for Henry's response, pedaling slowly down the narrow bike and pedestrian walkway.

Although we don't see each other often, my brother and I are still close. We talk every week or so, and I trust him to be calm, steady, and brutally honest, all things I need right now.

"Aw Mia, I'm sorry. That sucks." I hear genuine regret in Henry's voice. "I can't believe Ethan would do that to you. After all this time together, I just didn't see that coming." An instant later his tone slides into alarm. "No, don't eat that, Auden. Where did you get a glue stick? Spit it out, into Daddy's hand. Here, you want some Cheerios? Just spit it out for Daddy."

I wait patiently as Auden howls into the phone. I picture Henry prying a round of gummy glue stick out of Auden's wide-open mouth. Henry and I look alike, with similar eye shape and coloring, but he has straight brown hair worn long and little round wire-rimmed glasses, channeling a bit of a John Lennon vibe. These days he is usually covered in some pureed vegetable substance and looking both tired and a little harried. The shrieking dies down and Henry comes back on the phone. "Just a second. Keurig's ready and I'm beat." His voice trails away.

Halfway across the bridge I pause because the drawbridge is going up. A sailboat is waiting to enter the harbor. Cars back up on either side as the two lanes of asphalt split apart and lift high into the air. Below me white sailboats bob in salt water the color of cobalt glass. The breeze carries the scent of brine and underneath a hint of gasoline from the boats. Overhead the sky is patchy, clear blue peeking out from behind fluffy clouds, giving the promise of sun later. It looks like a perfect Seattle day, a perfect, disastrous day.

"Okay, I'm back. The caffeine is hitting my brain," Henry announces. I can hear him slurping coffee. "I just put the twins down in front of Baby Einstein. Don't tell Christine. They're not supposed to have any screen time until they're two. So if they don't get into Harvard, I'm holding you responsible." He chuckles darkly, then sobers. "I still can't believe it. I thought you and Ethan were a done deal. Okay, so let me get this straight. You're stuck waiting to see what he decides?"

"Yes! I feel like my entire life is crumbling around me, and I can't do anything to stop it. I'm just watching it happen." I straddle my bike and watch the sailboat slowly glide under the bridge. I pause, then ask quietly, "What do I do if he doesn't want me?"

Just saying the words feels like a punch in the gut.

Henry is quiet for a moment. "Mia, why are you letting Ethan have all the power? This is your life too. You don't have to passively just wait for him to decide for you."

"But I love him," I protest. "I want him to choose us again."

"That may not happen," Henry says gently.

I am silent for a moment. I know he's right, but I will continue to hope until I hear the words from Ethan's mouth.

"So what do you think I should do?" I ask miserably.

The crossing gates slowly lift and cars snake across the bridge once again. I don't start pedaling, just move my bike over to the edge of the narrow walkway and rest my arms on the bridge railing, looking down at the boats bobbing in the harbor.

"You remember that Mother Teresa coloring book you had when we were kids?" Henry asks.

"Sure." It was my favorite childhood possession, gifted to me by Aunt Frannie on one of her whirlwind visits back to the US. She'd been working in post–civil war Sierra Leone and dropped in to see us for a few days, enough time to fill my head with stories of her wild adventures and help me blow out the candles on my birthday cake.

For my favorite niece. Be brave and strong and true, just like Mother Teresa, she'd written on the inside cover in her bold, slanted scrawl. I took one look at the drawing of Mother Teresa on the front cover and claimed her as my hero too.

"What made you think about that?" I ask. That coloring book

had made a tremendous impact on my young mind and heart. I'd colored the border of Mother Teresa's sari Crayola denim blue, and used sky blue for the stream of water pouring from a ladle into the open mouth of an emaciated, dying man. I imagined myself in the picture, my hand holding the ladle, the goldenrod sun hot on the crown of my head.

"I was just thinking about you as a kid," Henry replies. "You used to tell everyone that you wanted to travel the world and be like Mother Teresa. Do you remember?" He chuckles.

"Saint Mia," I reply. That's what I dreamed of as a child. Saint Mia giving her life to help those in need.

"So when did you give up on that dream?" he asks.

"I haven't given up on it," I say, feeling a little defensive. "I just . . . haven't quite figured out how to live it out yet."

But as soon as I say it, I wonder if that's entirely true. Have I forgotten those childhood dreams? Are the dreams I have now more Ethan's than mine? Maybe a little. Maybe more than a little.

But I want the life Ethan and I have created together. It's a good life, an appealing life. I want to live it with him. But still, Henry's question niggles at me. It feels important. Why *had* I let my childhood visions dissolve? I'd known I was giving something up as Ethan and I moved toward a future with each other, but wasn't that normal? The result of two people compromising to make a life together work?

Had Ethan had to let go of any of his dreams? I've never considered that question before.

"You still there?" Henry clears his throat.

"Yes, sorry. Just thinking." I hesitate. "So what do you think I should do now?"

"Think about what you want for yourself, not just what you and Ethan planned together," Henry says bluntly. He doesn't sugarcoat things. "I know you hope it will work out between you, but what if it doesn't? What would a life without Ethan look like? What would you choose if it were up to just you?"

My mind immediately flashes to an airplane lifting off the tarmac into the sky, bound for some exotic locale. Like me, Ethan has only ever been to Canada. Unlike me, he's quite content sticking close to home. Hawaii for vacations, New York at Christmastime—those are the extent of his travel aspirations. We've wrangled and compromised, settling on the Caribbean for our honeymoon—maybe England and Scotland for the soccer and the Scotch distilleries someday. But he still doesn't have a passport. Those plans are all still just theoretical.

I think for one split second of a tiny airplane circling the globe. Of high windswept plateaus in Patagonia, the bitter aroma of mint tea in a dusty Moroccan souk. I think of the South Pacific, palm trees swaying in the breeze, sand as soft and white as icing sugar. I think of my passport filled with official-looking stamps.

"Where do I start?" I ask finally.

"Start with Saint Mia, start with the dreams you had before Ethan," Henry says gently. "At least that could help point you in the right direction. I think you need to start planning an alternate life."

An alternate life. I grip the bridge railing and blow a breath out through my mouth, a long slow exhale to quell my panic. I have no idea what that would look like. I want the life I've been planning on for six years. I want my apprenticeship at the bakery. I want Ethan. But Henry is right. I may not get the chance to live the life I've been counting on.

"Okay." For the first time since that disastrous Ferris wheel ride, I feel a spark of hope. I don't have to be the victim here, waiting on someone else to decide my fate. I can't control Ethan's decision, but I can start taking steps to control my own future. The idea gives me a wobbly sort of courage.

"Hey, text me and tell me how it goes," Henry says. "He's a fool if he lets you go. You deserve a man who sees how amazing you are. And Mia, remember, you're stronger than you think."

"I hope so." I clear my throat, trying to swallow the clog of tears. "Thanks, Henry."

After we hang up, I ponder his words. *An alternate life.* I roll the phrase around in my head; it's terrifying and liberating all at the same time. I still hope more than anything that Ethan chooses me, chooses us, but if he doesn't . . .

Dizzy with the magnitude of it, I swing my leg over my bike and pedal toward home, trying to wrap my mind around the idea. In the sky ahead of me, south toward SeaTac airport, I see an airplane lifting off into the pearly gray clouds, the nose pointed up and away, toward a far horizon. It looks like freedom. I think of my passport waiting in the suitcase I've never used. I think of a spinning globe, all the countries of the world a blur of colors as they whiz by. In an alternate life I could do anything, be anywhere. When I consider the possibilities, I can't quite catch my breath.

Chapter 7

"I got you salmon," Ethan says, unpacking our picnic from a brown paper Metropolitan Market bag. I sit beside him on a grassy knoll at Gas Works Park, facing a panoramic view of Lake Union and, beyond it, the city of Seattle. I feel preternaturally calm, but I have to clench my hands between my thighs to keep them from trembling. I desperately want to hear what he has to say, but equally I'm afraid for him to open his mouth. If he doesn't speak the words, they are not yet true.

Pulling out plastic trays of sushi, little packets of soy sauce, wooden chopsticks in white paper sleeves, Ethan arranges our picnic between us on his plaid wool picnic blanket. Tonight feels like a distorted mirror image of so many other peaceful evenings here, all of the same elements but none of the ease.

"Thanks." I clear my throat and take the tray with the salmon roll and a bottle of ginger kombucha. I pick at my salmon roll nervously.

"Listen, Mia, thank you for giving me space this week." Ethan sets down his chopsticks on his untouched tray of shrimp sushi roll and looks at me.

My heart plummets. *Don't do it,* I want to beg. *If you say it, you can't take it back.*

He gazes out at the jaunty white sailboats on Lake Union and sighs in a resigned way. "I think I've dragged this out long enough, and I want to be fair to you," he says. "I've been thinking a lot about us." He clears his throat, then turns to me, holding my gaze with those striking blue-green eyes, steady and resigned. "I just don't think it's going to work."

He says the words, and I stare at him numbly, holding a piece of salmon roll between my chopsticks. Not going to work? Those are words you say to someone when you cancel a dinner engagement or reschedule a doctor's appointment, not destroy your future together.

"What?" I ask in a strangled voice.

He looks pained. "Look at us, Mia. We're going different directions. I've been concerned for a while now, but I didn't know what to say. I've been offered a job with the investors who came out a few weeks ago, and I've accepted it. I'm moving to San Jose this spring. I know you hate the idea of Silicon Valley, that you don't want to live a corporate life, and that's okay. But I think we need to face reality. We're not the same people we were six years ago. It's not just the move. It's a lot of reasons." He looks down at his hands. "I just don't think we fit together anymore." He flexes his jaw as though willing himself to stay strong, to be a man and get through this meeting.

"Is there someone else?" I ask dully, putting the piece of salmon sushi back in the tray. I have no appetite.

He shakes his head, looking stung. "I wouldn't do that to you. You should know that."

"I'm not sure what I know anymore." It's mean of me to say, but it's how I feel. He has the advantage here. I have . . . nothing.

Below us on the water a rented hot tub boat glides slowly past, a happy couple in swimwear lounging in the hot tub sunk into the deck of the cute little craft. It hurts to look at them, so carefree and relaxed, arms twined around each other. I thought that would be us. I thought we were forever.

"Mia . . ." Ethan sounds pained. "Mia, listen to me." His voice drops, softens. "Look, I don't regret us. These last six years have been amazing. You're a wonderful person. I just don't think we'd be happy together. Can't you see that?"

I want to argue, to pull out a dozen reasons why this is not best, why us being together is best. But the only one I can come up with is that I still love him. It isn't enough that we can finish each other's sentences, that I can predict with 99 percent accuracy what flavor of ice cream he'll order at Molly Moon's (balsamic strawberry), or that we have a running six-year game of Scrabble scored on the back of an old Top Pot Doughnuts box. It isn't enough that he can quote the lyrics to Patty Griffin's greatest hits and I can do the same for all his favorite Beatles songs.

We stand or fall on the strength of our commitment, and I suddenly see that I am alone in this love. I am clinging to a man who has already let go of me. So in the end I don't say anything. I just nod, chin up, trying to be courageous in the face of this bombshell revelation.

"Do you want to finish your sushi?" he asks, and I shake my head, not trusting my voice.

"I'm sorry," he says, and I look away. There is nothing more to say. Fighting back the sting of hot tears, I fumble for my phone and order a ride from Uber. I can't let Ethan drive me home. It's too humiliating.

Abdi driving a blue Prius is four minutes away from collecting me when I stand. Ethan scrambles to his feet too. We face each other awkwardly across the picnic blanket, scene of so many carefree memories, the entire history of our relationship spelled out across the buffalo plaid.

"Are you going to be okay?" he asks, looking uncertain.

I gape at him. How could he ask me that question? Seeing his hangdog expression, I feel the first sizzle of anger, like cold butter in a frying pan. I glare at him for a moment, my anger and sorrow building in my chest like a sob. He just blew our future to smithereens. Of course I'm not going to be okay.

And then I hear it, Henry's voice whispering in my ear. *Why are you letting Ethan have all the power? . . . You need to start planning an alternate life.*

I hesitate for a brief moment, and in the space of that hesitation, something unexpected happens. I catch a glimpse out of the corner of my eye, a whirl of rainbow-colored saris, a whiff of cardamom and black pepper. Rosie's voice bubbling over with excitement. *India, Thailand, Mexico . . . It could be the chance of a lifetime.* And all of a sudden I know what I am supposed to do.

"I'm going away," I say abruptly, looking at Ethan with a sudden sense of purpose.

"What? Where?" Ethan pauses. He is holding open the Metropolitan Market bag, already tidying away the scene of our demise.

I glance away from him, over the water, to the skyline of Seattle and the Space Needle. It hurts to breathe right now. "On a humanitarian trip through India, Thailand, and Mexico with Rosie and a team of skilled professionals volunteering with the Humanitas Foundation." I sound like a travel brochure.

"The what foundation?" Ethan stares at me in puzzlement, our plastic sushi trays in his hand.

"I want my life to mean something," I say. "I'll be gone until July."

"Um, okay." Ethan stuffs the trays in the bag and gives me an astonished look. "Really? When did this happen?"

Why does it matter? I want to ask him. Instead, I shrug. "Recently." I attempt to look calm, hoping against hope that I am not too late, that they do indeed have a space for me on the trip. I have to go. I am destined to go. Suddenly I am ravenous for this alternate life.

A glance at my phone tells me that Abdi is one minute away.

"I should go." I gesture toward the parking lot.

Ethan hesitates, as though he wants to do something, say something, to make this easier and better than it actually is. For a moment he looks uncertain, regret mingling with relief. In the end he just says, "Take care, Mia." He gives me his sweet, endearing smile, tinged with sadness, with finality. This is excruciating.

My phone dings. Abdi has arrived.

"Goodbye, Ethan." It feels so unbelievably sad. I never thought this day would come. Like Ilsa in *Casablanca*, leaving Rick for the final time, I am brave and stoic. I walk over the hill alone. When I glance back, Ethan is standing on the picnic blanket, silhouetted against the Seattle skyline, head down and shoulders slumped, in relief or sorrow, I can't tell. Maybe both. I watch him for a moment, my heart breaking and breaking again.

In the back of the Prius, I tap out a hurried text to Rosie, my hands shaking. Is there still space on your trip? I'm in.

"Please, please, please let this work out." I mouth a panicked little prayer as I punch Send. Then I lean my head back against the seat and let myself fall quietly to pieces.

Chapter 8

"So, Mia, tell us a little more about yourself." Stella, the director of the Humanitas Foundation, leans close to the computer camera. A fortysomething wasp-thin blonde, she has sharp eyes and an intent, pinched expression. Beside her sits a younger, stocky man with thinning brown hair and a thick Boston accent. Bryant is the personnel relations coordinator for the Humanitas Foundation and the ideas guy. They appear to be in a luxury hotel somewhere, surrounded by marble walls and potted palms. Above their heads hangs a massive tiered crystal chandelier.

It's been two days since the fateful sushi picnic, and I am in a hastily arranged video call interview to see if I'm a good candidate to join the trip.

"Mia, we're looking for someone with good energy, positive vibes, you know?" Bryant bounces up and down in a deep wingback chair and massages a stress ball in one palm. "I spent five years working with aid organizations in Tanzania, and let me tell you, it takes a unique person to really flourish in those environments. Some people just aren't up to the challenge."

I sit up straighter in the floral armchair in the cottage living room, trying to project positive vibes, though I'm not exactly sure what that would look like. I hope my eyes aren't still pink and puffy from crying.

Across the room Rosie hovers out of sight of the camera, coaching me wordlessly with hand signals and facial expressions, like a high stakes game of charades. She filled out my application the night Ethan broke up with me. I lay curled on the sofa in a daze of grief and disbelief, woodenly responding to her prompts as she scribbled down my answers to pages of questions, everything from medical history to future aspirations. I drew a complete blank on that one, and Rosie tactfully suggested we just put, "Make the world a better place," and hope it would fly.

Apparently it did, because I've moved on to the next level.

"Mia, can you tell us why you want to be a part of this trip?" Stella asks.

Bryant passes the stress ball from hand to hand. They both watch me closely.

"Well . . ." I clear my throat nervously. Behind the computer Rosie stretches her mouth into a rictus of feigned delight, a reminder for me to smile. I paste on a smile and try to look positive.

"I've always wanted to travel . . ."

Rosie shakes her head vigorously, and I hurry on to the next point. "And I am passionate about social justice and helping to make the world a better place. I want to engage in genuine opportunities to bring about positive change."

Rosie gives me a thumbs-up. Stella and Bryant glance at each other. I can't tell whether they liked that answer or not. I feel a little like a pageant queen onstage during the question and answer portion. Smile. Look bright and sunny. Give pithy answers. Hope the judges give you a good score.

Bryant leans forward in his chair. "Great. Thanks, Mia. So, as I'm sure you are aware, one of the goals of the Humanitas Foundation is to help participants give back long term. We ask each volunteer to draw up a personal plan, something unique that they want to accomplish to make the world a better place. We love

Rosie's idea to create a jazz club for at-risk youth in New York, a place where kids can go to learn jazz and teamwork. That's the sort of project we're interested in."

I glance at Rosie, surprised by this revelation. It's the first I've heard of it. She nods and looks modest.

Bryant clears his throat and eyes me earnestly. "Mia, what long-term goal do you have to make a difference once the trip is over? We felt your answer on that part of the application was a little vague." He makes a tamping down motion with his hands, as though to reassure me before I get too nervous. "Now, we know you're applying late in the game, and so we don't expect you to have everything squared away just yet, but if you can just give us a rough idea of your future goals."

I open my mouth, but no sound comes out. The truth is I'm not sure what I can give the world other than a nice light brioche, and that certainly isn't going to wow anyone. Stella is watching me narrowly. Bryant is working his stress ball as the silence stretches long.

"Medical care," Rosie says firmly. She moves in front of the camera and gently nudges me aside, out of view of the screen, obscuring my blank look of surprise. "Mia wants to provide free medical care to disadvantaged women and children in the US and abroad. Isn't that wonderful?"

I stare at Rosie in confusion. This is a complete fabrication. I have no interest in medical care. Quite the opposite, in fact. I catch her eye and mouth, "What?"

She smiles encouragingly, then moves so she is out of view of the camera too. She presses the mute button so that Stella and Bryant can't hear us, hissing, "Well you have to say something." She turns, ready to get back onscreen.

"But I don't know the first thing about medical care," I protest. "I faint at the sight of blood. Why couldn't you pick something I'm actually interested in and good at?"

"Can you think of anything better?" Rosie gives me a pointed look. "Sugar, you are kind and smart and talented, but you have to give them something concrete, even if it's not exactly what you want to do. Don't worry, just go with it. It probably won't matter anyway. You can always change your mind later and design a project around something more suited to you."

I hesitate.

"Besides," she reminds me, "I know how much you admire your aunt Frannie and her dental clinic. You want to follow in her footsteps, right? Have that kind of impact? The heart is the same, isn't it? You can figure out the details as you go."

"Hello?" Bryant and Stella are staring at our empty couch. Bryant reaches forward and taps the computer screen, frowning. "I think you're frozen," he says.

Rosie punches the mute button off and pops back into view of the camera. "Sorry, y'all. We lost you for a minute. Mia?"

I hesitate for a split second. I'm a truthful person. I don't like to mislead anyone, but Rosie's right, I have to offer them something concrete. I can't tell them the pathetic truth, that I'm disoriented and brokenhearted and currently the only things on my life bucket list are perfecting my croissant technique, getting some stamps in my passport, and finally drinking an authentic cup of Indian chai tea. Oh, and figuring out my life's purpose. That too. They'll never accept me.

I poke my head back into view and smile wanly. "Yes, that's right. I think everyone should have access to free medical care, especially women and children." Which is totally true, I just don't happen to have any interest in personally providing that care.

Rosie moves away from the camera and mouths, "You're welcome."

"Well that sounds very promising," Stella says. She leafs through what appears to be a printout of my application form. "I don't see anything on here about medicine. Do you have any training?"

"Um," I stall, trying to think. "I volunteer with homeless women and children in a residential facility in downtown Seattle on a weekly basis. I did first aid training through my volunteer work there." To be precise, I spent a stultifying Saturday practicing CPR on a silicone dummy and bandaging imaginary wounds with the other volunteers to gain that mandatory first aid certification. "And I've been thinking about getting further training after the trip, but I'm not sure yet what that will look like." Since I've been let go from my apprenticeship, the thought of doing further schooling has crossed my mind. Not in anything medical related, but still . . .

"I see. Good." Stella and Bryant exchange a glance, and she nods slightly, then turns to me. "Mia, as you know, we recently had a female member of the team drop out for . . . personal reasons."

"Girl got caught being a mule for a Mexican drug lord—had a kilo of cocaine stuffed in her push-up bra when she came through US customs in San Ysidro—and now she is going to prison," Bryant adds cheerfully.

Stella shoots him a censoring look but doesn't break her stride. "So while we normally have a longer and more thorough vetting process for applicants, we are willing to expedite the process in this case, especially since Rosie has provided such a glowing recommendation for you."

She exchanges another look with Bryant, who leans over and whispers something in her ear. They confer for a moment while I wait awkwardly. Finally, Stella turns to me with a frosty smile.

"Mia, Bryant and I both feel you would be a great fit for the Humanitas Foundation's Global Experience. You are officially accepted as the replacement team member. Welcome to Team Caritas."

I breathe a huge sigh of relief, breaking into a genuine grin for the first time in days. "Thank you!" I enthuse, pushing aside the twinge of unease about my somewhat untruthful claim. As Rosie said, it probably won't matter in the long run anyway, right? I'll straighten out the details with Stella and Bryant later when I have a clearer understanding of what I actually want to do. The most important thing is that now I have a chance to figure that out. It's time to embrace my alternate life.

Chapter 9

End of April

I'll be out in a minute," Nana Alice calls through the bathroom door as I knock and slip into her studio apartment. "We're watching European Cake Week, is that right?"

"Yes, I think so." It's our last *Bake Off* viewing before I leave for my trip, a good episode to end on. I always enjoy the Old World splendor of "European Cake Week."

Sitting down at her tiny table for two, I notice a glass vase of pink roses and white gerbera daisies amid the litter of crossword puzzles and magazines. What are those for? It's not her birthday.

Curious, I sneak a peek at the card. It reads, "With great admiration, Albert." I blink, surprised. Albert Prentice, the old flame in the trilby? Is something romantic sparking between them? I've seen him now and then in the few weeks since he moved in. He sits at Nana Alice's table for meals, and she mentioned he joined her for bingo last week. A moment later Nana Alice comes out of the bathroom in her pink terry cloth robe.

"Those are pretty." I nod to the bouquet.

"They're from Albert," she says, two pink spots of color staining her cheeks, matching the roses. "Isn't that sweet?"

"What's the occasion?" I ask.

"Oh, no reason," she says vaguely. "We had dinner at Ivar's

Salmon House last night, and he brought me those flowers. I'm making chamomile tea. Do you want a cup?" She starts the water boiler and sets two mugs on the counter.

"Sure, thanks. So is something going on between you two?" I ask, delighted by the thought of a late-in-life romance for Nana Alice. She's been a widow for many years, since my Grandpa Harold's heart attack when I was still a toddler.

Nana Alice darts a sharp glance at me. "Nothing's 'going on.' We're just old friends." She puts a tea bag in each mug and drizzles in some of our West Wind Farm lavender honey.

"Old friends who go on dates to the Salmon House?" I prod gently.

She waves off the insinuation. "It wasn't a date. We were just . . . reconnecting. We're too old for romance."

"You'd better tell that to Albert, then. I think he may be smitten with you." I nod to the flowers.

"No romance," Nana Alice says firmly, pouring boiling water into the mugs. "It wouldn't be fair. The poor man has lost a lot already in his life."

I start to argue, to try to convince her that it's never too late for love, but then I decide to drop it. If Albert Prentice is half as charming as I suspect, he's quite capable of wooing Nana Alice without my help.

"Here, I brought you something to go with your tea."

I hand her a little white bag with a fresh Nutella brioche, a memento from my final visit to the Butter Emporium this morning to say farewell to my colleagues. I took Colleen's advice and declined the new owner's offer to work the counter again. I am starting fresh. Which is an optimistic way of saying I am currently unemployed. After the trip is over, I'll figure out what to do.

"Oh, this looks tempting," Nana Alice says approvingly, peeking into the bag.

"Good, I hope so."

Nana Alice has assured me that her tests and doctor's appointments went just fine, but I'm still a bit concerned. Last time I stopped in at the dining room, her fried chicken and vegetable medley looked untouched on her plate. And maybe it's my imagination, but she seems a little tired recently, not quite herself.

Ensconced in two blue recliners facing her television, we start the "European Cake Week" episode. My favorite contestant, Chetna, is still in the running, but Nana Alice's top choice, the down-to-earth Diana, has withdrawn due to health reasons.

"Are you ready for your trip?" Nana Alice asks over the music of the opening credits.

"I think so." I'm excited and anxious, but mostly just relieved. I've not heard from Ethan since he officially called us off almost three weeks ago, and the days have stretched long and heartsore. The only bright spot is the impending trip. Tomorrow Rosie and I fly to Florida for a week of orientation before heading out internationally with our team.

"Goodness me, it sounds exciting." Nana Alice sips her tea. "I envy you, Mia, getting to do all these things when you're young. What I wouldn't give to be young again, full of such possibility and promise. You must make the most of every moment. I'm so proud of you, especially after what that boy did to you. After six years. *Tsk.*" She presses her lips together and shakes her head in righteous indignation. She's still so angry at Ethan that she refuses to say his name. He's been labeled and relegated to the "people we only allude to" category.

After another humph of disapproval, she breaks off a piece of the brioche and bites into it. "Oh, this is perfect."

I'm relieved to see her eating. She's naturally petite, but now I can see the knobs of her collarbone under her blouse. She reminds me of a sparrow or a finch, all bright eyes and brittle bones.

We turn our attention to the episode. For the technical challenge, Chetna is attempting an orange savarin with cinnamon cream. Nana Alice's new favorite contestant, sweet-faced young Martha, is opting for a dark chocolate and almond liquor savarin.

"Ooh, Luis's cake looks over-risen to me," Nana Alice warns, setting the brioche aside, barely nibbled. "Careful, Luis."

The contestants take their cakes out of the pans.

"Nancy's looks a little flat, but Richard's shape is perfect," I observe, watching as carefully as if I were one of the actual judges. "Those slivered almonds baked in beautifully."

The bakers scramble to decorate their European cakes before the time is up. With one minute left, in the final flurry of frantic activity, Nana Alice sets down her mug of tea and turns to me. "Mia, there's something I need to tell you."

There's a gravity in her voice that snags my attention.

"What is it?" I glance up.

Nana Alice clears her throat. "I don't want you to worry or cancel your trip, but I got some unfortunate news from the doctor this week."

My heart skips a beat. "What's wrong?" I punch Pause, the screen frozen on a close-up of Nancy's tropical-themed rum punch savarin with coconut cream and exotic fruits.

Nana Alice sighs. "They did a pap test and then a biopsy. The results just came back. It looks like cancer of the cervix."

In the glare of the television, she looks tired and small. "I've got an appointment next week with an oncologist to discuss options." She meets my eyes, her own sympathetic.

I can't breathe. For a moment I think I'm suffocating. "Cervical cancer? What does that mean?" I focus on the television screen, trying to right myself. The rum punch savarin is decorated with a colorful paper cocktail umbrella and a tinsel palm tree. It looks garishly festive, at odds with this terrible moment and its devastating news.

"It's good news, actually," Nana Alice assures me, "as far as cancer goes. Cervical cancer is quite slow growing, and there are good treatment options for it. My odds are pretty high." She seems unruffled by the diagnosis. Suddenly her comments about Albert make sense. She doesn't want to enter into a romance when she's already sick.

I whip out my iPhone and type in cervical cancer, scanning the information from the American Cancer Society. She's right. It is a very slow cancer, and the recovery rate is high. It's one of the most successfully treated cancers, the website states. I slip the phone back into my pocket, slightly reassured.

Nana Alice reaches over and takes my hand. "Mia, my girl, don't worry. No matter what happens, I've lived a good long life. And I most likely have some fine years ahead of me yet. We'll see what the doctors say."

"You have to beat this," I say with conviction, although I'm trembling inside. "I can't . . . we're not ready for life without you. We'll get you the best doctor in Seattle, the best care. Does Dad know? Uncle Carl?"

Nana Alice shakes her head. "I haven't told anyone else yet. I'll call them both tomorrow. I wanted to tell you first before you go away."

"I'll cancel the trip," I say instantly. "Of course I'm not going."

Nana Alice grips my hand firmly. "Oh no, Mia. This trip is important. The time I lived in . . . women didn't do the things you can do now. I made the best of what was available to me, but my one regret was not doing more with my life—more freedom, more adventure. I want you to go on this trip not only for yourself but also for me."

I look at her, caught in indecision. She's neatly trapped me, and she presses her advantage.

"It's only a few weeks," she reasons. "I'm not going to waste away while you're gone. You'll be back before you know it, and while you're away I want to hear and see and smell and taste all of it. Please, Mia?"

I don't want to go. I want to stay by her side every step of the way, to keep her safe, to make sure that she is going to get well. But she is looking at me expectantly, her eyes bright with anticipation. It really is only nine weeks.

"Go, Mia," she urges. "Go on this grand adventure, for both of us."

In the end, there is really nothing else to say but a reluctant yes.

That night I dream of bees. A dozen are buzzing around my twin bed, alighting on the side table where my passport sits, empty and waiting for the promise of that first stamp on its blank white pages. But my passport is no longer empty. As the bees step gingerly across the pages, I glimpse dozens of stamps, the inked record of a globe-trotting life. The bees crawl across my visa for India, leaving dots of honey where they tread. I shoo them away, careful not to injure them, but they circle back and land again, crawling through the pages, over exotic stamps in a rainbow of colors. I sense that they are giving me their blessing, coming to see me off as I embark on this unanticipated alternate life.

Part 2

Sunbeam Key, Florida

Chapter 10

"Now this is traveling in style," Rosie says approvingly, surveying the cavernous inside of the Hummer limousine as we whiz south down Highway 1 away from Miami International Airport. Thirty minutes ago we arrived on a direct flight from Seattle, ready for the orientation week at the Humanitas Foundation's headquarters located somewhere outside of Miami. After gathering our luggage, we found this limo idling by arrivals and a driver holding a placard with our names on it.

"It's not what I expected." I glance around the interior of the limo in puzzlement and take a sip of the rapidly warming glass of champagne the driver gave us before we set off. I was picturing a serviceable fifteen-passenger van with the foundation's logo on it, with worn fabric seats and teeth-jarring suspension—like my summer camp experiences.

The information we've been given about orientation week is scanty. A packing list for our trip, a confidentiality agreement and liability waiver, and a plane ticket to Miami. I'm not sure what to expect, but being picked up by a Hummer limo already feels like a curveball.

I settle back against the seat and sip my champagne, determined just to enjoy the ride. My backpack is stuffed with all the items from the packing list. Nana Alice's cottage has been sublet to a pair of naturopathic medicine students doing a two-month course in Seattle. I am currently unemployed and single, so after the flurry of shopping and packing, there was actually little to say goodbye to.

"To adventure," Rosie says, holding aloft her glass of champagne. We clink glasses and drink. The bubbles tickle my nose.

"Ooh, look. A cheese tray and nut mix," Rosie exclaims, inspecting the contents of the well-stocked snack bar. "Here." She tosses me a packet of cheddar cheese squares and crackers. "Don't let the champagne go to your head." She peels the red wax off a mini wheel of Babybel cheese.

Under her sophisticated polish, Rosie is still a cattle rancher's daughter, born in South Texas in a hard-bitten portion of the state where the sun is relentless and conditions are severe. She was raised with a scrappy sense of self-preservation and an eye for scrimping and thriftiness.

"Doesn't this seem a little . . . extravagant?" I ask.

Rosie shrugs. "Maybe they just want to pamper us before the rigors of the trip. I think it's very considerate."

"Hmm."

"I can't believe we're going to Lars Lindquist's private island," she says, giving a little clap of delight.

"Who?"

"Lars Lindquist, founder of the Humanitas Foundation. Reclusive billionaire heir to the Lindquist breakfast food empire?" Rosie searches my face for comprehension, but I am at a loss. "The man who is funding this entire trip," she prompts.

"Oh, right." I remember Rosie and Stella mentioning him. "Lindquist. You mean like the microwave pancakes?"

Rosie nods. "The same."

Lindquist microwavable pancakes are healthy, tasty, and brimming with maple-y goodness, at least that's what the commercials from my childhood always advertised.

"With a touch of maple syrup baked into every bite," I sing quietly under my breath, the jingle coming back to me from long-past Saturday mornings watching cartoons. I remember the commercials, the happy maple leaf dancing beside a stack of pancakes dripping with golden syrup. Every childhood friend had Lindquist pancakes in the freezer and Lindquist golden maple syrup in its distinctive little yellow sunshine bottle in the pantry.

"Apparently Lars Lindquist decided to use his money to better the world by starting the Humanitas Foundation and sending out teams internationally to help people in need." Rosie nibbles her tiny wheel of cheese.

"How do you know anything about Lars Lindquist?" I ask, polishing off another cracker. I suddenly notice that I'm famished.

Rosie gives me a look of fond exasperation. "Honestly, Mia, do you live in a hole in the ground? I follow Lars Lindquist on Instagram. He's got over a million followers."

"Oh." I don't have an Instagram account. I'm not a typical twentysomething since I'm pretty uninvolved with social media. I prefer personal interactions, face-to-face.

"He's very handsome," Rosie adds. "And single." She twirls her finger around in the tin of mixed nuts, picking out the cashews. "He's been linked to Princess Theodora of Greece and Denmark, but I think they split up last spring." Rosie likes to follow the royals.

"How old is he?"

"Midthirties, I'd guess."

"Oh, that's young." I'd pictured the heir to a breakfast food fortune as being ancient, craggy and snowy-haired. "And he has a private island? How do you know that's where the orientation is?" I don't remember reading this in any of the materials. I realize, talking to Rosie, that I don't know a lot about this trip. It all happened so quickly that it seems I missed some pertinent details.

"I googled the Humanitas Foundation's address," Rosie says,

popping a cashew into her mouth. "It's on Sunbeam Key, which is the Lindquist family's private island."

Private island definitely does not sound like summer camp. I suddenly wonder if I've brought the right kind of clothes for this trip. On a three-hour visit to REI, the famous Seattle-based outdoor equipment store, I religiously followed the packing list and only purchased practical, versatile travel gear with the help of an enthusiastic salesperson who knew everything about performance fabrics and the SPF of sun shirts.

Munching a handful of salted almonds, I pull out my phone and quickly google Sunbeam Key. One look at the enormous, ornate mansion facing the ocean, and I realize with a sinking feeling that this is not the kind of place where you wear a shirt with built-in sun protection. When I saw the clothes Rosie had laid out to pack, I thought she was being overly stylish, bringing fashionable but not practical choices. I may have been wrong. Well, it's too late now.

We speed down the highway under the fierce sun, the landscape out the window brown and barren.

"Thank goodness for air-conditioning," Rosie says, stretching and relaxing against the opposite seat. Florida at the end of April is a world away from the moist chill of a Seattle spring. To pass the time, we ravage the snack bar and have another glass of champagne from the mini fridge.

A little more than an hour after we leave the airport, we pull into a private marina. The limo driver escorts us to a gleaming wooden Chris-Craft motorboat where a man in dark aviators waits at the helm. We clamber into the boat, and a moment later we are off, skimming the calm blue water, turning our faces to the sunlight, warm and bright. Two dolphins arc from the water, and I think for a moment that I could stay like this forever, with the wind tousling my hair and the sunshine undoubtedly freckling my nose.

Twenty minutes later we approach Sunbeam Key, a

picture-perfect island with a dock jutting from a white sand beach ringed by palm trees. Our driver moors the boat and helps us onto the dock, setting our luggage at our feet.

"Mia and Rosie, hi there!" Bryant calls as he and Stella hurry toward the dock. Bryant reaches us first and pumps our hands enthusiastically. "Ladies, you all right? How was the trip?" His Boston accent is even stronger in person, his *r*'s melting into *ahs*.

Stella touches my arm briefly. Her skin is cold, even in the Florida heat. "Welcome to Sunbeam Key," she intones.

Behind her a cameraman with a video camera is filming our arrival. Am I supposed to look at the camera or pretend it isn't there? Stella notices my discomfort.

"Just ignore it," she advises. "You'll get used to it. We use the footage for publicity purposes, to help promote the work of the foundation."

I nod uncertainly, trying to act normal and pretending I don't see the blank eye of the camera following our every move from just a few feet away.

Two strapping young men in tight white T-shirts appear and grab my backpack and Rosie's suitcase, following us as Bryant and Stella lead the way up a white crushed-shell path that winds through palm trees to a cluster of beach bungalows painted in candy-bright colors.

"These are the guest cottages. You're here in Lingonberry." Bryant stops in front of a bright red cottage with white shutters sitting picturesquely between two stands of palms. The white T-shirted men are already placing our luggage inside the front door. "Now, you two rest up, have a nap or take a swim. Dinner is at six, predinner drinks at five thirty by the pool. We'll have a presentation later tonight. Just follow the path around to the beach in front of the big house. Can't miss it."

"Casual chic attire is acceptable," Stella adds.

I open my mouth to ask what exactly casual chic attire is, but they are already heading back down the path to the beach, the cameraman loping behind them.

From the front steps of our cottage, I can see the dock through the palm trees. Another boat has just pulled up. Most likely those are some of our fellow participants. My heart skips a beat in anticipation. Suddenly it all seems so real.

Inside the guest cottage we unpack and get settled in. The space is perfectly appointed for both comfort and style. French toiletries in the tiled bathroom and Italian sodas in the mini fridge.

"I think I'll take a quick nap." Rosie yawns. "It was such an early flight. I can't keep my eyes open." She kicks off her shoes, pulls a satin eye mask from her purse, and falls onto one of the twin beds, red hair splayed across the white duvet cover like a flame. She is almost instantly asleep.

I'm too excited to sleep, so I uncap a lemon soda and take the slim orientation packet I found on our beds out on the front porch. Installing myself in the rope hammock hung between two porch railings, I glance through the packet, which only contains a welcome letter from Lars Lindquist and a weekly schedule.

The view from my hammock is enchanting—other guest cottages in mint green, canary yellow, and cotton candy pink nestle beneath the stands of palm trees. And beyond the cottages, glimpses of ocean and the soothing shush of the surf. There is no breeze, and the temperature is climbing, but in the shade of the front porch, the air is still comfortable.

I set the welcome packet aside and take a deep breath, trying to center myself, to be present and comprehend that I am actually here. I pull out my phone and, without thinking, start to text Ethan, then stop. I picture the look on his face as he was breaking up with me—regret mingled with relief. Ethan has made his choice to end our relationship. I have made mine to come here. It still hurts so much to think of him that sometimes I can't breathe, the pain sharp and piercing as a cracked rib. But I am determined not to wallow in grief. I will keep moving forward.

I text Nana Alice instead. Just arrived. Traveled in style in a limo with champagne. Gorgeous view! I snap a photo from my porch and hit Send. When I hugged her goodbye last night after our *Bake Off* session ended, she felt so frail in my arms.

For a moment my heart clenches with grief and worry, but I close my eyes and take a deep breath, trying to picture the worry and sadness sliding from my shoulders. Nana Alice insisted I come. I am here for her, too, not just for me. I take another slow, deep breath, feeling for the first time in weeks a flicker of contentment. A laugh bubbles up from somewhere inside, born of sheer relief. My new life starts now.

My phone dings. Gracious, such glamor. Enjoy the sunshine! XOXO, Nana

I spy movement through the trees, and a moment later a small group of people appear, walking up the path from the beach. Stella is marching ahead, trailed by the muscular luggage handlers. Bryant brings up the rear, talking and gesturing to a tall, lanky man with glossy dark hair pulled back in a man bun. I wrinkle my nose. Man buns are not my fashion trend of choice. Too pretend samurai. Guys with man buns seem like they're trying too hard to look cool. The ever-present cameraman is filming them as they walk. They stop at a canary-yellow cottage two doors away.

Man Bun glances up when he reaches his porch, and we lock eyes. He's striking—smooth, tanned skin and almond eyes that hint at East Asian heritage. He's wearing a baby-blue T-shirt featuring a green Godzilla holding a surfboard and making a "hang loose" gesture. His mouth quirks up into a small smile, and he gives me a nod. I can't help but smile back. He ducks his head to enter the cottage and doesn't turn around again. I wonder what team he's on.

Although I don't feel tired, the afternoon heat and sun are potent, and I must eventually drift off. I wake to Rosie shaking me, pointing to the time on her phone.

"Mia, up and at 'em, sugar. We slept too long. We're late."

We dash inside to get ready. It's time to meet our team.

Chapter 11

"Ooh, I hope we don't miss anything important," Rosie frets as we hurry along the crushed-shell path Bryant pointed out to us, which leads away from the cottages, farther along the island.

"I think it's just cocktails by the pool right now," I puff, struggling to keep up with Rosie's long legs. She looks gorgeous in a bright yellow sundress in a travel-friendly fabric. It floats around her, light as air. With her red hair falling around her shoulders, she looks like a sunset, vibrant and alive.

After assessing my new wardrobe I donned the only possible option, a knee-length ink-blue travel dress with capped sleeves, a pair of black flip-flops, and a small clutch I'm borrowing from Rosie. (Side note: Who brings a gold clutch on a humanitarian service trip around the world? That was most definitely not on the packing list.)

The best word to describe my travel wardrobe is serviceable. It's not going to win any style awards, but it feels practical, efficient. A fitting wardrobe for Saint Mia. My hair is going crazy in the heat, curling every which way. After my hasty postnap shower, I briefly considered containing it, pulling it back in a low messy bun, but then didn't bother. I like letting it go free.

We trot along the path, which winds through dense green foliage for a few minutes before suddenly opening up to a vast expanse of white sandy beach.

"Oh my goodness!" Rosie exclaims.

On our right is the endless aqua rolling expanse of the ocean, and on our left, across the wide swath of sand, stands an imposing white mansion with tall french doors open to a long veranda spilling over with pots of tropical blooms. An infinity pool glitters in the sunshine on a spacious patio situated between the front of the house and the beach.

Small groups of people holding drinks cluster around the pool. On one side of the pool, a calypso band is playing a jaunty tune, the musicians on their steel drums and maracas, guitars and trombones bobbing enthusiastically as they play. The music floats across the beach, and I feel my toes tapping before I even realize it. A pig is roasting on a spit over a fire pit dug in the sand, and the tantalizing smell of roasted pork wafts past us on the warm breeze as we approach the patio. Across the pool I spy Stella talking to a tall, whip-thin woman with blonde dreadlocks who is wearing black leather pants with metal studs down the legs. Bryant hovers by a tiki hut bar, handing out cocktails.

Rosie elbows me. "Just think, our teammates are here somewhere," she whispers excitedly.

She, unlike me, is primed and ready to find love. If she happens to find it in a gorgeous, exotic locale while helping those less fortunate, so much the better. We hover at the lip of the patio for a moment, unsure of what exactly to do.

"Ladies!" Bryant waves us over to the tiki hut. "Come get a drink."

The bar is manned by a huge Pacific Islander bartender with sleeves of tribal-looking tattoos. Rosie asks him for a cosmopolitan; the color complements her hair perfectly. I order a sidecar. If Rosie can match her hair, so can I. I'm not a girly drink fan. I much prefer the sour kick of cognac, Cointreau, and lemon juice.

"Thanks." I accept the sidecar and take a sip. Nana Alice was the person who introduced me to the sidecar. She ordered one for me on my twenty-first birthday, and we toasted my new adulthood on a windy rooftop patio overlooking Elliot Bay. I tamp down a stab of guilt at leaving her, focusing instead on my surroundings. She'll eat up all the details. I set my glass on the bar and fish my phone from the clutch, snapping a few photos to send to her later.

Bryant pops up in front of me and waggles a finger at the phone. "Naughty, naughty, Mia. Someone didn't read their non-disclosure clause. No outside photographs for any of the time you're with the Humanitas Foundation. Our photographers and videographers handle all media for the trip."

"Oh, sorry," I murmur, taken aback. Obviously I didn't read the confidentiality agreement carefully enough. It appears that I might have missed some important details. I hastily delete the photos, embarrassed.

"Mr. Lindquist likes to keep an eye on all publicity and media images related to the Humanitas Foundation," Bryant explains. "Everything from here on out has to go through the proper channels—that goes for videos, photos, tweets, everything."

I nod, cheeks flaming, and take a gulp of my sidecar. Five minutes into orientation and I'm already in trouble. Nice, Mia. Good first impression.

"Don't worry." Bryant claps me on the back in a brotherly fashion. "You'll get the hang of it."

"Thanks." I slip my phone into my pocket.

Rosie has wandered toward the pool and is animatedly talking to a sandy-blond man sporting a full lumberjack beard.

"Sorry, Mia, gotta go." Bryant sees some new arrivals near the patio entrance and hurries to greet them, leaving me alone. I sip my sidecar in what I hope looks like a coolly confident manner.

"Hey, how was your nap?"

I turn. It's our man-bun neighbor standing at my elbow, holding a can of Heady Topper IPA. "I came over to your cottage to say hi earlier, but I didn't want to wake you." He smiles, and I notice his eyes crinkle at the corners.

"Um, thanks," I mumble, disconcerted to think of this attractive stranger watching me sleep. I hope I wasn't drooling. Maybe I looked like Sleeping Beauty, all softly flushed cheeks and crescents of eyelashes. One can hope, right?

"I'm Kai." He reaches out and shakes my hand. Of course his name is Kai. How could he not have a cool hipster name? I bet he surfs. I suddenly wonder what my hair looks like right now and wish I'd put a little more effort into being party ready. A touch of lipstick wouldn't have gone amiss.

"Mia." I try for a firm, convivial grip to project self-assurance in the face of the possible drooling/insane clown hair scenario.

Up close he is taller than I thought, towering almost a foot above me, and I have to crane my neck to look up at him. His skin is tanned, cheekbones sharp, and his eyes are black. He's gorgeous in a laid-back, exotic way. He makes me think of sandy beaches, tropical breezes, and brightly colored cocktails spiked generously with rum. I take an instinctive step back, trying to put a little distance between us. He makes me nervous.

"So, Mia, what brings you here?" he asks, his throat at my eye level, a crescent of tanned skin above the neck of his T-shirt. He's changed; it's no longer Godzilla but an Indigo Girls concert tee, a choice that catches me off guard. They're one of my favorite bands but not usually popular with men of my generation. I want to know the story behind that shirt.

I take a sip of my sidecar and say with a touch of irony, "A broken heart and an epiphany."

"Wow." He regards me thoughtfully. "Cool . . . the epiphany, not the broken heart. Sorry." He takes a sip of his beer.

"What about you?" I ask. "Why are you here?"

"Trying to win a bet." He gives me a wry sideways glance. "I dropped out of law school at the University of Virginia after my first semester. My mom and stepdad are . . . not happy, to put it mildly. So we struck a deal. I take a year to get my not-for-profit up and running, and if I can't, I go back and finish law school."

Law school. Impressive. So he's smart. Probably really smart.

"How is this trip going to help you win your bet?" I ask.

He shrugs. "Well, since at the end of the trip Lars Lindquist is choosing one of the participants and fully funding their project for two years, I figured it was worth a shot to join and see if I win." He smiles with a touch of self-deprecation.

I look down at my flip-flops, focusing on something mundane to regain my equilibrium. He's just a guy, the first guy I've really talked to since Ethan broke my heart. A gorgeous, smart, sexy guy, granted, but still, just a guy. I'm single. I'm still shattered. I don't have any idea how to feel.

"So what will you do if you get the funding?" I hazard a glance back up at him. I can feel the sidecar going to my head, my cheeks growing warm under his intent dark gaze.

"Sustainable urban farming," he says. "Right now I'm working at Whole Foods and converting an old Lay's Potato Chip truck into a portable greenhouse, but I have a plan. I want to show kids where their food comes from and how they can grow it in a small urban space. I want to increase not just their nutrition but their connection to the earth and their ability to take care of it." He takes another sip of beer, and I watch his throat move, the fluid motion of his wrist as he lifts the can to his lips. He's wearing a hemp bracelet. Since when have I found granola crunchy men attractive? I've always leaned more toward the preppy L.L.Bean types.

I think of Ethan. He and Kai could not be more different. It occurs to me for the first time that all of Ethan's dreams for the future were at their core self-centered—the house we'd own, a favorite vacation spot in Maui, what model of vintage Porsche he'd buy. Never once did I hear him say what Kai has just said, that he wants to do something that makes the world a better place.

If this were a romantic movie, and I were the female lead, I would gaze up at Kai and say softly, "Me too." But this is real life, so instead I panic, gulp my sidecar, and mumble about having to find the restroom, then make a beeline for the first person I recognize.

Stella is stalking back and forth near a large potted fern by the wide veranda stairs, cell phone to her ear, berating someone about a mix-up with the appetizers. "Mr. Lindquist wanted Key West Pink Shrimp, sustainably caught, not that toxic Chinese farmed shrimp. He is your company's most lucrative customer, and if we don't see Key West Pink Shrimp on the table tomorrow at lunch, you can kiss your catering career goodbye."

I glance back. Kai is watching me from across the pool.

"Where's the bathroom?" I ask Stella, who looks annoyed at the interruption. She gestures toward the house. "In there," she hisses. "There are twelve. Take your pick."

I stash my cocktail glass behind one of the posts on the veranda and hesitantly enter the enormous house, expecting that at any moment someone will appear and stop me. The front hall, a vast and pristine white swath of marble, is empty. I peer into room after opulent room outfitted with crystal chandeliers and expensive furnishings until finally I locate a bathroom. There are tiny shell soaps in a dish, and the marble sink has gold handles shaped like ornate fish. My reflection in the mirror is underwhelming. I look pale and my hair is going a little crazy Medusa in the heat. I smooth it with a dab of hair salve from my clutch, then apply a slick of lip balm and bite my lips till they have a flush of color.

I'm shaken by my encounter with Man Bun Kai, and I'm not

really sure why. He did nothing out of the ordinary. Maybe it's just beginning to sink in that I'm single again, and over the past six years all of my single-girl skills have atrophied.

I stare at myself in the mirror sternly. "Get it together, Mia Alice West," I mutter in my best drill sergeant voice. "Now go out there and do what you've come to do."

I am such a mess internally, my heart like hamburger meat. I need to protect it. I need to remain free from encumbrances. Mother Teresa didn't have a man, and look what she managed to do. I gave my heart once and in doing so gave up my own vision for my future. I can't let that happen again, not if I truly want to be Saint Mia, not if I truly want to make a difference in the world. The thought steels my resolve. I square my shoulders and march back to the party, resolute. I will keep my heart safe and my eyes firmly on the goal.

CHAPTER 12

"Hey, folks, good evening." Bryant's amplified voice booms over a sound system just as I descend the veranda steps. "Come on into the tent."

I join the tail end of the crowd drifting toward the white tent where tables and chairs are set up for dinner. A small bevy of waiters in tuxedos waits at one side of the tent, poised for action. Two videographers are circling the crowd like sharks, filming everything.

"Come in, come in. It's great to see each of you in person. Welcome to the Humanitas Foundation's Global Experience kick-off dinner." Bryant is standing on a small stage at the front, holding a microphone. "Now just look around and find your team table."

I scan the crowd for Rosie. Everywhere I look there are cool, serious-looking people hunting for their tables. Some look like adventure guides or world travelers, a certain hard professionalism making them downright intimidating. A few of the other women I've seen walking around could be models or triathletes. I feel decidedly uncool in this crowd. I'm pretty, but I am not one of these flawless women who seem to glide through life, nor am I a hard-core rock-climbing superwoman. People find me more endearing than dazzling.

I turn at a tap on my shoulder to find Rosie standing next to me. "There you are."

We check two tables—Team Veritas and Team Fidelis—before we finally locate the Team Caritas table. Next to our table I spy a sign for Team Fortis. Veritas, Fidelis, Caritas, and Fortis. It's been a few years since my college Latin class, and I'm a little rusty, but I can still translate the words. All virtues—Truth, Loyalty, Charity, and Strength.

The tall blonde woman with the dreadlocks who I saw talking to Stella earlier is already sitting at our table. She appears to be in her midthirties, with a chiseled jaw and a hard stare. She would be pretty if she didn't look so jaded.

"Hello, I'm Rosie Jasper." Rosie offers her hand to our new teammate, using her best Texas charm.

The woman nods in a bored way and shakes Rosie's hand. "Winnie Jones." She has an accent, British or maybe Australian. I can't tell for sure.

Rosie cocks her head and studies Winnie for a moment, then asks. "Wait, are you *the* Winnie Jones?"

The blonde jerks her head in affirmation. "That's the rumor, yeah."

I am at a total loss. I shoot Rosie a confused look, and she leans close and murmurs, "Winnie Jones, lead guitarist and singer for Dynamite Kitty, the iconic Aussie all-girl punk rock band? She's like the Joan Jett of our generation."

"Oh," I say faintly, still clueless. I lean more toward the folk/Americana genre. "Hi." I reach out my hand, and Winnie eyes me with a touch of amused derision before shaking hands. She has unusually small pupils, almost pinpoints, which give her a narrow look of suspicion. She's wearing a men's white sleeveless undershirt, and her right arm is covered from wrist to shoulder in a colorful, eye-catching array of flower tattoos interspersed with daggers, skulls, a Hello Kitty character wielding a large stick of dynamite, and a decapitated Ariel from the Little Mermaid, holding her own head in an outstretched hand and brushing her long red hair.

I tear my gaze away from the disturbing tattoos and sit down in my assigned chair next to Rosie, eyeing Winnie Jones, celebrity punk rocker, across the table with a sinking heart. This is one of our six team members? I was hoping for someone channeling more Peace Corps and less heroin chic.

"Is this Team Caritas?" I glance up, and my heart does a funny little flip. Kai is standing next to me, reading our table name.

Rosie straightens her shoulders so her breasts are perky and smiles up at him. "It is. And you are?"

"Kai Nakamura." He gives her a firm handshake, then turns to Winnie, offering his hand across the table. Winnie shakes it, muttering, "Winnie Jones. Yes, the same one."

Kai stares at Winnie in puzzlement. "Great," he says.

Apparently I'm not the only one living under a rock. It's a cheering thought.

Winnie raises an eyebrow, then smirks when she realizes he doesn't recognize her. "Cool shirt," she says, gesturing to his Indigo Girls tee. "Those chicks are fierce."

"Um, yeah, thanks."

Kai takes a seat to my right, and Rosie leans over to me, saying in a loud, indiscreet whisper, "Well, isn't he a tall drink of water?"

I kick her swiftly under the table, and she widens her eyes at me and kicks me back, daring me to disagree. Which I can't. I don't know much about Kai Nakamura yet, but he is most definitely easy on the eyes.

Waiters buzz around our table, filling glasses from pitchers of ice water infused with raspberries, cucumber, and mint.

"I met one of our other teammates," Rosie says, taking a sip of water. "Milo. He's a sculptor from Wisconsin."

"That blond lumberjack-looking guy?"

Rosie nods, eyes sparkling. "He's a sweetheart."

I glance surreptitiously at Kai. With his T-shirt and man bun and surfer vibe, he's definitely not her type. Rosie goes more for urbane, well-groomed men with Swiss watches and an extensive knowledge of wine.

We have two spots left now. I survey the tent, but there are still a number of people looking for their places. Milo, the blond lumberjack, finds our table a moment later.

"Caritas. Dude, finally!" He gives us a jaunty mock salute. "Milo Olsen, reporting for duty." One of the videographers has followed him and films our introductions. Milo is charming in a millennial, lumbersexual way. Plaid button-down shirt, bushy but well-groomed blond beard, and a mischievous twinkle in his eyes. As he shakes my hand I note the absence of callouses. Definitely not a real lumberjack. He's had a recent manicure, actually. His nails look nicer than mine. I glance at Rosie and wonder if he knows anything about wine.

Milo slides into a chair between Winnie and Rosie and leans back, lacing his fingers behind his head, relaxed and comfortable in an instant.

"Can you believe this place?" he asks, looking around. "It's like being at a resort. I thought we'd be roughing it; I brought like four bottles of insect repellent."

"I'm sure it won't be this luxurious once we're on the trip," Rosie says, serenely sipping ice water with raspberries bobbing in it. "So we'd better enjoy it while we can."

"Oh, I'm enjoying," Milo agrees. "It's just not what I was expecting."

I like him. I'm nervous and jumpy around Kai and feel instantly wary of Winnie, but Milo seems easy to be around. Now only one empty place left. Who will fill it?

Just as the salad course is being served, a slender man with a narrow, intelligent face slips into the last chair. Although it's hot as an oven in the tent, he is wearing a dark blue suit and tie. His skin is the color of burnished bronze. He looks East African. Ethiopian, maybe? He rises slightly and shakes hands all around.

"I am Abel," he murmurs to each of us, meeting our eyes. His English is laced with a slight melodic accent. He resumes his seat, careful of his suit, as a waiter appears to fill his glass. On his other side, Winnie glances his direction, then ignores him, texting on her phone. He sits without speaking, observing the action around him with a keen interest.

Team Caritas is all here.

Chapter 13

The salad course is baby greens with goat cheese. Kai carefully lifts a forkful of lettuce and examines it intently. "Mache," he says, sounding surprised. "Interesting choice with the baby beet greens and arugula." He catches my bemused look and grins a touch sheepishly. "Mache bruises easily. It's not usually used in commercial mixes," he explains. "I like edible plants. Way more interesting than legal briefs."

I'm not sure that I agree, but I nod anyway. Both edible plants and legal jargon would rate fairly low on my scale of interest. To each his own, as Nana Alice would say.

"So Mia, I've confessed my geeky hobby. What's yours?" He gives me a sideways glance, still examining the salad on his plate.

"I love to bake," I reply. "I like making people happy with something I create with my own hands." I stop, a little embarrassed that it's not more profound. But then I guess I shouldn't worry. He just confessed to a love of lettuce.

"Cool," he says. "Is that what you want to do as a career?"

I shake my head, wincing at the still fresh sting of my apprenticeship's abrupt end. "Baking's just a hobby."

"Why?" Kai sets his fork down and looks at me curiously. "If you love it."

I glance away. How do I explain to him what I've known to be true since the age of twelve? That baking, while I love it more than anything, is not big enough to be my life's purpose. That I need to strive for something more.

"My grandma owned a bakery when I was little," I tell him finally. "I wanted to be a baker just like her."

When I close my eyes I can still smell it—the warm, distinctive scent of sugar, vanilla, and cinnamon mixed with the sharp tang of the homemade lemon-peel-and-white-vinegar cleaner Nana Alice used to keep the display cases sparkling.

"I used to pretend I had my own bakery. I served cardboard cakes and pies to all my stuffed animals. But my aunt Frannie, who I admire more than anyone on earth, encouraged me to think bigger, aim higher." I look down at my wilting salad greens, at the little round of goat cheese flecked with chives perched in the middle.

I think of that moment with a pang. Aunt Frannie was staying with us on one of her whirlwind visits home. The first morning after she arrived, I shyly offered her a blueberry muffin I'd baked myself. I was proud of it, the perfect conical dome glazed with crystalized sugar, the plump organic blueberries I'd picked with my mother.

"I want to be a baker, Aunt Frannie, like Nana Alice. I'm going to own a bakery too and call it Sweet Something."

Aunt Frannie took the muffin and studied me, a flicker of disappointment in her fierce green gaze.

"Oh Mia, you can think bigger than that." She set aside my perfect muffin and leaned forward intently.

I studied the tanned, freckled lines of her face, the mop of unruly ginger hair. She was both intimidating and awe inspiring. I hung on her every word like it was gospel.

"You are smart and strong. There's so much you can give and do if you want to. Don't settle for rolling out pie dough and making muffins. Aim higher, my dear girl. Shoot for the moon."

I felt the weight of her words settle onto my young shoulders, a conviction, a calling. If I wanted to be like her, I had to reach higher, seek better things.

I never forgot her words. For a few years I lost my way as I dreamed of a life with Ethan. Now I'm hoping this trip will help me get back on course and discover these better things, whatever they may be.

"So if baking's just a hobby, what do you plan to do for your profession?" Kai asks, breaking into my reverie.

I open my mouth for a split second, almost telling him the truth, that I don't know, that the only thing I really love is to bake and that I am searching for the right thing. But instead, I recite the pat answer Rosie gave Bryant, even though it is a lie.

"I want to provide free medical care to disadvantaged women and children in the US and abroad." Saying the words makes me cringe a little inside. Even if the heart is the same, I don't like being misleading about the details.

"Really?" Kai surveys me. "Huh." He looks surprised and maybe a little disappointed. "That's cool."

"Yep." My heart is beating fast in my chest. I hate lying. Why can't I just tell him the truth? "It will fill a real need." I try to muster enthusiasm.

Kai nods. "Yeah, sounds like it. Are you planning to go to med school or something?"

"I'm . . . considering my options after the trip is over." I deflect the direction question, brushing away a twinge of guilt over lying. I can't tell my teammates the honest answer. How disappointed they would be in me from the start. I don't want to be the vestigial teammate with no helpful skills. Taking a swallow of ice water, I avoid Kai's eyes.

During the main course we all take turns introducing ourselves, starting with the basics.

"I'm a barista by trade," Milo tells us over the slow-roasted pork with mango slaw, "but I'm also trained as a woodworker. I want to use woodworking to help juvenile offenders learn basic life skills. That's my plan after this trip. And I'm here because I've never been out of the US and I like the idea of helping people." He shrugs. "I want to see things in a new light."

Next to him, Winnie tips her chair back on two legs and stretches her arms above her head, cracking her knuckles, looking bored. When it's her turn she keeps it brief. "Winnie Jones. Rock star, recovering addict, Australian. I think that about sums it up." She laces her fingers behind her head and looks around the table at us with a mixture of amusement and insolence.

"What made you decide to come on this trip?" Rosie asks.

Winnie smirks. "My manager, Bruce. The band is taking a break and he signed me up, said it was this or another stint at a detox ranch in New Mexico. So . . ." She shrugs. "This is definitely the lesser of two evils. I've been touring with Dynamite Kitty since I was nineteen. There's nothing new under the sun for me. I'm just marking time till this is over."

No one says anything. Rosie glances at me and raises her eyebrows, channeling consternation. I speedily google Winnie on my phone under the table. Dozens of images spring onto the screen. Winnie onstage screaming into a microphone. Winnie making an obscene gesture to the camera. Winnie posing on the cover of *Rolling Stone* magazine with three other members of Dynamite Kitty, her long blonde dreadlocks and heavy black eyeliner her signature look. In every photo she looks angry or vacant or both. A few news headlines catch my eye—the release of the band's first smash hit album *Bang Bang Chaos*, and then a couple of gossip column articles about her stints in rehab for alcohol and drug abuse. Perturbed, I tuck my phone away as Abel begins to speak.

"I am a lawyer by training and am now a researcher for Amnesty

International," Abel tells us. "I was born in Kigali, Rwanda, but came to the US when I was a child. I hope to start my own foundation to help monitor and encourage fair criminal justice practices in developing world countries, specifically in African nations like Rwanda." He looks around the table solemnly.

I have a vague recollection of studying the Rwandan genocide in a college class. There were horrifying photos—piles of dead bodies, a line of blood on a church wall three feet high, the violence even more terrible because it was neighbor against neighbor, friend against friend.

I study Abel thoughtfully. I'd guess him to be no more than thirty or thirty-one. If I recall correctly, the genocide took place somewhere in the late nineties. That means he would have been a child when it happened. Did he flee the genocide and come to America? What has he seen and endured?

I glance around the table at my teammates, both impressed and intimidated. What am I doing here, the girl who can bake a fluffy biscuit, amid people like Abel and Kai who are motivated and equipped to change the world? I feel like a fraud.

When it's my turn to share, I try to be as honest as I can. I say a sentence or two about being from Seattle and gloss over the medical care for disadvantaged women and children bit with just a brief mention. Then I say what is really on my heart.

Rolling my glass of ice water between my palms, I watch the shreds of mint and slice of cucumber tilt from side to side. "I thought I knew what I wanted from my life," I say finally, focusing hard on the glass. "I had it all planned out. And then it all fell apart. I got my heart broken. So I guess I'm hoping to see a way forward, to find significance in the midst of loss, to discover a new and unexpected life and to make a difference in the world."

No one says anything. I look up to find all eyes on me.

"Good luck with that, Pollyanna," Winnie says, raising her water glass in a mock salute.

Abel meets my eyes. "It is possible," he says. "I know this from experience. It is not easy, but it is possible."

Rosie squeezes my knee under the table, and Kai lifts his water glass. "To possibilities," he says. We toast, even Winnie.

"To possibilities," I whisper, looking around at this group of almost complete strangers. I am about to embark on a journey I've dreamed about for years. For better or worse, these five sitting around this table will be my companions on the road.

Chapter 14

"Well, folks, now that you've gotten to know your teammates a bit, we're going to get started with the rest of tonight's program." As we finish dessert, Bryant takes the stage, microphone in hand. "In a moment we're going to hear from the founder of the Humanitas Foundation. He's the mastermind behind this entire trip, and a little birdie told me that he's just been named in *People* magazine's fifty most eligible bachelors list!" Bryant winks at the audience and a few people cheer.

"So let's welcome our gracious host, Mr. Lars Lindquist!" Bryant claps loudly, still holding the microphone. We all turn as a tall blond gentleman walks from the back of the tent and mounts the stage.

Lars Lindquist is strikingly handsome, with wavy blond hair curling over the collar of his white shirt and melancholy soft gray eyes. He looks a little like the Swedish actor Alexander Skarsgård. He's wearing a perfectly pressed gray linen suit and expensive Italian loafers. He's beautiful, Scandinavian, serene. I feel instantly underdressed. Rosie gives a little hum of appreciation, and I find myself drawn to him, too, like a magnet. He takes the microphone.

"Good evening." His manner and voice are refined and smooth. I expected glamor and showmanship, but he seems reserved, almost diffident. "Your presence here tonight is the culmination of a long-held ambition." He scans the room, gazing at each table. "Three years ago, in a life-changing moment, I made a promise that I would use the resources at my disposal to help change the world for good. Tonight marks the beginning of fulfilling that promise.

"You have been chosen for this trip because each of you possesses a gift that I believe can, given the right opportunity, make the world a better place. That is our aim, to work today for a brighter tomorrow. Thank you all for your sacrifice, your time, and your energy. I am truly grateful." He puts a hand over his heart and bows his head slightly, then hands the microphone to Bryant and walks between the tables to thunderous applause. He doesn't pause or look up, but disappears out the back of the tent.

"Thank you, Lars. You are truly an inspiration," Bryant says. We all applaud again, then he announces, "Cocktails and light jazz around the pool starting now. Breakfast and team orientation tomorrow at eight sharp."

Dusk is falling as we file out of the tent and spread out around the pool. The calypso band has been replaced by a trio of musicians in fedoras playing classic jazz.

The same waiters from dinner circulate through the guests, passing out martinis and mint juleps. I accept a mint julep and take a tentative sip, grateful for something in my hand to lessen the awkwardness of this social event. It's quite obvious that there will be no campfires and songs of peace and justice. So far orientation is luxurious, enjoyable, and seemingly incongruous for the start of a humanitarian trip around the world. Maybe this is just normal life for Lars. Perhaps it doesn't seem ostentatious to him. Maybe he doesn't know anything different.

Rosie is making her way around the pool, introducing herself, a martini in one hand. I look around for my teammates, but they all seem to be engaged in conversation with other people. I don't feel like socializing. I'm tired and emotionally drained. I'd rather go back to our cottage but don't want to appear as though I'm not a good team player.

Climbing the sweeping granite steps to the veranda, I lean over the wide stone railing, looking down on the scene. Dusk is falling, and around the house and grounds lights are winking on here and there, warm and yellow. The pool glitters like a sapphire, and beyond the wide strip of beach the ocean stretches vast to the horizon, the rhythmic sound of surf calming, almost mesmerizing.

I close my eyes and press my ice-cold glass to my forehead, where a tension headache is starting to bloom. It's been a long day. It's been a long month. I think briefly of Ethan, wondering what he is doing, what he would think if he could see me now, on this elite private island, about to embark on this grand adventure. I wonder if he cares. I wish I didn't feel so alone.

"Good evening."

I whirl. Lars Lindquist is standing slightly behind me, a mint julep in his hand.

"Oh, hi, good evening." I stumble over my words in surprise, removing the sweating glass from my forehead.

"Do you mind if I join you?" he asks, moving forward toward the railing beside me.

"Yes. I mean no, I don't mind, of course." I scoot toward a huge stone urn laden with creamy white gardenia bushes in full flower, their sweet, heady fragrance filling the sultry air.

He joins me at the balcony, leaning against the railing, and looks at me in puzzlement for a moment, as though trying to place me. "You're . . ."

"Mia West," I supply. "The replacement for the Colombian drug mule." I take a sip of my mint julep and try to act nonchalant even though he is standing so close. He smells delicious, like pressed limes and bergamot.

"I was going to say latecomer," he says with a smile. "I know who you are. Thank you for agreeing to join us on such short notice."

"Well, thank you for having me." Up close he is just as handsome as he was onstage. There are crow's feet at the corners of his eyes and his hair is thinning just a little at the front, but he cuts a stylish, urbane figure. He has the well-manicured and polished air of a man used to expensive and elegant things. *He* is an expensive and elegant thing.

"I wonder what will come of all of this," he muses, taking a sip of his julep. "I hope great things."

I get the feeling he is not talking to me. He leans casually against another urn of gardenias and stares out at the party. There is an air of calm around him, of stillness, but he seems a little sad. What could possibly make this handsome, successful billionaire look so wistful? I follow his gaze across the pool, and my eyes light on Rosie, who is standing near the jazz band talking to Milo.

"That is your friend, is it not?" he asks, his eyes on her. "The one who convinced you to join her on this trip? Rosalie Jasper?"

Surprised that he knows so much about us, I glance at Rosie, who is laughing and shaking her head at something Milo is saying. She is glowing in the golden lights strung up in the palm trees around the pool, shimmering in her yellow dress, so effervescent you cannot tear your eyes away from her. As we watch, Milo reaches out and takes her hand, and they perform a few swing dance steps to the catchy jazz tune. Rosie twirls into Milo's arms and out again, her yellow dress pooling around her knees like melted butter.

"Yes, that's Rosie."

"Extraordinary," Lars says, and there is a touch of wonder in his voice, as though he is looking at a Degas or a Renoir painting.

Has anyone ever watched me with an expression like that? I take a gulp of my mint julep and try not to think about my future stretching ahead of me, solitary, so alone.

Lars looks at me then, really looks at me, and smiles. "What are you doing up here, when all the energy of life is down below us?"

"I've never been great at parties," I admit. "Especially ones where I don't really know many people. And I'm a terrible dancer."

Lars nods as though I've said something profound. "It seems, then, that we are both watchers," he muses. "Perhaps we watch so that we do not feel so alone." He swirls the ice in his highball and takes a swallow of his drink.

I don't say anything. I can't quite get a bead on him. He's rich. He's beautiful. He has a million followers on Instagram, or so Rosie tells me, so why in the world would he feel alone? And why is he up here talking to me and not down there in the thick of his own festivities?

"You have a beautiful island," I say, searching for small talk.

He nods in agreement. "My grandfather came over from Sweden in the late 1940s and opened Lindquist's Pancake House in New York City. It was so successful that he kept expanding until he had fifteen restaurants from Pennsylvania to New Jersey. Then he started marketing the pancakes and waffles and syrups to grocery stores along the East Coast. He bought this island in 1957 and built the house later in life. It's been in the family ever since."

"That's quite a legacy," I say. "It's a magnificent place."

"It's a gilded cage," he says softly. "A beautiful, gilded cage from which there seems to be no escape."

I have no idea how to respond. A moment later he turns to me and dips his head in a small formal gesture. "Mia, it has been a pleasure. I will bid you good night."

"Good night," I say to his retreating back. I watch him walk away, puzzled and intrigued by the enigmatic figure of Lars Lindquist.

Chapter 15

"Good morning, y'all," Rosie calls, waving Team Caritas over to where she stands under a coconut palm bright and early the next morning. She has been designated by Bryant as our official team organizer for the week. "First thing we have is a team building activity," she announces.

It's eight thirty and our team is assembled on the beach after a light breakfast of fresh muffins and tropical fruit smoothies hand-blended at the tiki bar. Looking like a camp counselor from the 1950s in a pair of high-waisted khaki shorts and a crisp white button-down shirt, her bright hair twisted into a chignon, Rosie hands copies of the schedule around to us.

"Paddle boat races? You're joking, right?" Winnie squints at the paper and groans. She looks hungover, with pink, watery eyes. "It is waaaay too early for this." She pulls out a pair of large black sunglasses from the pocket of her cargo shorts and dons them, obscuring half her face.

"Paddle boats. Sweet." Milo, wearing a pastel plaid short-sleeved shirt that would look right at home in a Florida retirement community, stuffs his schedule into his pocket, picks up three coconuts lying in the sand, and begins to juggle them.

I scan the schedule quickly. For the next five days there are blocks of time for cultural and geopolitical orientation in the afternoon and team building in the mornings. The late afternoons and evenings are reserved for recreation and group social activities.

"What are these paddle boats you speak of?" Abel intently studies the week's schedule as though there will be a pop quiz at any moment.

"The name is kind of self-explanatory," Kai quips, leaning back against the trunk of a nearby palm tree, arms crossed, looking totally relaxed. "You get in the boat and paddle hard and eventually you go somewhere very slowly." Today he's wearing a Willy Nelson T-shirt with Willy's face sporting his signature braids down each side and a headband that reads Have a Willy Nice Day.

I giggle at both the T-shirt and his description of paddle boating, and Kai meets my gaze with an amused look. I share his opinion; I love being on the water, but paddle boats feel almost pointless. So much effort for so little reward.

One of the cameramen, Jake, a wiry Filipino man with a goatee, has been assigned to our team, and he crouches next to a nearby palm tree, fiddling with his video equipment and apparently waiting for us to do something publicity worthy.

"Okay, everyone, pick a partner, and let's head down to the water," Rosie urges us.

Milo springs into action, swiftly claiming Rosie as his partner. With a shrug Winnie beckons Abel to join her. "Let's get this over with," she mutters.

That leaves me with Kai. He raises his eyebrows. "You game to join me for the world's slowest boat race?"

"Sure." I nod, trying to act relaxed. Kai makes me nervous. He's just so appealing, so easy to like, and I don't know what to do with the plain and simple fact that I find him attractive. It is seriously throwing me off-kilter. I am determined to be a good team player, however, and I do have strong legs from cycling up all those steep Seattle hills. I will paddle like mad and make every effort to keep my feelings for him from developing into anything more than friendship.

We follow the other two teams down to the half dozen paddle boats sitting just above the tide line. One end of the island forms a crescent around a lagoon, and across the length of the lagoon lies an obstacle course marked out with floating buoys. The goal, Rosie explains, is to navigate the obstacle course in the paddle boats as fast as we possibly can. The team who reaches shore first wins.

"Ready. Set. Go!" Jake shouts to get us started.

Together Kai and I drag our boat into the water and jump in. We're already behind. Jake stands at the edge of the water, filming the race. I start paddling furiously as we inch away from the sand.

"Nice form." Kai glances sideways at me, looking both amused and a little impressed. He adjusts our course with the steering handle so we head straight toward the first buoy.

"I'm a cyclist," I pant, trying to keep up the fast pace. "But I sort of hate paddle boats. It feels like being perpetually stuck in first gear."

"Like paddle boat purgatory," Kai deadpans. I laugh, a little breathless from the effort of paddling.

We skirt the first buoy and are heading for the second when Kai looks down. "Uh-oh. I think we've sprung a leak."

I glance down. There are several inches of water in the bottom of our boat. I was concentrating so hard on paddling I didn't notice. Already it is sloshing around my toes. There's a crack behind my pedal, and water is gushing into the boat at an alarming rate.

Ahead of us Rosie and Milo are laughing merrily as their boat veers around the third buoy. Abel and Winnie are making surprisingly good time, right on their tail. We are definitely not going to win the time challenge. As it stands right now, I'm not even sure we can make it back to shore before our boat sinks.

"I think we'd better turn around."

I bite my lip, trying to assess our odds of reaching the shore.

Not good. We both paddle as hard as we can while Kai steers us around in a lazy circle. Slowly, slowly we start back toward shore.

"Hey, you're going the wrong direction," Milo yells at us as they pass us on the other side of the buoys, heading in for a first place win. "You have to go around all the buoys."

"We've sprung a leak. We're sinking," I yell back, still paddling hard and feeling a little nervous. I can swim, of course, but I'm not the most confident swimmer. I'm from the Northwest, where Puget Sound is a chilly fifty-six degrees at the height of summer. We northwesterners prefer to be on the water rather than in it. However, this is Florida. The water in the lagoon is warm and calm. We'll just swim to shore slowly and steadily. It will be okay.

Rosie leans around Milo and calls out, "Do y'all need a rescue?"

"No, I think we're fine," Kai replies.

"Are you a strong swimmer?" I ask, paddling like mad and trying to keep my tone light. We aren't in any real danger, but slowly sinking into the salty water is a little unnerving.

Kai nods. "Yeah, I grew up in Hawaii. My mom used to joke that I'm part dolphin. I could surf almost as soon as I could walk."

I smile. I pegged him for a surfer the moment I met him. I lean forward and paddle faster, not that it makes any discernible difference. We are definitely not going to make it to shore.

Abel and Winnie pass us on the other side of the buoys just as Rosie and Milo beach their paddle boat for the win. Our defective boat is riding lower and lower in the water, the nose almost under the surface by now. Water is sloshing up to my calves. Suddenly our boat tips forward. Seawater rushes in over the sides. We are officially swamped. With a shriek I dive over the side, and Kai does the same. We both swim clear of the boat.

"Mia, you okay?" I can see Kai's dark head on the other side of the sinking boat, his expression concerned.

"Yeah, I'm good," I say, feeling a little flutter of anxiety. We're in deeper water than I realized. My shorts and T-shirt are sodden, and I've lost my flip-flops. Thank goodness my iPhone is waterproof. Kai swims around to me. Just one corner of the boat is above the water now, a red fiberglass nub poking above the placid surface.

"We can still place third." Kai laughs, then turns and starts swimming toward the beach with long, languid strokes. "Come on."

I follow him as fast as I can with an awkward frog kick/dog paddle. Thankfully the water is calm, and now we have all the time in the world. The other teams are watching us from shore. I can hear faint cheering as we swim closer to shore. Rosie is waving and gesturing to us. The sun is warm on the crown of my head, dancing like diamonds on the surface of the water. Not what I had in mind for the morning, I muse as I swim behind Kai, but all in all not a bad way to spend the time.

When I glance again toward the shoreline, Rosie is gesticulating wildly, swooping her arms over her head in a jerky motion. Milo is leaning toward us, his hands around his mouth like a bullhorn, yelling something. Their posture is no longer jubilant. It looks . . . frantic. My heart skips a beat.

"Kai, something's wrong."

A moment later we draw into range, close enough to hear Milo's words. He's shouting as loud as he can, "Shark! Shark! Get out of the water!"

Time stops. For an instant I freeze in disbelief. This can't be happening. Kai swears under his breath. He glances behind us. I panic and go under for a second, sure I felt a bump against my leg. I swallow water and flail, clawing the air. In an instant, Kai is there. He grabs my arms and pulls me upright.

"Mia, put your feet down. You can touch here."

He's standing, the water just reaching his chest. He holds me upright, his hands strong around my rib cage, until I calm enough to draw a full breath of air and set my feet down on the bottom. I can just reach on tiptoe.

"Mia, Kai!" Rosie screams, pointing. "Shark!" The entire team is gathered on the shore, yelling and gesturing for us to hurry.

"Can you walk?" Kai asks tightly. He grabs my arm and pulls me with him. I glance back, but the surface of the water is deceptively still. I can't see whatever's out there. Kai pulls me toward shore, our progress excruciatingly slow.

"I can touch." I put my feet down, trying to match his pace. My heart is racing with fear and adrenaline.

"Walk fast. Don't swim," he instructs tightly. "Humans look like wounded sea creatures when they swim."

I obey, walking as fast as I can through water that's now at armpit level. Every step feels like slow motion. Kai stops and slips behind me, his hand on my shoulder. It takes me a moment to realize what he's doing.

"Are you putting yourself between me and the shark?" I pant, every muscle straining to go as fast as possible as we slog through the water.

"Yes," he answers shortly.

He's using his own body to defend me. That's downright heroic. But I'm not about to let a man lose his leg or his life protecting me. I'm not a damsel in distress.

I duck under Kai's arm so I'm beside him, not in front, then grab his hand. "We're a team," I say. "We go down together."

He glances at me for an instant, and I see a flicker of admiration in his gaze. We push through the water side by side.

Slowly, excruciatingly slowly, we gain ground. Every second I'm braced for an attack, expecting to feel razor sharp teeth latch onto me under the water. Kai's fingers grip mine so tightly I lose circulation. Now the water is to my waist, now my thighs. Our teammates on the shore are going crazy, cheering and screaming encouragement.

When we are in knee-deep water, Kai drops my hand. "Run!" he commands. We run, splashing and high-stepping, desperate to reach land. I don't stop until all I feel on my toes is warm dry sand, and then I stumble and fall, breathless and shaking. Our entire team surrounds us, their faces suffused with relief. My legs are trembling so hard Rosie has to help me stand. She wraps me in a towel and then gives me a long, tight hug, ignoring the wet patch I leave on her crisp blouse. Jake is filming the scene, circling us, catching all the dramatic footage.

"There, see it?" Milo points out at the water. I can just make out an ominous dark shape darting through the water between us and our sunken paddle boat. Kai whistles low. "That's a bull shark. At least six feet long. They're notoriously aggressive."

"He was chasing some fish, and then he doubled back and headed for you." Milo shakes his head. "We didn't think you were going to make it."

Sodden and weak-limbed, I watch the blurry shadow of the shark in disbelief. Rosie grabs a bottle of water and presses it into my hand.

"Did Kai put himself between you and the shark?" she asks, keeping her voice low so the others can't hear.

I nod. "He tried, but I told him we were a team."

"Oh my stars," Her eyes follow Kai as he and Milo stand a few yards away watching the shark. "That's so . . . heroic."

I take a swallow of water. "Yeah it is." He doesn't know me, didn't need to put himself in harm's way for me. But he did. The thought warms me. Rosie bustles off to get a bottle of water and a towel for Kai.

"You okay?" Kai comes over to me and puts his arm around my shoulders, pulling me against his side, solid and reassuring.

I lean into him a little, resting my head against his shoulder. The relief is starting to seep through my body, leaving me jelly-legged and light-headed, and a little euphoric. "Yeah, I'm okay. Thanks for sticking with me." My voice is hoarse from salt water and fear.

"Thanks for being brave," Kai says, giving my shoulder a squeeze.

Out of the corner of my eye, I spot Jake filming our interaction and drop my eyes to the sand, feeling awkward that such a personal moment will be on camera for Lars Lindquist and the entire world to see. Rosie returns with Kai's towel and a bottle of water, effusive and concerned. He thanks her, and then Milo calls him back over to watch the shark hunt for prey.

I sit down in the sand and drink some more water, feeling steadier. What an unexpected morning. I watch Kai for a moment, replaying the events of the past half hour. His actions were admirable, but I have come on this trip with one goal, to find my place and make a difference in the world. Kai is a teammate. Maybe he can be a good friend. Nothing more. I need to keep that crystal clear in my mind. There is no room for gorgeous, heroic Hawaiian surfers in my alternate life. Not even one who is willing to risk life and limb to save me. I don't need to be saved. I can stand on my own two feet.

Chapter 16

"*Sa-wah-dee-krap*." Facing Abel under the big white tent, I intone the traditional Thai greeting, then give him the *wai*, placing my palms together like praying hands and making a slight bow of respect. It is our third cultural learning session, and all the teams are practicing a few polite phrases for each country on our itinerary. I stumble over the foreign words of the Thai language, the sounds too acrobatic for my English tongue.

"*Sa-wah-dee-kah*," Abel replies in his soft, lilting accent, returning the bow solemnly.

"*Kob khun krup*," I say. Thank you.

"*Kob khun kra*," Abel replies, each of us using the appropriate phrase for addressing the opposite gender.

I like being paired with Abel. He's the most reserved member of our team, saying little but observing everything with a look of concentration on his narrow, clever face. He has a calm steadiness about him, a sense that he is always listening.

As all the teams practice the phrases under the watchful eye of our instructor, Jake circles Abel and me, filming.

"*Pood Thai mai* . . ." Seeing the camera lens breaks my concentration, and I forget the phrase for "I don't speak Thai."

"Just do your thing, and Jake will blend into the background.

You won't even know he's there," Bryant assures me in a whisper, coming over to where we are standing. He's been observing our lesson.

"Does he have to film everything?" I whisper back, still feeling annoyed about Jake recording the entire shark incident and its aftermath.

"We use a lot of it for publicity," Bryant explains. "We have a website and an Instagram account so everyone can track with the trip, almost in real time. And Lars likes to keep a close eye on the teams, to have a real sense of what's going on day by day. This is the first trip for the foundation, so we're really interested to observe what works and what doesn't, to see how it all plays out in real life." He waves a hand at Jake as though erasing him. "Act like he isn't there."

I try, but I still feel awkward with a camera lens pointed in my direction.

"Good effort with the Thai phrases." Our instructor, an Asian studies professor from Columbia University, claps her hands briskly and calls all the teams back together again. "Now please take a seat, and let's discuss the political climate of Thailand, particularly the issues surrounding the new king."

We return to our seats as the instructor begins her lecture onstage at the front of the tent. So far the lectures are interesting and informative, but we still have no idea what exactly we will be doing to help in the various countries. Stella assures us that we will be "practically assisting on-the-ground organizations in each location." Which sounds good but still seems quite vague.

Outside of the planned sessions, the members of Team Caritas gravitate toward each other, sitting together at meals and in the evenings. Somehow the shark incident has brought us closer together. We are still mostly strangers, vastly different in personality and outlook, but we have each other's backs. Thinking of what lies ahead in just a few short days, I find that reassuring. At least we will be going into the unknown together.

~

Our final night on Sunbeam Key, Lars throws an epic bon voyage party. Each team will depart in the morning for one of the locations. Teams Veritas and Fortis will start in Thailand, Team Fidelis in Mexico, and we on Team Caritas are heading for India.

By eight the party is in full swing—Brazilian barbecue with dozens and dozens of skewers of meat roasting on a huge grill by the pool, colored lanterns strung from the palm trees, fruity cocktails. The air is soft and warm, the colored lights around the pool reflecting on the water's surface, blurry and beautiful watercolors of themselves. As the sun sets, a half dozen of the white T-shirted muscular men wheel a baby grand piano from inside the house and assemble a trap set on the veranda. A man in a fedora and suspenders takes a seat at the piano and begins to play some light jazz. He's accompanied by guitar, drums, and stand-up bass. Several people start to dance on the patio, and others clump together in little groups, cocktail glasses in hand.

Just as the band starts into "Girl from Ipanema," Lars joins the party, looking impeccable in a white linen suit. I haven't seen him since the night we spoke on the veranda. He mingles with the guests.

I wander over to the tiki hut bar where Rangi, the tattooed Samoan bartender, is leaning against the counter watching the festivities.

"Hey, pretty lady, can I get you something?" he asks.

"Um, something tropical?" I ask. "Maybe virgin since I've got a long day of travel tomorrow."

He nods and whips out a coconut, the top already sheared off.

He pops a straw into it and hands it to me. "Can't get more tropical than this."

I take a sip. The liquid inside is sweet and slightly nutty flavored. Delicious. "This is quite a party," I say.

Rangi shrugs. "Pretty standard for around here."

"Really? How often do you have these sorts of things?" I'm surprised. I imagined we were getting some sort of special treatment.

"At least twice a month. Sometimes more," Rangi says. "They're different each time. Last August when it was hot enough to melt your face, Boss Man hosted a vodka and ice palace–themed party. Had tons of ice flown in from Alaska and an ice sculpture contest. It was crazy."

"Wow, really?" I sip my coconut water. The band has moved on to an upbeat version of "In the Mood." "Why did he have it here? Why didn't he just go to Alaska?"

Rangi gives me a sideways glance. "What do you mean? Boss Man doesn't leave the island. Everything has to come to him."

"What?" I stare at him in bemusement. "I thought Lars had a million followers on Instagram. I thought he dated a princess."

"That's right." Rangi nods, crossing his arms and leaning against the bar. "But it all happens here. Everything Boss Man wants to see and do he brings right here 'cause he can't leave. In the two years I've worked here, he's imported a Chinese circus troupe, a traveling ballet company from St. Petersburg, and a gourmet sushi chef competition. Once a month he has a weekend-long party with famous Hollywood celebrities. Justin Timberlake and his family stayed here for two weeks last year."

While all this is impressive, I'm stuck on one phrase. "Why can't he leave?"

"Don't know." Rangi shrugs. "Rumor is something bad happened to him a couple of years ago, and now he only feels safe on the island."

I scan the crowd until I find Lars' tall, lean figure. He's holding a martini glass in one hand and chatting with beautiful Korean twin sisters from Team Veritas. He can't leave the island? With consternation I think back to my first conversation with him, the air of elegant sadness that envelopes him. What did he call this place, a golden cage?

"Thanks for the drink." I raise my coconut in a little salute and wander toward the pool, still puzzling over this unexpected news about our host.

There's a flurry of activity by the piano on the veranda, and then the opening chords to "Fly Me to the Moon" fill the night air. Someone starts to sing, and instantly I recognize the voice. Rosie is leaning against the piano, serenading the patio in her fabulous, sultry croon. I pause to listen. I've heard her sing many times before, but her voice still stops me in my tracks. One glance around and I see that it is having the same effect on others. Most of the party guests have stopped what they are doing and are listening, heads turned toward her, cocktail glasses motionless in their hands. Clad in a lovely turquoise sundress, her hair loose around her shoulders, she looks alluring, enchanting. I feel a swell of pride as I watch her.

"She is truly captivating."

I whirl to find Lars Lindquist standing at my elbow, infusing the air between us with the light scent of bergamot, like Earl Grey tea. I sniff appreciatively, trying not to be obvious.

"Is she classically trained?" he asks. "Julliard perhaps?" He takes a sip of his martini, dirty with two olives, his eyes never leaving Rosie.

I laugh. "No, she's just naturally that good." I don't elaborate. People always assume things about Rosie—that she comes from Southern money, that she's highly trained at a fancy conservatory, that she was born with a silver spoon in her mouth. To look at her, no one would guess her humble roots.

"Marvelous." Lars shakes his head. He's entranced by her, and for good reason. She's sparkling and talented, not to mention strikingly beautiful. With her jade-green eyes and statuesque, bombshell figure, she looks like she belongs on a pin-up calendar from World War II.

Rosie has finished her song and descends the steps, laughing and flirting with a dentist from the Fidelis Team.

"Would you tell her how remarkable I find her voice?" Lars requests.

"Why don't you tell her yourself?" I wave and call to her across the pool. "Rosie!"

She sees us and gracefully excuses herself from the conversation with the dentist. She seems to float over to us, her smile radiant.

"Rosie, have you met our host, Lars Lindquist?"

"I have not yet had that pleasure," Rosie says sweetly, her accent seeming to grow thicker with every word, slow and golden as honey. She holds out her hand, and he takes it and presses it between his palms, almost reverently. Rosie meets his eyes and smiles demurely. I watch Lars melt. There's no other word for it. If he were an ice cube, there would be nothing left but a puddle in his expensive leather boat shoes.

"Thank you for gracing us with a remarkable performance," he says, his voice mellow and smooth with just a hint of a Scandinavian accent. "Your voice is truly a gift."

"Oh, that's so sweet of you to say," Rosie purrs. "But you must be used to far better. I heard a rumor that Diana Krall sang at your holiday party last year."

"Jamie Cullum came for Christmas," he corrects her with a slight smile. "Diana joined us for a Valentine's Day fête."

Rosie laughs delightedly.

I feel like I've stepped into a vintage romantic movie, where everyone is perfectly coiffured and delivers their lines with just the right amount of practiced zest and sparkle. I am not up to their caliber, that much is clear.

I clear my throat and hold aloft my now empty coconut shell. "I'm just going to get a refill. Either of you want anything?" They don't hear me. They're already discussing a Venetian carnival event Lars threw last year and how opera star Renée Fleming, a personal friend of his, whipped off her ornate mask and sang a surprise ballad just before the midnight supper.

I wander off to the bar, a little blinded by the sparks those two are making together. I wonder if Rosie knows Lars never leaves the island. I glance back at them. Rosie is laughing, her head thrown back, the slim line of her throat white and graceful as a swan. Lars is looking pleased and a little sheepish. He is everything Rosie is looking for in a man. Kind, handsome, ridiculously wealthy. And he seems like a genuinely good human being, a far cry from the louts Rosie has fallen for in the past. I can see the attraction between them. I should be celebrating it, but instead it gives me pause.

Rosie's chief ambition, besides to find the love of a thoroughly good man, is to pursue her dream of a career singing jazz in New York. And Lars cannot leave the island, for reasons that are a mystery. Therefore Lars is not a good match at all. Just another man with baggage who looks good on the surface but is hiding some flaw beneath.

I hesitate, watching them together, wondering if I should tell her what I know. Right now it's just a harmless flirtation. And besides, tomorrow we jet off to Mumbai, and Lars . . . Well, apparently Lars will be staying right here on the island.

Chapter 17

How r u today? What did doctor say?

Later that night, after the party has wound down, I slouch in the hammock on the deck of our Lingonberry cottage and text Nana Alice. She had her big oncology appointment today. I've been wondering about the results all evening but wanted to be somewhere quiet and private before asking her questions. I don't bother trying to call. It's bingo night at Sunny Days, and she never misses a chance to play.

I hear back from her a minute later. I'm good. Dr says great treatment options available. We're optimistic. More later. I'm one number away from winning a Twix bar!

I imagine her punching the letters of the text on her phone one at a time with her gnarled index finger, and my heart squeezes. I desperately hope she's doing as well as she claims.

For a moment I waver, tempted to get on a plane to Seattle instead of Mumbai tomorrow. But Nana Alice would never forgive me, or herself, if I gave up this adventure because of her. I will go to India, I decide. If she takes a turn for the worse, I can always leave the trip early and fly home. I glance at my watch. Ten till eight in Seattle and almost eleven here. Rosie isn't back yet. Earlier, as the party wound down, I passed Lars and Rosie climbing the veranda steps to the house with a bottle of champagne.

"Lars wants to show me his telescope," Rosie told me, her voice light and balmy as the evening air. "Don't wait up."

The sky this evening is clear, like blue velvet, a backdrop for a luminous swath of stars. They'll have an incredible view.

I text Henry next. Off to India tomorrow. Bravely charging into my alternate life. It's too late to actually call him in Chicago. The twins wake at five, and Henry has adopted an early bedtime for the entire family with a fervor that borders on the religious.

To my surprise, he replies a moment later. Go get 'em, tiger.

I imagine him drowsy and squinting at his phone in their king-sized Pottery Barn bed, trying to type without his glasses, Christine sleeping in an eye mask beside him.

I place a quick call to my parents, correctly guessing that they are just sitting down to dinner after another long day on the farm. They work sunrise to sundown, especially in the summer lavender season. I video chat with them for a few moments while they eat my mother's homemade lentil soup, my father regaling me with tidbits of eco-farming news from the latest *Acres* magazine and my mother filling me in on all the current news in Sequim. I tell them about my teammates and our week of orientation, glossing over anything that might concern them—like the shark incident. Finally, it grows late.

"Have a wonderful time," my mother tells me in parting. "We're so proud of you, sweetheart." Finished with supper, she is sitting at the dining room table, knitting socks for homeless veterans in Seattle, her cinnamon sugar curls a little wild around her head, her strong, bony hands holding the knitting needles with practiced ease.

"Don't drink the water," my taciturn father interjects from his scruffy plaid recliner by the fireplace. "Be safe and use your head." I can hear the rustle of his magazine pages. He's drinking his evening hot toddy, the lemon and whiskey laced with lavender honey from our bees.

"I will," I promise, bidding them both good night. "I'll call you from Mumbai."

After I hang up, I sit for another moment in the darkness, breathing in the warm salt air, centering myself. A light breeze rustles the palm fronds above the cottage, and through the trees comes the distant, rhythmic lull of the ocean.

Tomorrow I embark on a grand adventure, one I've longed for since I was young. I've never been on an international flight, never been surrounded by a culture and language different from my own. I've dreamed of this day for so long, and now that it is almost here, I'm filled with an anticipation, almost a lust, to dive in, swim in the current of the world, drink deeply of the new and exotic and different. I am thirsty for adventure, for experiences, for a wider, wilder life.

For a moment I picture Ethan, the image of his face accompanied by a pang of sorrow. I wonder what he is doing right now, if he thinks of me, if he misses me. The loss of him still hurts, although the past month has mellowed the intensity from excruciating to the dull ache of a slowly mending broken bone. I shake myself. Enough pining over Ethan. He has made his choice. I have made mine. I can only look forward now. The biggest adventure of my life starts tomorrow.

In the early morning hours I dream again of bees. I am not at West Wind nor on Sunbeam Key. The landscape is strangely familiar, barren and brown, the sun searingly hot on the crown of my head. It is the India of my Mother Teresa coloring book, the same spare scenery, the goldenrod sun. I see myself from afar, a halo of light outlining my frame as I sit on a rock under a spindly thorn tree. I am dressed in a simple white sari with a blue border and ringed by small brown barefoot children. I hold one on my lap and he plays with my curls. My face is suffused with peace and a radiant sense of purpose.

I hear the bees first, the low buzzing, and then see them, a small swarm on the horizon rapidly coming closer. I set down the little boy and shoo the children off. They scamper away to safety, but instead of running after them, I lift my arms toward the swarm of bees in welcome. A moment later they envelope me in their golden, buzzing energy. Gently they alight on my exposed skin—my clavicle, the bend in my elbow. I close my eyes as a few step gingerly across my cheekbones. I am covered in bees but they do not sting me. I stand still, illuminated and serene.

And then I understand it all. I am Saint Mia, the beatific version of myself. At that moment all is right in the world. I am benevolent. I am transcendent. I am exactly where I should be.

Part 3

Mumbai

Chapter 18

"Lord, have mercy, we're going to die!" Rosie crosses herself with one hand and grips the metal side bar of the auto rickshaw with the other as our driver bends low over the handlebars, guns the engine to a high whine of protest, and catapults us directly into the heavy flow of Mumbai traffic.

Nothing has prepared me for India. I realize this in an instant, sitting bolt upright beside Rosie in the back, stifling a scream as we race through an intersection and swerve sharply to narrowly avoid rear-ending a large red city bus. It's ten thirty at night, and this is the third close call we've had in the twenty minutes since we left the airport.

Zooming behind us in matching rickshaws are Abel and Winnie, Kai and Milo, and Jake, the cameraman, with Shreya, our handler for our time in India. A soft-spoken, young Indian woman with a long, dark braid and a hot pink sari embroidered with gold and turquoise flowers, she met us at arrivals after our long series of flights from Miami to Mumbai. She ushered us outside and promptly loaded us into a row of idling yellow-and-black auto rickshaws: tiny, covered three-wheeled vehicles with a seat in front for the driver and a bench for two in the back. They are open at the sides and there are no seat belts. Rosie and I are squeezed into the tight back seat, Rosie's suitcase and my backpack wedged between our knees, both of us holding on to the metal frame and trying not to panic. I glance at Rosie, who has a terrified grimace plastered on her face. Her knuckles are bone white as she grips the metal side rail.

As we hurtle through Mumbai, I turn my head this way and that, trying to take everything in. The sheer sensory bombardment is overwhelming, electrifying. Everywhere a cacophony of sound and movement—the streets teeming with vehicles and people even at this late hour. Horns and music blare in a discordant chorus. The air is thick, hot and humid—like breathing bathwater. I draw a deep breath, eager to take India into my lungs, inhaling car exhaust, dust, spices, and sweat. It makes me a little queasy.

An auto rickshaw passes us on the left, carrying Shreya and Jake. A moment later we almost plow into a family of four, including an infant and a toddler, jammed together on a motorcycle. I cry out in alarm as without warning they turn in front of us and pass within just a few inches of our front wheel. I swear the woman's orange sari actually brushes our rickshaw's single front headlight. For a moment she is illuminated, the gold threads on the edge of her sari glinting in the headlight's beam. When I glance up, Jake is leaning out the side of his auto rickshaw, taking his life into his hands as he photographs our near miss. I squeeze my eyes shut, heart pounding, and simultaneously swear and say a prayer for safety.

Twenty minutes later we turn into a quieter, more residential area and stop in front of a shabby cement building. A skinny dog barks as we disembark. My hands ache from my death grip on the metal frame, and I fumble with my backpack. Shreya hops out of the first rickshaw.

"Please come this way," she says to us in precise, crisply accented English, ushering us through a door and up a set of brightly lit stairs. "You will stay at this guesthouse. Very modest but clean. We hope you will be comfortable."

"Is there Wi-Fi?" Milo asks as we climb the stairs. In response Shreya makes a side-to-side tilting motion with her head, a head bobble that looks like a cross between a nod and a shake. I am not sure if it means yes or no. Milo glances back at me in confusion, but I shrug, as mystified as he is. What does a head bobble mean in India?

Inside, the guesthouse is worn but clean with tile floors and harsh fluorescent lighting overhead. In the reception area a pencil-thin young man with slicked-back hair and a hint of a mustache is sitting behind a laminate counter.

Shreya speaks to the man in a rapid-fire language that is not English, and he stands. "This is Jayesh," Shreya tells us. "He is the night manager. If you need anything, just ask him."

Jayesh bows slightly to us. "Welcome," he says carefully in English. "Come. I will show you to your rooms."

The narrow hallway smells strongly of spicy cooked food and a chemical cleaner. Kai and Abel are given the first room. Milo and cameraman Jake share the second. Rosie and Winnie and I are in a triple room down the hall. Three single beds are sardined into the space under a small window completely covered by an air-conditioning unit. On the other side of the room sits a square laminate table, two plastic lawn chairs, and a white porcelain sink the size of a skillet.

Winnie tosses her backpack into the corner and flops onto one of the beds with a groan. "I forgot how insane the driving is here," she says. "Oh India, I missed you."

Rosie opens the wardrobe and proceeds to empty the contents of her suitcase into it, taking most of the space and all of the hangers. I stand by the door, unsure what to do. I feel disoriented and overstimulated, as though my soul has not yet caught up with my body. My hands and feet and lungs and eyes are in Mumbai, but my brain seems to be still somewhere in the international air space between Munich and here. And my heart? Where is my heart?

Perhaps still in Seattle. I think briefly of Ethan, wondering what he would make of this. Ethan, who likes order and predictability.

I unpack quickly, stowing my belongings on the only empty shelf in the wardrobe. I need to remember everything about our arrival so I can tell Nana Alice. I wish I could take photos, but Jake will be posting videos and photos on the Humanitas Foundation website and on Instagram. Nana Alice will be able to track our progress from the comfort of her own armchair. I imagine her watching Animal Planet or *The Great British Bake Off*, then stopping to check Instagram, seeing the photo of Rosie and me in the rickshaw. She'll enjoy my facial expression, I'm sure.

A quick knock at the door and Shreya pokes her head into our room. "Are you comfortable?" she asks.

"Yes, just fine," Rosie assures her. Although she holds a deep appreciation for the finer things of life, she is remarkably adaptable when she needs to be.

"Good. I will come for you at nine tomorrow morning," Shreya says. "If you need anything in the night, Jayesh can assist you. Sleep well." She closes the door.

Looking around, I suddenly realize that the only thing I really need is the toilet. I slip out to find it. Inside the women's bathroom across the hall, I am stymied. There is just a white porcelain oval bowl recessed into the floor with raised ridged foot-shaped areas on either side. A spigot pokes from the wall next to the bowl, and under it sits a bucket of water with a red plastic cup bobbing inside. I glance around in puzzlement, then go for reinforcements.

"I can't find the toilet," I announce to Winnie and Rosie.

Sprawled on her bed, Winnie glances up from reading a worn paperback. "Great news," she deadpans. I glance at the title of her book. *The Portable Nietzsche*. Unexpected. I hadn't pegged Winnie as a reader, much less a reader of German nihilist philosophy. She's full of surprises.

"What do you mean you can't find the toilet?" Rosie asks. "Isn't it just across the hall?"

I motion for them both to follow me. Winnie rolls her eyes but complies, and we cram into the ladies' room. "See?" I gesture around me.

Winnie sighs. "You're looking at it," she says with a touch of asperity, pointing to the bowl set into the floor. "That's a squatty potty. You put your feet on the sides like this and go into the bowl. When you're done, flush it out with water." She nods to the cup bobbing in the bucket.

"How do you know that?" I ask, impressed.

"I did a three-month tour of Asia with Dynamite Kitty in 2010. We had some concerts here." Winnie shrugs. "A lot of the world uses a squatty potty." She rolls her eyes and turns to go, tossing over her shoulder at me, "Seriously, Pollyanna, it's not brain surgery."

"Only if you know how it works," I mutter at her retreating back.

"All those hours of orientation," Rosie says thoughtfully. "All the lessons on history, culture, political dynamics, and social structures, and no one thought to tell us how to use the toilet."

Together we observe the squatty potty, for a moment awed and a little intimidated by everything we do not know.

Chapter 19

Bright and early the next morning, Jayesh ushers us to a small restaurant around the corner from the guesthouse. It is simple—a handful of tables and chairs in a brightly lit, utilitarian space. Only one other table is occupied, two men sitting with round metal trays in front of them filled with unidentifiable dishes, tiny bowls of sauces, and bread rolls. They stare at us wordlessly as we take seats at two tables against the front window. Jake leans against the wall by the front door, wearing a baseball cap and aviators, camera at the ready to film our first Indian breakfast.

"Shreya will meet you here in thirty minutes," Jayesh tells us. "Enjoy your meal." He gives a slight bow and leaves. My stomach rumbles. It's been many long hours since the airplane food from the night before. Excitedly anticipating a real Indian breakfast, I look around. There is a menu posted on the wall. It is in English, but it might as well be in another language.

"Idli vada." I say the words aloud, marveling at their strange shape in my mouth. *"Rava Masala Dosa."*

I love Indian food, but as I scan the menu I realize that nothing looks familiar. The *naans* and *biryahnis* and *vindaloos* of Bombay Kitchen, my favorite Indian restaurant, are nowhere in sight. I have no idea how to feed myself. The thought makes me feel a little lost.

I thought I was ready for India, but so far I can't seem to do the simplest things.

A middle-aged man barges through a door at the back of the restaurant. Portly and unsmiling beneath a thick black mustache, he pours tea into glasses and sets one before each of us. "*Masala chai*," he says, jabbing his finger at the tea.

Relieved to recognize something at last, I pick up my glass and inhale the steam—cardamom, cloves, ginger, and black pepper. Out of the corner of my eye, I see Jake raise his video camera, and I instantly tense. Then I force myself to relax. So what if Lars Lindquist and the entire watching world see me taking my first sip of authentic Indian chai? Let them experience it with me.

The first sip is sweet and peppery and scalding hot. It's the best tea I've ever tasted. I inhale again, trying to cement this moment into my brain. I'm here, in India. I've done it. Gotten a stamp in my passport, gone on an adventure of my own.

Milo sets down his chai and makes a face. "Dude, do you think they do nitro cold brew here? I'm not feeling this tea."

The proprietor plods from the back, his arms laden with plates. He sets them down in front of us, points, and announces impassively, "*Kheema pav*," then disappears back the way he came. We examine the plates in silence. Two normal-looking bread rolls beside a mound of something minced and reddish brown. Meat? Vegetables? I can't tell.

Rosie purses her lips and examines her plate. "Y'all have any idea what this is?"

Kai picks up his fork and tastes the minced brown item cautiously. "It's meat," he reports. "Sort of like an Indian take on sloppy joe. It's good." He takes another forkful. I watch him for a moment, noting the clean line of his jaw, the casual air of confidence he exudes. I make myself look away.

Ladling some filling between two halves of a roll, I take a bite.

It is spicy and filled with a cacophony of flavors—delicious. I'm so hungry I devour it all and am wiping up a smear of sauce with the last bite of roll when Shreya breezes through the door.

"Good morning, Team Caritas," she says. Clad in a sari the color of a tangerine, she looks fresh and cheerful. "Come. Follow me, please. We do not want to be late."

Two identical yellow-and-black taxis are waiting outside, their metal roof racks stacked high with wrapped bundles. We gather beside the taxis and wait for Shreya's instructions. Around us the air is vibrant with the sounds of the city—car horns, a radio blaring Bollywood music from the salon on the corner. A cow wanders down the roadway, nosing a pile of garbage. Already it is growing almost unbearably hot, the sun beating down through a gray haze of smog above the roofs of the buildings. The air quality is notoriously bad in Mumbai, a far cry from the fresh, chilly salt breeze of Seattle.

"Hey, Shreya, what exactly are we going to be doing while we're here?" Milo asks the question I've been eagerly wondering since orientation week.

"You will be assisting in school enrichment programs for poor children in the slums," Shreya explains. "You will visit a different slum every day and provide a program with entertainment, education, and a special snack."

I glance around at the other members of my team, cheered by the description. Helping in enrichment programs for poor children in the slums seems like good, useful work.

Shreya gives us more details, reading off a list on her phone. "You will be divided into two teams. Team one is Winnie, Milo, and Kai. Team two is Rosie, Mia, and Abel. Jake will alternate between the teams. Today he travels with team one."

I'm relieved not to be paired with Winnie. I find her abrasive personality and lack of initiative frustrating, and given that she keeps calling me Pollyanna in a sardonic tone, I'm pretty sure she doesn't like me either. But I'm a little disappointed not to be on the same team with Kai. Probably for the better, though. Less distraction this way.

"What do we have to do?" Winnie sniffs, wiping her runny nose on the sleeve of a grungy T-shirt that says Dynamite Kitty in hot pink, flaming letters. Even though it's already sweltering, she doesn't seem to sweat, wearing the T-shirt paired with skinny black jeans with studs and her ever-present black lace-up combat boots.

"You and Rosie will provide musical lessons for the children," Shreya explains. "Kai and Abel will play soccer for physical education."

"How about Mia and me?" Milo asks.

"Ah yes," Shreya says. "You and Mia will be in charge of . . . pancakes."

"Pancakes?" Milo and I ask in unison, shooting each other a surprised look.

Shreya repeats the confusing Indian head bob. I decide it must be an affirmation. "I'm sorry that we do not have any opportunities for you to practice your"—she glances at her phone—"Latte art or medical skills. Instead, you will be providing these children with a special snack. Many come from very poor homes. Often they do not get enough food and may suffer from malnutrition. An American pancake is a treat for them. We have all the supplies you need. You will simply cook the pancakes and hand them out to the children."

For a moment I'm taken aback. I was expecting something a little more . . . important, more transformational, than making pancakes. At the same time, however, I feel a tiny bit relieved. At least it's not anything related to medicine. My lie sits uneasily on my conscience, but as long as no one asks my expert opinion or assistance in bandaging a wound or diagnosing an ailment, I might be able to put that ill-advised moment of untruth behind me.

Pancakes I can do.

"Now." Shreya claps her hands. "Team one, you will go in a taxi to your first location. My colleague Priya will meet you there. Team two, you will come with me." We squeeze into the taxis, four people per taxi, and head to the slums.

Although the driving is as perilous as last night, I think I must be adjusting to it—either that or my store of adrenaline is already used up. I barely blink as we swerve sharply to avoid plowing into a man pushing a four-wheeled wooden cart loaded with bananas.

I'm riveted to the scene out the window. Everywhere there are vehicles and buildings and people, people, people, a teeming mass of people. Families sleeping under bridges; wafer-thin men walking beside the roadway; women in dusty saris selling fruit and street food; children begging at every intersection, their hands outstretched, tapping on the glass, some of them handicapped, all of them ragged and clamoring for money from the line of vehicles stopped at a red light.

I start to roll down my window, fishing some coins from my satchel, but Shreya puts her hand on my arm to stop me.

"Don't," she says. "Many of those children are being exploited for profit by organized crime. Do not give money to them, as it simply goes into the pockets of criminals."

I roll the window back up, staring at the wide, dark eyes and outstretched hands tapping on the glass.

"But what can we do?" I ask. A woman wanders by, a baby hanging limply in her arms. She cups her hand and holds it out to me, but I shake my head remorsefully. She walks on.

"There are organizations that do good work among these people," Shreya replies. "Give money to them, and it will actually help the children."

The light changes and we pull away abruptly. There is so much that happens behind the scenes, I realize, so much I have yet to learn.

When the taxi finally stops on the side of a busy roadway, we all pile out. Two young men are standing on the berm of the road, a wooden handcart beside them. At a word from Shreya, they unload the bundles from the top of the taxi and stack them in a handcart.

"This way." Shreya motions for us to follow her. Behind us the men wheel the handcart as we enter one of Mumbai's slums.

I thought I knew what to expect—after all, I saw *Slumdog Millionaire*—but the reality takes me by surprise. We walk down a dusty path running alongside a sluggish brown river clogged with garbage and reeking of human waste.

"Oh good gracious," Rosie murmurs, breathing shallowly and pressing the sleeve of her blouse against her nose. The odor is overwhelming, and I follow her lead, breathing through the cotton of my short-sleeved shirt, inhaling the faint lavender scent from the sachet of West Wind lavender my mother gave me for my backpack. A fragrant token of home.

We pass a young boy with skinny haunches squatting on a board and defecating into a gutter that runs directly into the river. I look away, embarrassed by the sheer humanity of it, the lack of privacy for such a base function. Everyone defecates, but not everyone has to do so in public. There is garbage everywhere, mounds of it, drifts of it, like party confetti, a tattered, jaunty rainbow of refuse. And mangy dogs so skinny you can count their ribs, and flies, flies everywhere, buzzing in the doorways and over the piles of garbage.

We wind through dirt lanes lined with dilapidated buildings made from corrugated sheet metal and wood. Everywhere people are watching us, small children naked from the waist down, women in colorful saris squatting in doorways. It is both uglier and more normal, less sensational, than I had anticipated.

Shreya glances back at us. "About 6.5 million people in Mumbai live in slums like this one," she explains as we follow her single file down a narrow alley. "Over half of the total population of the city. Many people come to Mumbai from other parts of India for economic reasons but can only afford to live in the slums. There are many problems in these places—extreme poverty, malnutrition, domestic abuse, lack of medical care—but at the same time each slum is its own community just like any other community. There are families, small businesses, shops. It is home for many of us in Mumbai."

I walk close behind Shreya, aware of the dozens of eyes watching us impassively from every direction. Children run out of the open doorways and join our procession, chattering and waving. It feels like a parade, and we are the stars of the show. I have never felt more white or more privileged in my entire life. I feel ill at ease in the face of such stark deprivation, such poverty. I wanted this experience, pinned all my hopes on it, but I didn't anticipate my own reaction, the twin feelings of intimidation and discomfort.

"You okay?" Rosie whispers behind me.

I glance back at her. "I don't know. It's different from what I thought it would be. You?"

"About what I expected," she says. "Although the smell is worse."

I envision the beatific Mia in her sari, shining and holding small brown children on her lap. Embarrassed, I realize that in my vision the children were poor but well scrubbed. Everything was bathed in light. There was no odor, no dust coating everything.

I square my shoulders and smile at each person we pass, feeling naive and foolish and deeply uncomfortable. But today is not about me. I am here to help, and I will do the best I can.

Chapter 20

"Here we are." Shreya stops in front of a corrugated metal building with no door, similar to many of the others, and motions us inside. The classroom is bare but clean, with woven rugs on the dirt floor. It is just as hot inside as out, maybe hotter.

"This is where we run the before- and afterschool programs every school day," she explains as we let our eyes adjust to the dimness after the glaring sunlight outside. "In India it is mandatory that all children attend school, but children from very poor areas do not have the advantages of wealthier students. Many are not in school at all, and if they are, their education is often inferior. We help these disadvantaged students master the essentials—reading, writing, math, and also English, to give them a stronger foundation for school. It is summer break and the students do not have school now, but we are having a special program to celebrate your visit."

The two young men with the handcart unload the bundles in the middle of the floor, and we unpack them. A few deflated soccer balls and a pump. Two brand-new packs of toy instruments for children.

Rosie shakes a tambourine and eyes the other instruments thoughtfully. "I don't really know how to teach children music," she says. "I've never done it before."

"They will be happy to learn anything you can teach them," Shreya assures her.

I open a bundle to find boxes of Lindquist Original Pancake Mix and bottles of syrup. The happy sunburst shape looks cheerfully out of place. I also find two frying pans, ten eggs, and a bottle of cooking oil as well as a liter of bottled water. I'm all set.

Already a half dozen children are poking their heads around the doorway, giggling. I wave to them, and their heads pop back outside amid shrieks of laughter. Rosie sorts her instruments, humming a little jazz tune under her breath. Abel sits cross-legged in a corner, inflating the soccer balls. I help Shreya lug the pancake supplies over to a two-burner gas stove top sitting on a small table in the back corner.

"The people who live in this slum are fortunate," she tells me, fiddling with the knobs of the stove. "The government makes sure that each house has electricity and a gas stove. Also most residents have access to clean water. They have to pay to use the public toilets, sometimes three hundred people for every one toilet, but many of their basic needs are met."

"This is all new to me," I tell her, a little embarrassed. "I've never seen anything like it."

"Of course not," she says with a small smile. "You are from America." She shows me how to light the stove and adjust the flame.

"How did you start working with this program?" I ask her.

"I was raised in a slum here in Mumbai," she says. "My parents still live there. They worked very hard so that my brother and I could go to school and have an education. I had many good opportunities in my life, and I want to help other children in the slums have the same." She slants a sideways glance at me. "No matter where I go in life, or what I do, I am still a little girl from Dharavi. I cannot forget that, nor do I want to."

She turns off the gas burner and steps back. "There. Do you feel prepared to cook the pancakes on this?"

"I think so." The stove works similarly to the Coleman camp stoves we used on family camping trips when I was growing up. "I just have to figure out the ideal cook temperature, and then the rest is easy."

We arrange the ingredients nearby so I can access them easily.

"How do you like India so far?" Shreya asks as I hand her boxes of pancake mix and she stacks them on the table beside the stove.

"It's not what I expected," I confess, gingerly passing the eggs to her.

"How is it different?" She looks genuinely curious.

I hesitate, trying to formulate the words. I imagined the more colorful aspects of India, the postcard images, the novelty of it, the exotic beauty. But I was unprepared for its sheer overwhelming *otherness*, the myriad stares and unintelligible syllables of a foreign language, the garbage and the strange odors and the press of thousands of people in a city bursting at the seams with humanity. I was unprepared for different when different doesn't look like a magazine.

"I thought it would feel like the pictures," I admit finally, embarrassed. I hand her a bottle of syrup.

She smiles. "Life never looks like the pictures," she says, not unkindly. "Pictures are just a moment frozen in time, but this"—she sweeps her hand to encompass the slum community—"This is real life. If we want to help people, we cannot focus on their problems, on what we can see just on the outside, the garbage and poverty. We must enter into their lives, be a part of their community. That is where real change happens, person to person, day by day, when we live life together."

I look down at one of the happy sunshine-shaped maple syrup bottles in my hands, suddenly unsure. I've come on this trip because I want to do something that makes a difference in people's lives. If Shreya is right, what does this mean about the efficacy of our trip? We are only here for a brief visit, a few hours, a blink of time.

Can we really hope to change anything? If not, what are we even doing here?

The next hour passes quickly. Two student teacher volunteers arrive and usher about two dozen children into the room. The children are divided into groups that rotate through different stations. A beginners' English class led by one of the student teachers meets in one corner, a music class led by Rosie in another. Abel takes a third group outside to play soccer in the street. The alley is narrow and not conducive to sports, but through the doorway I can hear him running practice drills with the children, his instructions punctuated by their yells of victory or groans of disappointment as they make or miss their shots.

At a signal from Shreya, I begin to prepare the pancakes. In a large plastic bowl I combine oil, water, and eggs with the pancake mix, stirring energetically with a wooden spoon. I pour a little oil into the flimsy frying pans and start heating them slowly. It rights me somehow to be baking again, although, to be fair, making pancakes from a boxed mix can only loosely be considered baking. But it feels good to be working with flour and eggs, oil and heat. Life just seems better with a wooden spoon in my hand.

As I mix the batter, I watch the hubbub around the room.

"Here, here, like this. Watch how I do it." Rosie stands in one corner ringed by children sitting cross-legged on the floor. She plays "Twinkle, Twinkle, Little Star" on a sparkly green plastic recorder. "Now you try."

Rosie vainly tries to bring order to the pandemonium as the children enthusiastically shake, blow, and tap their various musical instruments. Their efforts don't bear any resemblance to an actual tune, but they appear to be enjoying themselves immensely. One little boy beats a tambourine on the floor. A little girl in a threadbare red dress and little gold hoop earrings jangles a triangle and bobs up and down.

In the opposite corner the children sit around the chalkboard, dutifully shouting out the English words the teacher is showing them.

"Monday," they yell with fervor. "Tuesday. Wednesday. Thursday."

The air is stifling in the enclosed space, smelling strongly of unwashed little bodies. None of the children wears shoes, and their bare feet are caked with dust. However, as I watch, I am struck by how universal childhood is. Their circumstances are vastly different from any I've seen back home, indeed a world away from the privileged life of my niece and nephews in Chicago, but their boundless energy and infectious grins are the same.

I ladle batter into both frying pans and turn down the heat a little, watching closely for the telltale bubbles to appear on the top, signaling that it is time to flip the pancakes. As the lessons and games progress, my stack of cooked pancakes grows. The room gradually fills with the scent of them, and the children turn every few minutes, eyeing them covetously.

When I take the last pancake from the skillet, Shreya moves to the center of the room. She claps her hands. "Children, it is time for our special snack. Line up here please."

The children obediently line up, squirming, wiggling, giggling, and poking those in front of them. I hand each child a pancake, pouring a thin stream of Lindquist pancake syrup on the top in sticky loops.

"Enjoy," I tell each one. I ask their names and tell them mine. They grin and chatter at me in Hindi and Marathi with the occasional English word thrown in for my benefit. Then they sit cross-legged on the floor, devouring their treats, hands and faces sticky with syrup.

As I watch them, I can't help feeling a warm glow of satisfaction. What we are doing here is not epic, not monumentally life changing, I know that, but surely there is value in these little things too?

Chapter 21

"Congratulations," Milo announces, opening the door to his room when we return to the guesthouse later that afternoon. "You've officially survived the hottest day of my life."

He waves us into the room. The rest of team one is already congregated there. The air conditioner is going full blast. Winnie sits in a plastic chair under the cold air, a wet washcloth over her eyes. Kai is sprawled in another chair, shirtless, holding a tall glass of some orange substance. He's wearing only a pair of basketball shorts with the words Charlottesville Black Knights emblazoned on them.

Jake is nowhere to be seen. Milo stretches out on his bed in a pair of khaki shorts, displaying freckled and surprisingly toned abs.

"You want a mango lassi? It's cold. Help yourself." He gestures to the small laminate table next to Kai. It is crowded with full glasses of the same orange beverage.

Abel, Rosie, and I each grab a glass. It's so hot outside that the thought of doing anything other than sitting right here in the cool comfort of this room is unthinkable. It must be in the midnineties, maybe more, but the smog and the still air make it feel much hotter. I feel wilted from the intensity of the sun.

Rosie sits gingerly on Jake's unmade bed and sips her lassi.

"Please, Mia, sit." Abel leans against the wall next to me,

gesturing for me to take the only open chair, across the tiny table from Kai. I do. The lassi is essentially a mango and yogurt milkshake—delightfully cool, creamy, and sweet. "Oh this is delicious," I sigh, sipping blissfully.

"Mmm." Rosie agrees appreciatively, holding the glass to her forehead.

We all sit in silence for a moment, wrung out by the heat and our experience in the slums. I think about the people we have just left, those who live day to day in these temperatures with no air-conditioning, no cool drinks for respite.

"How was making pancakes?" Kai asks me, stretching out in the chair and lacing his fingers behind his head.

"Great. It was fun. The kids were so cute." I concentrate on the glass in my hand as though it's the most interesting thing in the world, trying to keep my gaze away from the tanned, smooth plane of Kai's upper body. His shirtless state is unnerving. I can talk normally if I focus on something other than his bare chest.

"Did you play basketball in high school?" I ask, gesturing to his gym shorts.

He nods. "Varsity shooting guard, till I tore my ACL my senior year."

Chalk that up as another of Kai's hidden talents. Nana Alice would be so impressed. She loves watching men's basketball. I stare at the mango lassi, admiring the creamy orange color, the coolness of the liquid. I press the cold glass to my suddenly pink cheeks.

"Looks like you got some sun, Mia," Milo observes from across the room. "Us white kids have to be careful. We burn like Wonder Bread."

"I must have forgotten my sunscreen," I murmur, not looking at Milo. I turn back to Kai. "How did it go at your location?"

He shrugs. "Okay, I guess. We played soccer and gave kids pancakes. Honestly, I was expecting something more."

"Really, like what?"

He hesitated. "I don't know. I guess I thought we'd be doing something that felt more . . . impacting."

"You think what we did today doesn't matter?" After Shreya's words about being part of a community, I've been wondering the same thing myself. But it feels so good to bring a smile to the children's faces, even if it's just with a pancake.

"Seriously, Pollyanna?" Winnie pipes up incredulously, sitting upright in the chair and pulling the washcloth from her eyes. Apparently she wasn't sleeping. "You think teaching kids to play "Row, Row, Row Your Boat" on a plastic recorder and giving them a pancake is really going to change their lives?" She shoots me a caustic look. "Those kids have to deal with things we can't even comprehend. Nothing we did today is going to make any difference." She tosses the washcloth onto the chair and leaves the room without another word.

I sit motionless holding my lassi, stung by her tone, by how easily she dismisses our efforts. I glance up and find Abel watching me.

"She has a good point, but a harsh way of saying it," he says, his eyes kind. "Do not take it personally."

"I seem to rub her the wrong way." I frown, feeling embarrassed.

Abel tips his head, a brief gesture of absolution. "It is not you. That woman is an egg. Hard on the outside, but inside she is a soft, scrambled mess."

It's an unexpected analogy. "What do you mean?" I ask.

"I have known others like her," he says. "She tries to cover up her wounded places with a tough armor, but don't be fooled. Those tender places are still there."

I shake my head, still stinging from her rebuke. If there is anything tender in Winnie, I have yet to see it.

"Y'all!" Rosie shrieks, interrupting our conversation. She's staring at something on her phone. "A photo of our team is trending on Instagram. It's featured as a top post! Look!" She holds the phone out breathlessly, and we pass it around.

The trending photo is a shot of Rosie and me in the auto rickshaw from the night before. The lights behind us are just a blur, and in the foreground we are almost running over the family on the motorcycle. The woman's orange sari is illuminated in the single headlight, as are Rosie's and my faces, caught in identical looks of sheer terror. It is a captivating image, but I'm surprised at how many comments it's garnered. Two thousand in just a couple of hours.

I stare at the photo, amazed that so many strangers are interested in our team. I really thought no one would even know or care about us. Studying my horrified and slightly shiny face, I make a pact with myself to be camera ready anytime Jake is around. If my face is going to be plastered on Instagram for the world to see, I need to pay a little more attention to my appearance. Mascara and frizz control hair balm at a bare minimum.

I quickly scroll through the top dozen or so comments, curious to see what people are saying. A few offer humorous caption suggestions for the photo while several ridicule us for coming on this trip. But ten comments down, my heart stutters to a halt in my chest.

Careful, ladies! Stay safe. From Instagram user ethanwhite. Ethan is following our team on Instagram. I stare at his name for a long moment, stunned. What does this mean?

"Hey, Mia." I glance up to find Kai watching me, brow furrowed with concern. "You okay?"

I quickly pass the phone back to Rosie. She looks at me questioningly, but I shake my head. "Just reliving the terror of my first auto rickshaw ride," I say, making light of the moment. I paste on a smile, although my mind is racing.

Setting my glass of lassi on the table, I excuse myself after a moment. "Jet lag and the heat," I claim. "I'm going to take a little nap. See you all at dinner."

In the quiet of our room, I look up the photo and his comment again on my phone, staring at those four words until they blur. Careful, ladies! Stay safe.

Why is Ethan following our team? Why did he leave that comment? Maybe it doesn't mean anything. But then again—what if it does?

Chapter 22

Early the next morning I climb the narrow stairs of the guesthouse to the deserted rooftop terrace and call my mother. It's evening in Seattle, the best time to try to reach her.

"Hi, sweetheart." Her head bobs into view on the phone's screen as she picks up the video call. "How are you? How's India?"

She's in our farm shop. I can see sachets of dried lavender and beeswax candles hanging on strings behind her. I imagine the smell of the shop—beeswax and lavender and the salt tinge of the Sound. Suddenly I feel homesick, a sensation that surprises me. Funny, now that I've finally managed to leave home, I miss it.

"It's good, a little crazy. Not quite what I expected. Our team is really diverse, but it's working pretty well." I glance out over the terrace wall. The sun is just starting to peek weakly through the smog. From somewhere below me the smell of frying onions and spices wafts up through the muggy air.

"Oh, I envy you," my mother sighs. "I always wanted to go to India."

This surprises me. I wasn't aware that my mother had ever yearned to travel somewhere as exotic as India.

"How are you and Dad? Everything okay on the farm?" I want to hear that all is well, that everything is familiar and predictable and normal back home while I am embarking on this exhilarating but unnerving new adventure.

"Oh yes, everything's humming along as usual. Your father's out in the fields right now. Tourist season's in full swing." My mother pauses from her organizing. The light from the wall lamps illuminates her face, highlighting the laugh lines radiating from the corners of her eyes and her wild red-gold curls. She wears no makeup, and her skin is pale with just a smattering of freckles across her nose, like mine. I ache to hug her, just for a minute, to be enveloped in the scent of lavender that clings to the creases in her skin. The scent of home.

She briefly disappears from the camera view, and I hear rustling. "Just a minute, I'm restocking the jams. I made some strawberry lavender this week. It's your dad's new favorite."

Tears spring to my eyes, and I laugh a little. It feels so good to connect with her.

"We do have some news, though." My mother's head pops back into view. "Your father and I are taking a trip."

"Really, where?" Usually my parents take two weeks off in the slow late fall or winter season. One week they spend with Henry and Christine and the kids and the other visiting historic towns in New England or a national park somewhere around the country.

"We're going to volunteer for six weeks with an organization that helps exploited women and their families start fair trade lavender farms in Moldova." My mother beams into the camera, looking a little fish-eyed as she comes close to the screen. "Isn't that exciting? We were so inspired by what you're doing that we wanted to do something similar. Mary Ellen and her husband over at Purple Hill Lavender Farm volunteered with this organization last summer and said it was a life-changing experience. She signed up to go back this year but just had emergency gallbladder surgery, so she asked us to consider taking their place. At first we said no because of your Nana Alice's health issues right now. It didn't seem right to leave after we heard about her cancer, but when your father mentioned the opportunity to Alice, she absolutely insisted we go. We thought about it and decided, given the type of cancer it is and her good prognosis, that the opportunity was too good to pass up."

"Wow." I'm astonished by this unexpected news. My parents, my predictable, steady parents, are going to leave the farm for six weeks and jet off to a country I've barely heard of? Where in the world is Moldova exactly?

"Who's going to look after the farm while you're gone?"

My mother wrinkles her nose. "We haven't figured that out yet, but we'll come up with something. Your father and I think it's high time we had an adventure. We leave in two weeks," she adds.

Two weeks? My jaw drops. That's the start of the farm's high season. They're leaving the farm at the busiest time of the year? They'll miss the Sequim Lavender Festival. They never miss the Festival.

Seeing my expression, my mother laughs. "I know, so soon. It's been a bit of a whirlwind, but it just feels right. It's high time we did something a little crazy."

I don't know what to say. Apparently I'm not the only one thinking about an alternate life. It makes me feel strangely discombobulated. Instantly I feel selfish for even minding about the trip. I'm an adult. They're free to do what they want with their lives, but still . . . there is so much change in my life right now. I always think of my parents and the farm as steady and predictable, unchanging. To hear about these unexpected plans is a seismic shift, the ground suddenly unsteady under my feet.

"How's Nana Alice?" I ask, changing the subject. I figure my mother will have more specifics about the actual situation. So far Nana Alice has simply been doling out vague and optimistic-sounding assurances via text.

My mother sighs. "She says her oncologist has mapped out a good treatment plan and her prognosis is excellent. She says she feels better already." She pauses for a moment, then clears her throat, a quick look of unease flashing across her face.

"What?" I ask. "Don't you believe her?"

My mother brushes off my concern. "I'm sure it's nothing. She just seems so tired, that's all. A little . . . fragile. But she says everything is fine and that she's responding well to the treatments."

I slump back against the concrete railing, feeling conflicted. What if Nana Alice isn't okay? Should I go home?

"Don't be alarmed," my mother assures me. "She's getting excellent care. And your trip as well as ours is giving her something to look forward to. Apparently she's been tracking your travels on Instagram—is that what they call it?"

My parents are not particularly tech savvy. They have a website for the farm but otherwise spend very little time online, preferring to read or listen to NPR.

"She says she feels almost like she's there on the trip with you." My mother chuckles. She starts hanging bunches of dried lavender on hooks near the cash register, her arms filled with the powdery purple blooms. "I think your trip is giving her a new zest for life."

I'm surprised and pleased to hear that Nana Alice has figured out how to follow our adventures online. I texted her the pertinent information before I left Florida but didn't realize she'd managed to make it work.

Of course I also thought no one else was following our trip, but that was before I saw the photo of Rosie and me trending on Instagram last night. Apparently more people than I ever imagined are interested in our trip, including Ethan. I wonder again what his comment means. Why is he tracking my travels?

I turn my attention back to my mother. "Should I be worried about Nana Alice? Do you think I should come home?"

She pauses for a moment, considering. "No, I don't think so." She waves away the idea. "Alice is a resilient soul, Mia. She's stable, she's in good hands. She says she is getting well. Don't worry. Enjoy India."

"Okay." I take a deep breath. "But if anything changes . . ."

"You'll be the first to know," my mother assures me. "We can all be back at her side in short order if the need arises, but I think she's going to be just fine."

CHAPTER 23

"At last, a free Saturday," Rosie says happily as we walk to the restaurant for a late breakfast after sleeping in blissfully late. "Milo and I are going shopping at Palladium. It's supposed to be the most high-end mall in Mumbai. They have Jimmy Choos." Rosie beams. "Want to come with us?"

"I want to explore the city, find an outdoor market, see some historic sights." I give a wide berth to a mangy dog sniffing a soiled diaper in the gutter in front of the restaurant. "I'll ask at breakfast and see if anyone wants to come with me."

The café is fairly crowded this morning, and I scan our regular two tables, noting that the entire team except for Winnie is already there. Even Jake is present, sans camera, eating with the rest of the team. Winnie was gone from the room when we awoke, and I wonder where she went. She's generally not a morning person, a fact she attributes to her years as a rock star playing shows until late.

"Morning, ladies," Milo greets us. "Ready to see a new side of Mumbai?"

"Absolutely. I can't wait." Rosie sits down across from him.

I slide into an available seat across from Kai. "Good morning."

He nods to me, his mouth full of breakfast roll. A moment later the restaurant owner, Sunil, unsmilingly delivers chai to Rosie and me, and I take a grateful sip.

Even though we've been here ten days, this will be our first time venturing out into the city without Shreya or our handlers. We've been kept busy doing two enrichment programs a day in various slums around Mumbai. We return to the guesthouse at dinnertime each day, sweaty, exhausted, and wrung out by the heat and the working conditions. No one has felt like wandering back out into the city with the extreme heat and noise and traffic. Instead, we've spent the evenings on the rooftop terrace watching the sun set over the city, eating fruit from the neighborhood vendor, the sweet juices of ripe mangoes and melons running down our elbows, attracting ants and other insects to the sticky puddles.

"Ooh, what's this?" Rosie asks as Sunil sets a plate down in front of each of us.

"*Bun maska*," Kai says with a grin. "It will change your life."

"A truly delightful dish," Abel affirms. "This is my third plate."

I take a bite, chewing, analyzing. Bun maska, as far as I can tell, consists of a bun liberally spread with butter and fresh cream and sprinkled with sugar. I understand the appeal. The food in Mumbai is amazing, but every dish is an explosion of new flavors, a sensory overload. Sometimes it's nice just to have a sweet piece of bread smeared with butter and cream. Simple, uncomplicated, delicious.

It is already hot in the café, the air heavy with the smells of cooking. I wipe a trickle of sweat from the back of my neck and sip my hot chai. It seems counterintuitive to drink hot beverages in this kind of heat, but I can't seem to stop drinking this chai. It's addictive.

"So what's everyone's plan?" Milo asks, pushing away his empty plate. "Rosie and I are heading to Palladium if anyone else wants to come."

"I'm taking a Bollywood tour this afternoon," Jake says. It's weird to see him without a camera in his hand. I almost don't recognize him.

Abel polishes off the last of his bun maska and stands. "Sadly, I have research I must do for Amnesty. I will not go out today. Also, I saw Winnie this morning. She said she is meeting someone she knew from her past tour and not to wait for her."

So it looks like everyone has plans except Kai and me.

"Want to explore Mumbai together?" Kai asks, setting down his chai glass. I hesitate for one instant.

I should say no. Spending all those hours alone with him seems like a bad idea if I am indeed trying to protect my heart. But the thought of a day spent exploring Mumbai with Kai is too good to pass up.

"Let's go," I say, happily caving in to temptation.

"So this is it. The famous Gateway to India," Kai says an hour later as we stare up at the huge and ornately decorated archway, dubbed the Taj Mahal of Mumbai. We are standing at the Apollo Bunder waterfront in the Colaba neighborhood of Old Mumbai, taking in one of the top tourist attractions of the city.

"It's so ornate." I stare in awe at the imposing golden stone edifice facing out to the Arabian Sea. A tour group is clustered nearby in the shade of the Gateway, listening to a guide explain its historical significance. Kai nudges me, and we edge closer so we can hear the lecture, standing in the shade of the Gateway where it is marginally cooler. In the sweltering midmorning heat, I'm already sweating through my travel dress. May is the hottest month in Mumbai, Shreya told us, and the heat is oppressive, almost a living thing. Why the Humanitas Foundation chose to send us here in the hottest month of the year is beyond me. It seems like remarkably poor planning.

"The Gateway was built to commemorate the royal visit of

King George the Fifth and stands as a monument to colonial triumph," the guide intones in crisp British English. The tourists hold aloft iPads and snap photos, squinting in the glare of the sun. "It's constructed of basalt and is built in the Indo-Saracenic style," the guide continues.

"I didn't understand half of that sentence," I confess in a whisper, leaning in toward Kai.

"Really?" He glances at me through his Ray-Bans and smirks. "Which half?"

"Okay, busted. I understood none of it." I pull a wry face. "What's Indo-Saracenic?"

"Well this, obviously." He points up to the Gateway with a straight face, then throws me a cheeky grin and explains in a low whisper, "It's a style of architecture that combines elements of native Indo-Islamic and Indian design with the Gothic revival and neoclassical styles that the British favored in Victorian times."

"How do you know that?" I ask, impressed. It sounds like he's reading straight from a textbook.

He shrugs. "I like architecture. It's a durable historical record."

I stare at him for a moment and then glance away. I find smart men irresistible. It was one of the first things I loved about Ethan, his sharp intellect. That and the dimple. Unsettled, I gaze around us. The vast square in front of the Gateway is thronged with people, tourists and locals alike. Vendors are selling big colorful balloons and spicy snacks, and a number of photographers are taking photographs of tourists in front of the arch for a fee. The air smells like baking rock and fish and seawater. I am almost giddy with the exotic excitement of it all.

"Hey, look." Kai points to a sign advertising ferry rides around the harbor. "Want to take a ride?"

"Absolutely." I love being on the water and am eager to cruise the Mumbai harbor. We pay our fee and board one of a fleet of small ferry boats. Our ferry is an awkward vessel, rolling and ponderous, wearing a necklace of black rubber car tires to protect it from bumping against the dock. We clamber up a set of steep steps to the top observation level and sit in plastic chairs under a tattered green-striped canopy. The ride is approximately thirty minutes according to the man who sold us our tickets, a short pleasure cruise around the harbor.

"I could live on a boat," I sigh happily. "When I was a kid I loved going to Seattle because it meant we'd take the ferry over from the peninsula. And usually we'd see Nana Alice and visit her bakery. A ferry ride, my grandmother, and a homemade cookie equaled the perfect day."

Kai smiles. "I love the water. My mom used to say when I was little that I'd live in water if I could."

I can see that, a little Kai like a sleek seal in the warm Hawaiian waters.

Our boat pulls away from the dock and starts chugging into the harbor, which is clogged with boats of every size and description, from sleek expensive yachts to tiny open motorboats barely big enough for a few people. The Arabian Sea below us is grayish brown and the breeze smells a little like rotten eggs, but I am so delighted to be on a boat that the murky water doesn't matter. Then I think about our last disastrous boat ride together and cross my fingers, fervently hoping this lubberly vessel is seaworthy. I have a feeling you really don't want to swim in this harbor.

Our vessel is crowded, but most of the Indian passengers remain on the lower deck, flocking to the railings below us to take photos and videos on their phones. Only a few venture up to the top deck where we are, perhaps because of the glaring sun. We stay in our chairs under the awning, enjoying the small measure of privacy. It seems that wherever you go in Mumbai there are a thousand people there with you.

"Are you hungry?" Kai pulls out a Ziploc bag of trail mix from his small daypack and offers some to me, pouring the peanuts and raisins and M&Ms into my hand.

"Thanks." I fish out a yellow M&M and pop it into my mouth. Peanut butter. After a solid week of Indian food morning, noon, and night, the taste is gloriously familiar.

"Oh golly, that's good," I moan, devouring the whole handful with a speed that borders on gluttony. Even so, the M&M's melt in my palm, leaving dots of primary colors. Kai proffers the bag, a tacit invitation to eat more, and I shamelessly accept.

We sit munching companionably for a few minutes, staring out at the view. The smog is terrible today. Even in the harbor the air is thick and yellow. The distant boats are obscured by it, the black outlines of their masts just visible through the haze.

"How did you know you wanted to be an urban farmer?" I ask when I've eaten the last of the snack. The engine is loud below us, and we have to lean close together to be heard.

Kai stashes the empty bag in his pack, then stretches out in the plastic chair, long and lean, lacing his hands behind his head. He considers the question for a moment.

"At first I didn't have a choice," he says finally. "My dad abandoned us when I was six. He was . . . not a nice guy." A shadow flickers across his face. "After he left, my mom and my little brother, Sam, and I moved to Honolulu. Those were tough years. Mom worked as a waitress, but she made almost nothing. We were just scraping by. I remember more than once eating just saltines and ketchup packets she'd snuck from the restaurant for our dinner. But our next-door neighbor, Hiroto, knew a lot about foraging. He was Japanese Hawaiian, same as my mom, and about eighty years old. He started taking me foraging outside the city, showing me edible fruits and plants."

Kai takes a water bottle from his pack and offers it to me. I unscrew the top and take a few quick sips.

"The day I picked my first strawberry guava, it was like a lightbulb went off in my head. I realized I could help feed my family. After that we always had something besides saltines to eat, even on the days when Mom's paycheck didn't stretch quite far enough."

"Wow, that must have been such a relief, to be able to provide for yourself and your family like that." I hand him the water bottle, and he takes a swallow, then screws the cap back on.

"It was a powerful feeling for a boy with not a lot of resources," he agrees. "That's why I want to give other kids that same power. I want to teach them what Hiroto taught me, self-sufficiency and reverence for the land."

At his words I can feel my heart melting like butter, sliding into a sunny puddle right there on the deck. I sense the hardship that lies at the foundation of his story, the abandonment by his dad, the poverty and bare kitchen cupboards. He could so easily carry it like a wound, a liability, a limitation, but instead, he's taken those hardships and turned them for good.

I blink, realize I'm staring at him moonily, and glance away, trying to break the awkwardly long pause.

"That's so cool." I stare out at the bay for a moment, steeling myself. I could so easily fall head over heels for this man. But if I did, what then? Would I just glom on to his vision for his life because I still haven't developed one of my own? Become Mia the urban farmer? I can't make that mistake again. I have to find my own way first.

Chapter 24

"So what's your family like now?" I ask Kai as our ferry continues its slow, lolling circuit of the harbor.

"They're great." He chuckles wryly. "They drive me crazy sometimes, but I love them." He describes his mother and stepfather, Gordon, the law professor his mom met when he wandered into the diner where she was waitressing—a sunburnt, introverted tourist who ordered cup after cup of coffee until he summoned the courage to ask her on a date. Sam is now a junior at the University of Virginia, majoring in economics. And he has a younger half sister who is thirteen, Ruthie, named for Supreme Court Justice Ruth Bader Ginsburg. They live in Virginia, just a few miles from Charlottesville, on a farm with horses and a black Lab named Thurgood.

"They're pressuring me hard to go back to law school. If I don't win the funding for my idea, they'll get their wish." He frowns.

"Why go back to law school if you aren't passionate about it?" I ask. "If you know what you want to do, why don't you just do that instead?"

"I have to fund the project somehow. Being a lawyer would allow me to do that. It's not what I want to do, but I could practice law if it let me do what I'm really passionate about."

"Well, let's hope it doesn't come to that," I tell him. "Maybe

Lars Lindquist shares your love of lettuce and will choose to fund your project."

Kai laughs. "Yeah, I hope so."

The boat takes a lazy turn back toward the dock, and Kai points out the iconic Taj Mahal Palace Hotel standing imposingly near shore. "What about you?" he asks. "Were you always interested in medicine along with baking? Did you give your stuffed animals cupcakes and then operate on them?"

I chuckle. "Growing up I wasn't interested in medicine specifically," I skirt my fabricated passion and opt for the truth. "But I always admired my aunt Frannie, who's a dentist in Africa. I was raised on a lavender farm on the Olympic Peninsula, the most tranquil place you can imagine." I describe my family and Sequim and West Wind.

Kai looks impressed. "That sounds idyllic."

"It is," I agree. "But even as a kid I had this thirst for adventure. I dreamed of a life of selfless service to the poor somewhere foreign and exotic." I clear my throat. "Mother Teresa was my childhood hero. Aunt Frannie gave me this *Life of Mother Teresa* coloring book. It was my favorite thing in the world, my inspiration."

"Impressive." Kai whistles. "When I was a kid I just wanted to be a fireman or Superman. You know, the normal stuff."

I smile, leaning back in my chair as the boat trundles steadily through the brown water. "Yeah, I never wanted a normal life. I mean, don't get me wrong. Growing up on the farm was great. My parents are hardworking, honest people, and they raised my brother, Henry, and me to be socially conscious and industrious citizens. But life on the farm never felt exciting enough. I wanted to be Saint Mia and follow in the footsteps of Aunt Frannie and Mother Teresa. I always dreamed of better things."

I dart a glance at Kai, feeling a little vulnerable sharing my most deeply held dreams, but there is no skepticism or judgment in his expression, just a steady, attentive openness. "Better things," he repeats.

"Better things," I affirm, thinking suddenly of my parents, of their impending trip. They leave in just a few days. Apparently they are thirsting for adventure, for better things too.

We are heading back toward the dock now, though the shore is almost obscured in the smog.

"So how has the trip been for you so far?" Kai asks. "Is it what you were hoping for?"

I hesitate. I like giving the children pancakes, seeing their happy grins and sticky fingers. It feels good to help them. Each time we visit a new slum, I think of what Shreya said about true change coming through relationship. I try to engage as much as I can with the children, learning their names, making silly faces with them, laughing together. But given the constraints of the schedule and the language barrier, I have little opportunity beyond these simple things. Sometimes I wonder if we are making any difference at all.

"I don't know," I admit finally. "It's complicated. What about you? Is the trip still not what you hoped it would be?" I remember him expressing his doubts that first day and wonder if he's changed his mind.

Kai shrugs. "To be honest, I'm disappointed. I thought we'd be doing something that had more of a lasting impact. Lars has spent so much on this trip already, just to get us here. It's got to be tens of thousands." He pauses, frowning. "That money could have been used to really help these slum communities—funding kids' educations or building safe homes or giving families medical care. Instead of sending us around the world to hand out pancakes. I kind of think we're just wasting time and money so a reclusive billionaire can feel like he's doing something good. This feels like a lost opportunity to me."

"I guess you're right." I look down at my hands, mulling over his words. I've been enjoying the experience, loving the exotic adventure of India, but I haven't considered the financial cost or what we could do differently and better. Kai is correct. That money could be used in a dozen better ways, contributing to long-lasting change. I've just been concentrating on the children's happy smiles and on how wonderful it feels to give them something I made. Now I see how shortsighted that is. Perhaps I've been only playing at being Saint Mia, handing out my stack of pancakes with a halo of golden light around my head. I have been making myself feel good but probably not helping anyone, not really.

"Shreya said something the first day we were here that I keep coming back to," I say, brushing back a curl from my face. "She said we can't just focus on fixing the problems, that real change happens person to person, day by day, when we live life together."

"That sounds true," Kai says.

I nod. "I think so too." If I am honest, I know I have not entered in, not really. I have gingerly dipped my toes in life in the slums, posing for photos for Instagram, whipping up a batch of pancakes because it's easy and it's what I love to do. Not entirely worthless, surely, but nothing that will stick, nothing that will change things for the better.

The thought is disappointing.

Now that I'm here, assessing my experience in the hot gray light of a Mumbai afternoon, I see how self-serving my vision has been. I wanted to go into the world with zeal and compassion. Saint Mia. But now, faced with the complex reality of grinding poverty framed by an exotic culture and locale, I wonder if my zeal was more to have an adventure than to actually help transform lives. I thought I wanted to change the world—but did I actually just want to experience it, consume it?

"Hey, you okay?" Kai asks, shooting me a concerned look. I

smile and nod, although inside I feel hollow with uncertainty and dismay. Have I botched my alternate life already? I genuinely *do* want to help others. But how?

"I wonder if there's a way to change things in the time we have left," I tell him. "Maybe we can still make a difference, even if it's a small one."

The boat bumps against the dock, and we scramble to our feet, following the other passengers across the gangway.

"Hey." Kai turns to me. "I know this trip is disappointing. It's not what we hoped it would be, but we're here in Mumbai. It's our free day. Let's enjoy today, and tomorrow we can talk with Shreya and the team about changing things, okay?"

I hesitate, then nod. Tomorrow we will try to make a difference. For now Mumbai and the Colaba Causeway street market await.

CHAPTER 25

"Hey, Mia, are you hungry?" Kai asks. We've been browsing the market stalls for several exhilarating hours, and the late afternoon sun is slanting long shadows across the road.

"Famished," I confess. We find seats in a crowded local restaurant and stuff ourselves with *Hyderibadi biryani*, *chilli paneer dry*, and *dahi vada*. When the food comes we hardly talk, wholly bent on the delicious flavors. Afterward we order filter coffee and leisurely converse over the bustling noise of the café.

"When we first met I asked why you came on this trip, and you told me a broken heart and an epiphany." Kai leans toward me across the small table.

I nod. "That's right." I'm impressed that he remembers. I was too busy trying to pretend that I didn't find him ridiculously attractive.

"So who broke your heart?" He looks genuinely interested in my answer.

"Oh." I clear my throat and sit back, toying with my metal tumbler of coffee. *So we are going to have this conversation, are we?* "My boyfriend of six years, Ethan. We had our life all planned out, and then on our six-year anniversary he broke up with me as he was trying to propose. He had the ring in his hand, but in the end he just couldn't do it."

Kai winces. "Ouch. Sorry."

I nod. "I was devastated. All of a sudden the life I thought I wanted was gone, all the plans we'd made together. And I was left with . . . nothing." I spread my hands, revealing the blank space, the thin air between my palms.

"When did this happen?" Kai asks, his dark eyes intent on my face.

"Five weeks ago." I marvel that I am sitting here, so soon after Ethan broke my heart, discussing it all like it is ancient history. My heart still hurts, but so much has changed in such a short time. In one way it feels as fresh as yesterday, but in another like I am remembering another lifetime, another Mia.

"I learned a lesson though," I say. "I almost gave up my dreams once for a man. I can't do it again." I meet his eyes firmly, issuing a warning.

Kai holds my gaze steadily, seemingly unfazed. "Not every man would ask you to give up your dreams," he says slowly. "In a good relationship there's room for both people to do what they love. Otherwise it's not a great fit." He takes a swallow of coffee, setting the tumbler back in the matching saucer.

"Maybe not," I concede, "but I'm loyal to a fault. I loved Ethan so much. I was convinced we could make it work despite our differences, but in the end he wasn't as convinced as I was. So . . ." I shrug. "Here I am. And I think I'm glad. Still heartbroken but a little bit glad. I would have given up so much to be with him. I just didn't realize it at the time."

I look around the restaurant, taking in the high chatter of dozens of voices, the thick cooking smells, the gleam of light off the laminated red tables.

"What about you," I ask. "Any broken hearts littering your past?"

Kai shrugs. "A few girlfriends in college, nothing serious. I . . . have a hard time trusting people. After my dad left, it was a bad time for my family for a lot of years. It still surprises me that one man could mess up the lives of three other people so thoroughly, but it's true. He was physically abusive. He drank too much, and when he drank, all the anger he had pent up inside him would come out. It was better when he left. It felt safer, but the damage was still done. There were scars."

He sighs and tucks a loose strand of hair behind his ear, looking suddenly vulnerable.

"Even after my mom met Gordon, it took me a long time to trust him. I couldn't quite believe that a man could be honorable, could treat her or us right."

"That makes sense." I toy with my coffee. "You don't want to get hurt again."

He smiles, a little sadly. "Yeah, but I also haven't given up hope. I'm just waiting to meet someone I want to take the risk for, someone I can trust."

We lock eyes across the table, our confessions hanging between us, all the fears and insecurities related to love.

"Well look at us," I observe wryly. "We make quite a pair. The walking wounded of love."

Kai looks at me intently, his eyes dark and inscrutable. "For the right girl, I'd risk it."

I smile sadly. "I thought Ethan was the right one. I'll be more careful next time."

Kai lifts his tumbler of coffee. "To the next time," he says.

We clink and drink the last of the brew, laced with the faintest hint of bitter chicory beneath the sweeter caramel notes.

It is growing dark when we finally leave Colaba, taking a rickshaw back to the guesthouse. I grip the metal railing in front of me and lean out slightly, letting the hot breeze rush against my skin. Despite the disappointment of realizing that I am failing in my goal of making a lasting difference in Mumbai, today has been wonderful.

I glance at Kai beside me. I always pictured myself coming to India someday with Ethan, but the reality is that Ethan would have been a terrible companion today. He doesn't like spicy food or crowds. It is Kai who belongs in today. Kai with his Ray-Bans and his interest in the world, his willingness to try anything and his amiable shrug if it doesn't work. Kai who asks incisive questions, who listens carefully as I answer. I know he's been hurt, that he's leery of love, but still he offers honesty and authenticity in friendship. When he looks at me, I feel like the only person in the world. His attention is a gift. I've never felt like that with anyone before.

"I had an amazing time today," I yell over the high whine of the rickshaw. "Thank you."

As a testament to how acclimated I am becoming to India, I don't flinch as we narrowly avoid hitting two men in dress shirts sandwiched together on a motorcycle. The warm evening air blows around us, tossing my curls this way and that.

"Me too," Kai yells back. "Thanks for coming with me."

For a moment our eyes meet and something flickers in his . . . Interest, awareness, attraction? Whatever it is, I feel it cross the line between friend and something else entirely. It's a heady sensation. I think of his confession, his reluctance to trust. *For the right girl, I'd risk it . . .* What did he mean by that? Was it just a statement of fact? Or something more?

He reaches out and brushes a curl from my cheek, tucking it behind my ear. His fingers linger for a moment against my cheekbone. The gesture is strangely intimate, caring. I drop my eyes, suddenly self-conscious, unsure where to look. My attraction to Kai should be simple. He's so good, so easy to like, so true. But the soft places of my heart are still too tender and bruised. I am not ready to love another man, no matter how perfect he seems.

I glance back up, and he is still looking at me, his face half in shadow in the interior of the rickshaw. I want to say something, to acknowledge that I feel what is between us, but that it's complicated. I don't know what to say, however, and the moment passes, swallowed in the soft, muggy Mumbai night.

Chapter 26

"Mia! My dear girl." Nana Alice picks up my call on the fifth ring. She sounds surprised and delighted. In the calm before breakfast, the rooftop terrace is empty. I lean against the wall and press the phone to my ear. Nana Alice has been constantly on my mind, and we've been texting back and forth, but with jet lag and the twelve-hour time difference, this is the first opportunity I've had to call her at a decent hour. By my calculation, it is early evening in Seattle.

"How's India?" she asks.

What can I say? India is . . . a puzzle, by turns intimidating and disappointing but also enthralling. I don't know how to put it into words. And Kai. It's only been about ten hours since our rickshaw ride last night, and my emotions are still running high.

I look around in the early morning gray, at the uneven concrete floor of the terrace, the plastic lawn chairs, the few straggling tropical plants in pots.

"India is . . . complicated. It's great," I hasten to add, because I want her to imagine the trip she wants me to have, not the trip I'm actually having. I lean over the railing of the balcony and watch a man pushing a cart laden with brooms down the alley. I hear smooth classical music in the background over the phone and the low murmur of voices.

"Where are you?"

"Albert's nephew arranged for us to have a three-course dinner at the restaurant in the Space Needle," she says loudly into the phone. "It revolves. The view is top-notch."

"Wow, the Space Needle, huh?" I'm surprised that she and Albert are dining in the upscale revolving restaurant atop the famed Seattle landmark. It's both touristy and expensive.

"The wild salmon is a little dry, but the local Riesling is delicious," Nana Alice confides. She sounds ever so slightly tipsy, but perhaps she's just ebullient because of the special occasion. Or because of Albert. I hear him in the background telling her, "Alice, my dear, this nice waitress wants to know our choice for the dessert course."

He called her *my dear*. No way they're just old friends.

"I should go," Nana Alice says buoyantly. "I think I'll have the crème brûlée." I'm not sure if that last statement is directed at Albert or me. "Albert says, 'Safe travels.' We've been following your trip on the Instagram."

"So I heard." I'm amused picturing the two of them surfing the web.

"We saw a picture of you and Rosie in a little yellow buggy. You looked scared to death. And some photos of you making pancakes. That's my girl."

I shake my head, amazed by the speed and connectedness of technology.

"I'll let you go now," Nana Alice chirps into the phone. "Our dessert just arrived."

"Wait," I almost shout. "How is your treatment going? Any news?" I feel so helpless, so far away. I need to know that she is being taken care of, that she will be okay.

"It's going very well," Nana Alice assures me. "I'm feeling better every day."

"What does your doctor say?" I ask, but the connection falters.

"Oh dear, I can't hear you," Nana Alice says, the sound of her voice suddenly intermittent and far away. Then there's a click and she's gone.

I sit for a moment, picturing them dressed to the nines, Nana Alice in an A-line dress with a sweetheart neckline, Albert in a bow tie. The two of them sitting at a table as the entire room slowly spins above the glow of Seattle, Nana Alice and Albert sparkling as bright as any city lights below. I'm glad one love story seems to be going well.

"Lars wants to talk to all of us this morning," Rosie announces, reading a text on her phone as we get ready to go down to breakfast. It's just a few minutes after my call with Nana Alice, and I am distracted, still thinking about her and Albert at their romantic dinner atop the Space Needle.

"Lars is texting you?" I mumble, a toothbrush in my mouth. I reach for the bottled water to rinse. The water in Mumbai isn't safe even for brushing our teeth.

"Yes, I gave him my number when we were in Florida, and he's been checking in now and then." Rosie is still staring at the text, her expression avid.

"Really?" This is new information. "What does he want to talk to us about?"

"I've no idea." Rosie shrugs and texts Lars back to let him know that we'll await his call. Before we go to breakfast she pauses to apply some lipstick and smooth her hair. I pause for a moment and do the same, applying a pea-sized amount of hair balm to my wild mane and flicking on a coat of mascara, since Jake will be coming with us today and presumably filming.

Down in the restaurant we eat our breakfast quickly, keeping an eye on Milo's iPad propped on the edge of the table. We are about to head to another slum. The thought of doing another program seems pointless now that I see what a waste of time and money this trip is.

Just as I swallow the last of my chai, Lars calls. Only one other table in the café is occupied, two older Indian men sipping chai and talking in low tones. When they hear the call come in, they turn and stare at us wordlessly.

"Hello, Team Caritas?" On the iPad Lars leans forward and peers into the camera so that we get a wide-angle view of just his forehead.

"Hey, Lars, we're here," Milo says, chewing the last bite of *Parsi akuri*, Mumbai's flavorful version of scrambled eggs.

Bryant and Stella are sitting to Lars' left. They appear to be in the formal parlor of the Lindquist mansion. I recognize the white baby grand piano and palm trees out the french doors behind them.

"How's India? Hotter than blazes?" Bryant asks cheerfully. He's holding a glass of some fruity-looking beverage complete with bobbing maraschino cherries.

"We don't want to delay your work," Lars says, moving back so we can see his whole face and torso. He's wearing a pale blue polo shirt and a pink cashmere sweater draped across his shoulders; he looks like he's in a yacht commercial. I glance at Rosie, who is leaning toward the iPad in glad anticipation, eyes bright.

"I'm calling because an opportunity has presented itself," Lars says, choosing his words carefully. "I know that you are scheduled to leave for Thailand next week, but I am calling to ask you to consider a change of plans."

"Big change of plans," Bryant echoes, sipping his fruity drink. I exchange a curious glance with Kai across the table.

"Have you been following the breaking news in Europe?" Stella asks, chiming in for the first time. I shake my head. I've been too preoccupied to focus on anything outside of Mumbai.

"The refugee crisis?" Abel says, his face grave.

"I read about it on the BBC news site, yeah," Winnie pipes up suddenly.

I stare at her in surprise. I assume Abel knows about global current events from his Amnesty contacts, but I had no idea Winnie followed international news.

"That's right," Bryant says, nodding enthusiastically. "Big problem right now, thousands of people coming from conflict zones—Syria, Iraq, Afghanistan, driven out by Islamic State militants. And they're all coming to Europe, most in rubber boats from Turkey to Greece. Lots of children. Lots of drownings." He shakes his head, sobering. "Terrible stuff."

Taken aback, I glance around the table at Rosie, Milo, and Kai, who look as stunned as I feel. I had no idea this was happening.

"How awful!" Rosie says.

Lars nods. "These refugees are coming across the borders into Europe, thousands a day, seeking asylum." He pauses. "Right now there is a shortage of volunteers to help the refugees once they reach Europe. Many are arriving with nothing more than the clothes on their backs. They need everything—food, clothing, transportation, information, medical care—and they need it urgently."

"That's where you come in," Stella interjects. "We want to send you to Europe, to one of the border zones, to help the refugees."

Rosie and I exchange a surprised look. Go to Europe?

"Dude, but what about Thailand and Mexico?" Milo asks.

"If you are willing we will divert Team Caritas and its resources to Europe for the remainder of the trip," Lars explains. "This situation is very dire. Europe is facing a humanitarian crisis unprecedented since World War II. I feel very strongly that we should assist these people in whatever way we can."

"Why choose our team and not one of the others?" Winnie interrupts, crossing her arms with a hard stare.

A brief look of discomfort flashes across Lars' face, and Stella leans in, replying with a firm smile. "Teams Veritas and Fortis are having some . . . interpersonal conflict that would make them unsuitable choices to send at this time," she says crisply. "And Fidelis has been exposed to measles and is currently in quarantine. So your team is the only viable option."

Lars nods. "It's all very unfortunate and unforeseen." He frowns. "You don't have to decide immediately. Discuss it among yourselves. We will not force you to go, of course; this is not the trip you agreed to participate in. But I ask you to consider it very carefully." He looks at us soberly. "These people are in desperate need. We can help. Please let us know your decision as soon as possible."

After he hangs up, we are silent for a moment.

"Goodness." Rosie clasps her hands on the table and looks around at the group, assuming the role of moderator. "Well, we all heard Lars' request. What do we do?"

Kai is looking at something on his phone. He turns the screen toward us, scrolling through a series of photos—clusters of people crammed into small, inflatable rafts. Children without life vests held by mothers in head scarves. Exhaustion, fear, and worry etched into the lines of the women's faces. One man with a thick mustache like a bottle brush is crying as he lifts a young boy out of a raft onto land.

"He's crying because they didn't capsize," Kai says quietly, pointing to the caption on the bottom of the photo. "Because he and his family made it to Europe alive."

We are all quiet, looking at the photo. These are obviously desperate people in great need.

"Lars has asked for an answer as soon as possible. I think we should take a vote," Rosie says. "Go to Europe or continue on our normal route? Kai?"

"Europe," Kai says instantly. "I vote we go where we can help the most."

Rosie nods and ticks off his vote on her fingers. "One for Europe. Mia, what about you? Europe or our scheduled itinerary?"

I hesitate. On the one hand I'm disappointed to not be going to Thailand and Mexico, both countries I was looking forward to seeing. I think of riding elephants through lush jungles, slurping down plates of authentic pad thai, visiting Buddhist temples with spires of gold. But on the other hand, we can actually help people in crisis. The thought makes my pulse quicken. No more making pancakes for schoolchildren.

I think of the photo Kai just showed us, the desperate look of the man holding his son, the tears streaming into the deeply etched grooves of his face. Thousands of refugees a day, Stella said. Thousands of people who need our help. Perhaps it's not too late to redeem this trip.

"Yes," I say firmly. "I vote we go to Europe."

Milo glances at the photo on Kai's phone and shakes his head. "Man, that looks rough. I guess if we can be any help, we should do it."

Abel nods. "I agree," he says.

Now it is just down to Winnie.

She shrugs. "Anything beats trying to teach those kids to play the recorder," she says.

And just like that, we are going to Europe.

Part 4

Hungary

Chapter 27

A scant two days after our call with Stella and Bryant, I lean my head against the airplane window and stare down at the vast glittering swath of Mumbai as it grows smaller and smaller. Next to me, Rosie is trying to sleep, her head tilted back and a silk eye mask covering her eyes. It's so early in the morning, it's still pitch black. We are heading to Budapest now, a continent away.

"You okay, sugar?" Rosie turns to me and peeks out from under the eye mask.

I nod. "Just thinking about our time in Mumbai."

I sift back through the last two weeks, trying to embed Mumbai into my memory. I see it in snippets, snapshots, sensations—heat undulating from the buckled pavement as we alight from an auto rickshaw at the edge of yet another slum. A man passing our taxi balancing a twin mattress on the handlebars of his bicycle. The salty, crumbly flavor of dried *bombil.* The vivid black sheen of Shreya's braid as she walks in front of me down the alley toward one of the classrooms. The gap-toothed grin of a little girl in a soiled pink dress as I hand her a pancake drizzled with syrup. The scalding sweetness of cutting chai, burning my tongue, warming my throat with ginger and cardamom.

It is all Mumbai, and yet I know it is just a fraction of the whole. I caught a passing glimpse of the city, pulsing with millions of individual lives, a city of contradictions and juxtapositions. My Mumbai is just a sliver, a glimmer, a scanty sip.

"Do you think we did any good there at all?" I ask softly. A bell dings, indicating we are at cruising altitude, and the seat belt sign winks off.

Rosie yawns. "Maybe not," she says. "But at least we tried. That's something, right?"

I shake my head. I'm not sure that's enough. What have I left in Mumbai? A stack of pancakes to fill hungry tummies and make sticky syrup rings around little mouths. My naïveté in believing that somehow what I was doing would really matter. A savior complex that took only days to dissolve. What did I really do? I'm afraid the answer is almost nothing. As we fly away, life carries on in Mumbai, equally untouched by our presence or our absence.

"You should sleep," Rosie advises, slipping her eye mask back on and nestling down in her seat. "We'll be in Hungary before you know it."

She's right, but I can't.

Hungary. I roll the name on my tongue like a hard candy. It is unfamiliar and full of possibilities. When Bryant and Stella called back to confirm the location, I had to look it up on a map of Europe. The photos show a flat, agrarian land of red-roofed villages and placid farmland and vineyards.

I don't know what awaits us there, but whatever it is, I want to be ready. This time I will seek out opportunities to make a lasting difference. This time I will truly be Saint Mia.

"*Szia, szia.* Welcome to Budapest." Our handler, Laszlo, finds us as soon as we enter the airport arrivals hall and shakes hands enthusiastically. "How was your trip? Everything okay?"

"They've lost my suitcase!" Rosie exclaims, looking distraught. When we collected our luggage at baggage claim, her suitcase never came down the belt.

"Nem jo." Laszlo shakes his head. "Don't worry. We will find it." An upbeat, sandy-haired man in his thirties, he has a neat mustache and an honest face. According to Stella, he is a coordinator for Migration Aid, an informal network of volunteers across Hungary who are helping refugees as they cross the border from Serbia on their journey through Europe.

"Wait here. I will see about the suitcase." He heads in the direction of the Emirates Airlines desk. Fifteen minutes later he returns looking disappointed.

"It is missing in Dubai airport," he says. "They are trying to track it down now, but they are not hopeful." He claps Rosie on the back sympathetically. "Don't worry. We have everything here in Budapest. We will get you the things you need."

With that promise, he ushers a dismayed Rosie and the rest of us out the door and into a white passenger van waiting in the parking lot.

On the drive into the city, he gives us a brief orientation. "You will stay in Budapest in a hotel for tonight. Tomorrow we go to the Hungarian/Serbian border. There are many migrants there now, and more come every day. Most are from areas of war and conflict—Syria, Afghanistan, Iraq. Some others come from other countries, even poorer countries in Europe, for economic reasons. They see an easy way to get into Western Europe. They think the life and the money will be good, but most of the people who cross the border are refugees, fleeing violence and unrest." He shakes his head and glances at us in the rearview mirror. "The governments, they cannot stop these people and cannot do enough to help them either. It is up to us, the citizens of Europe, to do something. That is why you are here. We are doing what we can, but it is not enough. We need your help."

My heart thrills at those words. This is what I have come for.

As we drive through the outskirts of the city, I press my nose against the window, craning my neck to see every detail. Everything looks older than in the US, and more run-down. Even the roads look tired. But Budapest is a far cry from India. Traffic moves at a moderate pace and obeys all of the laws. There are no cows or heavily laden handcarts, no chaos and sensory overload. We reach the heart of the city, and I draw in a wondrous breath. The buildings become grander, with ornate arches and spires. There are leafy, green parks and cafés with tables set out under awnings.

"Wow, great examples of Austro-Hungarian architecture," Kai says admiringly as we pass building after building.

Rosie glances up briefly but then resumes texting on her phone. I wonder who she's texting. Is it Lars? She's missing the view.

The feel of Budapest is one of calm and order, of quiet contentment. It's a little puzzling. Where are the refugees, the people we are trying to help? Nothing I've seen in the city matches any of the news photos we've been following closely for the past few days. I ask Laszlo about it.

"The refugees aren't here in the city," he says, gesturing around him. "Some are gathered at Keleti train station, but most are at the Hungarian border, in the Röszke refugee camp. You will see them tomorrow."

We pull up to Hotel Central Basilica, an elegant cream-colored stone building with tall arched windows just a stone's throw from St. Stephen's Basilica. Laszlo handles the check-in process, and soon Rosie and I are ensconced, sans her suitcase, in a tastefully appointed room. Winnie is next door in a single, and the men have two rooms across the hall. From our window I can see the plaza and the magnificent basilica with its high dome and two spires. I want to pinch myself. It amazes me that people live with this beauty surrounding them every day.

Rosie flings herself onto one of the queen beds with a groan of dismay. "My suitcase! I have no clothes, no makeup, nothing," she exclaims. "What am I going to do?"

Just then the room phone rings. Rosie sits up and answers it.

"Yes, this is Rosalie Jasper." She listens for a moment. "Really? Are you sure? Well, thank you, I'll be right down." She hangs up the phone.

"They found your suitcase?"

Rosie shakes her head. "No, but the next best thing. That was Laszlo. Apparently Lars contacted him and had him arrange for a personal assistant to take me shopping to replace some of the things I lost. She's waiting downstairs. Isn't that the sweetest?"

"How does Lars even know about your suitcase?" I ask, starting to unpack my backpack. "You found out it was gone less than an hour ago."

Rosie blushes a little. "I texted him on the way from the airport," she confides. "I was so distraught. I don't even have a second pair of panties."

"Well, I sure hope you didn't tell him that," I mutter, wondering for a moment if there is more going on between them than I realized. Have they been texting often? Does Rosie know Lars' secret yet?

"Laszlo says we'll be back in time for dinner," Rosie says breezily, grabbing her purse and slipping on her shoes, the only belongings she has left now. "See you at the restaurant. When we meet again, I will be a brand-new woman."

Chapter 28

That evening we dine with Laszlo at a tiny restaurant a few streets away from the hotel. Rosie arrives wearing a new outfit she found at Zara—a daring jumpsuit in black and gold paisley that looks like a pair of very expensive, avant-garde drapes.

"We didn't have time to do much shopping, but at least I got a toothbrush and some mascara and a pair of pajamas," she tells me. "Oh, I do so hope they find my suitcase."

We squeeze around two cozy tables in the traditional Hungarian restaurant, and Laszlo orders the three-course fixed menu for all of us. The food is hearty and good—goulash soup, crispy duck legs with purple cabbage, and warm apple strudel for dessert.

As we polish off the last of the strudel, Laszlo outlines the plan for the next day. He will pick us up at eight o'clock from the hotel and drive us to the makeshift refugee camp. He sets down his fork and gazes around the table. "The border where we will go tomorrow is not like here. Budapest is very nice, very beautiful. The place you will stay, the camp where you will volunteer, everything is more difficult. Be ready for that." With this caution, he gestures for the bill.

After Laszlo leaves us, Milo, Rosie, and Jake opt to visit the rooftop bar of a nearby hotel for a nightcap.

"Anybody else want to come along?" Milo asks.

"Not tonight," Abel says, declining politely. "I think I must turn in."

Winnie yawns. "I'll pass." They head back to the hotel.

Kai glances at me. "Want to see the city?" he asks, and I accept immediately. There's something so genteel about Budapest, so stately and civilized. I can't wait to see more.

After admiring the basilica, we meander through the cobblestone streets and squares. All the shops are closed at this hour, but the cafés are open, spilling light and music onto the sidewalks. People linger at tables under café awnings, enjoying a cappuccino or a digestif. I am entranced by the soft music, the clink of wine glasses, the gentle burble of conversation. Hungarian sounds so different from Hindi, the words more bulbous and round. Hindi strikes me as a lilting, spiky language, beautiful but sharp.

We reach the Danube River and follow a walking path south. Lights rim the banks of the river like a luminous pearl necklace. Riverboats bob in the water below us, and small clusters of people dot the grassy riverbank, laughing and talking and drinking wine. The air is soft and smells of dusty paving stones and budding trees with a dank undercurrent of muddy river water.

We pause to admire the proud and imposing palace and the dreamy, fairy-tale spires of Fisherman's Bastion rising high on the other side of the Danube. As Kai points out a few notable architectural features, I suddenly catch a snippet of English conversation from a couple sitting a few yards away. They are facing the river, side by side on the grassy bank. Their voices sound familiar. With a jolt of recognition, I see it's Winnie and Abel.

Winnie has a bottle of beer in one hand and is gesturing with the other, animatedly telling a story. She takes a drink and sets the beer down on the grass, then leans back, her dreadlocks cascading down her back. She looks so at ease. I've never seen her like this. I gawk for a moment, feeling voyeuristic but captivated. Abel says something too low for me to catch, and Winnie laughs—not the harsh derisive laughter I've heard before from her, but a genuine laugh of amusement. The sound is rich and husky. It takes me completely by surprise.

I stare at the two of them, trying to fit the puzzle pieces together. Winnie and Abel? I can't understand it. But it is obvious that they are enjoying each other's company. I wonder what in the world is actually happening between them and how long this has been going on.

"Want to keep walking?" Kai asks. He doesn't seem to notice them, and I don't point them out. If they wanted us to know about whatever this is, they wouldn't have sneaked away together. I give them one last curious glance before turning to follow Kai back up the river.

A moment later all thoughts of Winnie and Abel are driven from my mind as Kai takes my hand, lacing his fingers through my own. It seems like the most natural thing in the world, and at the same time I can't breathe, can't think.

He's relaying some architectural fact about the palace having been destroyed six times in Hungary's long history of conflict and conquest, but I can't concentrate on his words. All my attention is on our joined hands. His fingers are strong and warm, entwined with mine. My heart is beating very fast. Our hands fit together, yet holding his hand feels so alien to me. This is not Ethan's hand; this is not Ethan.

We walk for a few minutes holding hands, but then I panic. What am I doing? I like Kai, so very much, but this is not the time or the place for a new romance to bloom. I bend down and make a pretext of adjusting the laces on my Converse sneakers. When I rise, I move away from him slightly, putting a little distance between us. I don't take his hand and he doesn't initiate again.

"I think I might need to turn in," I say. I'm starting to feel the effects of the long travel day and jet lag.

"Yeah, we should get some sleep."

Kai turns around and starts back the way we came, stuffing his hands in his pockets. He doesn't look at me, and I wonder if he feels rebuffed, or if he regrets holding my hand. Oh, it's all a muddle.

Wordlessly we retrace our steps. Already my mind is far away, focused on what tomorrow may bring, but walking beside Kai, keeping pace with his long, easy strides, I can still feel the warmth of his fingers laced through mine.

Back at the hotel, I see that I missed a call from Henry. Exhausted but worried that it might be about Nana Alice, I return his call while Rosie is in the shower.

Henry answers, shouting to be heard above the ruckus in the background. It sounds like the shrill siren of a toy fire engine punctuated by the high, tinny jangle of a kid's piano being pounded indiscriminately.

"Hey, tiger," Henry yells. "How's it going? Where are you?"

"Budapest," I say, pitching my voice loudly to be heard over the background noise. "What's up?"

"Just checking on you. Mom and Dad asked me to make sure you got to Hungary okay."

Not about Nana Alice, then. Relieved, I flop back on one of the beds, relishing the sensation of being horizontal after so many hours of travel.

"I'm okay. We just got here this afternoon." I kick off my shoes and stretch my toes. "Did Mom and Dad make it to Moldova okay?" I have to almost yell into the phone. One of the twins has begun singing the ABC song in a high monotone while also banging cymbals together.

"Yeah, they called yesterday. They got there safely, but they don't have good internet. They sounded fine, though. Better than fine. They sound great." Henry is using a pitch of voice generally reserved for TV reporters standing in the midst of gale-force winds. "Holy smokes, Oliver," he snaps finally. "Can you not play *all* the instruments at the same time? Choose one."

"Smokes!" Oliver shouts, the piano louder.

"I want to personally disembowel whoever invented those plastic toy pianos," Henry says. "They're a hand tool of the devil."

I laugh. The noise abates somewhat as Oliver apparently chooses just the cymbals.

"Hey, who'd Mom and Dad get to run the farm while they're gone?" I ask, suddenly remembering that I don't actually know. In the whirl of the last few days in India and then our travel to Hungary, I haven't kept up with my parents.

"Us," Henry says. "We're actually at the farm right now. We got here yesterday."

"What? You're at West Wind?" I'm astonished. Henry flew the coop as soon as he could. He always seemed to feel about the farm the way I do, glad we grew up there and glad he left.

"Yeah, Christine and I just needed a break from the city for a while. I want the kids to hike a real hill, play on the beach." He exhales loudly. "Last week I took the boys to the park, and Auden kept falling down on this little incline. I realized he's never climbed a hill. He's grown up with flat pavement and manicured backyards all his life. It was completely ridiculous. And sad." Henry interrupts himself to confiscate both the piano and the cymbals. "Here, look, Auden, Oliver. String cheese!"

Silence descends on the other end of the phone. Henry comes back on with a groan of relief. "I think the makers of string cheese should get a Nobel Prize. The boys would sell their souls for that stuff."

"Where are Christine and Maddie?" I ask, making myself get up and find my pajamas.

"They're running the shop right now while I ride herd on the boys. So far Maddie loves the farm. She says it smells like Grandma Meg."

"Wow. How's it feel to be back home?" I'm still trying to visualize them at the farm. My parents have visited Henry and Christine in Chicago every year since the kids were born, but I don't think the kids have ever been to Sequim. I shimmy out of my travel clothes and slide a soft cotton T-shirt over my head.

"Weird, good. Like time stopped here. It feels exactly the same." Henry sighs. "I'm glad we're here. We needed some time away. Christine's up for a major promotion at work. It'll be longer hours, more travel." He sounds weary. "We wanted to really talk about it, make sure it's the best decision for us."

"Sounds complicated." I sense a thread of discontent in his words. Henry has never loved Chicago, but Christine's work is there. I wonder what he would change if he could choose a different sort of life.

"Yeah, it always is," he says, then sharply, "Auden, stop stuffing Cheerios up your nose. Not cool, dude. Not cool." He comes back on, sounding resigned. "Sorry, got to go. I have to find the tweezers."

"Second shelf of the medicine cabinet, next to the Tylenol," I say automatically, picturing the tweezers in the place they've occupied for as long as I can remember. "Have fun playing farmer."

I pull on a pair of blue-striped cotton boxer shorts and shake out my curls. I am so ready for a solid night of sleep.

"Sure thing. Be careful out there," Henry admonishes. "We're watching the news. We're proud of you, sis."

Chapter 29

At 7:50 the next morning there's a sharp knock at our hotel room door. I'm already dressed, my backpack at my feet, ready to go. Rosie is standing in front of the bathroom mirror, pinning up her hair. She is wearing the same drapery-esque Zara jumpsuit from the night before, looking a little like a seventies lounge singer who's had a hard night. Her meager belongings are gathered in a plastic shopping bag on the bathroom counter.

When I open the door, a porter is standing in the hall. He rolls a huge shiny silver suitcase into the room. "For Miss Rosalie Jasper from Mr. Lars Lindquist," he says with a little bow.

"What's this? For me?" Astonished, Rosie comes out of the bathroom and accepts the suitcase while I fish around in my wallet for some forint coins to tip the porter.

When I close the door, Rosie is already on the bed, unzipping the suitcase. It is stuffed with bags from Nordstrom. She shakes out a Clinique makeup bag brimming with mascaras, blushes, and lipsticks in a rainbow of pinks and reds. She unpacks a sleek leather jacket, blouses, several pairs of jeans, and a stack of sundresses. "Citizens of Humanity," she announces approvingly, holding up a pair of jeans. Everything appears to be in her size and in colors that complement her skin tone.

"Lars sent you all this?" I ask, incredulous. Just how did Lars know her size and colors? And how in the world did he get it here overnight?

"Isn't he a dear?" she says with a dreamy sigh. "Look, these are Gucci." She shows me a pair of watermelon-colored suede flats with fringe. "I should lose my suitcase more often. These things are far nicer than the clothes I had."

"Although one could argue that watermelon suede flats might not be the ideal footwear for a refugee camp," I observe dryly. It looks like a suitcase of swanky items chosen by someone who thinks that cocktail hour is a daily part of life.

"True." Rosie frowns and holds up a Topshop dress in a succulent plum shade. "But bless his heart for thinking of me."

She rifles through the rest of the suitcase, pulling items out to admire. A silver leather clutch. A pair of Balenciaga cat-eye sunglasses in a tortoiseshell print. He must have spent thousands stocking this suitcase. What does it mean, that he has done this for Rosie?

Looking at the swath of expensive items on the bed, I feel a twinge of unease about the status of their relationship. I don't want Rosie to get hurt, thinking Lars can offer her everything she dreams of when in fact his condition would almost certainly make that impossible. I bite my lip, torn over whether to intervene, while Rosie happily organizes the contents of the suitcase into two piles.

"These I will admire in private, and these I will wear," she explains. The wearable pile is substantially smaller than the admiration pile. Two dresses, three tops, and two pairs of jeans. The leather jacket and sunglasses. A mascara and bright red lipstick. A pair of leather ankle boots, the watermelon suede flats, and a pair of flowered leather mules. She changes out of the jumpsuit and dons the dark plum dress and ankle boots, then stops to text Lars a thank-you before we head down to the lobby to meet the others.

"Rosie," I say, ready to deliver a warning.

"Yes?" Rosie looks up. She looks so happy, so delighted to be cared for that I can't complete the sentence. Let them figure it out between them. Rosie is clever and astute and does not suffer fools lightly. And Lars seems like a good man. Perhaps he could change, or they could work it out somehow. I shouldn't stick my nose into whatever is or is not going on between them. Besides, how serious can it be when they are a continent and an ocean apart?

"How do I look?" Rosie poses in front of me, then snaps a selfie, no doubt to send to Lars.

"Like you're definitely going to win an award for best-dressed volunteer at the refugee camp," I say, hoisting my backpack onto my shoulders and grabbing my satchel. It's a few minutes after eight. Laszlo and the team will be waiting for us in the lobby. "Now come on, we don't want to be late."

"Mia, if we have an accident, I will be crushed to death by cucumbers," Rosie whispers fifteen minutes later, eyeing several crates stacked beside her seat.

"What a way to go," I murmur. "I'll be buried under bread rolls."

Crammed into the white passenger van, we are headed west toward the Serbian border. Every available square inch of the van is piled high with food and supplies for the refugee camp, compliments of Lars Lindquist's generosity. We are wedged in among dozens of liters of bottled water, crates of apples and oranges, bags of white rolls, and packages of diapers, among other things.

As we leave the city behind, I stare out the window. While Budapest was elegant and cosmopolitan, the rest of Hungary is quiet, rural, and agrarian. We pass a handful of exits for small towns dotting the fields along the highway. Occasionally I catch a glimpse of red-tiled roofs or a church steeple, but mostly it is flat fields and clusters of trees. The air is warm and sweet, smelling of hay, of turned earth. Crows fly overhead, outlined black against a cerulean sky.

Ninety minutes later Laszlo takes an exit off the highway. "We are close to the Serbian border," he announces. "We will reach the camp in a few minutes."

I press my nose to the window, feeling a jolt of excitement and a flutter of nerves in the pit of my stomach. We are so close. I am eager to get on the ground and start helping people.

We pass a lone gas station, and a couple of minutes later Laszlo turns down a one-lane dirt road. There are no houses or buildings anywhere in sight, just fields on either side of the narrow road, a scrim of trees, and the wide blue dome of sky. We continue down the lane, passing news vans parked along the shoulder with cameramen and reporters holding microphones milling around. Farther along we creep past a line of Hungarian police vans parked beside the road, dark and silent. And then we reach the camp.

"This is it?" Milo asks, incredulous. A few dozen camping tents are scattered across a fallow field bordered by trees. The ground is black earth, churned to mud. The lane we are driving on bisects the camp into two sections. On the left, two large open-sided white tents are filled with stacked boxes. One tent contains food and the other clothing, Laszlo tells us. Two Porta-Potties stand a little ways beyond the tents. The camp looks haphazard, inadequate, just a few small tents in a field of turned earth. The ground is littered with trash. It reminds me of Mumbai. Shredded plastic bags, a single discarded tennis shoe, drifts and mounds of rubbish trampled into the muddy soil.

Police are everywhere, milling about at the edge of the camp, standing by the police vans, hands resting casually on the guns at their hips. Dozens of refugees, maybe more than a hundred, are spread out across the field. Some are going in and out of the camping tents. Others wait in long snaking lines at the food and clothing tents. A closed-sided tent on the right side of the field has the word *Medicine* printed in several languages in large red letters on the canvas. A straggly line of people waits there. As I watch, a lithe woman with cropped dark hair pops out of the tent and ushers a mother and child inside.

Laszlo pulls the van off to the side of the lane, landing the right two wheels in a shallow ditch. "Stay here," he instructs, jumping from the van. "I will find out where to unload the supplies."

At the far side of the camp runs a set of railroad tracks, and the refugees come walking along the tracks in small groups, a new set of two or three or four people trickling into the camp every couple of minutes. The refugees are coming from Serbia, Laszlo explained on the ride over. This camp on Hungarian land is the first time they cross into the Schengen Area, a group of twenty-six countries that have abolished border crossings and passport checks. When they reach Hungary they are almost where they want to end up. They have only to make their way north through the countries of the Schengen Area to their final destinations. Few want to stay in Hungary; they are just passing through, but Hungary represents hope and safety. They are almost to their new homes.

Laszlo reports back. "We can unload everything and take it to the tents." He points. "Food, clothes, and medicine. But first"—he gestures for us to follow him—"Come meet Szilvia. She is the boss while you are in the camp."

Chapter 30

At the food tent we shake hands with Szilvia, a stocky Hungarian woman in her midfifties with dyed blonde hair. She has sharp eyes in a kind, careworn face.

"You are welcome here," she says in heavily accented English. "Many organizations say they will send aid, but Medecines Sans Frontieres and Migration Aid are the only ones on the ground right now. We need help at every station."

Under Szilvia's direction we unload the supplies, stacking the food in the food tent and delivering the underwear, socks, hygiene items, and diapers to the clothing tent. I hand over the diapers and baby wipes to a harried-looking young Hungarian man who is attempting to communicate with the refugees waiting in the line. A young man in his teens, barely sprouting the scrubby line of a new mustache, waits with a little girl in a grubby blue dress.

"Socks? You need socks? Razor?" the Hungarian volunteer says slowly and clearly in English, pointing to the items. The young refugee looks confused and nods at every item. The volunteer throws up his hands and turns to me. "Do you speak Arabic? Pashto? Dari?" he asks hopefully.

I shake my head. "Sorry, just a little French."

He sighs in a long-suffering way and turns back to the young man. "Soap?" he asks again, emphasizing every word as though saying it loudly will make it more understandable. "Underwear for men or women?"

At the food tent Rosie, Winnie, and Kai are already hard at work under Szilvia's direction. Standing behind a set of folding tables in a U-shape, Rosie is handing out apples and oranges to people waiting in line, Winnie is slicing cucumbers in a cumbersome manner, looking as though she might never have held a kitchen knife before, and Kai is stacking and organizing crates and bags around the edges of the tent, keeping the others supplied with necessary items. Abel is assigned to the drink station in one corner of the food tent. Every adult gets a large bottle of water, and every child can have as much juice and milk as they want. Milo has been assigned to the clothing tent, Rosie tells me. I stand aimlessly for a moment, wondering what I can do to help.

Szilvia sees me and beckons me over to where she is taking inventory. "Many of these refugees, they have been on the road for weeks, sometimes months," she explains, counting the number of packages of oranges and marking it down. "They come from Turkey to Greece by boat, then by land up through Macedonia to Serbia and finally to us." She pauses her counting and makes a walking motion with her fingers, illustrating the route they take. "It is a long way, and many times they walk, days they walk. They are exhausted, hungry, no good food, not much water. Many children are sick from sleeping outside. We help them as much as we can before they leave to go north to Germany, Sweden, Norway. This is just a . . ." She searches for the word in English. "A pit stop. Then they go on to their new homes."

Her gaze alights on two people who have just arrived at the food tent, a heavy middle-aged woman with a younger man who looks like her son. He has her strong nose and dark curly hair. The woman sways and stumbles as they reach the front of the line, and Szilvia springs forward, catching her under the arm.

"Get water and food for them," she snaps at me, and I jump to comply. Abel hands me two bottles of water, and Rosie quickly gathers some fruit and packaged cookies.

Szilvia is speaking to them when I come back. She opens a bottle of water, pressing it into the woman's hand. "She has a problem with her heart and ran out of medicine, her son says. Here, take them to the medical station." She shoos me toward the tent on the other side of the lane.

We set off toward the medical tent slowly, the son and I both helping to support the woman. She moves ponderously, her skin ashen. She doesn't look good at all, and I cast nervous glances at her as we walk, hoping we can reach the doctor before she collapses.

The line at the medical tent is only about a half dozen deep. As we take our place at the end of the line, the woman I saw earlier pokes her head out of the tent and spies me. She is wearing a white lab coat and has a stethoscope draped around her neck.

"You," she calls, gesturing to me. "Come, I need assistance."

I hesitate, not sure I should leave my patient in need, but the lady in the lab coat again gestures impatiently for me to follow her.

Inside the tent the air is sweltering and smells strongly of antiseptic and unwashed bodies. I wrinkle my nose and try to not breathe deeply. A portly man sits on a white folding examination table, his arm held awkwardly out from his body. There is a deep gash in his hairy forearm, crusted with dried blood. I look away hastily, trying not to gag. Oh no. Why couldn't I have gotten the cucumber slicing gig? Anything but this. Wounds, blood, bodies, sickness—I am not cut out for this kind of thing.

"Hold his arm like this," the woman instructs, gripping the man's arm on either side of the wound. When I hesitate she jerks her head impatiently and I spring forward, holding the man's arm in a tight grip and staring at the ceiling, counting to one hundred in my head as she cleans and dresses the wound. I feel light-headed and bend my knees slightly. How unimpressive would it be if ten minutes into my first real assignment, I passed out in the medical tent? Surely Saint Mia has more grit and gumption than that.

I steel myself and concentrate hard on a few flies buzzing around the ceiling of the tent. The man flinches when she applies antiseptic but otherwise remains stoic. When she is done dressing the wound, she speaks to him in a torrent of beautiful words I don't comprehend, then ushers him out. When she comes back, she grips my arm lightly.

"Thank you." She smiles at me, and it feels like the sun breaking through the clouds, lighting up her face. Up close I see she is older than I am, probably late thirties. Her short dark pixie cut is tousled. She has bruised smudges under her eyes from fatigue, but even so she is striking, with a strong jaw and wide brown eyes fringed by dark lashes.

"I am Delphine Dupont." She sticks her hand out and I shake it. Her grip is strong and sure.

"Mia West," I say. "You're a doctor?"

"Oui."

"Oh." I brighten at the single word. "You're French?" I thought I detected a French accent.

She nods. "*Oui*. From Bordeaux."

"I studied French in high school," I say, feeling stupid as soon as the words leave my mouth. "I'm from Seattle."

"Seattle. Like *Grey's Anatomy*, *non*?" She starts tidying the examination area, wiping the table and getting ready for the next guest. Her supplies and tools are rudimentary. A folding examination table, a metal stool for her to sit on, and a small rolling cart stuffed with assorted medical paraphernalia.

Laszlo told us there is no electricity or running water at the camp, and I imagine how challenging it must be to keep things sanitary and offer assistance with such limitations.

"What were you speaking to that man when you bandaged his arm? It didn't sound like French."

Delphine nods briskly. "You are right. It was Arabic. My father was born in Tunisia, and I was raised to speak both French and Arabic, which is very helpful right now."

I'm impressed. She's the first person I've met in the camp who can communicate with the refugees.

"Are you here volunteering in the camp?" she asks me.

I nod. "For a few weeks at least. Maybe longer." Stella and Bryant have not given us a departure date, saying we would see how things looked when we got on the ground.

Delphine turns to me. "You came with the older woman, *oui*? You can bring her in."

While I go fetch my patient, Delphine leaves the tent and heads across the lane. She talks to Szilvia for a moment. I see her pointing back toward us. When she returns we are waiting in the tent, the woman sitting hunched on the examination table while her son stands nervously nearby.

"You will stay here and help me with the patients," Delphine announces. "You are my new assistant. Szilvia tells me that you want to provide medical care for poor women and children. This will be good practice for you."

Horrified, I stare at her for a moment, neatly trapped by my own lie. Laszlo must have told Szilvia about my medical aspirations. No wonder I didn't get the option to chop cucumbers. They think my medical skills are better used here. Too bad those prized skills are entirely fictitious.

"Oh, I don't really have that much training," I hedge. "I'm sure someone else would be more help." Like probably anyone else on the volunteer roster. I'm guessing most of them can at least handle the sight of blood. For a moment I panic at the thought of being stuck in this tent, forced to help with medical procedures. It's my own personal version of hell. It's also entirely my fault for allowing the Humanitas Foundation to believe a falsehood. Now I am paying the price.

Delphine fixes me with a stern stare. "This is a crisis," she says firmly. "Each of us must do all we can, and more than we can, to help."

After that, there is really nothing more I can say. I grit my teeth and get on with it. Delphine unwinds the stethoscope from around her neck and presses it against the woman's ample bosom, murmuring to her in Arabic. After a moment of concentration, she whips off the stethoscope. "Give me the blood pressure cuff," she orders.

Obediently, I rummage around the rolling cart, hoping I can correctly identify the blood pressure cuff. I locate what I think is the right equipment and pass it to her, resigning myself to volunteering in the very last place in the camp I'd choose to be.

Chapter 31

"Mia, are you in here?" Rosie pokes her head into the women's shared hostel bathroom later that night. "Can I brush my teeth?"

"Sure." Standing under the lukewarm spray of water in the shower, I lean my head against the cold tile of the shower stall and close my eyes. It has been a very long day.

Laszlo dropped us off at the hostel well after dark. Located in a small town near the camp, it is our new home. Rosie, Winnie, and I are sharing a large, basic room with bunk beds. The men have the same setup across the hall.

Rosie is quiet as she brushes her teeth. I lather and rinse, trying to erase the smell of antiseptic and dust and unwashed people that permeates my hair and clothes. I am bone-deep weary and footsore and want nothing more than to fall into bed, but even that simple desire makes me feel guilty. I can enjoy a soft bed and a good shower. The people we have come to help cannot. Tonight families, young children, and arthritic old men will sleep on the hard ground with nothing more than a thin fleece blanket to keep the night chill at bay. Fleeing war, violence, trauma in their own countries, they are now bunking down in an empty potato field as they wait for buses that the Hungarian government sends sporadically to transport them north to the border with Austria.

"Goodness, what a day," Rosie says, her mouth full of toothpaste.

"Yeah, you can say that again."

Rosie spits into the sink. "Did you see that mother with her teenage daughters walk into camp this afternoon? The one with the designer handbag?"

"I noticed them. What was the purse? It looked expensive."

The woman and her two daughters walked down the railroad tracks late this afternoon. They all wore hijabs covering their hair and stylishly cut manteaus (which look like long, fitted trench coats) in modest tan and navy blue. The older woman's pace was slow and dignified. Over her arm hung a beautiful purse in pale pink and rose gold.

"A Chanel," Rosie says, her tone reverent, tapping water from her toothbrush. "Python skin. That bag is probably worth about five thousand dollars."

"Wow. They walked all the way from Greece with a designer handbag?"

"I think it's the only thing they had," Rosie says. "The daughters didn't seem to have anything else with them. It makes me feel so ridiculous that I was so devastated about losing my suitcase when these people have lost everything."

I don't say anything.

Rosie pauses, the water still running in the sink. "I feel guilty parading around in these designer clothes Lars got me, but I don't have anything else to wear," she says soberly.

It's a conundrum. She can't borrow anything of mine as we're not remotely the same size, and even if Winnie was amenable to letting her borrow clothes, lace-up combat boots and Dynamite Kitty T-shirts would be just as jarring as designer wear.

"Maybe just try to tone it down a little," I suggest, rinsing conditioner from my hair. "That plum dress doesn't look too flashy. I think a couple things could still work." I want to help Rosie, but

I'm just too tired to think clearly. "At the end of the day I don't think what you're wearing matters as much as being sensitive to where people are coming from, what they've gone through, and what they've lost." I swallow hard, suddenly feeling tears spring to my eyes.

"You're right," Rosie agrees. "I just didn't realize it would be like this. To see people, real people, in these conditions, and start hearing their stories. It's . . . shattering."

"It is," I say quietly. There is no other word for it.

We don't say anything for a moment, the steady patter of the shower the only sound.

"Okay, sugar. I'm going to bed. I can't keep my eyes open anymore."

"Sleep well. I'll be there in a minute."

The bathroom door shuts behind Rosie, and I lean my head against the cold tile in the shower. I picture the woman with the Chanel purse and her daughters again. There were no men accompanying them, which Delphine noted was unusual. The woman's face was stalwart and weary. Something in her expression caught me, resigned but still proud. What had they gone through? What had they left behind?

The shower has run cold, but I am too tired to care. I stand under the chilly spray, overwhelmed by what I have seen today. The most poignant visitor to the medical tent was a little boy with shaggy hair who silently clutched a red toy car missing a wheel as Delphine cleaned an infected cut on his knee. His mother told us the car belonged to his seven-year-old brother, killed by a bomb in Damascus while the boys were playing in the street. When his mother found him at the hospital hours later, he was sitting by his brother's body, holding his limp hand. He carried the toy car with him from Syria, his only memento of his brother.

Silently I start to sob, unable to contain the grief. The little boy with the car, the woman with the Chanel purse—they are just two among thousands. Almost everyone who passed through the medical tent today had suffered loss—homes and jobs, fathers and uncles and sisters.

I stand with my face under the spray of icy water, letting my hot tears run free. I don't know how to hold all their stories, the reality of so much loss and pain. It is clear that there is so little we can do. Cucumbers and bottles of water pale into insignificance in the face of such great suffering. What they need is a safe place to start over, a reunited family, peace in their countries. No more war. I am ill equipped in the face of such trauma, such loss. I wonder how I can bear weeks of this. And it is just the first day.

The next morning I meet Maryam and Yousef.

"Your sister is sick, but this medicine can help her." Delphine stands by the examination table giving instructions and a packet of medicine to Yousef, an Iraqi man in his early twenties who is traveling with his younger sister. Maryam is not yet fourteen, a slender girl with a sweet smile. She does not talk, Yousef tells us, not since their parents died a few months ago. She and Yousef bear a strong resemblance to one another, their narrow, homely faces alight with good humor. Yousef studied English in university and translates Delphine's instructions into Syriac for his sister, who nods her understanding, glancing at us shyly from under long, dark lashes.

During the examination, I notice the gentle way he treats her. It is clear they adore each other. Their eyes are shadowed, but they are smiling, buoyed by their arrival on Hungarian soil.

"We are going to meet our older sister in Sweden," Yousef tells us. "We hope to be at her home in Gothenburg before Maryam's birthday next week."

"Your sister needs to rest and take this medicine along with liters of water," Delphine says firmly. "I don't like the sound of her cough. Bring her tomorrow for me to check her lungs. You are not to leave the camp until I say she can travel. Do you understand?"

Yousef nods, looking sober. "I will bring her here tomorrow."

Maryam ducks her head and smiles gratefully at us.

Delphine and I work ceaselessly throughout the morning. She and another doctor, Stefan from Switzerland, whom I have yet to meet, are rotating shifts around the clock to make sure that someone is always available to offer basic medical care. Delphine is on the day shift, 9 a.m. to 9 p.m., as am I.

We've seen all sorts of patients in just a few hours. Most have infected blisters from walking so far, or nasty-sounding coughs from sleeping outside in the rain on their journey. Many of the children are running fevers.

We are establishing a workable rhythm already, although I am far from an adept nurse. Delphine gives me a startled look when I confess that I have no idea how to take a patient's blood pressure. "What do they teach you in America?" she mutters with a shake of her head.

"Sociology," I reply, too low for her to hear. Nothing in my college education is remotely helpful in this situation. Nor has baking proven to be particularly useful either, unfortunately. My fake medical skills, however, are in very high demand.

Chapter 32

By early afternoon we finally have a slowdown in the line of people. Delphine sends me to restock our supplies and instructs me to take a ten-minute break and get some food in my stomach.

"You must take care of yourself, even in a crisis. Especially in a crisis," she admonishes me. "The need is always great, but you cannot run and run until you collapse. Then you are no good to anyone. You must take care of yourself so that you can care for others, *oui*?"

I nod and duck out of the tent, grateful for the fresh air and a few minutes to stretch my legs. At the food tent I ask Abel for a bottle of water.

"It's getting crowded," I observe as he tears the plastic on a six-pack of large bottles and hands one to me.

Several more groups of people are making their way down the railroad tracks toward the camp. As we watch, a family of five arrives—middle-aged mother and father, a girl of eight or nine, and a young man in his teens carrying an ancient woman on his back. She has her skinny arms wrapped around his neck, and he is hunched over, holding her slight weight. When they reach the camp, he gently lowers her to the ground, relief and joy written large across all their faces.

"This is the beginning of a new life for them," Abel observes.

"They know when they arrive here, they are safe. They are free." There is something in his tone, an understanding. I glance at him.

"Was it like that when you came to America?" I ask, twisting off the bottle cap and taking a long swallow of water.

Abel tips his head, a tacit agreement. "When I finally stepped onto American soil, I kissed the ground, right there at the airport arrivals curb. I thought I could leave all the sorrow behind me, all the things I had seen." He is watching the newly arrived family, but his tone of voice tells me he is far away. "But we cannot escape our experiences."

He smiles sadly, his eyes shadowed. "The memories are always with us, but sometimes we can ease the way for others. That is what we must do, use our pain to build understanding and empathy, not to build walls. Then it is transformed into a thing of beauty, then our suffering has value."

"That's a beautiful way to look at it," I say, capping the bottle and watching him closely.

"It is beautiful because it is true," Abel says. His eyes meet mine.

There is so much about him that I do not yet understand, a depth I find compelling. I want to know more of his story.

A moment later a father and son approach, looking for some milk for the boy, and I take my leave of Abel, stopping at the food table for a quick snack. Rosie presses an apple, a white roll, and a few triangles of processed cheese wrapped in thin foil on me. "You have to eat, sugar, to keep up your strength. We have tons, so don't think you're taking it out of the mouths of the hungry." She looks conspicuously glamorous in a white striped shirtdress with a wide leather belt and a pair of leather mules in a floral pattern with metal studs.

"How does this outfit look?" she hisses at me in a stage whisper. "Still too much?"

"Maybe lose the belt and the flowered shoes," I suggest. "The dress isn't bad."

"I gave half the stuff Lars sent me to them this morning." Rosie nods toward the back of the food line where I see the middle-aged woman and her two daughters from yesterday standing together. The mother has her Chanel purse clutched tight to her side; the girls are both dressed in their manteaus, but one is wearing Rosie's Balenciaga cat-eye sunglasses and the other holds her silver clutch.

"Good job," I say, admiring Rosie's generosity.

Beside Rosie, Winnie pauses from assembling sandwiches and eyes the girls. "Just what every refugee needs, a classic evening bag," she says caustically. Rosie rolls her eyes and gestures for the next person in line to approach. Jake lingers nearby, taking some photos and filming Rosie and Winnie at work.

Munching my snack, I drift around to the side of the tent where Kai is sorting and stacking bags of fruit and boxes of packaged snacks.

"Hey, how's it going over in medical?" Kai asks, taking a break from organizing.

"Okay," I say around a mouthful of apple. "I'm not a great medical assistant, to be honest, but the doctor, Delphine, is awesome. She's with Medecines Sans Frontieres." I unwrap a triangle of cheese and pop it into my mouth. It tastes creamy and a little slimy. "Actually, I should take some food back to her." I haven't seen her eat or drink anything since we arrived. Speaking of taking care of oneself, what is she living on, air?

"Here, let me." Kai assembles a quick snack from the items he's been organizing—a granola bar and an orange. "For the doctor." He hands the food to me, and I add two triangles of cheese from my own stash.

"Say cheese," Jake says from behind us, and we turn to find his camera pointed in our direction. Without thinking, I move closer to Kai, and he throws his arm around my shoulders. We both hold up the packages of cheese in our free hands.

"Cheese," we chorus, and then Kai adds, "Or processed cheese-like food product."

I laugh, then sober, aware that we are being photographed, that we are in a refugee camp and should perhaps not be so glib.

"I better get back to work," I say, taking a last bite of apple and gathering the snack for Delphine. "See you later."

"Bye, Mia." Rosie waves. Kai gives me a nod and a wink as I turn back to the stifling tent and the growing line of people waiting for our help.

That night at the hostel, after our shift is over, I slip into my pajamas, grab my phone, and climb into the top bunk. Winnie is already snoring quietly below me. Rosie is on the top bunk across the room, texting on her phone, her cheekbones illuminated by the soft glow of her screen. I check my email and send a message to Henry and my parents, giving them a quick update. All is well, I write.

I don't tell them the truth. That I am seeing an aspect of humanity I've never seen before, the devastation of war, the brokenness of trauma and loss. My heart and my head ache, both from the grueling hours of work and the emotional toll it takes. I feel wrung out but at the same time grateful to be able to help in whatever way I can. At least I am doing something, giving these people something to ease their way. It's not a panacea for their pain, but for those we assist on their journey, it does matter.

I open an email from Nana titled "Who's the cutie?" and find a screenshot of Kai and me at the food tent this afternoon, holding aloft our triangle cheese. His arm is draped casually around my shoulders, mine clasped around his waist. We are laughing. We look good together, like we fit.

Who's the cutie? Nana Alice writes below the screenshot.

That smile and those dark eyes . . . Treatment is going well. I'm feeling good. The doctors are pleased with my progress so far. Albert has asked me to go steady, but I told him we're too old for such nonsense. I will, however, go swing dancing with him on Thursday. Love and kisses, Nana A.

Who in the world taught her how to take a screenshot, I wonder? She never fails to amaze me. We haven't spoken since our conversation during their dinner date at the Space Needle. The past week has been too rushed as Team Caritas wrapped up our time in India and headed for Hungary, but I've been thinking about her every day. I should call her and check in, but I don't have the energy at the moment. I'm so tired I feel like I could fall asleep sitting up. Besides, the Internet connection is molasses slow in our room. I doubt it would support a call. I type a simple reply. Yep, you're right. Kai is a cutie. He's great, a good friend and a great teammate. Why don't you say yes to going steady with Albert? You're never too old for love!—Mia Then I set my alarm and gratefully fall asleep.

The next morning I'm scrambling to get ready for the day. Rosie, still in her luxurious jade-green silk pajamas from Lars' suitcase of mercy, is sitting in bed checking her phone. All of a sudden she gasps. "Mia, have you seen Instagram this morning?"

Curious, I stand on tiptoe and gaze at her screen. There is the photo of Kai and me from yesterday. Kai's head is bent toward mine, his fingers curled around my shoulder as we hold aloft our triangle cheese.

"Look." Rosie points. An hour ago AliceWest85 proudly and publicly commented on the photo, Mia, you're right. That Kai sure is a cutie. I can see why you're sweet on him!

I stare in horror at the comment. Nana Alice has outed my secret crush on Instagram. This is beyond mortifying. I meet Rosie's gaze, her eyes wide and startled.

"She sent me a screenshot of that photo and asked about him last night," I say, feeling like I have to defend myself. "I told her he's a friend and a teammate. She must not realize other people can see these comments."

"The entire world can see that comment," Rosie says, biting her lip. It looks suspiciously like she might be trying not to giggle, but she holds it in and opts for a sympathetic expression instead.

"Argh!" I groan. "The dangers of letting octogenarians loose on the Internet. Just as long as Kai doesn't see it." I cross my fingers for luck and hope against hope that he doesn't check Instagram.

Chapter 33

"We're out of painkillers again." Delphine clucks in annoyance, taking inventory of our limited supplies. It is late in the afternoon two days after the Instagram incident, and I am helping her disinfect and organize the medical station during a momentary lull in patients.

"Mia, can you tell Szilvia to put these on the Facebook supplies list?" she instructs. "Paracetamol and ibuprofen, and fever-reducing suppositories for children."

I jot the items down, making a mental note to give the list to Szilvia before the end of the day. She posts a daily list on the Migration Aid Facebook page detailing what items are needed. People then drop off supplies in Budapest, and volunteers drive the goods in trucks and vans to the border camp. Most of the volunteers are Hungarian—doctors, teachers, metro ticket takers, university students, all giving selflessly and sacrificially, to help refugees at their border.

"I just wish we could do more," I sigh, wiping the examination table with disinfectant. "I know this is just a pit stop for the refugees, but I wish we could make it feel more welcoming somehow."

Delphine pauses from her inventory and purses her lips, thinking. "Tea," she says abruptly.

"You want some tea?" I ask.

"No, we need to offer tea to the refugees," she says. "Tea is very important in many of these cultures. It signifies hospitality, comfort. It's a ritual of civility. My father drank two cups every day. Tea is the perfect thing. It is warming, hydrating, and will make them feel welcome. If you want to help these people feel more at home, we should serve them tea."

"Yes, perfect!" Spurred into action, I find Szilvia and request to leave my shift a little early to make a Tesco run for tea and the other supplies the camp needs. Kai and Milo volunteer to accompany me, and Jake tags along with his camera.

I'm secretly glad Kai offered to come with me. We haven't had any time together to talk since our evening stroll in Budapest. I often catch glimpses of him around the camp and we eat meals together with the group, but there's been no chance for personal conversation since the night he held my hand by the Danube. I keep an eye on him as he drives the van to Tesco. We chat about the events of the day, the people we've met, and the stories they've told us. He's acting completely normal, so much to my relief, I conclude that he didn't see Nana Alice's Instagram post.

In the vast bright expanse of Tesco, we split up the list. A van came from Budapest with supplies today, but a number of things we need at the camp were not in the load.

"I'll get everything that isn't food," Milo says, taking a cart and heading to the other end of the store. Jake follows him with the video camera.

"How about I get food and you get drinks?" I suggest to Kai. He takes a cart and heads toward the aisle with boxes of juice and milk.

I wheel two carts into the food section and stock up on bread rolls, oranges, and triangle cheese, then head to the tea aisle and start browsing the selections.

"Hey, look what I found." Kai wheels his laden cart into the tea aisle and shows me a dozen insulated white thermoses, the kind churches and AA meetings use for refreshments.

"Oh great! Those are perfect for serving tea."

"I thought so." Kai wedges the thermoses into his cart. "So I'm both useful and a cutie," he says nonchalantly. "Is that why you're sweet on me?" He shoots me a sideways look of amusement, and I want to sink through the floor.

Cheeks flaming, I focus intently on a row of medicinal-looking herbal teas, all labeled in Hungarian, trying to regain my composure. I've never been so embarrassed in my life. "That was my eighty-two-year-old grandmother. She misunderstood me. I'm sorry, it's not what you think." I'm babbling, my words tripping over each other in their haste to not make this awkward, to not own up to my embarrassing little crush.

"Hey, Mia." He stops me, his voice gentle. I look up at him in the fluorescent glare of Tesco. He has a smudge of dirt on the arm of his T-shirt, and his man bun is a little bedraggled, wisps of dark hair escaping around his cut-glass cheekbones. He puts his finger under my chin and tips my head up. When he smiles at me, the corners of his eyes crinkle in the most endearing way.

"It's okay," he says. "I like you too."

And then he kisses me. He tastes of green grass and something spicy, like chai tea, and his mouth is warm and gentle on mine. Our kiss deepens. Good heavens, he knows what he's doing. I forget where we are and wrap my arms around his neck, standing on tiptoe to reach his lips. I've only kissed one man for the past six years. Kissing Ethan was comfortable, sweet like a butterscotch candy. Kissing Kai makes me feel like I'm falling through space into a deep pile of feather pillows. I could fall forever.

"Um, guys." Milo clears his throat, and we spring apart abruptly. "I bought all the men's underwear in every size." He looks amused and a little embarrassed. He's pushing a cart loaded with clothing and toiletries. Jake is behind him, filming the entire scene.

"We were just . . . I mean . . ." I press my hands to my red cheeks, feeling guilty and embarrassed. What am I doing? Saint Mia would definitely not be kissing men in the tea aisle of Tesco. *Not men*, I amend internally. *Just one man—one perfectly wonderful man.*

I dart a quick glance at Kai, who doesn't seem perturbed at all. In fact, he looks like he's enjoying the situation. He's grinning.

"Hey," Milo says. "It's all good." He peers into my cart stacked high with the food items. "Think that's enough cheese?"

Jake lowers the camera. I'm pretty sure he got footage of our kiss.

"Jake, can you just delete that last part?" I ask pleadingly, trying to wheedle the footage out of him.

He is unmoved. "Sorry, Mia. No can do. Got to send it all to the boss. He likes to be kept informed about everything going on with the team, even the personal stuff. If it affects team dynamics, he wants to know." He shrugs apologetically. "But don't worry. He's got a soft spot for romance. I think he'll be cheering you on."

I give up. I signed up for this trip, after all, and agreed to all aspects of it, including the part about my private life becoming public fodder. Perhaps Lars Lindquist will enjoy watching the footage of our kiss from his Florida mansion late at night with a glass of brandy. Maybe it will warm his lonely heart. With a sigh of frustrated acquiescence, I turn my attention back to the list. I have more important things to think about than Lars seeing Kai and me kissing in the tea aisle.

"Okay, the last thing we need is tea and sugar. A lot of it." I stare at boxes of tea on the shelf. How many boxes of tea and how many bags of sugar will it take to help an entire refugee camp feel welcome in this new place? In the end I simply sweep the entire stack of Ceylon black tea boxes into my cart. Whatever we buy, I'm not sure it will be enough to make these people feel like anything more than strangers in a strange land.

An hour later we arrive back at the refugee camp. "Who wants to stay a little later and share some tea with the refugees?" I ask, hopping down from the van, full thermoses of tea in each hand. On the way back from Tesco we stopped by the hostel and, with the permission of the proprietor, made tea in the restaurant kitchen, filling all the carafes.

Although everyone on our team is hungry and tired and just finished their shifts for the evening, they agree to stay another hour—even Winnie, who grumbles but gives in. We split into teams of two, one man and one woman each, and take a carafe, a bag of sugar, and a stack of disposable cups and plastic spoons. I can't face Kai, not after our embarrassing spectacle in the tea aisle, so I partner with Abel. Each team circulates through the tents and the surrounding woods, offering tea to those we meet.

I am astonished by the effect. People accept the tea gratefully, sipping it and closing their eyes in relief. One or two even tear up. They invite us to sit with them. Over cups of tea, they begin to tell us their names and countries and bits of their stories in broken English. One hour turns into two. The thermoses run low.

At the tail end of the evening, at the far edge of the field, Abel and I stumble upon Maryam and Yousef. They are sitting together under a spreading oak tree, wrapped in thin fleece blankets from Ikea. The dew has fallen and the night is turning cool.

We are down to the dregs of tea in the bottom of the carafe, but I manage to fill their cups by the light of a flashlight Abel carries. Yousef invites us to sit with them, and we do. I squeeze an additional inch of tea into two cups for Abel and me, emptying the carafes entirely.

We sit together, sipping our lukewarm tea, the flashlight casting a mellow glow around their tiny makeshift campsite. I offer Maryam the sugar, and her face breaks into a smile as she helps herself to two heaping spoonfuls.

"She likes sweets," Yousef says with a fond smile.

"You travel alone?" Abel asks.

Yousef nods, dropping his eyes. "We left Iraq when Daesh overran our home city of Qaraqosh. We went first to Turkey and then to Greece."

I frown, recalling Delphine telling me that Daesh is another name for the radical militant group Islamic State. I cannot imagine what that would be like, to watch militant fanatics overrun your home.

"And what of the rest of your family?" Abel asks gently, his dark eyes intent on the siblings in the dim glow of the flashlight.

"Our father was killed by Daesh," Yousef says, his mouth twisting around the word. "He was strung up in front of his shop because he would not convert. We are members of the Chaldean Catholic community and therefore persecuted by the extremists. And our mother . . ." He stops, swallows hard. "Our mother died when she saw his body. A massive stroke in her brain. She fell down in the street and did not wake up. Three weeks she lived, but she never opened her eyes again."

Maryam hides her face with her hands. She coughs, a hoarse bark that sounds painful. Her shoulders shake. Yousef puts his arm around her, comforting her. To my surprise, Maryam reaches out and grasps my hand, her head still bowed. Her fingers are strong, her skin dry and a little rough. I can feel a tremor through her fingertips, suppressed grief and sadness. I grip her hand in mine and simply sit with them, bearing witness to their grief. I don't know what to say to make it better, but perhaps this is what they need right now, someone to hear their story, someone to assure them that they are seen, that their sorrow is not forgotten.

Abel leans forward and grips Yousef's arm. "You are not alone, brother," he says firmly. "I know this pain. I, too, lost my family—my mother, my father, and my older sister. It feels like the end of your heart, the end of life itself."

Yousef nods, his shoulders slumped with despair. "I do not know how to go on," he says. "We have only our sister now in Sweden. She is all we have left."

Abel gazes intently at Yousef. "You will see your parents again, brother," he says gently. "Death is not the end."

The sorrow is palpable, like steam in the air. I feel myself tearing up in solidarity, touched by the raw power of their grief. After a few moments, Yousef looks up and wipes his eyes, sniffing. In the weak yellow glow of the flashlight, I glimpse the sheen of tears on his cheeks.

"You are right," he says to Abel. "This is not the end."

Abel nods. "You must be strong," he says. "It will take great courage to build a new life in Sweden. Your sister needs you. Make your father and your mother proud."

Yousef takes a deep breath and nods again. He meets Abel's eyes, then mine, and straightens his shoulders. "I will try," he says solemnly.

Maryam untangles her fingers from mine and turns to him, her eyes shining when she gazes at her brother. It is clear that he is her protector and that she adores him.

"I will do it for Maryam," Yousef says. "So she can start over, a new life."

Abel nods and raises his cup. "To a new life for you both," he says. We drink the last drops of tea.

A few minutes later we gather the cups and leave Yousef and

Maryam for the night. It is growing late. We walk back to the van silently, picking our way carefully through the clods of dirt and trash that litter the ground.

"I didn't know about your family," I say haltingly. "I'm so sorry." I stop, unable to come up with any other words. What can I say, I who have known only comfort and safety and peace. I have no window into this magnitude of suffering, no way to comprehend what they have experienced. I'm both grateful and a little embarrassed by my privilege and good fortune.

"It was long ago," Abel says, his voice placing the loss far in the past. "Those I lost have been gone many years. I remember them and miss them still, but the years soften the pain. Life continues, and we must go on too." He looks at me steadily in the soft summer darkness, the outline of his face just visible. "I honor their memory with my life now, and I know we will meet again one day."

I walk quietly beside him back to the van. I don't know what to say. Such grief and such hope combined—it leaves me breathless. It breaks my heart.

Chapter 34

A few days later Delphine sends me on a quick errand midway through the busy morning. "Get baby wipes, and plenty of them," she instructs. "And tell Szilvia we need cough medicine."

I hurry out into the warm sunlight, scanning the camp, looking for Szilvia's brassy blonde head. I'm glad to be out of the stifling confines of the tent. Already the day is growing hot. It's going to be sweltering by afternoon. Breathing deeply the smell of mud tinged with human waste from the Porta-Potties, I finally spy Szilvia standing at the back of a van of supplies that arrived this morning from a Lutheran aid group in Munich.

"Put those in the tent. Hurry, hurry. The people are hungry," she calls loudly, flapping her hands at a few new Hungarian university student volunteers as they unload crates of fruit from the van.

Every day or so a new group or organization will show up with a van or car or truck loaded with donated supplies. Some just deliver their goods and leave, but a few open up their own temporary stations, beckoning everyone in the camp to come get whatever they are offering—free haircuts and shaves, a mobile phone charging station so the refugees can stay in contact with family back home or connect with those they are hoping to join in other parts of Europe. Just this morning a thin Hungarian man with a drooping mustache rode up on a bicycle and gave out fresh doughnuts from a wooden box attached to the back of his bike, handing them to refugees, volunteers, and police alike.

I stretch and look around me for a moment. The entire camp is a chaotic scene of goodwill and disorganization. Szilvia does her best to keep things at least somewhat organized, but the camp is makeshift, thrown together out of necessity. There is no authoritative source of information, and so rumors fly from tent to tent, handed down after phone calls to relatives in Sweden or Germany who try to keep abreast of the fluctuating European position on the refugee crisis. Every day it seems there is some new stance, some new rule or regulation from Hungary and the other nations in the European Union. No one knows what will happen next.

This morning a bus left the camp carrying some of the waiting refugees to the Austrian border. From there they can travel to their intended destinations, claiming asylum in Denmark, Sweden, or Germany. The Hungarian government sends a bus or two every day or so, but each bus could be the last. The borders could close without warning. The instability makes people nervous. They don't want to sit and wait for a bus; they are desperate to reach a place of safety and permanence.

"When you finish with the fruit, unload the rest of this into the clothing tent. Go, go . . . ," Szilvia calls to the volunteers as they troop toward the food tent, lugging crates.

I head toward Szilvia, keeping my eye out for Kai. We haven't talked since our kiss in Tesco five days ago. There's been no opportunity to be alone, but I am always aware of him, homing in on his presence around the camp even while I am busy doing other things. We're around one another constantly but never in private. I don't know what I would say if I did manage to steal a moment alone with him. My heart still aches when I think of Ethan, but it leaps like it's been electrocuted when I catch a glimpse of Kai.

As I head toward Szilvia, I notice Rosie standing in the dirt road a few yards away from the German van, talking to a man with straight blond hair whose back is to me. My gaze drifts past them and then snaps back to the man.

There is something familiar about him, the set of his shoulders in a light blue dress shirt, the way he leans toward Rosie as he talks, as though he knows her well. I stop and squint. It can't be. But then Rosie points toward me, and he turns. Even before I see his face I know. It's Ethan.

"Mia!" Ethan comes toward me, hands outstretched, as though we are long-lost friends. He stops in front of me, close enough to touch. His face is hesitant, hopeful. He sees my stunned expression and lets his hands drop. "Mia," he says again, his gaze searching mine, as though looking for something, some reassurance or sign.

"Ethan?" Standing in the middle of the field, I blink and blink again, shaking my head, dumbfounded. What is happening? Ethan is standing in front of me in a potato field turned refugee camp in rural Hungary. Ethan, who never wanted to venture far from home, who doesn't, to the best of my knowledge, even have a passport.

"What are you doing here?" I stammer. Out of the corner of my eye, I see Rosie standing in the lane watching us narrowly, her head cocked at an attentive angle. Beyond her Kai comes out of the food tent and heads toward the German van. He stops and looks toward us, his expression curious. Jake trots over and stands next to Rosie, video camera going. I wince, imagining Lars watching footage of this most interesting twist in his Caritas team dynamics.

"Mia, I came for you." Ethan's tone is gentle, almost pleading. I tear my attention from our audience and meet his eyes, those beautiful, clear blue eyes. I see a flicker of uncertainty in his gaze. He doesn't know how I'll react to his being here. For that matter, neither do I. I just stare at him in shock.

Taking my silence as some sort of assent, he gives me a sweet, pleading look. "Mia, I blew it," he says. "I never should have let you go. I knew I'd made a mistake as soon as you left Gas Works Park that day, but I didn't know what to do. You said you were going on this trip and you sounded so sure. I was confused. But I'm not confused now. Please, give me a chance to explain." He stops, waiting for my response, his expression hopeful.

I stare hard at the ground, focusing on a clod of dirt, thoughts racing. I turn it over with the toe of my sneaker and find an empty blister pack of pills underneath. All I can taste is green grass and chai tea. I don't know what to say. Why has he waited so long? Why has he come now, when my heart has just begun to heal, when my pulse quickens at the sound of a different voice?

My head is whirling with this unexpected turn of events. And my heart? My heart is torn. If I'm honest, this is what I wanted, what I secretly hoped would happen. I desperately longed for Ethan to realize his mistake and come back to me. But that was before—before India, before Kai, before I embarked on this alternate life. I was just starting to feel alive again. I shoot Ethan a perplexed look. In the midst of my myriad questions lies a kernel of curiosity. He has crossed a continent and an ocean to come for me. I have to at least hear him out.

"I can't leave my shift," I say, softening just a little. "I volunteer at the medical station. I'll meet you at the food tent about one."

He looks instantly relieved. "Thank you," he says quietly.

A dozen questions are buzzing around in my brain, as insistent and frantic as yellow jackets, but I need a little time to calm down and reorient before I say or do anything more.

"I'll see you at lunch," I say, then I turn and walk toward the medical tent, leaving him standing in the warm morning sun.

Chapter 35

At lunchtime we sit together, Ethan and I, on a little mound of flattened dry grass at the edge of the field. If I crane my neck, I can catch a glimpse of the rest of my team eating lunch beside the food tent. Ethan sits next to me, elbows on his knees, wearing skinny jeans and his favorite button-down shirt from Brooks Brothers. He looks incongruous sitting here in the dirt.

Someone has turned on a small radio in the food tent, and it's playing plaintive love songs from the nineties, sung in Hungarian. The current selection is a cover of Whitney Houston's "I Will Always Love You." The irony is not lost on either of us.

Ethan gives me a bashful smile. "She's reading my mind," he says.

I don't respond. I crunch a slice of cucumber, ravenous from my busy morning, and stare down the lane at the police vehicles and beyond them, the media vans. The reporters are still camped out there, covering the refugee crisis by venturing every so often into the camp to interview a refugee or take some footage. Otherwise they seem to loiter near their trucks waiting for something exciting to happen.

"Mia, I made the biggest mistake of my life when I let you go." Ethan gazes at me, his expression forthright and earnest. In the sunlight his hair gleams like gold. "It took me awhile to realize it, but when I did, I knew I had to come find you."

"How did you find me?" I ask, peeling an orange, slipping my fingernail under the dimpled rind.

"The night we broke up you mentioned the Humanitas Foundation, so I contacted them and told them the whole story. I sweet-talked Stella into at least talking to Lars Lindquist about us. Luckily, he seems to have a soft spot for lost love, because he agreed to help me come find you."

"You sweet-talked Stella? Lars is in on this?" I'm boggled by these unexpected revelations. "Okay, so you tracked me down, but why now?" I smear a triangle of cheese between two halves of a roll and take a bite.

Ethan doesn't touch his lunch. He sips from a bottle of water and keeps his attention solely on me. I can't remember the last time I had his undivided attention, other than when he was breaking up with me, which definitely doesn't count. Now that I am lost to him, he is fully present, fully engaged. Go figure.

"I saw a photo on Instagram of you and that guy." He nods to the food tent where Team Caritas sits. "The one with the man bun."

"Kai," I interrupt him. "His name is Kai."

"Yeah, okay." Ethan makes a slight gesture of dismissal, wiping Kai from the conversation. "I saw the photo of you two together, and I realized that I'd been an idiot. You're the most selfless, loyal, kind woman I've ever met. You're smart and beautiful. I knew I couldn't let you slip away. I had to come tell you in person, to say that I'm sorry and to ask you to give me another chance."

I stare at Ethan, the hank of blond hair falling over his forehead, that clean-cut, boyishly handsome face. He'll be handsome when he's seventy, like Albert, a heartbreaker with twinkling eyes. I feel my heart soften, ache, with his words. He is my first love. He broke my heart. And now he's asking for a second chance. Can I give it to him? Should I?

From the food tent, I can hear Rosie singing along to the

Hungarian version of Shania Twain's "You're Still the One" on the radio, and catch the low timbre of Kai's voice talking to someone. This is all so confusing.

"Did you see Nana Alice's comment on Instagram?" I ask.

Ethan looks puzzled. "Nana Alice is on Instagram?"

"Somewhat dangerously," I tell him dryly. So he didn't see her comment about me liking Kai. I take a sip of water and ask the question that's been on my mind since I first glimpsed Ethan standing with Rosie in the lane. "How are you even here? Did you finally get a passport, after all these years of us talking about it?"

"A man will do a lot for love," he says sheepishly. "There's an express option for passports now. And Valium is my new best travel buddy."

He grins, and I laugh in spite of myself, and for a moment it feels like it did in the beginning. Easy between us. Ethan is an easy man to like, to love. But apparently he did not feel the same way about me, at least not until he saw me with Kai. I guess jealousy can be clarifying. It can show us the hidden corners of our hearts.

The fact that Ethan came for me says something. But I am not willing to let him off so easy. I am not the same girl who ate take-out salmon nigiri and watched this man shatter my future and my heart on the shore of Lake Union. I've tasted a different life. I've grown. And I want to know why he thinks we will work a second time. He needs to convince me we could still be good together.

"You said we were going different directions. You said we don't fit together anymore." I cap my water bottle and pin him with a pointed look.

"I was wrong, Mia. We can make this work, I know it." Ethan has adopted his persuasive tone, the one that landed the sale of his start-up, the one that makes any plan sound reasonable and right. He reaches out and takes my hands, his fingers warm and strong and so familiar. My heart breaks a little. I've missed him so much.

"Are you still moving to San Jose?" I balk, not ready yet to be convinced but not sure I don't want to be. I slip my hands from his grasp and nibble my last slice of cucumber.

"No." He shakes his head. "I knew moving to San Jose would be a deal breaker for you, and I wanted to give us another chance. The company's agreed to let me work remotely from Seattle and just fly down every couple of weeks for a day or so to meet with my team. I start the end of this month. If we ever change our minds and want to move to Cali, I can always relocate at a later date."

This is unexpected. Ethan is both practical and ambitious. San Jose would be a smart career move for him. To turn it down for me, for the chance of getting me back, highlights just how serious he is.

"I didn't think you'd do that," I say, softening a little more.

He nods, face serious. "I'll do anything, Mia."

I toy with my water bottle and gaze out at the camp. "What you said about us going different directions, though—it's true. We want really different things." I meet his eyes, needing him to see how I've changed, how I've grown. "I've tasted a life I'd forgotten to even dream about, a life I wanted since I was a little girl, and I can't go back to our old plans now. My desire to make a difference and to have a life of adventure isn't going away. It's who I am."

Ethan spreads his hands, a gesture of surrender. "We can compromise. Isn't that what any relationship is about? We can keep the dreams we still want and build new ones if we don't. The Craftsman cottage in Green Lake? A Frenchie named Butterworth? If that's not us anymore, no problem. What do you want? A yearly humanitarian trip abroad? You want to start a not-for-profit in Seattle? We can make a life that works for both of us, Mia. I'm sure we can." His eyes are pleading, so sincere.

It's enticing, but is it enough?

"I love you," he says softly, earnestly. "And there's adventure and need everywhere in the world. Anywhere you go you'll make a difference. Let's do it together."

I hesitate. It would be so simple to slide back into the shape of our life together. But I am not that shape anymore. India changed me. The refugee camp is changing me. And Kai—if I'm honest, Kai has changed the shape of my heart too. Ethan is positive we can reinvent our future to accommodate the shape of my alternate life. I'm not convinced.

"I need to think about all of this," I tell him briskly. "I'll talk to you tomorrow."

I stand, brushing the dirt from my jeans, and Ethan stands with me. He looks a little surprised at being dismissed, but he recovers quickly.

"Sure, take all the time you need," he says. He leans over and kisses my cheek, just a quick brush of his lips against my cheekbone before I can react. "Thank you," he whispers. I glance up just as Kai emerges from the food tent. He freezes, his eyes focused on us, on Ethan's lips against my skin. He wheels around abruptly and heads back the way he came, his face set like granite, impossible to read.

Chapter 36

Late in the afternoon a Spanish charity arrives with a truck full of sodden donated clothing. They got caught in a rainstorm in the mountains on the way, and the canvas truck cover leaked. There is a lull in camp activity since the bus left with almost half the refugees after lunch. No one is waiting at the medical tent, and Szilvia seizes the opportunity to conscript all volunteers into helping in one of two ways. Half the volunteers are tasked with picking up trash. The other half of us are to sort through the wet clothes for anything helpful and then bag the remnants up to be hauled away as garbage.

I am assigned to the clothing truck, and although it looks like it will be a damp and unpleasant job, I'm grateful for the chance to focus on something other than my own internal drama. I need to do something else for a few minutes and give my poor psyche a break. In the dim and humid confines of the truck bed, Winnie stands on one side of me, Rosie on the other, sorting through soggy cardboard boxes of clothing. The clothes are unusable, sopping mounds of shorts and tank tops and strappy sandals, clothes that, even had they been dry, would not have been suitable for most of the refugees, who are predominantly Muslim and dress conservatively. Winnie holds up a glittery gold mini skirt.

"Start your new life in Europe like a Eurotrash disco queen," she remarks dryly, tossing it onto the garbage pile. I find a few pairs of socks and some blouses that are just a little damp and put them on the small save pile.

I'm fast learning in the world of disaster relief that good intentions do not always equal helpful results. We could have been using this time more productively, but instead we're here sorting through someone's kind but ill-conceived gesture of goodwill. I throw a red snakeskin bra on the garbage pile with a sigh.

"Oh my stars." Rosie holds up a pair of strappy black stiletto heels. "If this isn't the biggest waste of a trip. All the way from Spain to deliver stilettos to refugees." She tosses them on the garbage pile. While the comment is true, it is also a little ironic coming from a woman who is currently wearing watermelon-colored fringed suede Gucci flats, compliments of Lars Lindquist. She catches my eye and rolls hers ruefully. "I know, look who's talking."

To her credit she's been switching between the striped dress and the plum one, trying to be sensitive both to the refugees' situation and their expectations of women's modest attire.

"So what's the deal with you and Malibu Ken?" Winnie asks, jerking her head toward the open back of the truck. Ethan is just visible over by the tents, gathering trash with a rake and dumping it into a garbage bag. He is moving gingerly but working without complaint.

"He's, ah . . ." I pause, not sure how to summarize whatever Ethan is.

"He's Mia's ex-college boyfriend who strung her along for six years and then dumped her on a Ferris wheel when she thought he was going to propose," Rosie explains, summarizing my disastrous love story in one unpunctuated sentence. "He had the diamond ring and everything. And now he's had a change of heart and has come all the way over here to win her back, even though he's never set foot outside of America until now." She tosses a denim jacket on the save pile.

Winnie looks mildly impressed. "Wow," she says, surveying me. "Bold move. So are you going to give him a second chance?"

"I don't know." I frown at a purple cocktail dress, then glance over at Ethan. My heart speeds up every time I look at him, but I can't tell if it's from annoyance or anticipation. Maybe a mixture of both.

Rosie shoots me a sympathetic look.

"Don't," Winnie advises. "If it took him this long to figure out he made a mistake, he's either really dumb or he doesn't really want you. Either way you don't want to go down that road again."

Surprisingly sound advice from a woman who has a tattoo of a disturbingly anatomically accurate heart wrapped in yellow caution tape on her left bicep.

Kai suddenly appears at the mouth of the truck, his arms full of wet blankets. "Szilvia told me to bring these here. I guess someone's coming from Budapest to pick them up." He dumps the blankets in a mound by the door and then turns to go, giving me a brief confused look.

I wince and drop my eyes. I desperately want to go to him, to explain. But what would I say? I don't even know what I think about this whole situation. I have nothing to offer Kai, not until I know my own mind. He starts to go.

"Kai." I say his name before I can stop myself. He waits, but I don't say anything more.

"I've got to get back to work," he says, turning away, his jaw set and his expression stony.

Winnie whistles slow and low. "Looks like you've got yourself a regular love triangle," she says, tossing some more clothes on the trash pile. "This is getting fun."

I shoot her a black look, which she ignores.

"Take my advice, Pollyanna," she says. "Don't let a man decide your life for you. Be the captain of your own ship." She tosses a huge white brassiere trimmed with sodden feathers onto the trash pile.

I pause, considering her words. "Winnie, that may be the first thing we've ever agreed on," I say with a touch of irony. Then I force my attention from my disastrous love triangle and the two men who each seem to be occupying some portion of my heart and make myself focus on the task at hand.

Back at the hostel later that night, I listen to a voicemail from my mother as I brush my teeth. I'm still confused by my conversation with Ethan and my interaction with Kai, and I just want to hear her voice. She would know what to do with the mess I've gotten myself into. Oddly, we are actually quite close geographically. Only Romania separates Hungary from Moldova. We're practically neighbors, but right now my parents feel inaccessible to me in their unexpected new life. I miss them.

"Darling!" Her voice sounds bright and a little tinny from a bad connection, as though she's talking to me through an aluminum can. "We got your message. So glad it's going well with the refugees. Your father and I are having an amazing trip. It's truly inspiring to see what this program is doing to help the women and their families." She sounds exuberant, light and happy in a way I've never heard her sound before. There's some static, and her words trail off into garbled nonsense. I hear only the last sentence. "It's going so well we're tempted not to come home." She laughs, but there is something in her tone that makes me pause.

My homebody parents have cast aside every script I had for them and done the unexpected. What if they do indeed stay in Moldova? What would become of the farm? For a moment I picture

West Wind—the old white clapboard farmhouse, the rows of tidy lavender bushes spreading out across the fields, the very soil where I grew up. I want to freeze my family and childhood home in time and space, just for a little bit, so that something feels familiar and predictable. Everything is changing, my past suddenly unsteady, my future topsy-turvy.

I tap water from my toothbrush, suddenly missing my mother with a palpable ache. I need to hear her voice. I need to tell her about Ethan and get her advice. My wise, practical, steady mother will know just what to do.

I wander through the hostel in my pajamas, holding my phone aloft, searching for a stronger signal, and finally get one strong enough to make a call. It goes directly to her voicemail.

"You've reached Meg West's voicemail. I'm in rural Moldova and can only access my messages once a week when I get into town, but leave a message and I'll get back with you next week!"

Dismayed and disappointed, I hang up without leaving a message. How could I possibly explain the complexity of the situation in a few seconds? And by the time she is able to return my call, it will be far too late. I will have made my decision already.

Feeling a little orphaned, I head for bed. My head and heart are a muddle, but it looks like I'm going to have to figure this one out on my own.

Hurrying down the dark, narrow confines of the hostel hall, I clutch my phone, lost in thought. As I pass the men's shower room, the door flies open and Kai steps out into the hall. I startle, glancing up at him. He is bare chested with a towel knotted around his waist, his hair hanging loose around his face. He smells like soap and that spicy scent that makes me think of chai tea and his lips on mine.

"Mia." He looks surprised to see me. I freeze, trying to ignore the fact that he is shirtless again. Why do we have to be so different in height? I'm staring directly at his smoothly defined pecs. It puts me at a disadvantage.

"Kai, hey." I want to run, to make excuses. This is excruciatingly awkward, but I don't move. I can't just pretend nothing is happening. Kai looks down at me in the gloom of the hallway that smells like mildew and grilled sausages.

"Mia, what's going on?" he asks. The question to end all questions.

I stare at him dumbly and shake my head. I have no idea what to tell him. I have no idea what is actually going on.

"It's Ethan," I finally manage to say. "He came for me. He says he made a mistake, and he's asking me to give him another chance."

For a split second an unguarded expression flickers across Kai's face. Disappointment, hurt, betrayal.

"What did you tell him?" he asks.

"Nothing," I admit hesitantly. "I'm so confused."

Kai says nothing, just leans against the doorframe to the bathroom, crosses his arms, and watches me. The words start to trickle out of me, taking me by surprise.

"I don't know what to do," I say, focusing on the brown carpet in the hallway, a safe zone. "He's my first love. I've dreamed for weeks about this very thing happening—him coming for me, saying he'd made a mistake, that what he really wants is me, is us. But now that he's here . . . It's different than I imagined. I'm different. Things have changed." My voice trails away.

"What's changed?" There's a sharp edge to Kai's tone, challenging me to say the words. I glance up at him and then away, thinking of our incendiary kiss in the Tesco aisle, at what it has lit in me, bright and fervent as a struck match.

"Us," I say. "Me. I've changed. I started dreaming different dreams."

Kai straightens. "Like what?" he asks.

I shake my head, doubt creeping into my voice. "I don't know."

Kai stares at me for a long moment, his face set like stone. "You said you wanted better things," he says. "Now's your chance."

"I don't know what I want," I say, a whisper, a confession.

Kai gives me a long, searching look, his expression tinged with challenge and a touch of frustration. "Yes, you do," he says. And then he brushes past me without another word and shuts the door to his room.

I stand there for a moment in the dank hallway, smelling the faintest whiff of cardamom and freshly cut grass. I'm sick with apprehension, with anticipation, with a premonition of the truth.

Chapter 37

One in the morning. I sit up in bed with a groan of frustration, giving up on sleep. My thoughts are buzzing, angry and energetic as bees, around and around in my head. When I close my eyes I feel the agitated vibration of their wings, the ominous hum of their concern rattling my teeth. The bees are trying to tell me something, but I can't pinpoint what it is. I just know something is off-kilter.

With a sigh I throw on a hoodie over my pajamas and tiptoe from the room, making my way through the dark, sleeping hostel. The beer garden is deserted at this hour, and I slump into one of the metal chairs by a small gurgling fountain, trying to clear my mind. The air is warm and soft, the night absolutely still about me. I tip my head back and search the sky for the faint glow of stars, looking for inspiration.

"You okay, sugar?" I whip around, surprised. Rosie is hovering in the doorway, clutching a short silk robe around herself. It's cantaloupe colored with aqua cranes, one of the items from Lars that she did not donate to refugees. She's holding something in her other hand, but I can't quite make it out in the darkness.

"Yes," I say automatically, then shake my head. "No. I'm so confused."

Rosie fumbles along the wall for a moment and finds the

light switch, illuminating the garden in festive, soft-colored lights strung in long swoops through the spreading trees overhead. She sinks into a chair across from me and sets a small turquoise-striped box in the middle of the table. A Trophy cupcake box.

"For clarity," she explains. "It's hummingbird."

I lift the lid, amazed. "Where in the world did you get this?"

Rosie shoots me an opaque look. "Ethan brought it for you, a peace offering. He gave it to me after our shift today and asked me to give it to you."

I lift the cupcake from the box. Its coconut-dusted frosting is only slightly smashed at one edge. It is a thoughtful gesture.

"Share it with me?" I tear it gently, handing her half.

She sighs and leans back in the chair, nibbling the edge of the cupcake. "So what are you going to do?"

"I don't know." I bite into my half, the buttery frosting a generous inch tall. Butter and sugar always have a comforting quality. Let's hope tonight they also have revelatory powers. "You have any bright ideas?" My words are gummy with frosting.

Rosie shakes her head, her hair cascading like a living flame around her shoulders. "I think it comes down to what you really want." She licks frosting from her upper lip.

"I don't know what I want," I say without thinking, then stop. That isn't really true. I want it all, Ethan, Kai, and this new, unexpected life.

I glance over at the chair next to me, picturing Ethan sitting there, the bright gold of his head bent over his guitar. He's laughing at something, and I can see the dimple in his cheek. He looks so young, like the day we first met, when everything was possible and likely and filled with promise. My heart constricts just a little.

Maybe I'm being too shortsighted. Am I throwing away a perfectly good thing because of some idyllic daydream, the lure of the unknown? Maybe we can make it work, both get what we want from life. After all, he gave up moving to San Jose for me. We could still have it, the life we've dreamed of for so many years, with tweaks to accommodate this new direction I'm going, the new Mia. I do miss Ethan. I still care for him. I don't feel the quicksilver in the veins like I do with Kai, but when I look at Ethan I feel instead a tenderness, a gentle familiarity. We've spent so many years together, lived so much of life side by side. He is a part of me, of my life, and I can't ignore that.

"Ethan says we can compromise, that we can make it all work." I sigh.

"But you're not so sure," Rosie correctly surmises, giving me a thoughtful look.

I nod. "I have to think about it logically, not just give in to nostalgia and emotion. Could a compromise really work? Could we both get the life we want?" I scoop up a little frosting and consider the question. Yes, it could work if Ethan were more adventurous. If he could just develop his sense of social justice. If he longed for travel the way I do.

And then suddenly I see it. The truth, pure and simple.

If Ethan changed in all the ways I just listed, the ways I need him to change if we are going to make a life together now, he would not be himself; he would no longer be Ethan. With a jolt, I realize I am describing someone else entirely.

"It's not possible," I say slowly, with a dawning understanding. "I can't have Ethan and this new life. They don't fit together."

Rosie looks over at me, her expression sympathetic. "I know, sugar," she says gently. "I'm sorry."

Sitting in the empty patio that smells of spilled beer and cigarette smoke, my fingers sticky with hummingbird frosting, I know in my gut that I have made a decision. I want to share a grand adventure of a life with someone, but that someone is not Ethan. The life I want to live is no longer a life we can share.

In an instant I see the entire timespan of our love flashing before me. The moment I first laid eyes on him in line at Wow Bubble Tea. That dimple and his endearing smile. The way he would kiss the corner of my mouth and hold me to his chest, spinning us in a slow circle, humming "How Sweet It Is" in his best James Taylor impression.

I think of the little Craftsman cottage on Green Lake, waking up next to Ethan in the gray of a Seattle morning. Some other couple will live there now. Of Sunday mornings grabbing coffee and a morning bun at the Butter Emporium. Of the Frenchie named Butterworth. A life I will never have. A life I no longer want.

I sink my head into my arms on the table, feeling slightly sick with grief and frosting. "It's over," I murmur softly, tears springing to my eyes.

Rosie reaches across the table and places her hand on my head, a gesture of solidarity and comfort, a benediction.

"What about Kai?" she asks me.

I raise my head and look at her. "What about him?"

She slants me a knowing look. "I've seen how you look at him when you think he isn't watching. I've seen how he looks at you too. You're like magnets. You can't keep away from each other."

"We're just friends," I lie.

Rosie rolls her eyes. "Girl, you think I just fell off the turnip truck? You just keep telling yourself that."

"I'm scared," I admit bluntly. "I gave up everything for Ethan, including my own dreams. I'm scared I'll do the same thing again for a different man."

Rosie licks a curl of shaved coconut from the tip of her finger. "But Kai isn't Ethan," she says.

I nod. "I know, but I'm still so afraid I'll lose myself again if I give my heart away. I think I might love him. I'm in trouble."

Rosie tips her head and considers me for a moment. "It's only trouble if it leads you somewhere you don't want to go," she says finally. "Kai's a good man. He put himself between you and a shark. Remember."

I nod. "I like Kai so much that it scares me, but I have to figure out what I want first, just me. And I have to tell Ethan it's over."

As I say the words I feel a glimmer of relief, of excitement beneath the grief that lies like an oil slick on my heart. It fizzes up from the center of my chest like champagne bubbles, like joy. The buzzing in my ears stops abruptly, leaving a ringing silence, an empty calm. I know I have made the right decision. I cannot rewind time and go back to before, to who I was and what I chose the last time. And I cannot throw myself into another relationship before I know how to stand on my own two feet, before I know what this new Mia really wants in life.

I crumple the cupcake wrapper and stand, brushing the bits of shaved coconut from my pajamas. I am exhausted but peaceful. I will tell Ethan the news in the morning. In my heart I know I am making the right choice. In saying no to this old, good thing, I am saying yes to something even better.

Chapter 38

"Can I talk to you for a minute?" I find Ethan at the food tent during our midmorning break. The medical tent has been too busy for me to step away until now, and I've been dreading this conversation all morning.

"Sure, of course." Ethan sets down the apples he is sorting, his expression hopeful and a little nervous. I hate what I am about to do to him. He follows me from the tent, and I see Kai out of the corner of my eye standing at the drinks station watching us. We lock eyes for an instant before he turns away. I resolutely focus on the task at hand, ignoring all else. This isn't about Kai. This is about Ethan and me and all that we were and are not and will never now be.

It's hard to find privacy in the camp, and we finally have to settle for a secluded patch of ground behind the Porta-Potties. It's not the dignified setting I would have chosen. The end of a love should be poetic, not smelling like fetid human waste, not in a dry circle of grass next to two blue portable toilets.

We sit side by side, and I take a deep breath. I think for one brief moment of the other life I could have had, the one I am about to destroy forever. I look up and meet Ethan's eyes, those beautiful, familiar blue eyes. Ethan sees the truth on my face before I open my mouth.

"Mia." He puts a hand up as though to ward off what is coming, but I cannot be stopped.

"No," I say, my mouth trembling. "I'm sorry, Ethan. I can't come back to you. Not now, not ever. It's over."

He stares at me for a moment, and I see that he is both surprised and hurt. He thought I would return to him. Somehow the realization steels my resolve.

"Our futures don't fit together anymore," I say. "*We* don't fit together anymore."

"But we can compromise," Ethan protests, spreading his hands, using his best negotiator tone. "We can make this work. If we want something enough, we can make anything work."

I look at him, really look at him. Six years have changed him, changed us both. I notice for the first time that his hair is starting to thin at the top. I swallow the hard lump in my throat, as big as a duck egg; this is so bittersweet. Choosing to let a good thing go in order to make room for something better is harder than I anticipated. And scary. So very scary.

What if I never find love again? What if I am cutting myself free only to end up alone in this new life? It is a risk I have to be okay taking. No more guarantees, just wide open, endless possibility. And hopefully better things at last.

"That's just it," I whisper. "I know we could probably make it work, limp along, neither of us quite getting what we want. Maybe it would be good enough. But I don't want good enough. Not anymore."

He looks pained, suddenly comprehending the ramification of my words. It is truly over. I am guessing he never dreamed he'd be going home without me.

"Are you sure?" he asks. He isn't angry. He just looks sad.

I nod. I don't know exactly what I have just set in motion, but I know it is right. "Yes."

"Okay." Ethan nods. His tone is quiet, defeated. He rubs the bridge of his nose and sighs. The gesture is so familiar I have to bite back a sudden sob. What am I doing, letting this good man go? How can I let him just walk out of my life?

The only thing worse would be letting him stay.

Ethan reaches for me then, and I lean into his arms almost without thinking, out of habit. He enfolds me in a hug, and I start to cry. He rubs my back, a brief, familiar gesture of comfort.

Out of the corner of my eye I see Rosie flit by, casting us a sympathetic glance. A few seconds later Jake follows, his video camera pointed in our direction. I ignore him and bury my head in Ethan's shoulder. This is not fodder for the public. This is a private moment, a farewell to this man who held my heart for so many years. He smells of butterscotch candy, of first love, of my youth.

After a moment Ethan kisses the top of my head, then releases me and stands. I stand too. It is the last time I will feel his arms around me. I know this for sure. The knowledge makes me cry harder. Ethan's eyes are suspiciously pink, but he holds it together. "Be safe, Mia. Be well. I hope this life is everything you want it to be."

I nod wordlessly, tears streaming down my face. "You too," I manage to choke out. "Now you can move to San Jose. You can have the life you really want."

Ethan smiles sadly. "I would have given it all up for you," he says.

I nod wordlessly, crying harder. He turns and walks resolutely to the food tent. I see him talking to Laszlo, and a moment later he makes the rounds of the volunteers. It looks as though he is leaving. He gives Rosie a brief, awkward hug, shakes hands with Milo and Abel. When he gets to Kai he pauses, reaching up and clasping him on the shoulder. They exchange a few words, and then Ethan gets into the white van with Laszlo and drives away.

I watch him leave with a feeling of disbelief. From the food tent Rosie approaches me, her shoes crunching over the dry grass.

"You okay, sugar?" She stands next to me, and together we watch the van until it disappears from sight.

"I told him I couldn't go back," I say, almost in disbelief. "It's over."

She nods sadly and puts her arm around me. "Still think you did the right thing?"

"Yeah, I do . . ." I swallow hard but don't say anything further. In some way I feel like my heart is newly broken, but at the same time it is liberated too. Like a butterfly from a cocoon, a chick from an egg, my heart had to crack open to be set free.

~

Later that day I run into Kai as I leave the medical tent for a quick break. He's just coming in the tent door, and we almost collide. I step to the side quickly, confused and disoriented for a moment by his nearness. I stuff my hands in my pockets and try to act normal.

"Hey," I say, going for nonchalant.

"Hey." He holds out a stack of thin fleece blankets. "Delphine asked for these." He's wearing his Willy Nelson T-shirt, and he looks so uncertain that my heart squeezes with longing. *Stay strong, West*, I tell myself sternly. *Don't go there.*

"Thanks." I take the blankets and turn to go.

"Mia." His eyes search my face with concern. "Are you okay?"

For a moment I don't respond. "Yeah, I think I am," I say slowly, still a little amazed. I meet his eyes. "I did it. I chose better things."

He watches me intently, as though trying to divine the meaning behind my words. "Good," he says, but his expression is guarded.

I hurt him when Ethan arrived, I realize. We shared a kiss, there was a promise of something starting between us, and then I abandoned him as soon as Ethan showed up. What did Kai tell me during our dinner in Mumbai? That his greatest fear was of getting hurt, of trusting someone only to be let down. I've let him down. The realization gives me a pang of regret.

"I'm sorry . . ." I hesitate. How do I say this to him? "I'm sorry if I hurt you. I was so confused when Ethan showed up. I didn't know how to handle things well."

He shrugs, dismissing it. "It's okay. I get it." He looks at me. "So what happens now?" he asks, and I know he means us.

"I don't know," I say slowly, carefully. I want to be honest but not say too much or too little. Part of me wants to reassure him, regain his trust again, but I can't make promises I cannot keep. "I just knew I couldn't be with Ethan. Now I need space and time to figure out what comes next on my own. I spent so many years making decisions with someone else in mind. I have to learn what I want, just me."

"Are you sure?" he asks finally. His eyes are intent on mine, filled with questions he isn't asking.

"Yeah, I am." I nod, hoping he understands. This is not a rejection; it's a necessity. I have to know what I want before I can choose a companion for the journey.

"Okay," he says, a note of resignation in his voice, a wariness. Something shifts when he looks at me, something shutters in his eyes. Suddenly the inches between us feel huge.

"I hope you find everything you're looking for," he says. The statement feels scarily like a goodbye.

"Wait, Kai." I suddenly panic that I have inadvertently closed the door too soon on him. I don't want to lose him, but I know I cannot dive into another relationship, not yet. "I just need some time and space to figure things out," I repeat.

"Sure, I get it." He meets my eyes. "But Mia, I'm an all-or-nothing kind of guy. I can't do this halfway, you understand?"

"Yes," I say, feeling chastened and deflated.

"I'd better get back to my station." He turns to go.

"Hey." I stop him. "What did Ethan say to you when he left?" I've been so curious since I saw them together this morning, Ethan's hand on Kai's shoulder, his lips forming words I couldn't decipher.

Kai pauses, then looks up at the sky for a moment. "He said only a fool would let you go," he says at last, turning his gaze to me, his own dark and inscrutable. "He told me not to be a fool."

I open my mouth but have no idea what to say. Wordlessly, he turns and walks away.

Chapter 39

"Your sister is improving but isn't well enough to travel yet," Delphine announces later that evening, draping her stethoscope around her neck after listening to Maryam's lungs. Maryam is our last patient before Stefan starts his night shift.

Yousef nods, looking discouraged. "I see." They have been coming for daily checkups and hope to board a bus to Sweden any day now.

"Perhaps another few days of rest and lots of fluids," Delphine encourages. "She will be well soon."

I often see Maryam and Yousef around camp, standing in line at the food tent for breakfast or sitting together under their oak tree. Maryam always waves and smiles as though we are old friends. Yousef is constantly caring for his sister, plying her with bottled water and urging her to rest. Most of the refugees that were here when we arrived have moved on by now, but not Maryam and Yousef, not yet.

After they leave, Delphine asks me to refill the supplies before Stefan starts his shift. When I return carrying bottles of water, baby wipes, and medicines, I find the tent unexpectedly empty. I restock the rolling supply cart and exit the stifling confines of the tent, searching for Delphine.

The temperature has dropped after sunset, and a fresh breeze is blowing over the fields, bringing the scent of turned earth and growing things. The camp is quieting, people settling down for the night in tents or in the woods. I finally spy Delphine on a grassy knoll between the medical tent and a field of sugar beets.

As I approach I see just her outline, a blotch of white doctor's coat in the soft gloom. She is sitting with one arm slung over her knees. The glowing orange tip of a lit cigarette in her hand surprises me. She's a doctor. Surely she knows how harmful a habit smoking can be. She doesn't acknowledge me until I am just a few feet away.

"You smoke?" I can't quite keep the note of disapproval from my voice.

She chuckles low in her throat. "I'm French," she says. She gestures to a spot on the trampled grass beside her, and I sit facing the camp, clasping my arms across my legs. It feels good to rest. We spend long hours standing every day, and my feet ache constantly. Neither of us speaks. I hope I'm not intruding, but she doesn't seem to mind.

I see the white van roll slowly back down the lane. Kai and Milo returning from a Tesco run, bringing fruit and fresh bread for the morning. Kai turns the van so that the headlights shine on the food tent, and the other volunteers begin to unload.

"So what are you going to do now?" Delphine asks me suddenly, breaking into my contemplation.

"About what?"

She takes a draw of the cigarette. "You said goodbye to the man you loved today."

"Oh." I'm embarrassed that she knows about it. I'm sure the entire roster of volunteers was talking about it today, maybe the whole camp. "Yeah, I did." I feel the prickle of hot tears and an unexpected swell of sorrow.

"So . . . ?" She seems genuinely curious.

"I don't know," I answer honestly. "I just knew I couldn't go back to the girl I was and the life we'd planned together. I've changed, and now I've got to figure out what I want to do with this new life, this new me." I blink and swallow hard.

Delphine nods, grinding out her cigarette on the ground. "Well, whatever you decide to do, please do not consider medicine as a good option."

"What?" I gape at her, caught between a laugh and a gasp. "What do you mean?"

She smirks. "Szilvia told me you were interested in medicine. It's why she sent you to my tent. After two days I told Stefan I've never seen someone less suited to medicine in my entire life."

"Hey now," I protest, but she holds up her hand.

"But I also have rarely met someone as kind and selfless as you, Mia. It is a rare thing, a beautiful thing, to have a heart that is as open as yours is. Protect that gift."

"Thank you," I mumble, touched by the praise. "You're right. I hate medicine. I can't think of anything I'd rather do less." I hesitate then confess. "I lied on my application because I thought what I actually love to do isn't impressive enough."

"Hah," Delphine laughs softly. "So what is it that you really love?"

"Something that doesn't feel big enough, important enough," I say. The rest of my team is emptying the van, illuminated in the headlights as they carry and organize. Kai hands out the supplies to waiting arms. Winnie hefts two crates of fruit with ease while Abel unloads pallets of bottled water and stacks them like a game of Jenga.

"I love to bake. I love everything about it—measuring the ingredients, working the dough, the smell of tasty things baking in the oven. I love giving people something that I made with my own hands, something that makes them happy. But it feels foolish to love baking when things like this are happening all around me."

I gesture out across the camp. "I can't bake cookies while the world burns."

In the glow of the headlights, Milo stops and juggles oranges for a group of children who clap and laugh delightedly.

"Eh." Delphine tips her head, a Gallic gesture of polite disagreement. "It's true, a cookie is a small thing, but many small things make the world a brighter and happier place, do they not? Perhaps I am biased. In France we take our bread and pastry very seriously. It is the stuff of life. It brings people together around the table, it sustains our bodies and our souls. That is no light matter. It is the essence of a good life, *non*? I think these small things can change the world for good."

I've never thought of it that way, that food can bring people together, nourish body and soul. *Small things can change the world for good.* I like that phrase. It rings true.

"Hmm." I tip my head and consider her words. For the first time in a long time I wonder if perhaps baking *isn't* too flippant, just a pastime or a hobby while I'm waiting to discover my real calling in life. Maybe there's more to it than I've realized. Could it really be enough?

Two days later we have happy news to deliver.

"Congratulations." Delphine straightens and drapes her stethoscope around her neck. She grins at Maryam, who is perched on the edge of the examination table. "You are well enough to travel now."

Yousef beams and Maryam claps her hands excitedly when he translates Delphine's pronouncement.

"It is Maryam's birthday on Friday," he explains. "We hope to leave on a bus before then. It would be a great gift knowing we are on our way to our new home."

I smile at their excitement. It feels good to be able to share in some happy news. The last few days since Ethan's departure have passed in a monotonous blur. The camp numbers continue to swell with more people arriving every day and only a bus or two leaving sporadically. The line outside the medical tent stretches long at all hours of the day. I put my head down and work until I am numb from exhaustion, glad for the chance to not think about what I have done, glad to ignore my bruised heart.

I have not seen Kai except in passing. Once or twice I look up from a hasty meal to find his eyes on me, his expression wary and opaque, but he does not approach me, and I do not seek him out. I have made my decision. I need to figure things out for myself first. Kai is . . . too tempting. It would be so easy to just fall head over heels in love with him, but then I could end up back where I started, piggybacking on someone else's dreams. I have to make my own way first, and then I can focus on matters of the heart.

Chapter 40

"Yousef, Maryam!" Early Friday morning I spot the pair standing exactly where I left them last night. I shift the white bakery box in my arms and wave. It's been three days since Delphine cleared them to travel, and they have been waiting in the long line every day since, hoping for space on a bus to the Austrian border. A few times a day I stop to chat with them, spending a few minutes trying to make them laugh and relieving the tedium of their long hours of inactivity.

But this morning is different. It is Maryam's birthday, and I have a surprise for her. Holding the cardboard box with its precious cargo, I head toward the siblings and stifle a yawn. I was up late using the restaurant kitchen (with the hostel owner's permission) to make a carrot cake with cream cheese frosting from ingredients I scrounged up at Tesco.

Even using unfamiliar units of measure and an oven marked in centigrade, I loved being back in the kitchen. I stifle another yawn. Definitely need some tea at the break, if I can make it that long without caffeine.

When I reach them, Maryam throws her arms around me, hugging me fiercely.

"Happy birthday, lovely girl. It will be your turn soon." I kiss her cheek. They are only a dozen or so people back from the front of the line. Surely they will get a seat on the next bus out.

"Look." Yousef points to the three buses that rolled down the lane early this morning. A handful of policemen in navy blue uniforms and jaunty blue caps guard the buses while others gesture people forward in line and direct them to find seats inside. Two are already full, and the last one is being loaded now. "They will leave for the Austrian border as soon as they are full." Yousef looks hopeful. "Perhaps we go today, a birthday present for Maryam."

Maryam nods excitedly, her eyes eager.

The line inches forward a little.

"I bet you'll get on today," I encourage them. Now there are just two groups in front of them. The last bus looks like it is filling fast, but surely there will be space for the two of them. A cluster of young men are allowed to board. Now they are second in line. The young family in front of them is allowed onto the bus.

"We are next," Yousef says, beaming with relief. "Finally."

The police officer gestures them forward, and Maryam squeals with excitement. Yousef gives their names and documents to the officer, who glances at the bus behind him, then frowns and shakes his head. "No room," he says, pointing back toward the camp. "You wait."

"But we've been waiting for three days," Yousef protests. "We are going to Sweden. Our sister is there."

The officer shakes his head, granite-faced, and gestures back toward the camp. "No more room. You wait."

Beside me, Maryam bursts into tears, covering her face with her hands. They've already been here far longer than anyone else because of her illness. Now there will be another interminable delay, and on her birthday. It seems doubly disappointing. I peer up at the bus and through a back window spy two empty seats.

"There's space," I tell the officer, pointing, surprised by my own boldness. "They can fit."

The officer doesn't look behind him, just shakes his head. "You wait," he says.

Yousef puts his arm around a sobbing Maryam. On impulse I lift the lid of the box and hold it out to the officer in what I hope is a tempting manner.

"Are you sure there isn't space for them?" I ask sweetly, before I have a chance to reconsider my course of action. *What are you doing?* a voice in my head shrieks. *Are you really trying to bribe a Hungarian police officer with a carrot cake?* I almost pull the box back, mortified, but before I can do so, the officer peers into the box and then looks up at me, his face stern. For a moment we lock eyes.

"My mistake. There is room," the officer says abruptly, closing the box and taking it from me. He places the cake gently at his feet. For a moment I gape at him, flabbergasted that my harebrained scheme worked. Maryam shrieks with joy, and Yousef clasps my hand warmly, his face alight with relief.

"Thank you," he whispers.

"Happy birthday," I murmur in Maryam's ear, hugging her tightly. *Well, what do you know?* I think as I step back. *See, Aunt Frannie, sometimes baked goods really can change the world.*

"Go," I urge them, "before the policeman decides he doesn't like carrot cake." Yousef grabs their backpack of meager belongings, and they run for the bus.

"Wait!" I scramble in my satchel and find an old airline ticket, quickly scribbling the address of Nana Alice's cottage on it. I run after them and thrust it into Yousef's hand just before they board. "Send me a postcard when you're settled in Sweden."

He takes the paper and tucks it carefully into his pocket. "We will," he says solemnly. "Goodbye, Mia. Thank you."

I watch them until they are settled in their seats, until Maryam presses her face to the window and blows me a kiss, until the bus pulls away, carrying them toward the Austrian border and the new life ahead of them. They are carrying with them a little piece of my heart.

When I imagined this trip, imagined a life of service like Mother Teresa's, somehow I didn't factor in the people I would meet. I pictured how I would touch their lives, but I never thought about how they would touch mine. Yousef and Maryam have become friends.

Watching the bus trundle down the rutted lane in a cloud of dust, I think of Shreya's words that first day in the slums in Mumbai. *If we want to help people,* she told me, *we must enter into their lives, be a part of their community. That is where real change happens, person to person, day by day, when we live life together.*

How right she was. In some small way I have changed Yousef's and Maryam's lives, if only with a carrot cake and friendship. And by their friendship they have changed my life too.

CHAPTER 41

"The buses are coming back from the border!" A few hours later a Hungarian student volunteer pokes her head into the medical tent where I am helping Delphine weigh a chunky Afghani infant. "Austria did not let them through," she exclaims breathlessly.

Delphine and I glance at one another in puzzlement as the girl dashes off to tell others the news. Austria didn't let them through? What does this mean?

An hour later all three buses return to the camp with every passenger on board. They were turned back at the Austrian border, the drivers tells Szilvia. A new regulation is in effect as of this morning. Refugees must now register in the country where they first enter the Schengen Area. For everyone at the camp, this means registering in Hungary. They are stuck at the border until further notice.

The refugees file off the buses, faces tight with worry and frustration. An older woman weeps into her hands, falling to the ground outside of the bus steps as her son and daughter-in-law try to comfort her.

My heart sinks when I see Maryam and Yousef disembark from the last bus. Maryam glances up and sees me. She waves but does not smile. Yousef's expression is crestfallen.

I hurry over to them. "I'm sure they'll get it sorted out soon," I say, hoping I'm right. "Come on, it's almost lunchtime. You should eat something." They follow me to the food tent wordlessly, dazed and disconsolate.

At the food tent the volunteers are scrambling to organize a quick meal for more than a hundred people we thought we would never see again. I work feverishly alongside Rosie and Winnie, handing out meager allotments of food.

"Last of the cucumbers," Kai reports as we eye the long line snaking around the tent. Then ten minutes later. "One bag of apples left."

"I'll post an update on Facebook asking for supplies," Szilvia says, already whipping out her phone.

"I'll drive to Tesco and get what we need before dinner," Kai volunteers. He hasn't looked at me once since I got to the tent. It's become the new normal, and it makes me so sad.

We work late that day, far past dark, helping people get resettled and organizing for the morning.

At the end of my shift, I make the rounds of the other tents, gathering items to restock the medical tent for Stefan's shift. When I return, arms full of supplies, I find Delphine outside the door, leaning against one of the poles, smoking. I can just see the outline of her face. She is sober, preoccupied. I quickly put the items away inside and join her.

"You know those things aren't good for you, right?" I ask, only half in jest.

"Of course," she says in her sleek accent. "I know they are bad for my health." She waves away my silent consternation. "But so is war, so is displacement, so is treating patient after patient with insufficient supplies. This world is bad for my health." She sighs heavily.

I lean against the other tent pole and say nothing. She's right. A woman passes nearby, leading a small child by the hand toward the woods, a thin stack of blankets in her arms. It is chilly tonight, and many families are sleeping in the open. There were clouds earlier, piled up against a fiery orange sunset. I cross my fingers and pray against rain. There is no shelter for those who are sleeping outside. The camp is already at capacity, with more people arriving all the time. In addition to the three busloads of returned refugees, more are coming down the railroad tracks every few minutes. This evening the police patrol the edges of the camp, trying to ensure that no one leaves before they can be registered, although it is unclear how the registration process is supposed to happen.

"This is going to end badly," Delphine says, taking a draw on the cigarette. "I can feel it."

"What do you mean?" I ask, following her gaze across the camp, over the tents and groups of people bedding down in the open for the night.

"This crisis." She gestures with the cigarette. "It will end badly if the governments cannot come up with a better plan to handle the people who are coming. No one is prepared. But still they come. They will continue to come. We must be ready for them." She sighs and glances at me. "This is just the start, you know. They will move on from here in a day or week or month, and then the real work begins. How to house them and feed them and teach them a new language and find them employment. How do we help them become at home in Europe? It is a very difficult thing. Some would say an impossible thing."

"I've never thought about that." The crisis is what people are talking about. The news is full of it, the perils of the journey, families fleeing for their lives from war-torn countries and bombed-out cities, crossing the turbulent water in overcrowded rubber boats. But Delphine is right. Their perilous journey is just the beginning. The harder work begins once they reach their destinations. What will it take to integrate thousands of displaced people into their new countries? Many are traumatized. Most have suffered great loss. Who will help them navigate a new language and culture and learn to make it their home? How long will it take?

"Do you think it's possible?" I ask.

She laughs, a puff of air through her nose. "*Oui*," she says after a moment. "I am proof that it is possible. My father, my mother, a cross-cultural marriage. And me, I am a French woman to the bone although Tunisian blood runs through my veins. It is possible, but it is a long and difficult thing." She gestures to the camp, to the tents. "They are not ready. We are not ready. No one has any idea what is coming."

After my shift, armed with a carafe of tea and a flashlight, I seek out Maryam and Yousef. Dots of light spread out around the rest of the camp as other volunteers take tea to the restless, disappointed occupants. I find the brother and sister under the oak tree once more, their makeshift home a jumble of blankets and their scanty belongings.

Yousef sits with his head in his hands, Maryam hovering beside him. They look up at my arrival, their expressions bleak.

"Here, I brought some tea." I crouch down next to them and pour tea into three disposable cups, spooning a generous quantity of sugar into Maryam's, leaving Yousef's black, the way he prefers it.

They take the tea, and we sip in silence for a few moments.

"We were so close," Yousef says, closing his eyes as though it pains him to speak the words.

"I know. I'm so sorry." No amount of carrot cake can help them leave this place now. There are no buses, no open border. We do not know what will happen next, but for now they are stuck here. Everyone is stuck here.

"Maybe they'll open the border again soon," I say, trying for optimism. "They'll figure out what to do." I sincerely hope I am right, though Laszlo does not seem hopeful. His opinion of the European government's efficacy is low.

Yousef toys with his cup of tea, rolling the liquid around the inside. "What if Sweden will not take us? We have nowhere else to go." I hear a thread of panic in his voice. He glances at Maryam, who watches us worriedly, trying to follow the conversation in English. "I just want a safe place for my sister, a country where we can try to make our home again."

"You'll find it." I cup my hands around my tea, feeling the warmth spreading through my fingers. The early summer night is soft around us, alive with the sound of insects and the low murmur of voices. "It may take some time, but you'll find it. I know you will. Don't give up."

Yousef smiles grimly. "If only you were in charge of the policies, we would all be home already, Mia."

"I'd bake carrot cakes for every EU country and—*voilà!*—citizenship for everyone!"

Maryam giggles, understanding enough to get the joke.

"You are right," Yousef says. "We cannot despair. Even in the darkness, we must have hope."

"Do you still hope?" I ask, curious. I think of his father, strung up for refusing to convert, and his mother, struck down in the street by the grief and shock. After what Maryam and Yousef have endured and seen and lost, I'm surprised they have any hope left.

"Yes," Yousef says slowly, as though testing the word himself. "As long as there is breath in my body, I must choose to hope, for Maryam, for a new life."

He glances at Maryam, and she takes his hand, holding his knuckles to her cheek for a moment, her face sad. Yousef briefly touches her face, then turns to me.

"Thank you for helping us, Mia, for being our friend. With you here, we do not feel so alone."

"Of course." I wave away the thanks. "You are not alone, and you will get to your new home. I know it."

Yousef smiles, a brief, sad smile. "Then we will wait for this miracle. Even when we do not see the way. We will wait and hope."

Chapter 42

The next few days pass in a blur of exhaustion and activity. No buses leave the camp, and the police are tasked with making sure everyone stays put while the government works out a way to register and process the new arrivals.

Every morning the volunteers gather in the food tent while Laszlo briefs us on the latest developments. He has a friend who works in the Hungarian parliament and keeps him abreast of any new developments.

"Austria and Germany are threatening to shut their borders," he tells us grimly. "The Hungarian government is scared they will get stuck with all these refugees." He gestures to the sprawling camp that has grown larger even just overnight. "So Hungary is threatening to close the borders too. Effective today, only Syrians can come through the Hungarian border and register, and only a few at a time."

"What happens to anyone who isn't from Syria?" Kai asks from behind me. There are many Syrians in the camp, but also Iraqis, Afghanis, Kosovars, Albanians, even a few men from Bangladesh and countries in Africa. Most can't go back to their home countries. What is the alternative if they are not allowed to continue their journey, if Hungary kicks them out? Where in the world will they go?

Laszlo shrugs. "No one knows. But for now, we must concentrate on helping where we can. Only a few Syrians can leave this camp, but more refugees arrive every hour. We need to be ready for many more to come."

His words are prescient. Morning and night, people arrive, filling the camp still further and stretching our already meager resources. The camp swells gradually, the boundaries sprawling out into a neighboring field and the surrounding woods to accommodate the growing numbers.

Some of the refugees do not wait for the government to figure out what to do with them. They take matters into their own hands and go through illegal channels to reach their destinations.

"See those men?" Delphine points them out to me as we pay a call to a mother and newborn in one of the far tents. The small group of men is standing just outside the bounds of the camp, half hidden by trees.

"Who are they?"

"Smugglers. Pay them a few thousand euros and they promise to get you to Germany." She swears elegantly in French, her expression disgusted. "We must warn people not to go with them. They are dangerous men who care nothing for these lives. Sometimes they put the people in refrigerated trucks, packed in like little fish. It is very dangerous. It could be their death."

I glance at the men, at their wary faces and hard eyes.

I've seen more than one group of people disappear into the woods when the police are not looking and not return. I think of the refugees' desperation, their hunger to reach a safe haven, and I understand why they would take the risk.

The atmosphere in the camp has changed since the buses returned. People are confused, scared. Rumors fly thick and fast. Tensions mount with each passing hour.

The police, too, are wary now, hands always on the guns at

their hips, eyes alert. More and more police arrive at the camp, dressed in black riot gear with helmets and protective shields. The news vans multiply, and reporters mark time at the periphery of the camp, interviewing people as they pass, looking for an angle, for a story. Everyone is on edge, waiting for something no one can quite define.

"I do not like this," Delphine mutters darkly as we leave the tent after checking on the new mother and baby. "I've seen this before. Fear breeds violence. We need to be ready." She begins to stockpile medicine, bandages, bottled water.

The next morning Szilvia announces at our volunteer briefing, "We have to start limiting food now. Last night we ran out of bread, cheese, and milk. Some people went away empty-handed."

Kai and Milo made a late-night Tesco run and restocked the food tent, using Lars' generosity and credit card to buy the most essential items, but by lunchtime today we will be in the same situation again. Szilvia continues to make a daily plea on social media, and donated supplies are still arriving from around Hungary and beyond, but the amount of time, energy, and material goods needed to keep the camp going with the swelling population is daunting.

"This camp is not equipped to handle even a quarter of this population," Delphine observes a day or two later, glancing out the door of the tent at the sprawling mess. "This is a human rights violation. The EU should be ashamed." She continues her diatribe against governmental policy, rattling off lengthy phrases in French, only a smattering of which I understand.

I study the camp for a moment, feeling unease ripple in the pit of my stomach. It is just a field with a few tents. There are no showers, no running water, no facilities to make people comfortable. Trash piles up thick on the ground. Sick babies wail day and night. The lines for the medical tent stretch all the way across the dirt lane from morning till evening. We are struggling to keep the peace, keep people comfortable, meet the most basic needs, but it is not enough.

The atmosphere is growing increasingly tense and ugly. The air crackles with discontent and mounting unrest day by day. Volunteers and supplies are stretched thinner and thinner. There is no relief. I go about my duties at a frantic pace, a little knot of panic lodged in my throat, sharp as a peach pit. We sleep little and work late, dropping into our beds leaden from fatigue. I dream of agitated bees, of storm clouds rolling across the wide bowl of the sky, of lightning spiking down into fallow fields, of rain that smells like home, salty and cold like the sea.

"Kai, we need more bread." It's lunchtime and I'm manning the sandwich station with Rosie. Delphine has started lending me to the food tent during meals because it's usually a slow time at the medical tent and there are a huge number of people who have to be fed now.

I reach into the bread bin and hand a swarthy young man in a hoodie the last roll. There are still dozens of people waiting to be served. "Kai?"

Kai comes up behind me. "No more bread," he says, pitching his voice low so only I can hear. "We're out."

"I'm sorry," I tell a haggard-looking father and son next in line. "No more bread."

The dozens of hungry, frustrated people still waiting react badly to the shortage. "They can't keep us here like animals," a young man in a red windbreaker protests from halfway back in the line. "We want to go to Germany."

Others echo his sentiment, the entire group stirring, muttering. A few more young men call out, "Germany, let us go to Germany."

"Here, give them granola bars." Kai grabs a box and sets it down on the table in front of me. Beside me Rosie is prepping portions of fruit and cheese as fast as she can, as though an apple and a triangle of processed cheese will stem the tide of discontent. Nervously I grab a handful of granola bars, my hands shaking as I sense the crowd's frustration. It is not our fault. We are only trying to help.

"Give us bread," someone calls from the back of the line, and the crowd takes up the chant. "Bread, bread, bread."

"We're out," Winnie yells back, angrily, brandishing a cucumber at the protesters. "Stop whining and shut up."

Kai moves to stand between Rosie and me, his presence solid and steadying. "If this escalates, go find Laszlo and get in the van," he murmurs to us, his mouth set in a flat line as he surveys the disgruntled lunch line. I think of the bull shark in Florida. Once again Kai is putting himself between me and danger, although this time we're not even really speaking to one another. I'm grateful for him beside me, comforted by the sense of wary calm he projects.

"Stop! Stand back." A few police officers come running, hands on their guns, their faces stern. Quickly the fervor dies down to a discontented murmur. Within minutes, under the policemen's watchful eyes, the lunch line resumes its slow shuffle forward.

"Are you okay?" Kai asks, touching my shoulder, his forehead creased with concern.

I take a deep breath and nod. "Yeah, thanks. That was scary." I hand a large family from Afghanistan a fistful of granola bars.

He nods. "It happened fast."

Winnie *hmphs* and scowls at each person as they pass. "Ingrates," she mutters.

Crisis averted, Kai retreats to his supply station behind us. I dole out granola bars, buzzing with adrenaline, relieved and ashamed of feeling relieved. Since when did we become the enemy to these people? Without us there would be nothing for them in this camp but mud.

"Oh my goodness, that was intense," Rosie whispers. "Do you think we're in danger?"

"I don't know." I feel on edge now, seeing how quickly things can turn ugly. "We just need to keep our eyes open, I guess." I swallow hard, trying to tamp down my rising sense of unease, and keep handing out granola bars until the last person in line has been served.

Although the unrest at the lunch line is quelled quickly, it reveals the true state of the camp. The air is thick with fear and frustration, a potent mixture that seems to pulse stronger with every passing hour. Every day a handful of Syrians are taken to a processing station by bus. They do not return, presumably allowed to travel on to their intended destinations. As for the rest of the camp, they are going nowhere.

Delphine presses her lips together and shakes her sleek dark head when I tell her what happened at lunch. "The pressure is building," she says warningly. "This will not hold."

Chapter 43

Delphine's words prove prophetic. The next morning the camp reaches the breaking point. It begins peaceably enough.

"We are going to walk to Budapest," a young man tells us, eyes alight as Delphine examines his sore throat. "From there you can get a train to Austria. They can't stop us, not if we all go."

Delphine shoots me a concerned look. "And so it begins," she murmurs under her breath.

By lunchtime the entire camp is buzzing.

Szilvia tries to persuade the refugees not to carry out their plan. She and Laszlo go tent to tent with carafes of hot tea to speak with the eldest men, urging patience, forbearance. But people have been patient long enough. More than a week has passed since the buses returned from Austria. In eight days the camp has tripled in occupancy. People are tired, hungry, sick of waiting, sick of traveling, sick of politicians in faraway European Union capitals making policies that define their dreams and freedom.

At two o'clock on a Wednesday afternoon, right after we run out of bread for the second time in twenty-four hours, the refugees begin to gather along the dirt lane. I stand by the food tent to watch them, craning my neck at the back of the crowd. Men and women. Children carried on their fathers' shoulders. A hunched old man with white hair and a cane. I catch a glimpse of Yousef and Maryam near the edge of the crowd toward the front, and I wave, trying to catch their attention, but they do not see me. There is a hum of energy emanating from the crowd. It rises in pitch, gathering momentum.

All around the camp the police suddenly snap to attention. They come running, massing in front of the crowd. Their commander barks an order in Hungarian, and they form a barrier across the road, holding up their clear plastic riot shields, cutting off the exit. The reporters, who have been cooling their heels for days, spring into action. I spy Delphine on the other side of the lane, standing at the mouth of the medical tent, watching grimly, her arms crossed.

"To Budapest," someone in the front yells, a rallying cry.

"To Budapest," a few hundred voices cry out. The crowd surges forward as one. Cameras roll as the refugees begin to advance on the barricade.

Someone jostles me and I stumble. A strong hand grabs my arm and pulls me back to the edge of the tent. "Stay here," Kai warns, his tone serious. "I have a bad feeling about this."

I stand close to him, and we watch the altercation unfold with mounting trepidation.

The group of refugees is slow and ponderous and purposeful, the entire roiling mass of them moving step-by-step along the lane. I'd estimate there are almost four hundred people in the crowd. Old men, young mothers with nursing babies, everyone. When they are almost nose to nose with the policemen, they stop and wait.

"Move! Let us go to Budapest," a young man yells from the front. Others echo the sentiment. The police stand unmoving behind their shields, staring straight ahead unflinchingly.

"Budapest, Budapest," the crowd chants, raising fists in defiance. At a sharp command, the police draw their batons.

"Get back," a police commander yells in English. "Stop. You have been warned."

Someone throws a rock. It hits an officer on his helmet. A moment of stunned silence and then all hell breaks loose.

The crowd surges forward. Flying rocks, screams, harsh commands in Hungarian to fall back, to come no farther. Young men at the front of the crowd throw full water bottles, stones, brandish tree branches they've torn from the trees along the edge of the camp. The police part down the middle. They have a water cannon and train it on the crowd, pushing them back a little. The old man with the white hair falls, his cane spinning away from him in the force of the water. I gasp, horrified and transfixed. Kai grabs my hand, lacing his fingers through mine, holding on tightly.

Two young men grab a police officer and try to wrestle his shield away. Other officers come to his aid, striking the young men hard with their batons. They fall. The police fire tear gas into the crowd, then use the water cannon again. The air is filled with screams and the spray of water and a choking cloud of tear gas, the odor like gunpowder and something vaguely sweet. A woman in a hijab curls on the ground in a fetal position a dozen yards away from us, clutching her throat. A father comes running from the crowd holding a little boy no more than four. The child is gagging and choking, mucus streaming from his nose.

"Help him," the father begs, holding out the boy. "Please, help him!"

I freeze, my mind a complete blank. I have no idea what to do.

"Get him to Delphine." Kai springs into action. He races across the lane to the medical tent, the father carrying the child at his heels. I follow, choking a little from the tear gas in the air. It makes my eyes water worse than freshly cut onions, and we are a hundred yards away from the source of the gas. I can't imagine what it feels like up close.

Delphine and Stefan are in front of the medical tent, hurriedly prepping the area for emergency care. There are bandages laid out, big bottles of water lined up outside the tent, sheets spread on the ground for the wounded.

"Bring him here." Stefan motions for the father to set the child down outside the tent. The boy is the first patient.

From the front of the camp, we can hear screams and yells but cannot see much more than a seething crowd of people.

"Mia, come with me," Delphine orders, her mouth set in a tense line. "Kai, go gather the other volunteers and bring them here. There will be many more patients."

Kai sprints away, quickly returning with Rosie, Miles, Winnie, and Abel at his heels, along with a Danish volunteer, Frederik. People begin to stagger from the crowd, clutching their eyes. Two young men carry a third, unconscious and bleeding from a gash in his head.

Delphine barks orders. Fresh clothing for those who have been tear-gassed. Bottled water for flushing out eyes. The wounded go in one area, tear gas victims in another. I hurry to comply. I am shaking so hard I can hardly hold the water bottles.

And then I see Maryam. She is struggling toward the medical tent, holding up Yousef. He is gagging, his face slick with tears and mucus. Maryam is sobbing, but I can't tell if she's been gassed as well.

Delphine ushers them quickly past me. "Water, now," she snaps, and I tear into the packs of bottled water, unscrewing bottle after bottle as she flushes Yousef's eyes and nose and mouth. Maryam is making horrible choking sounds, crying uncontrollably.

Beside me Kai and Rosie are doing the same for other victims. I act as the water runner, keeping the others supplied with open bottles of water within their reach. Old, young, men, women, children—so many affected.

We work ceaselessly, feverishly. Delphine is a wonder of efficiency and purpose, treating the tear gas victims one after another. Milo and Frederik hand out fresh clothes, while on the other side of the tent Winnie assists Stefan, triaging anyone who is wounded. Winnie is amazingly calm, I notice, glancing over at her for an instant. She doesn't look shaken or panicked as she hands out bandages to staunch the bleeding and bottles of water to cleanse wounds. Jake loiters nearby, filming, as do many of the news crews, like vultures looking for carrion.

The noise seems to be dying down a little now. I glance up. The crowd is starting to disperse. The water cannon and tear gas seem to have been effective, deflating the fervor of the mob. People begin to retreat, falling back to tend their wounded. The resistance is broken in less than twenty minutes. No one will go to Budapest today.

Some of the refugees sit down on the ground, heads in their hands, crying. Others stare off into the distance, seemingly in shock. At the triage station Yousef is recovering. He stumbles to his feet with Maryam's help, and they head back toward their makeshift camp under the oak tree. Maryam carries their backpack, soaked from the water cannon. She turns once and meets my eyes, lifting her hand in what looks like a farewell. She is still crying.

"Mia, more water," Delphine commands sharply, and I focus once more on my task.

An ambulance arrives, its siren piercing the air, and the police wave it through the barricade. It trundles slowly up the dirt lane through the dwindling crowd. One man has a broken arm, and two people have concussions. Stefan is sewing up a gash over a young man's eye with Winnie's assistance. Two Hungarian paramedics load the man with a broken arm onto a stretcher. The concussed man and woman follow the paramedics, looking dejected.

I go through the motions, handing out water, assisting Delphine, but internally I feel paralyzed. What just happened? I can't quite wrap my mind around it. When my legs start shaking like Jell-O, I have to sit down. Delphine sees me and hands me a bottle of water.

"The first time is always the hardest," she tells me matter-of-factly. "It's the adrenaline. You are in shock. Put your head between your knees and rest a moment. It will pass." Then she turns back to the next person waiting for help.

Chapter 44

Feeling guilty that I've become a burden and not a help, I stumble around the side of the tent and sink down with my back to the canvas, sipping water and putting my head between my knees as instructed. My whole body is trembling and I feel cold, even though the sun is hot on the crown of my head. A few minutes later I feel a touch on my shoulder and look up. Rosie is crouching next to me, her face pale, her usually effortless composure rattled.

"You okay?" she asks in a low whisper. There's a streak of mud on her cheek, and her dress is soaked with water.

I shake my head. "I hate this," I confess, my voice tremulous.

"Oh Mia, I know. That was absolutely terrifying."

"It was," I agree, then say in a small voice, "but Rosie, I mean I hate all of this—volunteering at the camp, helping in the medical tent. I hate what I'm doing every single day. I've hated it since the minute we got here."

There, I've said it. The truth. "I don't hate the people. I love the people, but I don't think I'm cut out for this kind of work." I stop, dismayed by my own admission. "Do you know what the highlight of my time here has been? Baking and then bribing a police officer with a carrot cake."

Rosie raises her eyebrows in surprise. I didn't tell anyone about exchanging the carrot cake for bus seats.

"There's no shame in realizing you don't like something," she says, trying to comfort me. "You just find something else you like instead, something that helps people in a different way."

I look at her doubtfully. But what about Saint Mia? I thought this work would bring me joy and meaning, but so far I just feel constantly sad and anxious and tired, so tired.

"Sugar, you'll figure it out. I know you will." Rosie squeezes my knee sympathetically. She's still balancing on the balls of her feet in the dirt, wearing those ridiculous watermelon-colored Gucci flats. Her cell phone dings and she glances at it. "Lars wants to know if we're all right. He's seeing the news." She types a response quickly, then gets to her feet. "Are you feeling okay?" she asks. "I'm going to call him and come right back."

"I'm okay," I assure her, although truthfully I am not okay in a whole host of ways. I am still stunned by what we've just experienced and by my own self-revelation. I get up and brush dry grass from my clothes. I don't have time to consider all the implications of what I've just admitted to myself. Right now there are people who still need help.

Just as I turn to head back to my post, I notice Abel. He's sitting across the lane near the clothing tent, his head in his hands. As I watch, Winnie approaches him and squats down, putting her arm around his shoulders and urging him to drink some water from a bottle. He shakes his head but she insists, staying with him until he finally looks up at her, his expression bleak. I wonder what this scene has resurrected for him. I imagine he has known trauma far worse than this, and I wonder if he's reliving it all again.

In the next fifteen minutes tensions in the camp calm down significantly. Szilvia opens the food tent for an early lunch. People don't queue in line but approach the tables in twos and threes, taking food back for families and groups huddled together. The mood in the camp is discouraged and sullen. Other than the ambulance, the police are not letting anyone in or out. We are on total lockdown.

Kai finds me gathering empty water bottles from the triage area, my arms full of them. "Hey, you okay?" he asks, touching my shoulder gently. "You look like you've seen a ghost."

I hesitate, still stunned by the violence we just witnessed. "I think the riot just blew a hole right through my alternate life," I admit.

Kai looks confused. "What do you mean?" His hand on my arm is warm, steadying me.

If I close my eyes all I can see and hear is what just happened. The slash of scarlet from a gaping forehead wound, blood dripping over a man's eye. The screams and wails of terrified young children, a woman holding her infant to her chest and running from the tear gas, choking and crying, her face frozen in terror.

"Hey." Kai's voice brings me back to the present. "I came to find you. Lars just texted Rosie. The riot's all over the news. The Humanitas Foundation is pulling us out. We're leaving Hungary and heading back to Florida as soon as we can get out of here."

I hear the words, but it takes a moment for them to sink in. We are leaving the camp? I feel a profound sense of relief, closely followed by a wave of guilt and sadness. The refugees are still coming, and their situation is more precarious than ever. Who will take our place? Yet I long to go home where life is safe and peaceful and predictable.

"When?" I clear my throat, trying to wrap my mind around such an abrupt departure.

"Laszlo's on his way with the van. As soon as he can get into the camp, we're going to the hostel to pack for the airport. Within the hour, I think. Maybe sooner. I told Rosie I'd let everybody know."

Kai squeezes my shoulder and lopes away toward the clothing tent. I watch him go, thinking of our incendiary kiss in the tea aisle of Tesco just a short while ago. Have I lost everything now? Saying no to Ethan, no to Kai, embracing a life it seems I do not actually want. What is left for me? And what will happen to the people I am leaving behind?

I look around, unsure what to do in the few minutes we have left here. Do I try to be useful until the last possible second? Do I say goodbye?

In the end I head to the oak tree at the edge of the camp to find Maryam and Yousef. Their blankets are folded neatly at the foot of the tree, but they are gone. I ask a few others nearby, but no one has seen them. One man points toward the woods where the smugglers lurk, waiting for an offer from the desperate.

My heart sinks. Did they grow too weary of the waiting? At this very moment are they on their way to Sweden in the back of a refrigerated van? I close my eyes and say a brief prayer for them, asking for traveling mercies and for them to reach their sister and their new home safely.

Then I head back toward the center of camp to say my last farewell. Delphine is in the now empty medical tent, resting on the examination table with a wet washcloth over her eyes. There are no more patients for the present.

"Delphine," I whisper, in case she's asleep. She sits up and pulls the washcloth from her face. There are dark smudges under her eyes; she looks exhausted.

"Feeling better?" she asks. "It is a shock, no?" She swings her legs over the edge of the table and leans forward, giving me a once-over with a practiced eye.

I nod, looking down at the ground, feeling embarrassed. "We're leaving," I tell her. "The foundation that sent us is pulling us out. Laszlo's on his way to come pick us up." I wish I didn't feel so relieved to think about quitting this place. "I'm sorry to leave you with all of this," I say, gesturing to the camp.

She shrugs away my concern. "Eh, the work is never done.

Don't worry. Besides, this was never where you were meant to be. Your heart's passion lies elsewhere."

Her words sting a little, but I know they are true. I'm not cut out for the medical tents of refugee camps. "I'm sorry," I say again.

"Don't be. You were as helpful as you had the capacity to be, and now you are free to give the world what you were meant to." Her smile is warm, softening the acerbic edge of her words. She hops off the table and gives me a quick peck on both cheeks, then pulls back and cups my face in her strong hand for one quick instant.

"Remember, Mia, your place in this world is the space where your greatest passion meets the world's great pain," she says firmly. "Go now and find that place."

When we pull away from the camp some twenty minutes later, I turn and take one last look. I see that already Delphine is conscripting Frederik into service at the medical tent. I glance around the camp, cementing the picture in my mind, my heart filled with a potent cocktail of regret and relief. I have never been so sad to leave a place; I have never been so glad to drive away.

Part 5

Florida and Seattle

Chapter 45

Sunbeam Key

"Team Caritas, welcome home." Lars opens the door to the mansion himself and ushers us inside, his expression solicitous. Seated in the opulent marble and white columned front room overlooking the pool, a sweating cold cocktail pressed into my hand, I look around me, exhausted and bewildered by the twenty hours of travel and searing Florida summer heat. I am supposed to be in Thailand making pancakes for school children and eating pad thai wrapped in an omelet thin as tissue paper. I am supposed to be at the Röszke refugee camp helping Delphine salve an infected wound on the leg of an Iraqi man who has walked all the way from Greece. Instead, I am sitting in Lars Lindquist's lavish home, listening to a young Jamaican man play Chopin on the gleaming white grand piano and drinking a piña colada so strong it makes my head spin.

I glance around at my teammates. Abel sits on a white leather ottoman near a gigantic potted palm, his head in his hands. Ever since the riot he's been distant and unresponsive. Winnie's become his guard dog, sitting with him on the plane, shooing away the flight attendants with their offers of water, their cloying concern. She seems to have handled the riot unfazed. While we waited in the check-in line for our flight from Budapest, Rosie asked her how she was doing.

Winnie gave a small shrug. "I'm a punk rock musician. I've been touring with Dynamite Kitty since I was nineteen. My first tour, a guy got knifed in the front row right in front of me during my opening number. It was in Jacksonville. I got blood spatters on my T-shirt—that's how close he was. Screaming crowds and violence are nothing new."

I sip my drink slowly. Every time I close my eyes, I see it all again, the desperate shouts, the sting of the tear gas, like gunpowder, like vinegar and apple blossoms. I can't shake the shock of those images, the blind panic I felt as I unscrewed caps on water bottles and frantically prayed that we would all survive.

Stella and Bryant arrive as Lars is finishing mixing the drinks.

"Team Caritas," Bryant booms, clapping his hands as though we are heroes. "So glad you're safely back with us."

Stella nods. Her blonde bob never moves, or rather it moves only with the motion of her head, like a helmet. They take a seat on a long white lacquered bench, and Lars presses icy cocktails into their hands. The pianist stops playing at some unseen cue.

"We were relieved to hear that you were all uninjured," Stella says, taking a token sip of her drink, "but we know that experiencing something like a riot can be traumatic." She sets the drink aside and looks around the room at us. "Effective immediately, Team Caritas is no longer on field assignment. Tomorrow you will begin a week of debriefing here on the island before returning home. We have hired one of the best trauma specialists in America to guide you through this week." For a moment her frosty demeanor softens. "We regret that you had these difficult experiences and hope this week will help you process whatever trauma has occurred."

"Stella, may I?" It is Lars holding a lowball filled with ice. With a brief nod, Stella sits back and Lars stands in front of the piano. He gazes at each of us. His eyes, those soulful gray eyes, are tender and tired.

"I know that this is not how any of you would have chosen to end your time with Team Caritas," he says soberly. "I want you to know that I am honored by your service to the Humanitas Foundation, and I sincerely hope that this week will mark not the end of the trip but another chapter in your experience of giving back to those in need."

He pauses for a moment, clinking the ice in his glass. "The purpose of this trip was to help bring positive change to places of need. We have learned a great deal through the experiences of each of the four teams. Teams Veritas, Fortis, and Fidelis will be finishing their allotted time abroad while your time ends here. But rest assured, your team's work will not be any less valuable for being cut short. We will be reassessing and seeking to improve our model of service for future teams, and your experience on the field will help us do that."

He looks around the room. "Out of respect for the difficult circumstances that necessitated this week, Jake won't be filming any part of this debrief. Please remember, this may be the end of our time together, but it doesn't need to be the end of sowing goodness in the world. I wish you all the best as you begin your last week here on Sunbeam Key."

I listen to Lars' words with a mixture of astonishment and grief. This was not at all how I pictured this trip going. Indeed, I think I can say that it has gone about the opposite of all I hoped for it. I dart a swift look at Kai, who is gazing thoughtfully at Lars. I don't know how to process it all. What in the world has happened to my alternate life?

"Good morning, Team Caritas. Let's come to the circle and begin this morning's session."

After breakfast the next morning, esteemed trauma counselor Dr. Carolyn Danley begins guiding us through various exercises meant to help us process our experiences. We sit in the same extravagant front room from the night before. Everyone participates, even Winnie, although Abel seems withdrawn, silent and unengaged.

Dr. Danley has a thick strawberry-blonde braid, gentle blue eyes, and an empathetic way of speaking that makes me feel that somehow she is peering inside my soul.

"Write down everything you're feeling right now in your emotions and your physical body. You can use words or draw a picture or express in any way that feels most helpful to you." She hands us blank paper and pens. I write down the words that come instantly to mind—*fear*, *anger*, *sadness*, *guilt*, and then in letters bigger than all the rest, *LOSS*. It overlays all the other emotions—the remembered horror of the riot, the sadness of leaving before the work is done, the guilt of feeling that I have failed. I finally got what my heart longed for, this alternate life of my childhood dreams, only to find that it isn't what I want after all. I do not have what it takes to be Saint Mia. I stare at my paper, unable to see a way forward. Everything tastes like defeat.

"Would anyone like to share their paper with the group?" Dr. Danley asks. "It's all right if you prefer not to, but sometimes it is helpful to share with others, to have our voices heard. Often we find that others are experiencing similar things and that sharing what's going on inside can help us not feel isolated."

We look at one another, and for a long moment no one volunteers. Then Milo shuffles his feet. "I'll go," he says. He holds up his paper, a cartoon drawing of a man, arms akimbo, with a giant question mark above his head.

"What does that mean to you?" Dr. Danley asks.

"I feel confused," Milo replies. "Everything happened so fast. Not just the camp, the whole trip. But definitely how things ended with the riot and all." He shakes his head, looking bewildered. "It wasn't what I thought it was going to be, and I'm just confused about the entire trip, honestly."

Rosie volunteers next.

"Selfish." She holds up her paper. I recognize the drawing. It's the pink Chanel purse from the refugee camp with a giant eye inside, complete with eyelashes and eye shadow. "I went on this trip for pretty selfish reasons. I didn't really think about the people I'd meet or what I'd encounter." She pauses, looking a little embarrassed. "But I realize now that my motives were self-centered. I went on this trip for my own gain, but at some point I started to see other people—their needs and hurts and pain. I think it was the woman with the Chanel purse, actually. I realized that it wasn't just about me anymore. I have to think about others, too, about doing what I can to help them. It's a responsibility I've been ignoring, but not anymore."

Dr. Danley nods. "That can be a painful realization, can't it? But also ultimately very good."

Winnie's paper looks blank. "Pass," she says, not making eye contact.

"Do you want to tell us a word about how you're feeling, then?" Dr. Danley presses gently.

Winnie shrugs. "Nah." She glances at Abel out of the corner of her eye.

"Are you sure?" Dr. Danley presses gently.

Winnie shakes her head as though she's getting rid of a pesky fly. "Yeah." She refuses to say more.

"Disappointed," Kai states, not showing his paper when it's his turn.

"Do you want to say more about that?" Dr. Danley asks.

Kai meets my eyes for an instant. "No." His jaw flexes and he looks away. I glance down at my paper. How did everything turn out like this? Such potential in the beginning and then things went so horribly wrong.

"Abel." Dr. Danley's gentle voice breaks into my thoughts. I glance up. Abel is sitting across the circle from me, head in his hands, hunched and rocking back and forth. A low groan escapes him, a chilling sound that makes the hair on my arms stand up. Winnie vaults from her chair and crouches next to him.

"Abel, can you hear me? Can you tell me what is going on right now?" Dr. Danley asks, approaching his seat, but Abel is unresponsive. Winnie's eyes are locked on him. I've never seen her look scared before. We are all silent, watching the drama unfold, unsure what to do. Suddenly he drops his hands and stands, bowing slightly to Dr. Danley but still looking away from all of us, focusing on a spot on the floor to his left.

"Forgive me, please," he says, and then he bolts out of the room.

"Excuse me for one moment," Dr. Danley says. She pulls out a cell phone and hurries through the french doors onto the veranda, holding a quick muted conversation. When she returns, she looks grave.

"As you've noticed, Abel is experiencing some distress. Rest assured, he is safe and being well taken care of. We will find a way to help him."

Chapter 46

We finish the session, but it feels weird to be missing a team member. Winnie is agitated, distracted. The rest of us try to participate, but I can tell we are all thinking about Abel. When we gather again after lunch, he does not join us. Dr. Danley announces that he will not be back.

"As you may already know, Abel is a survivor of the Rwandan genocide," Dr. Danley explains, glancing around our circle. "He lost several family members in the violence. His own sister was murdered in front of him by a neighbor with a machete. The events of this past week have brought much of this unresolved trauma to the surface again, and Abel is finding himself struggling to cope. At my recommendation he has chosen to seek treatment for post-traumatic stress disorder at a residential center in the Ocala National Forest here in Florida. His treatment will be fully funded by the Humanitas Foundation. He has already left for the facility, as they had a spot for him immediately."

At this unexpected news, I glance at my teammates in astonishment. Abel is gone? I wish I could have said goodbye. The team feels incomplete now. Winnie looks aghast; all the color has drained from her face.

"He wanted to say goodbye to all of you but felt it was better if he left immediately," Dr. Danley explains. "He didn't want to slow down your own process or distract the team in any way. That was his choice."

At her words, Winnie jumps from her chair. It clatters backward onto the marble floor. "I'm leaving too," she says abruptly. "I'm not staying here. I need to see Abel."

Dr. Danley displays no surprise, just a quiet curiosity. "Why do you feel you need to leave?" she asks.

Winnie darts a look around the room. She seems trapped, desperate. "I'm shooting heroin again," she says, her tone defiant. "See." She shucks off her ever-present combat boots and socks, spreading her toes and pointing. In the webbing between her toes there are tiny red marks. "I've been using the entire trip," she says.

Rosie leans over to me. "I wondered if something like that was going on," she hisses in my ear. "I kept finding cotton balls in the trash can, and she was always so secretive."

"I just thought she didn't like us," I whisper back. My eyes slide to Winnie's long, pale bare feet. Her behavior on this trip makes so much more sense now—the moodiness and irritability, the secrecy. She's been hiding this from all of us.

Dr. Danley surveys Winnie calmly. "Why are you showing us this now?" she asks.

"I need to go with Abel," Winnie says. She sounds panicky. "He's the only person who understands me. I want to stop using, but I can't do it without him." Winnie's eyes glitter with unshed tears. I've never seen her so rattled. "To be alive is to suffer," she says, her voice trembling, "but we survive by finding meaning in the suffering."

She's paraphrasing Nietzsche. I recognize the idea from my college philosophy class. I glance at Winnie in astonishment. I didn't see it coming, this attachment between her and Abel. I saw them together that evening by the Danube, but I had no idea their bond had grown so deep.

"I'm trying to find meaning in the suffering," Winnie says, looking for one moment vulnerable and broken. "But I can't do it alone."

"All right," Dr. Danley says gently. "We will get you the help you are asking for, Winnie. I'm not sure we can get you a place at the same treatment center as Abel, but we will help you. I can promise you that."

Winnie nods. Her shoulders slump in defeat or relief—I can't tell which. She picks up her socks and boots. "Okay," she says, taking a deep breath. "Okay. I want to go today. And I have to talk to Abel. I've got to tell him that I want to get clean."

"Let's break until after dinner, shall we?" Dr. Danley suggests, looking around the room at the rest of us. "This has been a big day. There's a lot to process. We'll meet up again at seven." She stands and shepherds Winnie toward the door.

Winnie is crying but trying to hide it. She looks back at us, her eyes pink, her dark eyeliner smudged. "I'm sorry," she says. And then she is gone.

We are silent for a moment. "Dude," Milo says slowly, voicing the sentiment we all seem to be feeling. "I did not see that coming."

"If I'd known what she was struggling with . . ." I trail away. I would have what? Liked her more? I doubt it. Had more understanding and empathy? Perhaps. I hope so.

"What a remarkably strong woman to function so normally while carrying such a secret," Rosie says, shaking her head in astonishment.

I agree. As damaged as she obviously is and unpleasant as she can be, Winnie is both strong and resilient. I feel a grudging sense of respect for her, belatedly, and a touch more empathy.

I glance around our group. We are one-third fewer than when we started. A few more sessions and there may be no one left. Kai catches my eye and raises his eyebrows. I nod. This entire experience has an unreal quality to it, like I am caught in a Twilight Zone. Perhaps in another dimension I am in Chiang Mai wending my way through the street market, eating succulent pork satay and ripe yellow pineapple spears from a bag. Perhaps in another dimension I am still at the refugee camp, unwrapping foil from triangle cheese or helping Delphine weigh and measure a chubby Syrian infant. I can't quite believe this is all happening.

That evening as we start our last session of the day, Dr. Danley gives us an update. "Winnie has been admitted to a center especially for heroin addiction," she tells us. "It is a cutting-edge program in North Carolina, and she is on her way there now. Our thoughts and prayers are with her as she begins the brave and difficult journey of recovery."

The rest of the evening session inches by. Dr. Danley's material is good, but I am distracted, thinking about Abel, thinking about Winnie, wondering what in the world I am going to do now that my alternate life is in tatters. It is deeply disconcerting, this realization that I do not want the life I desired for so long.

After the session, Milo, Rosie, Kai, and I head back to the guest cabins. No one feels much like socializing; the loss of our teammates and the six hours of jet lag are wearing on us.

"Dude, all I want is a shower and then to sleep forever," Milo says with a yawn.

I agree. It's been a very long, fraught day.

"I'll be there shortly," Rosie tells me, hanging back as we reach the beach in front of the mansion. "I think I'll sit by the pool and look at the moon for a few minutes, just to clear my head a little."

"Okay, see you soon." I join Kai and Milo for the short walk back to the guest bungalows but halfway there remember my satchel. I can picture it in the front room, tucked under a white lacquered chair with a cushion hand-embroidered with birds of paradise.

"Forgot my bag. I'll be right back."

Milo offers to go with me, but I wave him off to bed. It will just take a minute. I reverse directions and jog back to the main house. Intent on my errand, I almost run into them. Rosie and Lars are sitting together on a chaise lounge in the shadow of a coconut palm by the pool. Rosie's head rests on Lars' shoulder, and he is holding her hand, his other arm circling her waist protectively.

"Oh." I stop abruptly, taken aback.

Rosie lifts her head, and her voice floats to me in the darkness, languid and sure. "Everything okay, sugar?"

"Um, just forgot my bag," I stammer, flustered at interrupting this intimate moment. I skirt the pool and take the wide steps to the veranda two at a time.

Chapter 47

When I return with my satchel, Lars is gone and Rosie is sitting on the chaise lounge, dangling her toes in the pool. A huge full moon hangs low in the sky over the ocean, bright and luminous as a pearl.

"Lars had to take a call from Singapore," she says dreamily, "but the evening is so nice I don't want to go to bed yet. It's been such a strange day." She tilts her head and looks at me. "Oh Mia, Lars is such a gentleman. I think I'm falling in love."

I'm alarmed by the strength of her feelings. Falling in love? Does she even know him? Does she know about his problem? If she doesn't, she needs to learn the truth before she becomes too attached. I have to tell her.

"Rosie," I say hesitantly, perching on the edge of a chaise lounge next to her. "You know Lars has a . . . limitation, right?"

She stills, her foot poised half in the water. "Limitation? What do you mean?"

I take a deep breath. "During orientation week Rangi told me Lars doesn't leave the island, not ever. He can't, apparently. Some kind of trauma in his past."

She tilts her head and looks at me thoughtfully. Her profile is beautiful, rimmed in silver moonlight. "Do you know what happened?" she asks.

"Allow me to enlighten you on that point." Lars materializes from the shadows of the veranda, descending the last few stone steps soundlessly, a highball in his hand. He startles both of us. Rosie lets out a little yelp, and I jump instinctively. I wonder how much he heard. I hope he isn't offended.

"I'm sorry," I say, hastening to explain. "I wasn't trying to meddle. I just . . ."

He waves away my words. "Please, don't apologize. You are simply watching out for your friend. I understand. I would expect nothing less." He sighs and sits on an empty chaise lounge across from Rosie, putting his elbows on his knees and swirling the ice in his glass. "Mia is right. I don't leave the island. I haven't set foot off this place in more than three years." He looks up at us frankly, the planes and hollows of his face illuminated in the light of a full moon. "Please understand, this is not something I am proud of. I want to be able to continue my former life—jetting to Paris for the weekend, attending a soccer match in Rio on a whim. It was an exciting life, a full life, and then it all was shattered in a moment."

"What happened?" Rosie asks, leaning forward curiously.

"My life as I knew it ended on April 20, 2012, in the Sulu Sea off the coast of the Philippines." Lars's voice is melodic, soothing as he weaves his tale. "I was on a week's yachting excursion with friends, celebrating my thirty-second birthday. We had just cut fresh pineapples in lieu of cake, and they were singing to me. I remember that because we didn't hear the boat approaching." He gazes across the pool, out toward the ocean, as though seeing the moment playing out before him once more.

"We were boarded before we could even sound an alarm. Pirates, members of the Islamic militant group Abu Sayyaf, looking for anything of value on the yacht. They took our wallets, watches, even the women's high-heeled shoes. And me."

"Oh Lars," Rosie exclaims, sounding distressed. "How awful!"

Lars takes a sip of his drink and grimaces. "When they realized I was someone of means, they took me as a hostage. What followed were the most terrifying few weeks of my life."

He swirls the ice in his glass. "I was taken to an island somewhere farther south, in Abu Sayyaf–held territory, and kept in a dirt-floor shack, tied up and blindfolded. It was fetid—sweltering and overrun with rats and insects. My wrists were chafed raw from the ropes. Each day they would pull me out and interrogate me. Who was I? How much was I worth? They wanted all the details so they could demand a high price as ransom. By the end of the second week, I was desperately sick with diarrhea and vomiting, and almost delirious with dehydration. I thought I was going to die."

"Oh Lars," Rosie breathes, her hand fluttering to her throat. "You poor thing."

I nod in agreement, transfixed by the tale.

He closes his eyes as though the memory still pains him. "It was excruciating, yet it had a silver lining. At my very sickest, when I thought surely I would die, I lay on the dirt floor in a puddle of my own vomit and made a bargain with the Almighty. I was raised Lutheran but had not darkened the doors of a church for many years. But there in that shack I swore that if God let me live, I would turn my focus from myself and spend my time and money making the world a better place." Lars' voice cracks with the memory and he stops, clearing his throat.

Rosie reaches over and puts her hand on his knee in tacit sympathy.

"So what happened?" I ask. "Were you rescued?"

"In a manner of speaking." Lars takes a sip from his glass. "I became so ill my captors worried I might die. A dead hostage would be useless to them. So when my business manager finally offered them one-tenth of their asking price for my freedom, they took the money and dumped me in front of a burger café in Davao City, blindfolded and hog-tied. I guess they thought a burger joint was as close to America as they could get." He laughs softly, bleakly.

"I never knew you'd been kidnapped," Rosie exclaims incredulously. "Why wasn't it in the news?"

Lars shakes his head. "It was all hushed up, taken care of quietly. The US government didn't want news of a ransom being paid for my release to encourage other kidnappings of US citizens. So we kept it out of the media. Only a handful of trusted people knew."

He clinks the ice in his glass and continues. "It was quite traumatic, as you can imagine. I was treated at a private hospital until I was well enough to travel, and then the US embassy arranged transport back home. I set foot on this island a little more than three years ago . . . and I haven't left since. I have had all the best therapy, the most cutting-edge treatments for trauma, but I am still a prisoner of my own mind. Somehow I feel that only here am I truly safe." He makes a futile gesture with his glass. "Pathetic, is it not?"

Rosie squeezes his knee. "Understandable," she says gently.

I nod. Understandable, but so very sad. He is a good man, a man with the best of intentions, but a man crippled by his own fear. I look around at the tall windows of the house spilling warm yellow light onto the wide stone veranda, at the vast black expanse of the ocean. A gilded cage, he called it. Now I understand why.

"So that's why you formed the Humanitas Foundation?" I ask. "So you could keep your promise even if you can't leave?" And why he wanted everything filmed, so he could feel as though he were a part of it, too, I'm guessing.

Lars nods. "Precisely. I intended to keep my end of the bargain, but of course I had to come up with a different way to do it. Imagine that, a global philanthropist who cannot leave his own backyard." He sighs in resignation. "I had such high hopes for the foundation, but as you know, things have gone quite awry. However, I am not deterred. We shall simply assess and adjust until we find a format that actually achieves our aims. I still intend to fulfill my promise, despite these initial setbacks."

"You should talk to Shreya, our handler in Mumbai," I tell him. "She'll have some good ideas for you about how to make changes that can really help people. And there's a doctor at the refugee camp, Delphine, with Medecines Sans Frontieres. She also would have some great input about helping refugees adjust to their new lives."

"And maybe stop sending suitcases of designer clothes to your volunteers," Rosie says lightly, with a note of fondness in her tone.

Lars chuckles. "I did that only for you, my dear. You told me you appreciated them."

"Very much," Rosie replies. "And somewhere in Europe two teenage girls from Syria are starting their new life off very stylishly with most of the contents of that suitcase. I did keep a few things," she admits. "Those Gucci flats were just too yummy."

I realize I have become a third wheel and rise to go. I clear my throat, but neither of them hears me. Rosie has moved to sit beside Lars, her head bent close to his. I wander back to the guest cottage, leaving them in peace.

Chapter 48

The next morning when I wake I see two missed calls and several text messages from Henry.

Call me ASAP. It's an emergency, the last one reads.

Heart pounding, I slip out onto the porch, careful to not rouse Rosie, who is asleep in the other twin bed, just the top of her head visible above the sheet. I have no idea how late she came in last night. I punch Henry's number, my hands trembling. Is it my parents? One of the kids? Nana Alice?

Henry picks up on the second ring. "Mia." His tone is tight with worry.

"What happened?" My heart skips a beat.

"It's Nana Alice," Henry whispers into the phone. In the background I can hear the rhythmic beep of some machine. "She's taken a turn for the worse. I don't want to scare you, tiger, but I think you need to come home now."

"What?" I panic, feeling utterly blindsided. "But she told me she was recovering, that she was feeling better every day."

Henry is quiet for a moment, then says heavily, "She's been lying to us all about her cancer, Mia. She's really sick."

I sit down on the deck with a thump, my legs giving out from under me. Henry explains the situation briefly. "She told everyone she had cervical cancer, that it was slow growing and under control, but that isn't true. She has stage four pancreatic cancer and it's metastasized. Pancreatic cancer is . . ." He hesitates. "Not good. It's fast moving and really difficult to cure, especially when it has spread like hers has. She caught a cold last week, and then last night she fainted while putting on her pajamas. She was dehydrated and her blood pressure was very low. The hospital gave her an IV of fluids and she stabilized, but she's really weak. They're worried about it turning into pneumonia."

I feel like I've just swallowed a bucket of ice cubes, the cold dread sliding down my throat at Henry's words.

"What's her prognosis?" I whisper.

There is silence on the other end of the line. "Even if she pulls out of this, she doesn't have much time," Henry says gently.

I give a strangled little sob. For a moment I gaze out at the palm trees waving gently in the breeze, listen to the chirp of birds punctuated by the roar of the surf. The ocean through the trees is dazzling, early morning sunlight sparkling off the water like diamonds. But my tears blur the scene, making the palm trees smudges of green. I feel as though my heart is breaking in two. Nana Alice has been lying to us all. Nana Alice is dying.

"I'm on my way," I say, already scrambling to my feet.

"Of course you must take the jet," Lars insists when I rouse Rosie, who calls him. On speakerphone his voice is sleepy but firm. "I can have it ready in an hour. I'll arrange a boat to pick you up, and I will come see you off myself."

Rosie helps me pack. I'm ready to go in fifteen minutes but can't leave until the plane is ready. Rosie holds me while I sob.

"I didn't know," I wail, face slick with tears. "I wouldn't have left her if I had known."

"Of course not, sugar," Rosie soothes, pressing my face against her shoulder and rubbing my back as though I am a child. "That's the way she wanted it. She didn't want you to know. She wanted to watch you have a big adventure and get to live a little of that adventure through you. She was trying to set you free."

I can't stop crying, fueled by a potent cocktail of emotions—guilt and anger, and most of all fear. I am deeply afraid of losing Nana Alice for good. What if I don't get there in time?

Rosie checks her watch. "You've still got twenty minutes. Do you want me to make you some breakfast? Want to walk on the beach for a few minutes to clear your head?"

I shake my head. There's just one thing I need to do before I go home. I have a confession to make.

Kai answers the door of the canary-yellow guest cottage wearing only a pair of faded gray boxer shorts. I stare at the smooth, tan expanse of his chest. Why is he always shirtless? It makes this so much harder. His hair is loose, black and shiny and falling below the plane of his shoulders. He smells like sleep and chai tea—cardamom and pink pepper and a hint of sweetness. My heart swells in my chest, a feeling of regret laced with a hint of bittersweet memory.

"Mia, hey." He scrubs his hands over his face, surprised to see me, but his smile fades as he takes in my pink eyes and strained countenance. "Are you okay?"

I shake my head. "I'm going home to Seattle. It turns out Nana Alice has been lying about her cancer. It's bad, really bad." I stop, my voice breaking, and clear my throat. "I'm leaving this morning. I don't want to miss a moment more with her, and there's not much time." My eyes fill with tears, and I dash them away with the back of my hand. "But I had to see you before I left."

"Just a second." Kai ducks back into the cottage and grabs a T-shirt and shorts from his bed. He comes out on the porch. I see

Milo at the tiny two-person table inside, eating Cap'n Crunch and watching us with interest. Kai shuts the door behind him and pulls on the clothes, then leans against the porch railing and watches me curiously. "What's up?"

I hesitate, then decide to plunge right in. I don't have anything to lose. I'm leaving in a few minutes, and we might never see each other again, if that's what he chooses. But I can't go before I tell him the truth.

"I lied to you," I tell him. "I've never been interested in providing free medical care for disadvantaged women and children. I'm horrible at medicine, and I faint at the sight of blood. Rosie made up that story for Bryant and Stella so they would accept me on the team. I went along with it because I desperately wanted to go on the trip, and I felt like I had to offer something that sounded grand enough to change the world. But really, this is the truth: I love to bake. And I love to help people. That's it. That's all I've got."

I spread my hands, an admission. "And I feel like I've failed at this new life. I've been living with a beatific vision of myself, Saint Mia who would save the world, but the riot at the camp made me realize that this isn't what I want to do at all. I'm not Saint Mia. I'm just plain Mia, just me." I shrug. "And that terrifies me because I don't know what I have left. It feels like I've lost everything, and I'm more confused than ever."

He's watching me impassively, arms crossed over his chest. He doesn't look surprised.

"I guessed as much," he says finally.

"About what?"

"I saw you working in the medical tent," he says, quirking a small smile. "You didn't seem like a natural, to be honest. I think it might have been when I saw you cleaning blood off the exam table with your eyes squeezed shut." Then he sobers. "Why are you telling me all of this?"

"Because I want you to see the real me. I don't want to leave with you not knowing who I really am." *No matter how pathetic the truth is.* I look up at him, but his expression is difficult to read.

"Okay." he says. That's it. Nothing more.

"Mia," Rosie calls from the porch of our bungalow, pointing toward the dock. "Lars called. The boat's here. He's meeting us at the dock."

"I've got to go." I hesitate. "I'm sorry I lied to you. You deserve so much more."

Kai tips his head and considers me for a moment. "Yeah, you're right," he says. "I do, but it's okay." He reaches for me, and I instinctively step into his embrace, warm and solid. His arms are tight around me, and I burrow my face into his chest for a fraction of a moment, pretending I belong there, pretending I don't ever have to leave.

"Thanks for telling me," he murmurs against my hair. I nod, then reluctantly step back, throat clogged with regret and tears.

"I guess this is goodbye." I gaze miserably up at him.

He shrugs. "I'm not that into goodbyes. Let's just say, 'See you around.'"

I give him a searching glance, trying to read the meaning in those words, but his expression is hard to gauge.

"Okay, then. See you around." I smile slightly, a little bubble of hope floating through the fog of sorrow surrounding my heart.

"Go," Kai urges me, nodding toward the boat. "They're waiting for you."

I go.

Chapter 49

Sprinting through the halls of Seattle's Swedish Hospital, I frantically murmur, "Don't let me be too late, don't let me be too late," over and over like a litany, a supplication. I've been trying to reach Henry since my flight landed, but his phone has been off, which is making me panic, imagining the worst. When I finally locate Nana Alice's room, I stop short in the doorway, panting for air. Nana Alice is sitting up in bed, brandishing a biscuit at Henry.

"This," she is saying, "is not a baked good." She holds the biscuit aloft with a look of contempt.

Henry, who is standing by the head of her bed wearing a long-suffering expression, just nods.

"It's got the density of plaster," she says. "Did they blend these in a cement mixer?"

"I'll bring you some better biscuits for breakfast tomorrow," Henry says patiently. They both glance up as I knock lightly and enter the room, trying to catch my breath from my dash through the hospital.

Nana Alice looks very ill. I bite back a gasp of surprise at the contrast in just a few weeks. She's lost even more weight; the bones of her wrists and the knobs of her collarbone stand out prominently beneath the thin cotton hospital gown. Her skin is a waxen color.

But she is sitting up and feeling well enough to critique the hospital baked goods, which I take to be a good sign.

"Mia, sweetheart!" She holds out her hand and beams at me. "Henry told me you were coming. What a lot of fuss for nothing."

When I hug her it feels like hugging a little stick figure, as though a breeze might snap her. I draw back and search her face. The whites of her eyes look yellowed.

"I came as soon as I could," I say in a rush. "I was afraid I'd be too late."

Nana Alice waves away my concern. "Oh, I'm not dying yet. Everyone's getting worked up about nothing. I'll be fine. Just a little cold. Come, sit." She pats the bed beside her. "You look hungry. Henry can run and get you a sandwich."

"Hey, tiger." Henry comes around to my side of the bed and gives me a firm hug. "You need something to eat? The cafeteria has a terrible turkey club, but the pastrami isn't bad."

I nod. "A sandwich would be great." I skipped breakfast and only had a granola bar in my satchel. "Hey, your phone was off when I tried to call. I thought something terrible had happened."

Henry checks his phone. "Sorry, had it on silent." He clicks the sound back on, then slips from the room.

Nana Alice clears her throat and takes a sip of water, then leans back against the pillows. She looks tired. The room is quiet for a moment, the only sound the steady *beep beep beep* of a machine beside the bed.

"Why didn't you tell me?" I ask softly. I know I should probably leave this conversation for another day, but I can't. I feel so betrayed.

She sighs and takes my hand in her own, her skin papery but reassuringly warm. "I'm sorry I lied to you about my cancer, Mia," she says, looking me in the eye. "It was the only way to get you to go on that trip, and I knew you needed to go. After Ethan strung you along for so many years, well, you needed a fresh start. I wanted you to be able to do the things you've always dreamed of. I was afraid if I told you the truth, you'd never leave." Her words are matter-of-fact but her gaze is beseeching, asking for understanding, for absolution.

I clear my throat. "You should have let me make my own decision about going," I say, my voice cracking. "You took that choice away when you lied to me."

Nana Alice presses her hand to her chest, looking pained. "I know. I'm so sorry," she says, a frail penitent in a faded blue-print hospital gown. "Will you forgive me?"

"Of course." I press my cheek against the soft pouf of her hair, a little flattened on one side but smelling as always of extra-hold hair spray from her weekly salon set and blow out. At this moment I will forgive her anything in the world. "But don't do it again, okay?"

"Oh I doubt I'll have the chance, but I promise," Nana Alice says ruefully. "Now"—she pulls back from my embrace and folds her hands in her lap—"Tell me about the trip. I want to hear all the details."

At some point Henry returns and hands me a pastrami sandwich, then sits on the other side of the bed texting Christine while I detail the entire story of Mumbai and our unexpected detour to Hungary, Ethan's surprise appearance, and then the riot at the refugee camp.

Nana Alice hardly touches her dinner when it comes. She's glued to my words, enjoying all the drama. She seems particularly intrigued by the romance surrounding Rosie and Lars, and she asks a lot of questions about Kai.

When I finish, she looks perturbed. "My goodness, what an unexpected ending to your trip." She looks thoughtful.

"Yes," I admit with a touch of regret. "So much of it wasn't how

I imagined it would be. Not just the end, although that was scary and traumatic and unexpected, but all of it."

"In what way?" Nana Alice asks me, eyes bright, curious.

I settle back in the chair and ponder for a moment. "I think I went expecting some big revelation, expecting to change the world in a grand way. And what I found instead was how small I am, how little impact I really had. It was . . . humbling. The times I felt most useful were actually when I was baking."

I think of the pancakes, of the carrot cake in a box. "And even those times, I don't know if they really helped in the long run. I thought I would go on this trip and find my big thing, but I didn't."

I gaze down at the empty sandwich wrapper in my lap, tasting again the bitter disappointment, as acrid and gritty as coffee grounds at the bottom of a drained cup. "All I found was myself, stripped of everything I thought I wanted. I didn't get answers. I just lost all my illusions."

"Well, that has its own value," Nana Alice says thoughtfully. "You have to be able to see a thing for what it really is before you can understand its true purpose. I know you're disappointed, but this may turn out to be a blessing in disguise. I am worried about you leaving things with Kai the way you did, though." Nana Alice surveys me closely. "He seems like a real gem."

I nod, a little wistful. "He is."

"Well then." She purses her lips. "You have to win him back."

"How?" I spread my hands. "I don't have anything to offer. I lied to him. I pretended to be someone I wasn't, to be more skilled and important than I actually am."

"Pshaw." Nana Alice waves away my protestations. "Mia, you are worth so much more than what you think. I bet Kai sees it. We all see it, but you don't."

I stare at her, trying to digest these words. I wish I could believe them, but my value has always been tied to what I thought I should be able to give and to do, and now that I've failed, that I realize Saint Mia is just an illusion, I don't feel I have anything left.

The bedside phone rings and Henry answers, mouthing, "Albert?" to Nana Alice.

"Tell him to call back in a few minutes," she says. "I want to finish this talk with Mia."

Henry relays the message and hangs up.

Nana Alice sighs. "I know what he's calling about anyway. He's just going to try to convince me to marry him again."

"He what?" I gape at her. "How do you know?"

Nana Alice shrugs. "He's been asking me every time he sees me for the past month."

"So what do you tell him?"

Nana Alice looks shocked. "I tell him to stop asking me."

"You haven't said yes? Why not?" I exclaim. Albert is sweet, gentlemanly, and obviously adores her.

"Because I'm dying, and probably quite soon. It isn't fair to the poor man. He's already lost a wife." Nana Alice folds her hands in her lap and looks stubborn.

"But he loves you," I clarify.

"Yes." Nana Alice nods soberly. "He does."

"And presumably he knows you're dying?"

"Oh yes, I've been very up-front with him from the start."

Well at least she didn't lie to someone, I think, a touch bitterly.

"Well then, why in the world would you deny him the happiness of spending the . . ." I stop and swallow hard to get the words out. "The time you have left, together? If he wants to marry you, I think you should let him!"

Nana Alice cocks her head and considers me. "Well, honestly I hadn't thought of it like that."

A few minutes later the phone rings again. Albert. I rise and Henry does too. It seems like a marriage proposal should be a private thing, even if it is a daily occurrence. Besides, Nana Alice looks tired.

"We should let her get some rest," Henry murmurs, ushering me from the room as Nana Alice takes the phone.

"If he asks again, say yes," I hiss over my shoulder. Nana Alice waves me away with a smile. I can hear her talking to him as we leave the room, tired but happy. Outside at the nurses' station we find my uncle Carl, who has just arrived and is getting an update from Nana Alice's nurse.

"Dr. Cho feels that Mrs. West is out of danger and stable right now," the nurse assures us. "We'll call you if anything changes, but her vitals are strong and she's improving."

Carl is staying with her through the night, and Henry and I agree we will return in the morning.

As we leave the hospital, it occurs to me that I have nowhere to go. The cottage is still sublet. I'm homeless, jobless, and suddenly feeling a little lost.

When I tell Henry he smiles wryly, then jerks his head, looking so like John Lennon I almost start humming "Imagine."

"Come on, little sister. Let's go home to West Wind. You can bunk with Maddie in your old room."

I nod, grateful and a little surprised as I clamber into my parents' old Subaru and we head to the terminal to catch the ferry to the Olympic Peninsula.

So it has all come back to this, I muse, staring at the lights of downtown Seattle as Henry drives, John Denver on the radio, and the smell of salt and rain seeping through my open window. I traveled the world to end up back where I started, in Sequim, at West Wind Lavender Farm. All the dreams and grand aspirations. They are gone now, and I am just Mia, nothing more, nothing less.

CHAPTER 50

The next morning when I arrive at the hospital, revived by a solid night of sleep, I find Nana Alice already awake and sitting up in bed, wearing her clip-on pearl earrings, her raspberry lipstick applied boldly. She has a visitor. Albert is holding her hand, and from the looks on their faces, I'd say they have reached an agreement.

"Mia." Nana Alice beams at me as I walk into the room. "We were just talking about you."

Albert stands and clasps my hand warmly. "I hear I have you to thank for changing her mind," he says, his blue eyes twinkling.

"We have news," Nana Alice says, holding out her left hand. I see a simple gold band with a pearl flanked by two small diamonds. "We're getting married."

The look they give each other is so filled with love that it makes my heart ache. They will love each other fully and well for as long as they have.

"Congratulations," I say, trying to swallow the lump in my throat. "When's the wedding?"

"Two weeks," Nana Alice says. "We don't want to wait. I don't have much time."

"But we'll enjoy every moment we have together," Albert says, gazing at her, his eyes filmed with a sheen of tears. Nana Alice reaches up and gives him a kiss on the lips, and he cups her cheek. She turns to me.

"We have a favor to ask of you, Mia," she says.

"Anything." I blink, trying not to cry at the scene before me, which is so impossibly sweet and so heartbreakingly sad all at the same time.

"I want you to make our wedding cake," Nana Alice tells me. "Lemon cake with cream cheese frosting. You can use my original recipe. I won twenty dollars in a *Seattle Times* baking contest in 1967 with that recipe. It's a winner."

The next morning I wake late. I stayed up past midnight tinkering with Nana Alice's lemon cake recipe and baking a test layer of the cake for practice. Yawning sleepily, I wander down to the kitchen to find it empty except for a familiar ginger-haired woman bent over my test cake on the counter, eating one corner.

"Mom?" I blink, befuddled. My parents aren't due in from Moldova for another ten days. Henry miraculously managed to get ahold of them yesterday and told them about Nana Alice's true prognosis and the upcoming wedding, and they immediately booked tickets home. They're scheduled to arrive three days before the wedding.

The woman turns, a fork in her hand. It's not my mother.

"Aunt Frannie?" I stare blankly at her for a moment, wondering if I've conjured her up or if I'm still half asleep.

"My favorite niece!" Aunt Frannie exclaims. She sets her fork on the counter and pulls me into a strong hug. She smells exotic, like red dust and chili peppers, salt and cloves. I sniff the collar of her shirt, inhaling the unfamiliar odors.

"What are you doing here?" I haven't seen her in nearly four years. She's been working in Ethiopia or Eritrea—I can't quite keep up. Her communication, never a strong suit at the best of times, has been sporadic as she travels with her team in remote places with limited Internet access. I'm thrilled to see her, as always, though aware that she's going to be sorely disappointed by what I'm doing with my life currently.

Aunt Frannie grins. "I'm just passing through, flying out tonight on my way to Cambodia for a dental conference. I decided to go at the last minute, so I didn't really plan anything in advance." She rolls her eyes. "I know, story of my life. Anyway, I got hold of your mom after I bought my tickets and she told me the whole story about Moldova and the farm. She gave me Henry's number, but I got so busy I forgot to tell him I was coming. I just texted when I landed in Seattle last night and asked if I could crash here for the day."

I pull back and look at her. Except for more laugh lines around her eyes and some silver streaks in her hair, she doesn't seem to have aged at all. She's as vibrant, brash, and larger than life as ever.

"Have you seen Henry and Christine?" I ask.

Aunt Frannie nods. "Passed them when I got up this morning. They were going into town. Those kids are certainly cute."

"Yes, they are. Want some coffee?" I scoop Stumptown coffee into a French press and hit the button on the electric water boiler.

"Sure thing." She yawns. "I'm still on Ethiopian time." She straddles the back of a kitchen chair and watches me measure out the grounds. "So your parents are in Moldova, huh? Who'd have thought?" She shakes her head. "Meg and Henry, saving the world one lavender plant at a time." Her voice is tinged with fondness.

I dread the question I know is coming next.

"What about you?" she asks. "Your mom told me you and Ethan broke up and you went on a trip around the world."

"I did. I went to Mumbai and Hungary with a team from the

Humanitas Foundation. It . . . didn't really work out the way I expected."

"How so?" Aunt Frannie sounds genuinely interested, so I give her the short version, leaving out some of the more embarrassing details.

"Wow," she says when I finish. "That sounds intense. So what are you doing now?"

"Baking cakes." I wince, not looking at her, sure I'll see disappointment. "I'm making Nana Alice's wedding cake. She's getting married in two weeks."

Aunt Frannie cocks her head and surveys me. "Cakes?"

"Yes, cakes." I press my lips together and pour the coffee.

"Well, that's the best cake I've had in years." She points to my test cake on the counter. "It's perfect. I'll be dreaming about that cake all the way back to Addis Ababa."

"Thanks." I'm pleased despite myself. "At least I can still bake well. Even if baking can't change the world, it's something, right?" I hand her a mug and sit down across from her.

Aunt Frannie looks at me curiously. "What do you mean, baking can't change the world? Who told you that?"

"You did." I glance at her in surprise. "When I was twelve years old, you told me that baking wasn't enough, that I should aim for better things." I wait to see if she remembers, but her expression is blank. "You might not remember saying that, but it stuck with me. I wanted to be like you, the next Mother Teresa. Saint Mia. It was my highest goal in life."

I take a sip of coffee, watching her face. She's listening carefully, brow furrowed.

"The problem is, Aunt Frannie," I explain, "I love to bake, and I don't seem to be as talented at anything else. I think this may be all I have, the thing I'm actually good at." It feels like a confession. It feels like the truth at last.

Aunt Frannie considers me, her slanted green cat eyes astonished. "Mia, are you telling me you've been avoiding doing the thing you love all these years because you thought I wouldn't approve?"

"Well, yes." I set my mug down, almost indignant. "I idolized you. I wanted to be just like you. You told me I needed to aim for better things, to think bigger than baking. You told me to shoot for the moon, but the problem is that I really just love to bake." I bite my lip, surprised by my outburst, and watch her miserably.

"Oh for Pete's sake, girl." Aunt Frannie takes a sip of scalding coffee. She looks at me with fond exasperation. "My dear, bright, wonderful niece. You can do anything you put your mind to. And anything you do, you will touch people's lives. It's who you are. I was wrong. I shouldn't have said what I did. I wanted to encourage you to reach as high as you could, to reach for the stars. But I didn't mean to limit your choices, and I'm afraid I've done just that." She pauses, then asks, "Do you know why I'm a dentist? Why I've spent my life traveling across Africa, setting up clinics in dusty schools and church sanctuaries, doing thousands of cleanings and extractions with just a folding portable dental chair and a headlamp?"

She waits for my response. I hesitate. "Because it's useful work and really needed?"

"Wrong." She shakes her head. "Because I love it. I love being a dentist. I wanted to be a dentist since I was a child. Your mother and I used to play house. Meg always wanted to play pioneer woman, farming like we were in *Little House on the Prairie*. And do you know what I was?"

I hazard a guess. "Her dentist?"

She nods. "So whatever I said about baking not being enough, that was nonsense. In the right hands, a cookie or pie or biscuit can be a powerful tool. It's not about the baked goods. It's about your heart. Almost anything can change the world if it's done with love, if you use it to comfort, encourage, or strengthen someone. Even dental crowns and routine cleanings. Even piecrusts."

She sits back and takes a sip of coffee. I stare at her, stunned by this paradigm shift. Her words are turning my entire world on its head.

"You really think so?" I ask.

She nods. "Absolutely. If baking is what you love, then that's what you should do. Figure out how to make baking benefit the world, and then go for it. End of story. Now, how about some more of that cake?"

And just like that, the spell of her words from my childhood, the false lesson I believed for so long, is broken. I no longer have to work so hard to find something else worthy of my time, worthy of my effort. What I love, who I am, is enough. Speechless, I cut us both generous slices of cake.

As Aunt Frannie tucks into hers with relish, I perch on the edge of the chair and stare at my wedge of cake, astonished by this morning, by the appearance of Aunt Frannie, by the direction the conversation has taken. I take a small bite of cake. Moist, laced with coconut and lemon zest. She's right. It is perfect.

Aunt Frannie scoops another bite of cake up with her fork and sighs contentedly. I am amazed by the change her words have wrought, what they unlock in my heart. All these years I was laboring to do enough, to be enough. But I've been missing the truth all along.

I think of what Delphine told me when I said goodbye to her that last day at the camp. *Remember, Mia, your place in this world is the space where your greatest passion meets the world's great pain. Go now and find that place.*

I have found my right place, with a cup of sugar and a stick of butter in my hand, but how do I let this passion meet the world's great need? That is still the question. I am free to do what I love, transform the world one baked good at a time, but how exactly do I do that?

A honeybee buzzes in through the farmhouse's open window, landing on the remainder of the layer cake and walking gingerly over the icing. I don't shoo the worker bee away, just let her continue her slow parade across the cake. I have the strangest feeling that I am on the correct path, despite the appearance of being back where I started. I have returned to the kitchen of my childhood home, but this time I know it is the right place to be. I am finally free to do what I love. But there is still a piece I cannot quite see.

Chapter 51

The next two weeks fly by in a whirlwind of wedding preparations. Nana Alice is discharged from the hospital and turns her studio apartment at Sunny Days into a hub for wedding planning. I stay at West Wind and take the ferry back and forth from Sequim every day. It's a long drive, but it feels unexpectedly good to be back home, sleeping in my childhood bed, walking the fragrant lavender fields heavy with morning dew. It feels like coming full circle.

Rosie and I text back and forth during my daily ferry commute. After debrief week finishes, she gently breaks the news that she will not be returning home to Seattle. She's going to stay on the island with Lars (in her own guest cottage, she hastens to assure me). They want to explore the possibility of a future together. I'm thrilled for her, though saddened by the thought of losing her as a roommate. I will miss her loyalty and care as well as the drama and pizazz she brought to our little home.

One morning I'm busy in the farmhouse kitchen, testing and perfecting the frosting for the wedding cake, when my phone dings. I glance at it as I zest a lemon rind. Kai. My heart leaps as I read his text.

Lars just agreed to fully fund my greenhouse project for two years!

Hastily wiping my hands, I text him back. Congratulations, great news! No more law school!

My phone dings again. Yep, huge sigh of relief. Time to focus on getting the portable greenhouse project up and running. Heading back to Virginia tomorrow.

Sounds exciting. Safe travels. I stare at the Pyrex bowl of creamy frosting, debating, then type. I miss you. Wish you were here. I hesitate, unsure if I should send that last text. It's true, I do miss him, but it feels vulnerable to put it out there. As my finger hovers over the Send arrow, a honeybee lands on my hand, gingerly walking the length of my outstretched finger. I take it as a sign and send the text, my heart skipping a beat. I wait ten seconds, a minute. No answer.

With a sigh I brush the bee out the open window and put my phone away. Regret lies dull and heavy in my chest. I wish so many things had turned out differently. I turn my attention back to the frosting, to the task at hand.

As one day slips into the next, I find solace in our old farmhouse kitchen. As I sift and stir and tinker alone in the familiar space, zesting lemons and measuring dollops of cream cheese, sifting flour and sugar, gently shooing away the honeybees that keep buzzing in through the open window, I feel my equilibrium gradually returning.

In those quiet, productive hours, early in the morning or later after my return from Seattle, while my mind is occupied with the technical aspects of getting the cake just right, my heart is slowly sorting through the events of the past weeks. My time in Mumbai, Shreya and the children in the slums, the Röszke camp, kissing Kai in the tea aisle of Tesco, Ethan's surprising arrival and our final goodbye, the debacle and terror and my epiphany the day of the riot, Maryam and Yousef. Every time I picture their faces, I say a little prayer for them, that they made it safely to Sweden, that they are finding their feet again in their new home.

Slowly, slowly, eased by the gentle rhythms of the kitchen, those complex and painful memories soften and my heart slips into a place of stillness, of acceptance. The trip was not what I had dreamed of. I wanted to be Saint Mia, to see the world and change it for good. But what changed was my own heart.

Funny that a trip around the world led right back to my own kitchen. I am starting to be grateful, to slowly move past regret and disappointment and see the bigger picture. Bit by bit I make peace with my life. For the moment it is enough to just be here, just be me.

Chapter 52

The morning of the wedding dawns bright and sunny. I slip into my daisy yellow sundress and very carefully load the lemon butter cake into my dad's old Ford truck. I take the ferry to Seattle and drive to the wedding location, the beautiful Admiral's House on Magnolia overlooking Elliot Bay and the Space Needle. Henry and Christine will follow later with the children, closer to the ceremony start time. Sunlight dances on the Sound below, bright and silver blue. Seattle in the summer is an overabundance of beauty.

"This looks perfect." I greet Aunt Karen, Uncle Carl's wife, who has been handling the flowers and decorations.

"It's a miracle we got it done," she says. "I've never seen a wedding come together so fast, but everything is ready."

Rows of white chairs are arranged in the garden for the thirty or so guests in attendance. An archway covered in greenery and blush-colored spray roses stands at the front. The Reverend Waters from the Lutheran church where Nana Alice has been a member for forty years will preside over the ceremony. And afterward there will be a reception on the lawn with dinner and dancing. A three-piece band in tuxedos is warming up near the archway as I gingerly carry the cake to the outdoor reception area, teetering on my wedges.

"That cake is pretty as a picture." Aunt Karen bustles over to admire my handiwork.

Situated on a card table covered in a lace cloth, the wedding cake looks perfect. Its cream cheese frosting is luscious, and I piped white frosting flowers with sugar pearl centers around the top and bottom. It looks dainty and elegant and vintage, in keeping with the rest of the wedding. It was a joy to make, and after all those test runs, it turned out beautifully. I pinched a tiny crumb from the underside of a layer and tasted it while the frosting blended in my mom's trusty KitchenAid mixer. Perfect.

Little by little, guests start to arrive. My mother and father flew in a few days ago from Moldova. They've been staying with Uncle Carl and Aunt Karen in Seattle in order to be close to Nana Alice. So far they've spent all their free time with her, so I haven't really gotten a chance to catch up with either of them yet. I give them both hugs and let them go mingle with the other guests, all friends and family they haven't seen in a while.

Henry and Christine arrive with the kids in tow. Maddie wears a white lace dress and carries a white patent leather purse, very prim and proper and ladylike. The twins look grouchy in tiny herringbone vests and bow ties.

"Oliver is refusing to wear pants." Henry kisses my cheek, and behind him Christine pulls a face. Oliver, clad in only a diaper on his lower half, tugs on her hand and points to the cake.

"Dis, dis," he hollers.

"Here, Ollie, do you want a cheese stick?" Christine asks, pulling string cheese from her purse and trying to distract him from the cake. Meanwhile Auden has wandered off into the yard and is crouching down, putting something in his mouth.

"Ew." Maddie grimaces, pointing to him. "Brother's eating a bug."

Henry dashes off to pry the bug from Auden's mouth, and I

turn at a tap on my shoulder, expecting to see an old family friend or a distant relative. My eyes travel up, up, and my mouth drops open. Kai is standing directly in front of me, wearing a smart navy blue suit and a sheepish smile on his face.

"You!" I stare at him as though he's been conjured up by magic. He is holding a bouquet of white daisies, my favorite flower. "What are you doing here?" I gape at him, delighted and baffled. He holds the daisies out to me.

"Alice messaged me through Instagram last week and invited me to come." He grins, leaning down and giving me a quick kiss on the cheek. "She wanted it to be a surprise."

"I'm so glad to see you," I say fervently, leaning in and giving him a long hug. My heart is doing a happy little jig in my chest, and I feel like crying. Also giggling a bit at the thought of Nana Alice navigating Instagram for the sake of my heart. All at once I'm immensely relieved that I wore waterproof mascara.

"I'm glad to be here." He meets my eyes, his own crinkling at the corners in that endearing way. "Hey, Mia, I know we have a lot to talk about," he says, sobering just a bit, "but today is about celebrating Alice and Albert. Let's just concentrate on that. We'll have plenty of time to talk later. I just want you to know something." He turns and faces me, gently cupping my face in his hands so he's staring into my eyes. His expression is earnest. "I'm not Ethan. I won't make you give up the dreams you have in your heart. Do you hear me? Whatever happens, I promise to help you find your better things."

I nod, blinking back tears, amazed by those words. He's making me a promise. He thinks we have a future together, one where we can both live out our dreams. I exhale with relief, letting go of a breath I didn't even realize I was holding. "Thank you," I tell him, eyes shining.

Kai drops his hands and grins, looking relieved. "So can I meet your family?"

I spend the next twenty minutes in a haze of happiness, introducing Kai to friends and family, marveling at his presence beside me. He is witty and self-deprecating, perfectly at ease. I am so head over heels for him. I feel like I'm floating on air.

When the music starts we scramble to our seats in the second row behind my mother, aunt and uncle, and Albert's two sons and their wives. Beside Reverend Waters, Albert is waiting, looking dashing in a sand-colored linen summer suit with a bow tie and a Panama hat. He also looks, adorably, a little nervous.

The band strikes up Pachelbel's *Canon in D*, and we all stand.

"Here she is," my mother murmurs, dabbing her eyes. Nana Alice is radiant in a sheath dress of ivory lace with a corsage of blush roses pinned at her breast. She wears a jaunty little ivory pillbox hat festooned with a tiny veil decorated with pearls. My father walks by her side, in case she needs a hand, but she does not. She walks slowly down the aisle between the chairs, leaning heavily on *Greased Lightning*. She doesn't look to the left or the right. She only has eyes for Albert.

The ceremony is short and sweet. Nana Alice perches on a little stool, and Albert stands tall by her side. They exchange vows and rings, promising to be true to each other. Albert's voice is stalwart as he promises "in sickness and in health, till death do us part."

I blink back tears. We all know the sickness part of the vow is already a reality. There will be no health. And death will come soon, how soon no one knows. But despite the somber future, there is still a feeling of joy, of celebration. They have found one another before it is too late. They are celebrating their love, and we are celebrating with them, today and every day they have together, for however long that may be.

As they exchange a surprisingly passionate first kiss as Mr. and Mrs. Prentice, Kai hands me a crumpled but clean handkerchief from his pocket. "I came prepared," he whispers, and I dab my welling eyes.

"I'm so glad you're here," I whisper to him. "Life is better when you're around."

He nods, and tucks my hand under his arm. "Funny, I feel the same way. Maybe we should do something about that."

My heart thrills at his words. He looks down at me and gives me a wink, then rests his cheek on the crown of my head. The band strikes up a rendition of "A Kiss to Build a Dream On" as Albert and Nana Alice walk back down the aisle, now husband and wife. There's not a dry eye in the garden.

Chapter 53

"Here, cake for table two." I hand Kai glass plates with slices of wedding cake, and he ferries them to the waiting guests. An hour after the ceremony, the reception is in full swing. After a meal of cold Alaskan salmon with fresh asparagus, rosemary sea salt bread from the Butter Emporium, and champagne, Nana Alice and Albert cut the cake and then hit the small square dance floor for a very slow, very sweet first dance to "When I Fall in Love." Nana Alice leaves her walker at the side of the dance floor and clings to Albert. Together they sway as the band plays. I watch them as I cut the cake and plate it for guests.

"Two tables down, four to go," Kai reports, as he returns for more cake. I just gaze at him for a moment. Hope and anticipation make a soft, warm spot in the center of my chest, sweet as a sunrise breaking over the horizon of my heart. I think I'm in love. I grin, delighted and amazed. No, scratch that. I'm most definitely in love.

"Mia, this cake is perfect." My mother taps me on the shoulder, gesturing to her slice of half-eaten cake. She looks wonderful, tanned and invigorated. Moldova seems to be agreeing with her. She comes and stands beside me. "What a beautiful celebration."

We both watch Nana Alice and Albert for a moment as they rest from the dancing. Nana Alice is out of breath but laughing, and Albert hovers at her side, equal parts solicitous and proud.

"Look at how he adores her," my mother observes. "I'm so glad they found each other."

Kai returns, and I hand him four more plates, our fingers grazing in the transfer. He meets my eyes, his dark gaze warm. When he turns away, I clear my throat. "How's Moldova? When are you coming home?"

"Well, we want to talk to you about that," my mother says, tapping her fork against her lips. Something in her tone makes me glance up. "We're not coming back."

"What?" My hands still over the cake. "What do you mean?"

"We've been asked to head up a new lavender growing program in India, specifically to help widows with children start small lavender farms. And we've said yes!" My mother's face breaks into a delighted grin. "Can you believe it?" she asks, sounding amazed and almost giddy.

I am stunned. My parents are leaving Sequim and moving to India? This is far more unexpected than their up and leaving for Moldova for a few weeks. The implications are more serious too.

"But what about the farm?" I protest, head spinning with the sudden changes around me.

"Well, happily enough, Henry and Christine have agreed to take over the farm." My mother takes a bite of cake, shooing a honeybee off a frosting flower, and motions toward Henry, who is wrestling with Oliver over by the punch bowl. "Your brother is showing a surprising aptitude for lavender farming. I guess all those hours your father forced him to work on the farm actually did some good after all. And Christine wants to expand the business side of things. It's really ideal for them. They've decided they want a slower pace of life for Maddie and the twins. Sequim will be perfect."

I cut another slice of cake and slide it onto a plate, performing the functions automatically while my mind whirs through this new information. Henry and Christine are leaving Chicago to run West Wind? That piece of news brings relief. The farm will stay in the family. Henry had hinted that they were unhappy in Chicago and seeking a change; Sequim can certainly provide that. But my parents. My parents aren't coming home? My parents are moving to India? I feel a sudden dart of panic. They've always been there on the farm, stable, steady, predictable. I've always known I could go home and things would be chugging along as they have since I can remember. All that is about to change.

"When are you leaving?" I ask.

"It's a two-year commitment initially." My mother takes another bite of cake and savors it for a moment. "This is delicious," she says approvingly. "It tastes just like Alice used to make it. Even better actually, but don't tell her I said that. We're not sure quite yet when we'll leave." She nods to Nana Alice. "It all depends on how things go here."

She doesn't elaborate. The doctors have told us that there is no way of knowing how much time Nana Alice has left. We know it isn't much.

Everything is changing so fast, and yet it feels right, too, as though things are falling into their proper places. Everyone knows their place, it seems, but me. How ironic that my parents, inspired by my actions, have done what I have as yet failed to do. They are using their talents to change the world for good. Someday, maybe, I will be able to do the same.

"I really like Kai," my mother says, watching him deliver a piece of cake to my dad, laughing at some undoubtedly dry joke my father is making. "Your father likes him too."

"Well, that makes three of us," I agree. "I like him a lot, Mom." More than a lot, if I'm honest.

"I'm so happy for you, sweetheart." My mother gives me a firm hug and a kiss on the cheek, then wanders off to talk with her cousin from Bend. I linger at the table, trying to wrap my head around all the ways in which my family is changing. What is it Nana Alice used to say? *There's nothing constant in life except change.* How true.

I cut two pieces of cake and look around, hoping to locate both Kai and a quiet alcove where we can sit for a few minutes. I don't see him anywhere, but I do notice that Nana Alice and Albert are resting from dancing at an empty table and somehow have not been served cake. Cutting two more generous-sized slices, I take plates over to them.

Nana Alice takes a tiny nibble and savors it. "Oh, that's perfect," she says, closing her eyes. "Moist, tart, exactly right. You make it better than I ever did, Mia." Albert is polishing his off in a few swift bites.

"Thank you," I say, meeting her eyes, suddenly choked up with emotion. "And thank you for believing in me. And for inviting Kai."

Nana Alice's face lights up, and she looks around until she spots him just coming around the side of the house. "Oh Mia, I think he's a keeper. Just like this one." She pats Albert's arm, and I have to look down at the ground, blinking away a prickle of tears. No crying on this happy day.

"I want to meet this man who's stolen your heart," Albert declares. "I believe Alice is a little sweet on him too."

"I do like a man in a good navy suit." Nana Alice nods approvingly. "Now go get your fella so we can say hello."

Chapter 54

Enjoying our cake, Kai and I sit and chat with Nana Alice and Albert, the conversation flowing easily around the table. Kai fits in so well, like he's been here forever. Nana Alice gasps as he tells her about us being chased by the shark.

Albert gives me a wink and a thumbs-up. I sigh happily. Kai and I hold hands under the table, and my toe taps to the beat of the music. A few honeybees buzz around my slice of cake, trying to light on my dress, on the fork, on the cake itself. I shoo them off gently, and they take flight for a moment but return, alighting on the edible pearl center of the frosting flower. I decide to let them be. I have a feeling they are here for a reason.

Keeping one ear tuned to the conversation as Albert quizzes Kai about his portable greenhouse, I watch a few couples whirl around the dance floor, humming along to the music. "I've Got the World on a String." The lyrics are ironic considering how much of my life and family situation seems to be in limbo or changing right now. I don't have the world on a string, but I do have Kai—beautiful, kind, affable Kai. And I feel happy right now, despite the changes and uncertainties. I have a lot to be grateful for.

One of the servers from the catering company stops at the cake table and glances around as though looking for whoever is supposed to be manning the table. I untangle my fingers from Kai's. "Be right back."

I approach her. "Can I help you?"

"It's beautiful," the server says, eyeing what is left of the cake. Her hands are full of dessert plates rimmed with the remnants of icing and crumbs. She is about my age, tall and slim with light brown skin that reminds me of Abel. She looks familiar, and I stare for a moment, puzzled, trying to place her.

"Thanks, I made it. My first time baking a wedding cake. You want to try some?"

She hesitates, then nods. "We're not supposed to eat the food, but since it is the baker who offers . . ." She sets the dirty plates down as I cut a piece and slide it onto a plate for her. She scrutinizes it for a long moment, then takes a taste and nods in approval. "It's very good."

Her name tag says Tsehay. I tilt my head, trying to recall where I have seen her before. There it is. Hope House, the women and children's shelter in Seattle. She was a client for a few months back when I first volunteered there. If I remember correctly, she got into permanent housing shortly after I started at the shelter. In the whirl of the wedding plans, I haven't yet returned to my volunteer position. I make a mental note to contact them next week.

"Tsehay," I say, "I think we've met before. Did you ever stay at Hope House?"

She looks surprised, then nods. "For a few months, yes. My two daughters and I." She studies my face, and then her eyes light up. "I remember you," she says. "You made cookies for everyone at the house and brought them in a silver box."

I nod. "That's right. How are you?" I am delighted to see her again. She was a staff favorite, always conscientious and kind to the other women. I rack my brain for her country of origin. Eritrea. I think she's originally from Eritrea.

"I am well," she says, placing her dirty cake plate on the stack at her feet, then blowing gently on a honeybee that is walking back and forth on the handle of her fork. "You know, back home I was a—what's the word?—a baker. I made cakes like these, very fancy cakes for weddings and parties."

"Really? I had no idea you were a baker. Do you still bake?"

She shakes her head. "No. When I came to America as a refugee five years ago, it was very hard to find a job. I have twin daughters, and my husband is dead. I had to take whatever I could find." She shrugs. "This catering job is okay. It is not what I want to do with my life, but it pays and I can afford an apartment, not living at Hope House like some of the other refugee women I know." She hesitates. "But still I miss it. Sometimes when I sleep I dream I am back in Eritrea, baking cakes like this." She gives me a quick sideways smile, tinged with wistfulness.

"It's good to see you." I reach out and clasp her hand.

Tsehay glances back at the house. "I should get back to work. It is good to see you, too, Mia." She gives a little nod and picks up the dessert plates, balancing them in front of her. "Thank you for the cake," she says. "It was delicious."

I watch her walk carefully toward the kitchen of the house, and something stirs in my mind. I think about sitting with Delphine on the rise of earth at the edge of the refugee camp. The harsh smell of cigarette smoke and Delphine's voice floating through the darkness, the contours of her face lit by the orange glow of the cigarette as we watch the refugees. What had she said to me? That this was just the start. After they were settled in their new homes, the real work would begin. How to house them and feed them and teach them language and find them employment? How to help them craft a life with a new language and culture? How to help them create a new definition of home?

I watch Tsehay walk into the house, her posture upright, almost regal, carefully carrying the stack of glass plates. A few honeybees buzz after her, perhaps drawn by the scent of sugar. A baker with no way to bake. A refugee trying to find her place in a strange new land. As I watch her retreating back, I have the first stirring of an idea, inchoate, vague, but lit with a flicker of excitement. What if there was a way to help women like Tsehay find their place in this new country? What if baking could play a part? And what if I am the one to do it?

I am just starting to turn the idea over in my head, letting my scattered thoughts coalesce, when Kai finds me at the cake table. He offers his hand to me.

"May I have this dance?" he asks, and I let him lead me to the tiny square of a dance floor. Nana Alice and Albert clap and whistle as we take our positions and the band begins to play an old Sinatra classic, "The Best Is Yet to Come."

"Earth to Mia," Kai whispers in my ear while he whirls me around the dance floor with more enthusiasm than ability. "You're a million miles away. What are you thinking about right now?"

I glance up at him, the idea crystalizing in my brain, quick and bright as a flashbulb. A way to do what I love and help women like Tsehay build a new life in America.

"I think I just figured out what I'm supposed to do with my life." I feel a little shaky with the newness of it, the wonder.

As we twirl around the dance floor, neither of us paying much attention to the actual dancing, I briefly tell him my plan, sketching out the rough idea, still unsure of the details.

"What do you think?" I ask, looking up at him as the final notes of the song die away, suddenly nervous. "Is it good, terrible?"

We slow to a stop, and Kai stares at me hard for a moment, thinking it through, and then he says solemnly, "It's good, Mia. Better than good. It could really help a lot of women. You need to talk to Lars and see if he'll fund the project. He feels so bad about how things went with Team Caritas that he's said he'll fund any project that seems worthwhile."

I stare at him, astonished. I can't stop the smile that spreads, slow and sweet as golden honey, from ear to ear. "You think this is worthwhile?" I ask.

"Yeah, I think so." Kai hoots in excitement and then twirls and dips me, planting a firm kiss on my lips as I hover in his arms above the ground.

"That's my girl," he says, grinning at me. I laugh with delight, exhilarated and so very relieved. After so long a wait, agonizing over my life purpose, in the end I am astonished that it has come so easily. It seems so simple and natural, this recognition of the path I was meant to walk. It feels so right.

Epilogue

Seattle
Eighteen months later

My phone rings just as I am touching up the displays in the glass bakery case.

"This is Mia," I answer without looking at the caller on the screen. I stand back and slightly adjust the angle of a vintage ivory platter of *ka'ak,* a famous anise cookie from Syria.

"So today's the day. How are you feeling?" It's Kai. I grin at the sound of his voice and nudge a pyramid of organic lavender honey shortbread cookies—the lavender and honey sourced from West Wind Farm—so that they are not lopsided but perfectly symmetrical.

"Great! Everything's ready. Where are you? Are you over the pass?" There was snow in the Cascades, and Snoqualmie Pass was closed yesterday.

"Over the pass and headed your way. I'm fifteen minutes out, tops. I'll be there in time for the grand opening. Wouldn't miss my best girl's big day."

I grin and wave away two honeybees that are buzzing around the inside of the display case. Although it's January and I'm in the middle of the city, miles from any hives, I am not surprised to see the bees. I know why they are here. These fuzzy little helpers are my guides, my beacons, enlightening me step-by-step along the path. They guided me around the world and through the terrain of my own heart until I reached my rightful place. How appropriate that they would be here today to celebrate the fulfillment of this destined dream.

"It's all happening for real," I say, taking a deep breath. After eighteen months of planning, training, and preparations, it has all come down to this day.

I set out a teacup saucer of sugar water for the bees and survey the front room. Everything looks perfect—delectable and inviting. The long glass case gleams in the rare January sunshine streaming through the tall windows of our storefront location on the outskirts of the International District. A few white painted tables and sunny yellow chairs dot the small eating area. Across one of the big front windows in beautiful looping script is the name Alice's Place, and in smaller letters "Artisanal bakery. All are welcome."

"Alice would love what you've created," Kai says, the noise of the highway humming behind him through the phone.

"I'm thinking about her so much today," I say softly. I haven't stopped thinking about her since the moment I opened my eyes this morning. She's been gone almost a year now, but I still miss her fiercely every single day.

"She was an amazing lady." Kai's voice is gentle.

I'm so glad he got to know her in the last months of her life. I dash away a few salty tears. Nana Alice would be so proud of what this day represents. I only wish she could have seen it completed.

"How'd the truck do in Boise? How was the presentation?" I stack rounds of freshly baked *hembesha*, an Eritrean bread subtly flavored with coriander and fenugreek, in a basket on top of the display case, then step back and check the results. All the baked goods look and smell tantalizing. The spices in the *hembesha* are authentic, sent from Ethiopia by Aunt Frannie as an opening day gift, a blessing of sorts.

"It was great. I'm a big hit with fifth graders. I have to plant more Swiss chard, but otherwise the presentation was spot on."

With funding from the Humanitas Foundation, Kai has been touring economically disadvantaged areas all over the West with his portable greenhouse truck, giving demonstrations about sustainable urban agriculture and food awareness at schools and youth programs. I miss him when he's gone, but it's what he loves, and his joy and enthusiasm are infectious. Besides, I've been up to my ears getting Alice's Place ready to open as well as earning a certificate in pastry from a culinary institute here in Seattle. Now all is ready. It's time to start this new season.

"Hey." Kai's voice is soft in my ear, a caress. "I'm so proud of you."

"Thanks." I can feel myself growing pink with pride. "But it's early yet. We have to see if we can keep it afloat."

"You will," Kai says confidently. "And you know why? It's a great business model. Who in the world doesn't like baked goods and supporting a good cause?"

"That's true." I hasten into the kitchen in the back and scramble in my satchel, trying to locate my lipstick, then give up and opt for some tinted Burt's Bees lip balm. I'm not really the lipstick type anyway. I smooth back my curls. "Okay, I'll see you soon. Drive safe." I hesitate, still savoring the newness of these words, still feeling a little shy saying them. "I love you."

I still can't believe my good fortune. Kai is one of the best things to ever happen to me. One day soon, perhaps at the end of the touring season, he will join me in Nana Alice's cottage, which she left to me in her will. I smile in anticipation. Every day is sweeter with him by my side.

"And I love you, Mia Alice West," Kai replies. "Now go get ready."

I hang up and pause for a moment, trying to catch my breath. It has been a whirlwind eighteen months since Nana Alice's wedding, where I first hatched this idea. And now here we are—about to open our doors for the first time.

This is my dream. A bakery staffed entirely by refugee women. We have a six-month baking apprenticeship program, and when the women graduate they can work in the bakery or move on to other baking jobs. It is the only bakery in Seattle focused on training and equipping these women.

I glance at the big white vintage clock over the doorway. Five minutes till we open the doors. My gaze catches on a postcard pinned to the bulletin board by the door. "Greetings from Gothenburg," it says in cheery red letters. On the back it simply reads, "We are safe in our new home. Maryam says hello. Your friends in Sweden, Yousef and Maryam." I press my hand to my heart for a moment. All this effort, the insane hours and sleepless nights, the brainstorming and planning and sheer determination to keep going despite setbacks and disappointments; I am doing it all for women like Maryam.

I brush away a tear, imagining what Nana Alice would think of all this. She was so excited by the idea of it. The bell over the storefront door jingles.

"Mia? Are you in here?" It is one of my two employees. Yara is our first apprentice baker. Originally from Aleppo, she and her widowed mother fled after her husband was killed fighting the Islamic State. She has a two-year-old son named Hassan.

"I'm here," I say, laughing through my tears.

"There's a crowd of people outside the front door, pressing their faces to the glass like children," calls my other employee in a mock chiding tone. "Don't you think we should let them in?" Tsehay peeks into the kitchen and grins at me.

When I decided to make Alice's Place a reality, I tracked down

Tsehay through the catering company and offered her a partnership in the program. She now runs the baking apprenticeships while I handle the operations of the actual bakery.

"Yes, it's time." I smooth my dress, the same sundress I wore to Nana Alice's wedding, this time with a cream-colored angora cardigan over it for warmth. "Let's go."

A small crowd of about twelve people have gathered at the front of the bakery. I see Henry and Christine and the kids. The twins have their noses pressed to the windows and are making silly faces. So much for the sparkling clean glass. I give them a wink and a smile.

Christine waves to me excitedly. She's provided marketing advice for us free of charge and has been an invaluable resource for talking through the logistics of starting a business. West Wind is thriving under her and Henry's care, and their family seems to be loving life in Sequim as well. Colleen and Hector from the Butter Emporium are here, dusted with flour, grinning and giving me a thumbs-up.

Rosie is missing, and I feel her absence keenly. She and Lars sent five dozen yellow and white roses, which are lavishly gracing the tables inside the bakery. They have been engaged now for eight months. Renowned violinist Joshua Bell serenaded them with Pucchini's "O Mio Babbino Caro" under the stars as Rosie said yes.

She's been encouraging Lars to moderate the extravagance of his life so that he can focus even more resources on the Humanitas Foundation, a suggestion he is trying to take to heart. They seem blissfully happy together. She has, for now, put her dreams of New York on hold, although she tells me that every week she takes a trip into Miami and volunteers at a jazz enrichment program for kids from tough urban neighborhoods. She's not giving up on her dream, just shifting the geography south a little.

Lars has not yet left the island, but in my last video call with

Rosie, she confided that they were planning a trip to Key West for their honeymoon. Which might seem strange for any other billionaire who already owns his own island, but I understand. Perhaps now, with Rosie by his side, Lars is ready to start venturing into the world again.

I scan the crowd, looking for Kai, but stop when I spot Albert, his familiar dapper figure standing slightly off to one side. He's wearing a bow tie and his fedora. I meet his eyes, and he gives me a small nod and a fond, sad smile.

Beyond him, the familiar shape of the portable greenhouse truck comes barreling down the road. Kai deftly maneuvers it into a parking spot across the street in front of a Pho restaurant and leaps out, loping over to stand beside Albert and giving me a jaunty salute. I grin and open the door. It's time.

"Good morning, everyone. Thank you so much for coming to our opening." I hover behind the white satin ribbon stretched across the entrance. My heart is beating in my ears and I lick my lips nervously, eager to get to the fun part, eating all the things Yara, Tsehay, and I started making at four this morning. "Alice's Place grew out of a dream—two dreams, in fact: my desire to do something meaningful with my life and my passion for baking. Nana Alice loved baking, and she passed that love on to me, but even more than baking, Nana Alice believed in living life to the fullest."

I nod at Albert. He tips his hat and returns the nod. He's looking older, frailer, but he still has a twinkle in his bright blue eyes.

"A wise friend once told me that the place you are to occupy in the universe is the space where your greatest passion meets the world's great pain."

I pause, thinking of Delphine and of the somewhat disastrous adventures of Team Caritas. Last I heard, Abel and Winnie are living together in Venice Beach, California. Abel opened a beachside

Rwandan coffee stand and is studying to be certified as a trauma counselor, and Winnie is working as a surf instructor and has taken up hot yoga. Milo manages a trendy coffee shop in Milwaukee and runs woodworking programs on the weekends at a center for juvenile offenders. For just an instant I think of Ethan too. He relocated to San Jose last year and is engaged to an Apple marketing executive named Ashley.

"That place for me is Alice's Place," I continue. "It honors the memory of a remarkable woman and seeks to empower other courageous women who are finding their way in a foreign country and creating new lives. So thank you all for coming. And without further ado—" I clear my throat, grab Nana Alice's pinking shears from the pocket of my sundress, and snip the ribbon, which falls in two swirls of white to the pavement. "Welcome to Alice's Place."

The small crowd cheers and claps enthusiastically.

"Please come in, taste and enjoy!"

I hold the door wide open, enveloped in a waft of that familiar, wonderful scent—sugar, vanilla, and cinnamon. In an instant I am a child again in Nana Alice's bakery, asking for a butterscotch oatmeal cookie. An instant later I am here in the present, a grown woman offering those same cookies to a waiting world, offering hope and a taste of good things to come. I stand aside as the first guests stream through the door, my heart bursting with gratitude, with anticipation, with joy. I have found my place in the universe. It was right here all along.

A Note from the Author

Dear reader friend,

Several aspects of this story are surprisingly autobiographical. First and perhaps most unbelievably, I was actually chased by a bull shark in Florida a few years ago! It makes a great story now but was absolutely terrifying at the time. I was also broken up with my senior year of college just as I was expecting a marriage proposal. And, just like for Mia, this drastic change in my future plans set me on the most marvelous path to discovering a remarkable alternate life.

This new life has taken me to some fifty countries across the globe, from the slums of India to the refugee camps on the border of Hungary doing international humanitarian aid work with the wonderful man I've been married to for almost eleven years. It has been the most remarkable adventure!

However even in the midst of the adventure, part of me always longed to write stories. I struggled for years believing that writing novels was not big enough, important enough, or sacrificial enough to be part of my life's purpose. I believed that I had to do something so much more grand and important to really change the world. I think I was wrong.

The more I see and understand of the world, the more I realize that we can ALL spark change by doing the things we love with passion and compassion. EACH of us has the capacity to make a positive change through giving the gift of our time, talents, and presence right where we are!

I believe the sweet spot in life is the place where our passions meet and kiss the world's pain. I've found my sweet spot—international aid work and writing stories like the one you're reading right now. My great hope is that you can find your sweet spot too. Then we can truly transform the world for good one bit at a time.

Rachel

Acknowledgments

Writing this book has been a true delight! I owe so much to so many who have helped it along the path to publication, contributing their time and talents to make this story shine. In addition to giving many of them good chocolate, I want to say a great BIG thank you to . . .

My lovely editor, Kimberly Carlton, who somehow manages to combine a keen editorial eye with empathy, approachability, and kindness! Also marketing guru Paul Fisher, digital master Matt Bray, and publicity queen Allison Carter. Kristen Ingebretson crafted a cover so snappy and vivacious I want to wear it as a bathing suit! I am so thankful for the entire Thomas Nelson team who consistently exhibit such professionalism, dedication, and warmth to their authors. I am beyond grateful!

My super agent, Chip MacGregor, whose pragmatism, wry humor, unflappability, and book smarts are truly invaluable. Chip, I'm so glad you're in my corner.

My wonderfully honest and smart test readers—Sarah Smith, Adelle Tinon, Sarah Wolfe, and Allison Jordan. Their constructive criticism and keen insights helped this story become better, sweeter, and stronger.

Purple Haze Lavender Farm in Sequim (ignore the *e*, it's

pronounced Skwim) and Macrina Bakery in Seattle, my yummy inspiration for the Butter Emporium.

The Migration Aid volunteers I met and worked with in Hungary who sacrificially and selflessly aided so many thousands of refugees as they came across the border from Serbia. And the refugees in the Roszke border camp who inspired me to write a story highlighting both their plight and their courage.

And most importantly my precious family. My dear husband, Yohanan, who is my strongest supporter, an insightful first reader, and a thoroughly good man. You are my very favorite! And my sweet Ash and Bea. You make the world a happier, brighter place. I'm so glad to be your mama.

Discussion Questions

1. "Do small things with great love," was a favorite motto of Mother Teresa. How do the characters demonstrate this motto in the story? How does Mia learn to live it out?
2. What role do bees and dreams about bees play in the story? What do you think the bees represent for Mia?
3. Do you think Mia's motivations to go on the Humanitas Foundation trip are selfish or altruistic? How so?
4. Mia goes on the trip to find her "alternate life." Does she succeed or fail? How does her view of her "alternate life" change by the end of the story?
5. How do Kai and Ethan differ in their life goals and their relationship with Mia? How do her interactions with each of them influence her choices in life?
6. What are three pivotal interactions that Mia has in the story that change the course of her life?
7. Which character in the story do you identify with the most and why?
8. What does Mia learn through her relationships with the strong women around her (Shreya, Delphine, Aunt Frannie, Nana Alice, etc.)? What strong women have influenced your life and how?

9. Shreya states that real change happens "person to person, day by day, when we live life together." Do you agree with this? How does Mia's experience in Mumbai and the refugee camp highlight this?
10. How does young Mia's conversation with Aunt Frannie about baking influence her view of herself and her decisions about her life? How does her adult conversation with Aunt Frannie challenge and change those earlier decisions?
11. Mia wants to become "St. Mia." In what ways does she accomplish her goal? In what ways does her goal change by the end of the story?
12. Mia learns that the sweet spot in life is the place where your greatest passion meets the world's great pain. Do you believe this is true? Why or why not? What is your sweet spot in life?

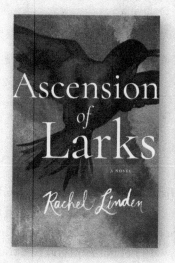

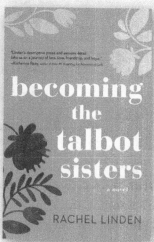

About the Author

Photo by Mallory MacDonald

Rachel Linden is a novelist and international aid worker whose adventures living and traveling in fifty countries around the world provide excellent grist for her stories. Currently, Rachel lives in beautiful Seattle, Washington, with her husband and two young children. Rachel enjoys creating stories about hope and courage with a hint of romance and a touch of whimsy.

Visit her online at rachellinden.com
Instagram: rachellinden_writer
Facebook: authorRachellinden